P9-EMR-794

BLOODLINE

ALSO BY F. PAUL WILSON

Repairman Jack
The Tomb
Legacies
Conspiracies
All the Rage
Hosts
The Haunted Air
Gateways
Crisscross
Infernal
Harbingers

The Adversary Cycle
The Keep	*Reborn*
The Tomb	*Reprisal*
The Touch	*Nightworld*

Other Novels
Healer	*Implant*
Wheels Within Wheels	*Deep as the Marrow*
An Enemy of the State	*Mirage* (with Matthew J. Costello)
Black Wind	*Nightkill* (with Steven Spruill)
Dydeetown World	*Masque* (with Matthew J. Costello)
The Tery	*The Christmas Thingy*
Sibs	*Sims*
The Select	*The Fifth Harmonic*
Virgin	*Midnight Mass*

Short Fiction
Soft & Others
The Barrens & Others

Editor
Freak Show	*Diagnosis: Terminal*

BLOODLINE

A Repairman Jack Novel

F. PAUL WILSON

A TOM DOHERTY ASSOCIATES BOOK • NEW YORK

This is a work of fiction. All of the characters, organizations, and events portrayed in this novel are either products of the author's imagination or are used fictitiously.

BLOODLINE: A REPAIRMAN JACK NOVEL

Copyright © 2007 by F. Paul Wilson

All rights reserved, including the right to reproduce this book, or portions thereof, in any form.

This book is printed on acid-free paper.

A Forge Book
Published by Tom Doherty Associates, LLC
175 Fifth Avenue
New York, NY 10010

www.tor-forge.com

Forge® is a registered trademark of Tom Doherty Associates, LLC.

Library of Congress Cataloging-in-Publication Data

Wilson, F. Paul (Francis Paul)
   Bloodline : a Repairman Jack novel / F. Paul Wilson. — 1st hardcover ed.
      p. cm.
   "A Tom Doherty Associates Book."
   ISBN-13: 978-0-7653-1706-3
   ISBN-10: 0-7653-1706-0
 1. Repairman Jack (Fictitious character)—Fiction. 2. Private investigators—Crimes against—Fiction. I. Title.
   PS3573.I45695B56 2007
   813'.54—dc22

                                                                    2007018784

First Edition: October 2007

Printed in the United States of America

0 9 8 7 6 5 4 3 2 1

Once again,
to
Mary

ACKNOWLEDGMENTS

Thanks to the usual crew for their efforts: my wife, Mary; my editor, David Hartwell; Elizabeth Monteleone; Steven Spruill; and my agent, Albert Zuckerman.

TUESDAY

1

It was happening again . . .

In the driver's seat, hands on the steering wheel, gunning the panel truck across Second Avenue toward the blond woman and her little girl . . .

. . . gaining speed . . .

. . . seeing their shocked, terrified expressions as he floors the gas . . .

. . . feeling the impacts as he plows into them . . .

. . . watching their limp, broken bodies flying as he races past, never slowing, never hesitating, never even looking back.

Jack awoke with his jaw locked and his fists clenched. He forced himself to relax, to reach out and lay a hand on the reassuring curve of Gia's hip where she slumbered next to him.

The dream again. Easy enough to interpret: He blamed himself for the hit-and-run, so his mind put him behind the wheel. Obvious.

What wasn't obvious was the timing. The dream occurred only under a certain condition: It meant the watcher was back.

Jack slipped from her bed to the window. The blinds were drawn against the glow from the streetlights. He peeked around the edge and . . .

There he was.

As usual he stood at the corner, facing Gia's townhouse, wearing his customary homburg and overcoat; his right hand rested on the head of a walking stick. His position silhouetted him against the lights of the traffic passing on Sutton Place and caused the brim of his hat to shadow his face.

A big man and, if the slight stoop of his shoulders was any clue, elderly. Jack had first seen him outside his own apartment back in January . . . just days before the hit-and-run. And lately he'd been showing up outside Gia's.

Jack had never been able to catch the guy. Not for lack of trying. He'd gone after him dozens of times, but the old guy seemed to know when Jack was coming.

Somehow the watcher always managed to stay one step ahead. If Jack waited inside the front door, dressed and ready to give chase, or sat in his car or hid in a doorway, watching the corner, the guy didn't show. Last month Jack had waited ten nights in a row—inside and outside, from uptown, downtown, and crosstown vantage points.

Nothing.

On the eleventh night he called it quits and went to bed. That night he had the dream again and, sure enough, a peek through the blinds confirmed the watcher's presence.

Deciding to give it another shot, Jack grabbed his jeans and hopped into them as he headed for the hall. He hurried down to the first floor and jammed his bare feet into his sneakers where they waited in the front foyer. Then out the door in a headlong dash across the street to the corner.

The empty corner.

But Jack didn't break his stride. This had happened every time—in the half minute or less it took him to reach the street the guy in the homburg disappeared. All it took was a few steps to put him around the corner and out of sight, but there was more to it.

Jack reached the corner and kept going, racing along Sutton Place for a full block, peering into every nook and cranny along the way. Tonight's attempt ended the same as all the others: *nada*.

His breath steaming in the night air, Jack stood on the deserted sidewalk, turning in a slow circle. Where did the son of a bitch go? Maybe a sleek Olympic-class sprinter could race out of sight in that short time. But some big old guy with a cane?

Didn't make sense.

But then, why should it? Nothing else did.

Check that: Events of the past year did make sense, but not in the usual way. Not the sort of sense that the average person could understand—or want to.

Jack rubbed his bare arms. It might be spring—mid-April—but the temperature was in the low forties. A bit cool for just a T-shirt.

He took one last look around, then hurried back to Gia's warm bed.

2

Someone said you might be able to help me. I need to keep my daughter from making a terrible mistake.
Christy P.

Jack stared at the last of the messages forwarded from his Web site, repairmanjack.com. None would have been of much interest even if he were working now. He'd blow them off later.

He'd looked into starting a site on MySpace because its sheer size provided an anonymity of sorts, but he'd almost bailed when he discovered that domains repairmanjack, repairman-jack, and repairman_jack were already taken. What the hell? He'd finally had to settle for www.myspace.com/fix_its.

But after setting it up he realized only other MySpace members could contact him there, so he'd kept his original as well.

"Jack? Can I bother you for a minute?"

Though he was in the study and Gia upstairs, Jack could hear the distress in her voice. He had a pretty good idea what was wrong.

"Be right there."

He took a quick sip of coffee and glanced at the computer's time display. Vicky was going to miss her bus if they didn't hustle.

He took the stairs two at a time to the second floor.

"Where are you?"

"Vicky's room."

Figured that.

He walked in and found the two loves of his life sitting on the bed, Vicky facing away, Gia behind her, holding on to her long dark hair.

"I can't do it," Gia said, looking up at him with American-flag eyes: blue on white with red rims. "I still can't do it."

Gia looked too thin. Her weight was still down since the accident. She'd lost a lot during the coma and the early recovery period, but wasn't regaining it now that she was almost back to normal. Though not exactly sunken, her cheeks weren't as full, giving her a haggard look. She still cried now and then but, despite her therapist's advice, resisted taking an antidepressant.

She'd let her blond hair grow to the point where it was now longer than he'd ever seen it, covering her ears and the nape of her neck.

But at the moment Vicky's hair was the problem: Gia had started weaving the back into a French braid but had botched it badly. Not as badly as she had in preceding weeks, but still . . . she used to be able to do this in thirty seconds—with her eyes closed. Now . . .

"Look at this mess."

Jack crouched beside her and kissed her cheek.

"You're getting better every day. Just keep at it. You know what Doctor Kline said."

" 'Practice, practice, practice.' " She sighed. "But it's so frustrating sometimes I want to scream."

And sometimes she did. But never when Vicky was around. Jack would hear her in another room, from another floor. He wondered how often she screamed when she was here alone.

Vicky half-turned her head. "Am I going to be late for school, Mommy?"

"You'll be fine, honey."

Some things had improved in the three months since the accident, but by no means had life returned to normal. Jack doubted it ever would. The broken bones had healed, but scars remained, on the body, the brain, the psyche.

Vicky had the best chance of leaving it all behind. The unborn sister she'd been waiting for would not arrive, and she'd accepted that. Emma had been no more than a bulge in her mother's belly and an image on an ultrasound monitor, not a little person she could see and touch.

Not so Gia. Three months ago she'd stepped off a curb as a mother-to-be and awakened days later to learn she'd lost the baby. Emma had been very real to Gia, a little person who'd turned and kicked inside her. More real to Gia than to her father, Jack.

Gia's scars ran deep.

And not being able to care fully for Vicky slowed their healing.

Her motor skills hadn't returned to normal yet, though they were worlds better than when she'd come out of her coma. With physical and occupational therapy she'd recovered about ninety percent of her manual dexterity, but it was the missing ten percent that was killing her.

She couldn't braid Vicky's hair.

And she couldn't draw or paint—at least not like she used to.

Which meant she couldn't make a living. Graphic art paid her bills, but her personal paintings soothed her soul. She worked daily at both in her third-floor studio, but didn't like much of what she produced commercially, and wouldn't show Jack her private paintings. He worried she'd one day explode and he'd find her splattered all over her studio.

"Am I going to be late for school, Mommy?"

Gia said, "You just asked me that, remember?"

Vicky frowned, then nodded. "Oh, right."

Vicky's only deficit was her short-term memory, but that was steadily improving. The neurologist said she'd be back to normal in a few more months. Her teachers were taking that into account and cutting her some major slack.

Jack looked around at the bookshelves lining the wall of her high-ceilinged bedroom. The good news was that Vicky was still a voracious reader. He glanced at her Jets banner—she remained a devoted fan—and at the four too-handsome faces crowded onto her Boyville poster—still her favorite music group, unfortunately.

Gia was unraveling the botched braid.

"You'd better do it or she'll be late."

As she rose to let Jack take her place, he gripped her elbow.

"Okay, but coach me. I still haven't got this down."

Not true. He'd helped so many times he could do it in his sleep.

So she stood over his shoulder and talked him through brushing out the hair, separating a nice fat lock, then poking his index and middle fingers through to divide it into three fat strands. Then the tricky part of keeping the strands in the webs of his fingers as he picked up new strands while braiding.

"Now . . . which one do I start with?"

He felt a gentle punch on his back and heard a soft laugh from Gia.

"As if you didn't know."

She kneaded his shoulders as he worked.

"Boy, if the guys at Julio's could see you now."

"Why do you say that?"

"Well, I doubt this is the guy they know."

"Maybe not. But you wouldn't hear a peep out of them."

"No rib nudging? No wisecracks?"

"Uh-uh."

"Why not?"

He looked up and winked at her. "Because of the guy they know."

He finished the weave—something very comforting about working with Vicky's hair—and tied it off with a blue elastic band.

"There. Not bad for a guy, ay?"

Gia bent and kissed his cheek. "Actually it's great. And thanks for being so patient."

He looked at her. "Patient? What's patient got to do with it?"

"Everything. It's not one of your strong points. Just . . . thanks for putting up with me."

As she hurried Vicky downstairs, Jack remained on the bed, staring out Vicky's window at the still-bare trees and feeling low. Worse than low. Like a rat. And a cowardly one at that.

Patient? Of course he was patient. He would be patient with her under any circumstance. And considering how he was the cause of all the trauma that had befallen her and Vicky, how else could he be?

But she didn't know that. Because he hadn't told her. Yet.

Gia, the accident that killed our baby, that almost killed you and your daughter, that left the two of you with broken bodies and battered brains, was no accident.

When would be a good time to say that? When would it be okay to tell her it had happened because he cared for them, because they mattered to him, because the baby carried his bloodline?

Would there ever be a right time?

"Dollar for your thoughts?"

Jack jumped. "Hey."

Gia looked down at him. "You seemed a million miles away."

"Just thinking."

Her eyes bore into his. "Didn't look like happy thoughts."

He shrugged. "They weren't. Can you think of much to be happy about?"

She smiled. "I'm alive, Vicky's alive, and it's been great having you stay with us. So look on the bright side."

Yeah. The bright side: moving in here to take care of them after they were released from rehab. Not easy, but maybe the most rewarding thing he'd ever done.

She kissed the top of his head. "Okay, we're heading for the bus stop, then I'm off to OT."

"Want me to drive you?"

She shook her head. "A cab'll have me there by the time you degarage the car. See you for lunch?"

"It's a date."

"Got anything planned for the morning?"

"Probably hang with Abe."

She looked down at him. "No business?"

"No business."

"What about that lady who wants help for her daughter?"

"Hmm? Where?"

"I just saw it on the screen downstairs. She sounds worried."

Jack shrugged. "I'm on hiatus."

"You're bored is what you are. You've made our troubles your troubles, but we're coming out of those troubles. You need a break."

Couldn't argue with that. The less and less Gia and Vicky needed him, the more restless he'd become.

Gia squeezed his shoulder. "Why don't you see what she wants."

He looked up at her. "I believe I'm having an out-of-Gia experience."

She laughed—a sound he didn't hear nearly enough these days.

"Seriously," he said. "This doesn't sound like you."

"Maybe it's a new me. I know spending all your time hanging around here or at Abe's isn't you. I know who you are. I thought I could change you but I realize I can't. I'm no longer sure I want to. You are who you are and I love who you are, so why don't you go out and be who you are?"

Jack stared at her. She meant it—she really meant it. A crack about the lingering effects of brain trauma leaped to mind but he quashed it. Not funny.

"Maybe I'm not so sure who I am anymore."

"You know. It's in your blood. See what the lady wants."

"Doesn't sound like my kind of thing."

"Maybe not, but it's her *daughter*."

The last word hung in the air.

Daughter . . . like Vicky was to him, emotionally if not legally . . . like Emma would have been if not for . . .

He remembered the message: *I need to keep my daughter from making a terrible mistake.*

Like what? Getting involved with a guy like me?

No . . . he wasn't going there again. He'd been there too many times.

"Maybe I'm not on hiatus. Maybe I'm retired."

A wry smile: "Then why are you checking the Web site? As a matter of fact, if you're retired, why keep it up and running at all?"

"Maybe I just haven't got around to shutting it down."

"And maybe you need a diversion, Jack. Go on, give her a call. If it's not in your ballpark, simply beg off." She kissed him and headed for the door. "Gotta run. Think about it."

He sat a moment longer. When he heard the front door close he forced himself to his feet. Lots of inertia lately. Too long since he'd awakened with his own agenda for the day.

He ambled downstairs and into the study where he stood and stared at the screen.

Someone said you might be able to help me . . .

She'd included her phone number.

What mistake do you think your daughter's going to make, lady? And why do you think a stranger will be able to do anything about it?

Okay. He'd bite. Couldn't see any down side to giving her a call.

3

"Nu?" Abe said as Jack approached his perch at the back of the store carrying a paper bag. "Two days in a row—what's the occasion?"

A lot had changed in Jack's life since January, but not Abe's place. The Isher Sports Shop—with its high shelves precariously jammed with dusty sporting goods that no one ever saw, let alone bought, the scarred counter at the rear, the four-legged stool where the proprietor perched in his food-stained white half-sleeve shirt and shiny black pants—remained a constant star in his firmament.

"Nowhere else to go."

"And on me you chose to bestow your presence."

"I figured you'd be lonely."

"So this is charity?"

"It is." He emptied the bag onto the counter. "And so's this."

Abe picked up the package of bagels and stared. His raised eyebrows furrowed his largely naked scalp—his hairline had started retreating with the glaciers.

"What's this? Low-cal bagels you bring me? What's a low-cal bagel? And whipped low-fat cream cheese? Why do you torture me?"

Jack ignored the question because Abe already knew the answer: His ever-expanding waistline concerned Jack. Not for aesthetic reasons—a skinny Abe would be a frightening sight—but he worried it would shorten his best friend's life.

"Have you weighed yourself recently?"

"I was on the scale just yesterday."

"And? What did it say?"

"I couldn't see it. My belly was in the way. They should design these things so people like me can read them."

"Come on, Abe. If it could speak it would have screamed in pain."

Abe sighed. "I did see the number. Very high."

"As much as one of the moons of Jupiter, I'll bet."

"When I read it, I had to face an inescapable fact."

"That you need to diet, right?"

"No. That I need a new scale. My old one is obviously broken."

Jack closed his eyes and shook his head. "You sucked me right into that one, didn't you."

"What can I say? I'm shameless."

"Why do I even try? Next time I'll stop at Muller's on the way."

Abe grinned. "An elephant ear you'll bring me, right?"

"Right. Maybe we're due for some comfort food."

" 'We'?"

"Had that dream again last night."

"Oh." Abe opened the bagel package, adding, "It could be maybe you'll keep on having it until you tell her."

That startled Jack. Could it be? No . . .

"Doesn't explain the watcher and how he seems to trigger the dream. But I fully intend to tell her the whole story. I just need the right moment, the right circumstance."

He'd been searching for that moment and circumstance for months now. Was it simply cowardice?

"You're afraid of her reaction?"

"You think I should be?"

"I don't know. A terrible thing was done to her—to both of you, and Vicky as well. You're not to blame, but . . ."

Yeah . . . but. His only blame was loving her, but would she see it that way?

"She's lost her baby and almost robbed of her livelihood. She's having a hard enough time accepting those losses—and that's while believing herself the victim of a terrible accident. So how the hell is she going to handle knowing. . . . ?"

Abe stared at him. "The truth?"

"Yeah. The truth: That the hit-and-run was intentional, and not simply to hurt her, but to kill her and the baby simply because of their connection to me, because they mean something to me." Something, hell—everything. "What's that going to accomplish besides causing more pain, and more fear?"

"If truth she wants, truth she should have. The longer you wait, the harder it will be when this right moment you mention comes—if it ever does. Maybe it's come and gone already."

Maybe it had.

"She's improving, getting closer and closer to where she'll be able to paint and illustrate again. Once she can do that she'll feel she's able to exert a little more control over her life."

"Why? She should be different from everybody else?"

"I hear that."

Jack polished off his bagel and grabbed Abe's copy of the *Post*. He flipped through it in silence while Abe studied *Newsday*.

"Here's something," Abe said. "A fellow named Walter Erskine died in Monroe Hospital the other night."

Jack frowned. "So?"

"Says he's survived by his sister, Evelyn Bainbridge, of Johnson, New Jersey. Your hometown already."

It hit with a flash. "Crazy Walt! He lasted this long? I thought he would've boozed himself to death long before now." He shook his head. "Harmless guy, but nutty as a Payday."

"Says he's going to be buried in Arlington."

"Yeah, he was a vet. Medic in Nam, if I remember."

Too bad. He had fond memories of Crazy Walt, and unaccountably warm feelings for him . . . a vague recollection of Walt saving his life as a kid. Or maybe not. Kind of a blur. So many things from back then were blurred.

Rest in peace, Walt. You sure didn't have much when you were alive.

After a while Abe said, "Oh, I got a call last night from Doc Buhmann."

"Who?"

The name rang a bell but Jack couldn't place it.

"My old professor. I sent you to him when that Lilitongue thing was causing all that trouble."

"Right, right. The guy from the museum."

Peter Buhmann, Ph.D., associate conservator of languages in the division of anthropology at the Museum of Natural History, professor emeritus at the Columbia University Department of Archaeology. Blah-blah-blah. They'd met only once, briefly, at his office in the museum.

"How's he doing?"

"Well enough. Getting ready to retire to Florida come the end of the year. He was asking about you."

"Me? Why?"

"Since he met you he can't stop thinking about the *Compendium of Srem*."

"Oh?" Jack felt a prickle of unease across his nape. "Why is that?"

"Something about you intrigued him, he says. A scholar you weren't, yet you were asking about legends only scholars—and damn few of them—have even heard of."

"I guess I neglected to mention that my interest was personal and my knowledge firsthand."

"Yeah, but he sensed something, a feeling that you were speaking from experience. He wants to know if you ever found the Lilitongue or the *Compendium*."

Jack knew Abe was the soul of discretion, but Buhmann was one of his revered professors from college. He might have said more than he should have.

"What did you tell him?"

Abe shrugged. "What else? I said I'd ask."

Jack's small lift of relief annoyed him. Should have known better. But the last thing he needed was a bunch of academics sniffing around, looking for him and whatever he might have found.

"Tell him I've got zorch."

"Lie to that old man? He hasn't got long to live, you know."

"What's wrong with him?"

"I should ask? But he told me he didn't have too long left, and how he'd go to his grave happy if he could see the Lilitongue of Gefreda or the *Compendium of Srem* before he died."

"Well, I can't help him with the Lilitongue—no one can—and as for the *Compendium* . . ." Jack shook his head. "Probably best if I keep that under wraps."

"From an old and fading man you're hiding it? Isn't he the one who put you on to the *Compendium*? As I recall, if you hadn't found it, you never would have known how to—"

Jack held up his hand. "Point taken." He scratched his jaw. "You think he can keep his mouth shut?"

"Like a clam, he'll be. Like a stone. He just wants to see it, touch it maybe. This is for him, not for posterity."

Jack considered. He did owe the old man . . .

"All right then. Maybe I'll drop in on him this afternoon and let him have a peek."

Abe clapped his pudgy hands and grinned.

"Excellent. This is a mitzvah you do. You won't regret it."

Jack hated when people said that.

4

Jack stepped into his apartment and sniffed. The air carried a musty tang. Not all that unusual after being closed up for a while. The old wood and old varnish on his Victorian wavy oak furniture gave off subtle but pleasant odors. The must came from the other junk arrayed on the walls—treasure in his eyes, though most other people would consider it junk. Or maybe *junque*.

He jammed his finger into the soil in the pink Shmoo planter as he passed. Nothing stuck. The little ivy plant was thirsty. Had to remember to add water before he left. He glanced at the framed official membership certificates in The Shadow and Doc Savage fan clubs and straightened the Don Winslow Creed on his way to the oak secretary.

Once there, he angled it out from the wall and removed its rear panel. An array of pistols adorned the top, side, and rear walls of the hidden space within. A rolled-up ten-by-twelve-inch flap of skin lay to the left, next to the *Compendium of Srem*. A Ruger SuperRedhawk chambered for .454 Casulls rested atop that.

Jack slipped the book free. Big and heavy, its covers and spine made of some sort of stamped metal.

With the secretary closed and returned to its original position, he placed the *Compendium* on the paw-foot oak table but did not open it. Something about the way the characters blurred and swam for an instant whenever he peeked inside made him queasy.

Instead he pulled his Tracfone from a pocket along with a slip of paper. He dialed the number Christy P. had left. She picked up on the third ring.

"Yes?"

"Christy? This is Jack. You left this number on my Web site."

A pause, then, "Oh, yes. Repairman Jack." Her tone was hesitant. "Interesting name. Did your mother pick it?"

"No, and neither did I. But it gets the job done. You mentioned something about your daughter and a mistake?"

"I think I'm having second thoughts about hiring someone for this via the Internet."

Smart lady.

"Consider having third and fourth thoughts while you're at it. But my site isn't the sort people find by accident. Someone must have sent you. Who?"

"Jeff Levinson. You know the name?"

"I do."

Jack had hired on a few years ago to take care of a recurrent swastika problem at Jeff's delicatessen.

"He speaks very highly of you. But still . . ."

"Your call, lady."

"I don't know . . ."

He could almost hear her chewing her lip.

"Maybe I can help you make up your mind if you tell me what you need done."

"How's that going to work?"

"Because maybe I'm not interested."

A brief pause. "Interesting tactic, playing hard to get."

"Not a tactic. I am hard to get."

Especially these days.

"I like that. I suppose we should meet then. I want someplace public because—"

"You haven't told me yet what you need done."

"So you're really serious about that."

"Some fixes I can do, some I can't. No sense in both of us wasting our time."

Even this phone call was beginning to sound like a waste of time.

She sighed. "Okay. She's involved with an older man."

Hoo-boy. Jack glanced at his watch. How much time had he just wasted?

"So?"

"He's old enough to be her father."

"So?"

"Can you say something else?"

"I'm waiting to hear something I can do something about. Affairs of the heart do not fall into that category."

"Dawn's eighteen and he's in his mid-thirties. Twice her age."

Jack's age.

He tried to imagine a relationship with an eighteen-year-old. What the hell would they talk about? What could he have in common with someone who hadn't finished her second decade, who was basically a high school kid? Sure, fantasy cheerleader sex and all that, but you needed something more to fill the down time.

Or did you?

He guessed coming so close to being a father—of a daughter, no less— could be affecting his perspective.

"I don't see how hiring me is going to help, Christy. What are you looking for? Someone to break his legs? Shoot him? That's not the way I work."

At least not unless someone really had it coming.

"No, nothing like that! I want to get something on him. Something that'll let my little girl see him for what he really is."

"You already know what he really is?"

"Well . . . no. But there's got to be something. There's *always* something, right? Besides, I get a bad vibe from this guy."

Time to end this.

"I suppose. But what you need is a private investigator. Someone who can—"

"I've already been that route."

"And?"

"Long story. Look, Jeff said you were tops—pricey, but tops—and just the guy I need. Can't we just sit down and talk over the details? I probably shouldn't say this, but money isn't an object. I've got money. It's results I want."

"I don't think I'm your man."

"If nothing else, maybe you can get my retainer back from the investigator I hired." Out of the blue she sobbed. Once. The sound took Jack by surprise. He hadn't seen it coming. "Please? I'm really, really worried about my little girl."

Her little girl . . . she might be eighteen, but he guessed your little girl was your little girl forever.

Like Emma would have been.

"Okay. We'll meet. I'll listen. But I'm not promising anything."

A sniff. "Thank you. Where? No offense, but I'll feel safer if it's a public place."

Jack laughed. "So will I. Where are you located?"

"Queens. Forest Hills."

Fairly ritzy neighborhood.

"That means it's no big deal to get into the city."

"I'm in all the time."

He doubted he could help her, but he could hear her out and maybe point her in the right direction.

"Can you make it in this afternoon?"

He was testing. If she wouldn't meet this afternoon, he'd know it wasn't as important as she'd made it seem.

"Sure. Tell me when and where."

Well, that settled that.

"There's this bar I know in the West Eighties . . ."

5

Jack stepped into the open door and knocked on the frame.

"Doctor Buhmann?"

He'd called ahead to make sure the professor would be in. The man glanced up from his desk.

"Oh, yes. Mister . . . I must confess I've forgotten your surname."

Wrong. Jack had never told him.

"Just Jack'll do fine. How're you doing?"

Not well, if his appearance meant anything. He looked even thinner and sallower than on Jack's December visit. And his office seemed even more cramped and claustrophobic. What courses had Abe taken from him in his Columbia days? *How to Cram Amazing Amounts of Junk onto Shelves 101?*

The old man waggled his hand. "So-so. No use complaining." His wrinkle-caged gaze was fixed on the plastic shopping bag dangling from Jack's hand. "You said you had something to show me?"

"Remember that mythical book you told me about?"

He licked his lips. "*The Compendium of Srem.* Don't tell me . . ."

"Before we go any further, we need to agree on some ground rules."

"Conditions? Yes-yes. Anything, anything." He reached toward the bag. "Just let me—"

"First condition: Not a word of this to anyone."

"You want to keep your ownership a secret? Yes, of course. I can understand that. The means by which antiquities change hands can at times be—how shall I say it?—controversial. I assure you, your name—which I don't even know—will not be connected with it."

He thinks I stole it, Jack thought.

Well, in a way he had.

"No. When I say not a word, I mean just that: You speak to no one about this. No one is to know the book exists. It remains a myth."

The professor looked shocked. "That is much to ask. I cannot even speak of what I've seen?"

"I'm doing this as a favor to Abe because of his high regard for you, and as payback for your giving me a little guidance when I needed it."

The *Compendium* had helped save Vicky from . . . what? He still didn't know exactly. But he did know that if not for this book she'd be gone now.

"Then surely you can allow me to lord it over my colleagues that I've touched something they've denied existed, seen something they haven't and most likely never will."

"And when you can't produce it, they'll think you're either going senile or you've lost your mind."

"Yes, I suppose they will."

"And then, to defend your reputation, you'll tell them about the guy who brought it to your office. And maybe someone will believe you. And maybe I'm on a security tape entering and leaving the building. And maybe someone will start looking for me."

Jack had honed his skills at spotting security cameras. When he couldn't avoid them, he'd wear a baseball cap—today's was emblazoned with the Mets' orange *NY*—and kept the peak low over his face.

But no tactic worked one hundred percent. If one of Buhmann's younger, aggressive colleagues knew Jack's face and went looking for the *Compendium* . . .

Jack lived not far from here. What if the guy got lucky and spotted him on the street and followed him home?

No thanks.

"You're a very cautious young man. I might hazard to say overly cautious."

Jack smiled. "You wouldn't be the first to say that."

Buhmann sighed. "Very well. I will go to my grave without uttering a word about what you're going to show me."

Jack thrust out his right hand. "I have your word on that?"

The professor gripped it. His skin was dry and papery.

"My word as a gentleman and a scholar." He blinked at Jack. "Now, may I please see what's in that sack?"

Jack pulled the thick volume from the bag and, despite the care he took, its weight made a *thunk* as it settled on the desktop.

"Here you go. A real, live myth."

Buhmann sat and stared, saying nothing. Jack stared too, watching as the doodles embossed on the metallic cover blurred and shifted into the word *Compendium* in large ornate letters; below that, smaller, the word *Srem.*

Buhmann looked up at him as if to say, Did you see that?

Jack nodded. "It gets better. Open it."

The old man's gnarled fingers trembled as he lifted the cover. He froze, blinking as the squiggles on the first page morphed into words.

"Incredible."

"Yeah. I know. You don't expect something this old to be in modern-day English."

"If this is truly the *Compendium of Srem,* English wasn't even a language when it was written."

Back in December the prof had given him a crash course in the legends surrounding the ancient book: Written in the First Age, filled with the lore of a civilization predating known history, and virtually indestructible. Legend had it that Grand Inquisitor Torquemada had consigned it to the flames as heretical and blasphemous. And when it wouldn't burn he ordered it hacked to pieces. And when axes and swords failed to get the job done, he buried it in a deep pit in Avila and built the Monastery of St. Thomas over the spot and lived there until his death.

Jack had found all that pretty hard to swallow. Even harder had been the legend that its text conformed to the native language of the reader.

The *Compendium* hadn't stayed buried. Somehow it fell into the hands of a globe-spanning cult. And from there, into Jack's.

He'd soon learned that all the tales were true.

Buhmann stared at Jack; tears rimmed his eyes. "It's in German! I . . . I was born in Vienna and came here when I was ten. English has been my language for over seventy years, but I grew up speaking German. What language do you see?"

Jack knew the answer but took a look, just to be sure.

"English."

The prof turned back to the book and began leafing through it.

"Does it list, as I told you, the Seven Infernals?"

"It do."

"And the Lilitongue of Gefreda? Did you find it?"

"I did."

His head shot up. "No! You did? Where is it? I must see—"

"Gone. And don't ask where because I don't know." He pointed to the book. "You'll even find an animated page in there."

Jack hadn't been through the whole book. It seemed to have far more pages than even its size would account for, and little of what he'd read made much sense. At least not to him.

The prof fixed his gaze on Jack. "Can we try a little experiment?"

Wary, Jack said, "Like what?"

"I want to see what happens when I photocopy a page. We have a copier just down the hall."

Though not crazy about the possibility of someone in the hall spotting the book and asking about it, Jack decided he'd like to see that too.

"Okay. But let's not make a production out of it. Down the hall and back, lickety-split."

Buhmann rose and, with the book clutched against his chest like a child's teddy bear, led the way into the hall. He nodded and smiled and said hello to a Maggie and a Ronnie, who looked like secretaries, and to a Marty whose mop identified him as a janitor.

When they reached the copier, the prof looked all around to make sure no one was near—in the process making himself look either sneaky or guilty or both—then opened the *Compendium* to a random page, pressed it against the glass, and hit the button. As the light bar made its transit, Buhmann did another three-sixty scan of his surroundings. Jack looked at the ceiling to keep from laughing.

The prof pulled the copy from the tray. After giving it a quick once-over he pumped his fist in the air.

"Yes! Yes!"

A few seconds later they were back in his office. Buhmann's hand shook like he had Parkinson's.

"Look! The translating property—it doesn't work with a machine. What you're seeing here is the handwriting of the original author."

Jack stared at the vaguely glyphic squiggles.

"Srem?"

The prof shrugged. "We don't know anything about Srem—does the word refer to a man, a group, a location? Who knows? But what we're looking at here is a language of the First Age."

"How do you know?"

"Because I've studied languages all my adult life. There is no known human language that even approximates this." He looked at Jack. "And I can't tell a soul?"

Jack took the sheet and ripped it in half, then in quarters, then stuffed the pieces in a pocket.

"Not a soul. Eyes only, remember?"

The prof heaved a sigh. "Very well. How long do I have to study it?"

Jack glanced at his watch. He'd arranged to meet Christy P. at two. He could get that done, then be back here by four.

"I can give you a couple-three hours."

Doc Buhmann's eyes widened. *"Hours?* I was talking weeks!"

Should have known. No good deed goes unpunished.

"Hey, prof, the idea was just to let you have a peek. According to Abe, all you wanted was one look before you passed on to meet the Great Curator in the sky. Isn't that what you said?"

"Yes . . . yes, I suppose I did. But this is the find of a lifetime."

"We're not going to argue, are we?" Jack reached for the book. "Because in that case—"

The prof's hands hovered protectively over the book.

"All right, all right! A few hours it is. Which means I haven't a moment to waste."

He sat, turned his back to Jack, and began flipping pages.

"Remember," Jack said. "The book stays right here. No sharing, no photo-copying. Agreed?"

The prof fluttered a hand at him without looking up. "Yes-yes. Agreed. Now allow me some peace and quiet, please. I must make every minute count."

Jack stepped to the door, then hesitated. He looked back. Was he going to regret this? He did owe the guy, but would this little kindness come back to haunt him?

Or was he being too much of a tight ass? How much could it hurt to lend him the damn book for a week or two? Jack wasn't doing anything with it. It was just taking up space in his apartment.

He shook his head. Too risky. He didn't know what was in the weird book, and someone might find something they could put to use in a bad way.

A couple of hours . . . he'd give the old man a couple of hours, but that was it.

6

Like Abe's shop, Julio's bar was another constant star in the chaotic firmament of Jack's life. The dead potted ferns and such still hung in the window; Lou and Barney still stood at the short curved bar, keeping it from tipping over; the dim interior carried the familiar tang of tobacco smoke and spilled beer; and the FREE BEER TOMORROW . . . sign still hung over the stacked liquor bottles.

Lou looked up, ready to stamp out his cigarette if he saw a stranger.

"It's okay," he announced to the other smokers. "Just Jack."

Julio let the regulars smoke when only other regulars were around. The anti-smoking laws pissed him off: If people didn't like a smoky atmosphere they could go to one of the bars down the street. But he wasn't stupid—all it took for a big fine and maybe license problems was one phone call from a stranger who'd stopped in for a taste and encountered fog.

"'Just Jack'? That's a helluva welcome."

Lou wore dusty work pants and a denim jacket. He flashed a gap-toothed smile and raised a pinky.

"For a second there I mistook you for some panty-wearing yuppie dropping by for a glahss of shah-doe-nay."

Jack raised a menacing fist. "You're cruisin', Louie."

Lou laughed and turned back to the bar. Jack continued on to his usual table against the rear wall. From behind the bar Julio raised his hands: a coffeepot in one, a green bottle in the other. Jack pointed to the Yuengling lager. Used to be Julio would hold up a Rolling Rock but Jack had abandoned the brand after Anheuser-Busch bought it and closed the old Latrobe brewery. The American beer wars: If a smaller competitor is making a better beer, don't try to outdo them, just buy them and shut them down.

Up yours, Budweiser.

As Jack was settling himself with his back against the wall, Julio arrived with the Yuengling. A short man whose bulging muscles filled out his white Flying Spaghetti Monster T-shirt, Julio sported a pencil-line mustache and another of his awful colognes.

Jack sniffed and made a face. "What is it this time? *Perfume de Muerte?*"

"It's called Aztec God. Great, huh?"

"Swell. Look, I'm expecting a customer in about ten—"

"Really?" Julio broke into a grin. "You getting back into business? Tha's great, meng!"

Jack realized he shouldn't have said "customer." He was pretty sure she wasn't going to be one.

"We're just going to talk."

"Yeah, but tha's how it always starts. Pretty soon you gonna be fixin' stuff again."

Maybe, maybe not.

Impending fatherhood had placed Jack in a position where he couldn't see much choice but to ascend from underground and put himself on the world's radar. Abe had set up a new identity for him and Jack had gone as far as taking the first step toward becoming a citizen when the hit-and-run changed everything.

With Emma's death the need for a new identity had lost its urgency and he saw little use in pursuing it. Easier to stay where he was . . . out of sight and out of his mind.

"We'll see."

As Julio headed back to the bar, a well-dressed blonde stepped through the door and froze, wrinkling her nose. Jack saw Lou stub out his butt and hide the ashtray under the bar. Julio spotted her and veered in her direction. A few whispered words and then he was leading her back toward Jack.

"Someone here to see you," he said as they stopped before the table.

Jack rose and offered his hand.

"Christy? Jack."

She took his hand gingerly and gave it a squeeze.

Julio said, "You want beer? Wine? Coffee?"

She looked the cosmo type, and like she wanted one, but she shook her head.

"No, thank you."

Jack indicated the opposite chair. "Have a seat."

She sat—gingerly. She rested her handbag on the table—gingerly. She touched the tabletop—gingerly.

Jack hid a smile. The furniture did tend to be a little sticky and Miss Priss had probably never been in a workingman's bar.

He gave her a quick once-over. He didn't know much about women's clothes, but her light blue skirt and jacket looked pricey. So did the semi-sheer white blouse beneath. No question about the diamond rings and bracelets: the real thing. She wasn't dressing for success; this was the way success dressed.

She wore her bobbed, ash-blond hair—not the real thing, like Gia's— parted in the middle, and had eyes almost as blue as Gia's. Maybe she had a nice smile, but Jack couldn't tell. Right now she looked tired and grim.

"Usually places on the Upper West Side are . . ." She seemed to be searching for a word.

"Nicer? Julio's is a holdover from the times when you came to this neighborhood to *save* on rent." He sipped from his Yuengling. "Sure you wouldn't like a drink?"

Her expression stayed tight. "I'd love one—I'm a Diet Pepsi addict—but I'm not sure my immunizations are up to date."

Oooh, a regular Margaret Cho.

"Okay. You wanted to talk. The floor is yours."

She leaned back, looking even more tired.

"Where to begin? Dawn's a good kid. Turned eighteen in March, graduates Benedictine Academy next month with honors."

"B-A, huh? Must be smart."

"Great academic smarts—though you'd never guess it by the way she speaks—but no common sense, apparently. She's been accepted to Colgate. She's got a wonderful future ahead of her, and then this son of a bitch comes along and . . ." She shook her head. "Sorry."

Jack shrugged. "Don't be. Tell me about him. When did he come along?"

"Right after the first of the year. Started showing up at the Tower Diner where Dawn works."

"The Tower Diner?" Jack knew a lot of diners but not the Tower. "Where's that?"

"Queens Boulevard in Rego Park. Close to home."

"No offense, but you don't look the diner type."

She leaned forward and tapped her index finger on the tabletop.

"I grew up waitressing in diners and Waffle Houses and IHOPs and God knows where else. Nothing wrong with the Tower, and nothing wrong with waiting tables there. It's good for a kid to have a job. Teaches them what the real world's like. Lets them see what kind of hole their government leaves in their check every week. And waiting tables sharpens your people skills."

Jack remembered a now-extinct Little Italy trattoria where he waited tables when he first came to town. Made some friends on the staff, but didn't think he'd added to his already abundant charm.

"You're telling me you don't come from money, I take it."

Her laugh was bitter. "I come from *nothing*. Never went to college, at least not formally. Took courses here and there along the way, though. But most of what I know I learned on my own, and *all* of what I own I've *earned* on my own."

"How?"

Here was something Jack wanted to know.

"Day trading."

"Really." Hadn't expected that. "I heard most folks had dropped out of that."

"Because they lost their shirts, most likely. But I seem to have a knack for it. I started with a little money back in the nineties when you couldn't lose. I made it grow, and kept it growing even after the bubble burst in 2000—learned you could make money even in a down market if you knew what you were doing."

"Good for you."

"And you know what? It's the perfect job for a mother. You do it from home. I'd finish my trades and be logged off before Dawnie walked in the door. I was there for her every day, ready to take her anywhere she needed to go. No having to go through what I did growing up. I gave her every opportunity to maximize her potential—and she has a lot—and now this."

Okay. Now to the heart of it.

"So now this older man comes into her life and . . . what?"

"He all but takes over, that's what."

"How does a guy in his mid-thirties take over an eighteen-year-old's life?"

She looked away. "I think they're having sex. In fact I'm positive they're having sex."

"Lots of eighteen-year-olds are having sex. Probably most of them."

"Not with men twice their age."

Yeah, Jack could see how the thought of your teenage daughter in bed with a guy her father's age could upset you. But since the girl was past the age of consent, you couldn't use the system to pull them apart. You had to go outside the system.

Where Jack operated.

"What's her dad think of this?"

"He's not in the picture," she said, her tone matter of fact. "Never was, never will be."

He drained his Yuengling. "Okay. Give me the *Reader's Digest* version. She's working at this diner and he's what—a regular?"

Christy nodded. "His name is Jerry Bethlehem and he began showing up sometime in January. After a while he started asking to be seated at one of Dawn's tables. I remember her telling me about this really interesting guy with the cool job who was a great tipper."

"What sort of cool job?"

"A freelance video game designer."

Jack nodded. That did sound pretty cool.

"Dawn's never been into video games, for which I'm glad—nothing but time wasters—but that's just what allowed him to set his hook into her."

"I don't get it."

"Neither did I at first. He's clever. He told her she was just the person he needed to talk to because she was an untapped market for games. If he could design a game that appealed to non-playing girls and young women like her, he'd have every video game company in the world pounding on his door."

"And if she helps him design it, he'll cut her in."

"Full partnership—fifty-fifty. She'll be queen of the video game industry. Or so he says."

Money and fame . . . quite a siren call.

"So he lures her over to his apartment—"

"Oh, no. He's too smooth for anything so obvious. A move like that would have set off Dawnie's alarm bells right away. And he has a townhouse, by the way. What he does is suggest they sit down and brainstorm the project at *her* house so he can meet her folks and assure them that he's not some nut case with bad intentions."

"Which you believe he's had all along."

"I don't believe. I know."

"How?"

"I . . ." Suddenly she looked unsure of herself—the first time since she'd walked in. "I just do."

Jack's skepticism must have shown.

"Don't look at me like that," she said. "A mother knows. This man is a seducer."

"So you've met him?"

"Right in my own living room. Bold as day. 'How do you do, Mrs. Pickering.' 'You have a wonderful-brilliant-beautiful daughter, Mrs. Pickering.' But Mrs. Pickering wasn't born yesterday."

Jack now knew what the P in Christy P. stood for. Something familiar about "Pickering" . . . from a long time ago.

Anyway . . . a single mother with a guy her own age making a play for her daughter. Sure, the protective instinct comes out, but Christy Pickering seemed to be protesting a tad too much. Maybe more than a tad. Envy, maybe? Jealousy? A little *hey-what's-wrong-with-me?* thing going down here?

"Is this Jerry Bethlehem good looking?"

She shrugged. "He's no Matthew McConaughey, if that's what you mean, but he's not bad looking. Mostly it's his eyes. He's got these piercing blue eyes that seem to look into your soul and let you feel you're looking into his."

"And what do you see there?"

"If you're naïve, you see truth."

"And if you're not?"

"Ice."

Whoa. "That so?"

"You're giving me that look again. His eyes can convince people who haven't been around the block that everything he's saying is the truth, but I've read Charles Manson has eyes like that."

Jack had read that too.

"Has he got some sort of cult thing going? Preaching revolution?"

"No . . . he's not even promising the moon with this video game scheme, but he's a bent wire. I feel it in my bones. He plays at being this charming, folksy Southerner but deep down he's a redneck hick and I can't believe he designs video games."

"But if they're hanging out in your living room, how—?"

"If only! That's where they started, but then they began meeting at his place because he has a better computer. Now Dawn's talking about moving in with him."

"But she'll be going off to Colgate—"

She threw up her hands. "College? Who needs college when you're going to conquer the video game world?" Her voice rose in pitch. "'It's a twenty-seven-billion-dollar-a-year industry, Mom, and Jerry and I will be its king and queen.'" She returned to normal. "So what's college going to do for her?"

Her lips quivered as she blinked back tears. She pulled a tissue from her purse and dabbed her eyes.

"Sorry. It's just that our life has been kind of a Hallmark card until now. And okay, maybe I've been living vicariously through Dawn, giving her all the opportunities I never had, giving her every possible chance to be everything she could be. And so, yes, seeing her throwing it all away on some video game pipe dream with a guy twice her age is killing me. But it's more than that. There's something wrong with Jerry Bethlehem. He's hiding something. I want to know what it is—I want *Dawn* to know before it's too late. Before he . . . hurts her."

"Hurts her how?"

She dabbed her eyes again. "I don't know. But he's got something bad planned for her. I just know it."

Jack didn't know the truth of that in the real world, but sensed it was very real to Christy.

"So you hired this PI to get something on him."

"Right. Michael Gerhard. His specialty is divorce work—getting the goods on cheating spouses."

A million of those guys around the city. A lot of them ex-cops.

"And he found . . . ?"

"Nothing. At least nothing I know of. He's not returning my calls. He came to my house, seemed very organized and professional. I wrote him a re-tainer check—which he cashed the next day—and haven't heard from him since."

"When was that?"

"Two weeks ago."

"Not so long—"

"He said he'd contact me in a few days with a preliminary report. He called four days later and told me that since Mister Bethlehem—he was very formal about the creep—was a freelancer without a nine-to-five job, it was tak-ing a little longer to build a database on him. When I didn't hear from him af-ter that, I gave him a call. No answer, no call back." She flashed Jack a defiant look. "I paid him good money and I want results—I want them before Dawn moves out."

"Is she headed that way?"

"Not yet, but she's been fiddling with the suitcases in the basement. Time's running out."

"Because you feel it will be easier to keep her from going than to get her back?"

She nodded. "But Gerhard hasn't returned one of my calls."

"He have an office?"

"No." She chewed her lip. "The address I thought was his office turns out to be a Mailboxes R Us or something like that. His phone is a cell."

"Might just mean he's keeping his overhead down."

Not every PI had a wisecracking receptionist and kept a .38 in the top drawer and a bottle of scotch in the bottom.

But they should.

"Do you think . . . ?" She paused, then, "Do you think he could have found out something about Bethlehem and be blackmailing him?"

Possible, but . . .

"Well, if he's that much of a crook, he'd be calling back and stringing you along for a few extra payments."

"What if Bethlehem bought him off? Or . . ." She leaned forward. "What if he found something and Bethlehem killed him?"

"That's a helluva *what-if*."

Though not an impossibility.

"Find out for me, will you? Find Gerhard, see what he knows about Bethlehem."

"And get your money back?"

"Anything you get back you can keep. As a bonus. On top of your fee." She patted her purse. "Which I have right here."

Jack considered. Finding Gerhard seemed doable. Brace the guy and get him either to finish what he'd started or return the retainer. Or tell Jack what he knew about Bethlehem so Jack could pass it on to Christy.

Piece of cake.

Yeah, sure.

But Jack had to admit Christy had piqued his curiosity about this Jerry Bethlehem. What games had he designed? Shouldn't be too hard to track that down. A Google or two would probably do it.

Christy Pickering was staring at him, a pleading look in her big blue eyes.

"Can you help me? Please?"

Oh, why not? He needed something to do. A small project like this was perfect. Take a couple of days, tops.

"Okay, I'll give it a shot."

"Thank God! Thank *you*!"

"Don't thank me yet. I'll take the Gerhard angle and that's all. Here's how we'll work it . . ."

7

Back in the saddle, Jack thought as he strolled up Central Park West. For only a short ride, true, but it felt good.

When he reached the museum he stood aside to let a horde of school kids crowd through an exit door in a brownstone arch and swarm toward their idling yellow buses. Once they were past he headed for the museum offices. The receptionist remembered him and passed him through.

On the way up the stairs he checked his watch. A little after four. The prof had had almost three hours with the *Compendium*. Jack knew he was going to face pleas for more time but he'd done his good deed for the day-week-year-whatever. Time to collect his book and go home.

Again came the thought about letting the old guy keep it longer, and again he pushed it aside. He'd needed the *Compendium* once. Never knew when he might need it again.

He knocked on Dr. Buhmann's door, then opened it—and froze on the threshold.

The prof sat slumped forward in his chair, his arms hanging limp at his sides, his right cheek against his desktop.

Jack leaped to his side.

"Doc!" He shook his shoulder. "Doc, you okay?"

But he wasn't okay. The chair rolled back and the old man would have tumbled to the floor if Jack hadn't caught him.

"Christ!"

Emaciated though he was, he was still dead weight. As Jack eased him to the floor he noticed he was still warm. And when he stretched him out on his back he saw him take a breath.

Still alive.

But what had happened?

He did a quick search for a wound or a bump on the head but found nothing. Then he noticed how the right side of the prof's face sagged, compared to the left.

Stroke?

He jumped up and dashed into the hallway.

"Hey! Anybody here? We've got a problem!"

An elderly woman stuck her head through a doorway. "What's the matter?"

"Doctor Buhmann. Something's wrong with him."

"What?" She hurried toward him. "Where?"

Jack stepped aside to let her see. "I think he's had a stroke."

"Oh, dear!" The woman jammed her hand against her mouth. "I'll call nine-one-one!"

As she hurried back into the hall, Jack dropped to a knee beside the prof. Yeah. Still breathing.

Eye level with the desktop now, he glanced across it. He saw a couple of sheets of paper, but no book.

"Oh, hell!"

He jumped to his feet and searched the desk and the area around it. No *Compendium*, but he did find a couple of Xeroxed sheets. One was filled with the squiggles they'd seen earlier, the other showed a strange design surrounded by its own squiggles.

What was it? Some sort of spider? But it had only six legs.

As he stared at the figure, a strange feeling stole over him. He was sure he hadn't seen this thing before, but it seemed familiar. It triggered an odd twinge inside, as if something he hadn't been aware of, something sleeping within him had stirred.

Then he realized what these sheets meant.

"Oh, hell!"

The prof had promised no copies, but obviously he hadn't kept his word. Bad enough. But what had he done with the damn book?

Or had somebody stolen it?

He checked the prof again and found no sign of injury. But no sign of the book either.

Jack folded and pocketed the sheets, then waited for the EMTs to show.

What had happened here?

8

He hung around until the prof had been wheeled away. When everyone else followed the stretcher down the hall, Jack stayed behind and searched the office, opening every drawer and checking all the shelves. A book that size would be hard to hide and, with its metallic cover, even harder to miss. But he came up empty. No *Compendium of Srem*.

Out in the hall he drew one of the secretaries aside. She was young with black-dyed hair, dark mascara, and pale makeup.

"I brought in a book for Doctor Buhmann earlier. He was going to look it over and then, um, give me his opinion on it."

"I'm afraid I can't let you take anything from his office."

Jack had seen that coming, but it was a moot point at the moment.

"I can understand that, but the problem is, I don't see the book anywhere."

"What did it look like?"

"Not like any other book you've ever seen. You'd remember if you saw it."

She shook her head. "I did see him bring a book to the copier, but I didn't get a look at it. And I know he didn't leave it there because I used the copier right after him. I saw him go straight back to his office. So it has to be there."

"It's not. Trust me."

She frowned. "Are you saying it was stolen?"

"I left him reading it at his desk. I come back and find him out cold and the book gone. What would you think?"

She made no reply, but something in her eyes . . .

He said, "Have you had other things go missing lately?"

"Maybe you'd better talk to Security."

Just about the last thing Jack wanted to do, but he didn't see that he had much choice.

9

Dark had fallen by the time Jack made it back to Gia's. No sign of the watcher—not that he'd expected any. But inside he found Gia sitting in the library with a familiar-looking woman—slight with fine pale features and glossy black hair.

Alicia Clayton, M.D., medical director of the St. Vincent's Center for Children with AIDS. The sight of her banished thoughts of men in homburgs and stroked-out professors.

Smiling, she rose and hugged him.

"Long time, Jack."

True. Well over a year since she'd hired him to retrieve some Christmas toys stolen from the center, then again for a more personal problem echoing from the horrors of her childhood.

"How're things at the center?"

She shrugged. "You know how it is: Never good, but not as bad as it could be."

Jack nodded. When dealing day after day with kids with AIDS . . . maybe that was the best you could hope for.

"What brings you uptown?"

"Me." Gia rose from her chair and stepped toward them. She looked tired. "She wants me to go back to volunteering at the center."

Gia used to be a regular down there, holding and rocking and feeding the AIDS infants. She'd stopped with the pregnancy. But now . . .

"How do you feel about that?"

Gia shrugged. "I don't know if I'm ready."

"Well, only you can decide that," Alicia said. "But your visits brightened many a little life."

Gia bit her lip. "Yes, well . . ."

Alicia slipped her arms around her. "When you're ready for us, we're ready for you."

Gia returned the hug without speaking. Alicia broke it off.

"Gotta go. I'm dragging Will to a fund-raiser for the center."

"Will the cop?" Jack said. She was still going out with Detective Will Matthews?

Alicia laughed. "Don't worry. I've never mentioned you."

Gia was lifting the tea tray from the table.

"I'll put this away and get your coat."

As soon as she was out of sight Alicia grabbed his arm.

"She's changed, Jack."

"You should have seen her two months ago."

"I can imagine. But inside and out—she's not the same."

Jack didn't want to hear that.

"She will be. She's tough."

"I know she is. But get her back to the center if you can. I think it will be good therapy. Holding a newborn might be tough as hell for her at first, but once she gets past that, I think it will do her a world of good."

"I'll do what I can. Nice of you to visit."

"After all her trips to the center, it was the least I could do. I would have come sooner but I didn't want to intrude."

And then Gia was back. Jack helped Alicia into her coat and together he and Gia waved good-bye as she hurried up to the top of the block for a cab.

Jack hitched Gia closer. "What do you think of her idea?"

"Sounds good, but I don't think I'm ready. I might drop one of those babies." She kissed him on the cheek. "Got to get dinner ready."

As she moved away he searched the street, looking for a homburg-wearing man with a cane. But the street was empty.

WEDNESDAY

1

"You were right," Abe said as Jack approached the store's rear counter. "A stroke. A bad one. He's still in a coma and might not come out."

Jack had called Abe with the bad news yesterday.

"How do you know?"

"From his doctor, who else? Just now, before you came in, I was on the phone already."

"I thought that kind of information was supposed to be privileged."

"It is. But not from a worried son calling all the way from Florida."

"I see. No sign of injury or foul play?"

"Because of what you told me about the missing book I asked just that, and the doctor says no. A spontaneous thing." Abe shook his head. "A good man. A brilliant man. Such a thing shouldn't happen to a dog."

"Here's a weird thought: Do you think the book could have caused it?"

"Your *Compendium*? How can a book cause a stroke?"

"Maybe he read something that got him so upset or horrified or whatever that he stroked out."

"His doctor—the neurologist who's taking care of him—said it was a brain hemorrhage."

"All right then: Could something in the book have pushed his blood pressure so high he blew out an artery in his head?"

Abe shrugged. "Me? A lowly merchant? I should know?"

Jack held up a white paper bag, darker in spots where grease from the contents had soaked through.

"Figured you'd need some comfort food."

Abe's eyes widened. "From Muller's?"

"Where else?"

Abe wiggled his fingers. "Let me see. Let me see. You brought me an elephant ear? Please say you brought me an elephant ear."

Jack had to smile as he deposited the bag on Abe's pile of morning newspapers. Some people are so easy to please.

"Got two—one for you and one for me."

Abe's fingers fairly trembled as he pulled the sack open and peeked. He pulled out a flat, oblong donut. Elephant ears from Muller's weren't the sugared fried dough usually associated with the name. These were like a flattened cruller, thick-glazed and dusted with some sulfurous yellow powder.

Abe took a big bite. He closed his eyes and made guttural Muttley noises as he chewed. Parabellum, his parakeet, must have been conditioned to those sounds because a light blue streak swooped out of nowhere and landed on the counter, ready to catch the inevitable crumbs.

Jack pulled out the other elephant ear and tossed a bit to the bird.

"'Splain this to a confused old man," Abe said around a second mouthful. "On some days, rabbit food you bring me; and others—like today—an artery plug. Why?"

He wasn't sure. Maybe the prof's stroke got him thinking that life was too short and too unpredictable to keep denying yourself what you really enjoy. He might feel differently tomorrow, but today had felt like an elephant-ear-for-Abe day.

Jack shrugged. "Don't know. It's a mystery. Like the whereabouts of that damn book."

"You keeping after the museum?"

Jack nodded. "Yeah. Talked to one of the security guys again this morning. They haven't found it. But one of the maintenance crew didn't show up today—the one who'd been working on the prof's floor yesterday. They checked his locker but no book."

"Probably not him. Think of all the curios and artifacts a janitor must see around the museum on a regular basis. He should risk his job and whatever else to steal a book?"

"Not just any book—a one of a kind."

"And a maintenance man's going to know that?"

Good point, Jack thought, but . . .

"The security guy said a funny thing this morning. Said they found a book in the maintenance guy's locker, but it wasn't mine. Then he said, 'Looks like he's a Kicker.' Any idea what he was talking about?"

"Probably means the book they found was *Kick*."

"Never heard of it."

Abe's eyebrows rose. "Really? It's something of a phenomenon. I saw an article on it in yesterday's *Post*. Don't you read the papers?"

"Sometimes. A little—usually right here. But I don't study them like you do."

Abe slid off his stool and rummaged under the counter, finally coming up with a tabloid. He thumbed through it, then folded it back and turned it toward Jack.

"There. Big as life."

Jack glanced at the header—*Kicking Back with Hank Thompson*—and saw a photo of a guy he assumed was the author. Below that was a picture of the book's cover—

He snatched the paper from Abe's hand.

"Christ!"

Ice water trickled down his spine as he stared: The word *Kick* ran across the top, the author's name along the bottom, and between them . . . a chillingly familiar insectoid stick figure.

"Nu?"

Jack dropped the paper and dug into his back pocket. He pulled out the sheets he'd found on the prof's desk and unfolded them, then held the figure copied from the *Compendium* next to the reproduction of the cover.

The same . . . exactly the same.

And again, that feeling of familiarity, of connection.

"What the hell?"

2

"He's something of a phenomenon," Abe said as Jack skimmed through the article. "He self-published the book two years ago and sold tens of thousands of copies over the Internet. One of the New York houses picked it up and it's become a bestseller."

"But what is it?"

The article wasn't much help. It mentioned the author's "troubled youth" as if everyone knew about it. And Hank Thompson's quotes about searching inside for the true inner you and then breaking down the barriers that blocked you from your real self sounded trite.

> *"Aldous Huxley said to open the doors of perception." He laughs. "I dropped out of school in the tenth grade. I know about Huxley through the Doors. Jim Morrison—the Lizard King—has always been a personal hero of mine. But I say, don't be satisfied with just opening those doors—KICK THEM DOWN!" he shouts in the oratory style that has packed his speaking engagements across the country.*

Jim Morrison was his hero? Jack looked at the picture and figured, Yeah, he must be. With that long, unruly, wavy dark hair, Thompson could be what Morrison would have looked like if he'd survived into his late thirties. Except for the eyes. He lacked Morrison's piercing dark eyes.

"Of all the possible people through human history to look up to, he picks Jim Morrison?"

Abe frowned. "Jim Morrison . . . who's Jim Morrison? Is he a customer?"

"Never mind. Is this guy for real?"

An Abe shrug. "I should know? Apparently lots of people think so."

> *"I tell them to KICK down those doors and let in the light—new light, new air, a new world awaits. The future is calling—ANSWER!"*

Jack looked up. "People buy this stuff?"

"By the ton. Apparently he's a mesmerizing speaker."

Jack read on and stopped at another quote.

"It is time to separate yourselves from the herd. You know who you are. You know who I'm talking to. You don't belong with the herd. Come out of hiding. Step away from the crowd. Let the dissimilation begin!"

"'Dissimilation.' That's a new one."

"You should remember it. Adopt it even. It's what you've done with your life already."

Jack thought about that. He supposed he had. But he got the feeling Thompson wasn't talking about living under the radar.

When I ask him what he has to say about claims that an unusually high percentage of his followers—known as "Kickers"—have criminal records, his face darkens.

"First off, they're not 'followers' of anyone. When you're dissimilated you follow your own path. As for the rest—half truths spread by jealous rivals who see me as a threat to their little self-help empires! But their kind of self-help really boils down to helping themselves get rich on other people's hard-earned money. We have Kickers who are corporate CEOs, housewives and secretaries. I'm not out to accumulate a fortune or start an empire."

I press him about the criminal record, because it's a subject that concerns a lot of people.

"My message speaks to the disadvantaged as well as the advantaged. If there's a large number of what some people like to sneer at as 'lowlifes' among the Kickers, it's because I started getting the word out by going to bars and halfway houses and AA meetings and just talking. I'd say my piece, sell a few copies of the book, then move on.

"I connected with those people. I come from where they come from, and I've lived through what they've lived through, survived what they survived. No one else speaks to them or for them. They know I care about them and won't lie to them. And they listen to me because they know I'm a man with a mission."

I ask him what that would be.

"Why, to change the world, of course."

Jack looked up: "Jack's Law: Never trust anyone who wants to change the world."

He stared down again at the head shot of Hank Thompson. The same strange figure was either painted or hung on the wall behind him; the way it framed him, a few of its appendages seemed to be jutting from his head. Jack tapped the cover reproduction and then the figure on the Xerox sheet.

"What is this thing? It looks like a spider."

"Two more legs a spider should have. To me it looks like a four-armed man—or woman."

"Let's hope it's not a woman . . ."

Jack remembered the painting of a four-armed goddess—Kali—in the horror-filled hold of a freighter floating off the West Side.

"The 'Kicker Man,' Thompson calls it."

"Whatever it is, it's ancient."

Abe frowned. "How so?"

"Despite promises to the contrary, your professor friend copied this from the *Compendium*."

Abe looked offended. "Oh? You were there when he copied it?"

"No, but—"

"Then how do you know?"

Abe seemed to be taking this personally so Jack explained about their copying one of the pages together. He pointed to the squiggles accompanying the figure.

"That's what the original First Age writing looks like when you photocopy it—when it can't mutate into English or whatever your native language is."

Abe frowned. "You've told me this before but how do you know it's true?"

"To the prof's eyes it was written in German."

"A joke you're making, right?"

"I kid you not. The upshot is that this figure is O-L-D. You studied all kinds of ancient languages and stuff with the prof. Ever come across anything like this?"

Abe shook his head. "Never. But Doctor Buhmann might have. That was maybe why he copied it. Or he'd seen the cover of this guy's book and wanted to compare them, see how close they were."

Jack studied them. "Line for line, they're damn near identical. Question is, where does a high school dropout come across something like this? Where else can you find it besides the *Compendium of Srem*?"

"Yours is maybe not the only copy?"

Jack gave the counter a shot with the heel of his hand.

"Damn, I wish I had the book. I'd like to read up on this thing, get the story behind it."

"Nu? You care?"

"Doesn't it do anything to you?"

Abe looked confused. "It should do something to me? What already? It's just a stick figure of a four-armed man."

"It doesn't make you feel . . . funny inside?"

"Not at all. The only funny-inside feeling I have is the need for another elephant ear."

Jack took one last look at the figure, then refolded the sheets.

"Got a phone book?"

"Only yellow."

"Fine."

Abe reached under the counter, came up with a fat one, and dropped it with a thud on the counter.

"You're looking up Muller's to order a delivery, right?"

"They don't deliver. I need info on a PI named Gerhard."

Abe shook his head as if to clear it. "He knows about the *Compendium*?"

"No, this is another matter. Although, the way things have been going lately, he just might."

He had contact information from Christy but wanted a look himself. Under *Private Investigators and Detectives* he found the Gerhard Agency, and listed under that was Michael P. Gerhard. The address was a "suite 624" on West 20th here in Manhattan, but the 718 area code of the phone number was the same Brooklyn number Christy had given him.

He pointed to the computer on the counter.

"Do me a favor and look up Michael P. Gerhard in Brooklyn."

Abe's pudgy fingers flew over the keyboard, then he adjusted his glasses and squinted at the screen.

"Plenty of Gerhards. No Michael P. but there's a Gerhard MP on Avenue M."

Avenue M ran through a number of Brooklyn neighborhoods.

"Can we narrow that down a bit?"

Abe pushed out his lower lip. "Can't say for sure, but I got a feeling that's a Flatlands address."

"How can you tell?"

"Old uncles I had used to live out there when it was predominantly Jewish. Now it's predominantly not Jewish."

Jack pulled out his cell phone and called the number Abe gave him. After four rings he was shunted to voice mail. He listened to the standard message—*"Hi, this is Mike, blah-blah-blah"*—and hung up. Then he called the office number and got voice mail again. A more formal message this time: *"Hello. You have reached the Gerhard Agency . . ."*

No question: Same voice both times.

Jack left a message: "Mister Gerhard, this is Jack—"

He needed a last name. He glanced around, saw *Nike* on a shoebox. No. Saw *Prince* on a racket.

"—Prince and I wish to engage your services. Please call me as soon as possible. It's an urgent matter." He left his Tracfone number.

There. All he had to do now was wait for his callback, arrange a meet, and convince him to square his accounts with Christy Pickering.

But while he was waiting, why not check out his "office."

3

Jack hopped the A train down to 23rd, then walked over to the address of the Gerhard Agency. As Christy had said, a mail drop. Jack used a number of them himself, in Manhattan, Brooklyn, and Queens, but this one was new to him.

He peeked through the window of box 624—Gerhard's "suite" number— and found it crammed with mail. Too bad this wasn't the drop Jack used a few blocks from here. He was sure he could wheedle a look at Gerhard's mail from Kevin, the guy who ran that place. But here, knowing nobody, he wouldn't even try.

His cell started to ring. He smiled as he pulled it from his pocket.

Mr. Gerhard, I presume.

But no. Abe's voice came through instead.

"I just called the hospital. Doctor Buhmann is awake and speaking. Shall we pay a visit?"

Oh, yeah. He had a few questions he wanted to ask the good professor.

4

"One-sixty-one."

Jack stared down at Doc Buhmann. He seemed to be fading into his pillowcase. The right side of his face drooped. The thin fingers of his left hand plucked absently at the bedsheet while the right lay limp at his side. Once he'd come to they'd moved him out of intensive care to this semiprivate room. Jack was glad for that. If he never saw the inside of an ICU again it would be too soon.

"I said, it's good to see you awake," Abe repeated.

The prof gave him a weak, lopsided smile. "Three-twenty-nine." The words slurred like someone at the end of a long bender.

Abe looked at Jack across the bed and muttered. "Three-twenty-nine? What's with these numbers already? I ask him a question, he gives me a number."

"Numbers are all he's said since he came to," said an accented female voice.

Jack looked toward the door and saw a heavyset nurse with coffee-colored skin approaching. She stopped at the foot of the bed.

"Is this usual after a stroke?" Abe said.

She shook her head. "First time I've seen it, but Doctor Gupta didn't seem too surprised."

"That's his neurologist, right? The one I spoke to. Where is he?"

"Down the hall. He should be here soon." She grabbed the small tent made by the prof's right foot and wiggled it. "Can you feel this, Peter?"

He gave her a watery stare. "Forty-nine."

"See?"

The prof was obviously responding to questions, but why with numbers instead of words?

Creepy.

A lean, dark-skinned man with a Saddam mustache strolled in carrying a chart.

"I am Doctor Gupta." His voice was high pitched, with a lilting Indian accent. "Which one of you is this man's son?"

Abe seemed to be in a trance, staring at the prof. When he didn't answer, Jack pointed to him.

"He is."

Jack wondered how Dr. Gupta could buy that fiction. Hard to imagine a less likely father-son pair.

Abe shook himself. "What? Oy. Yes. I'm him." They shook hands. "Tell me about this stroke."

"It's worse than a hemorrhagic stroke, I am afraid, although that would be serious enough. Your father has a brain tumor. That is what hemorrhaged."

"*Gevalt!*" He turned to the prof. "You never told me!"

"It's not exactly a brain tumor because it didn't originate there. It's metastatic from a lung mass which is in turn metastatic from a renal carcinoma. At least that is what we assume because his right kidney was removed not too long ago. Where would we find his medical records?"

Abe looked flustered. Jack knew he'd kept in touch with his old professor but this was obviously all news to him.

Jack jumped in: "But why is he speaking in numbers? I've heard of speaking in tongues, but—"

"The damage reached the Wernicke's area on the left side of the brain and thus has caused a form of receptive aphasia."

"Want to try that again in real-people talk?" Jack said.

"His speech is preserved but the content is garbled. He is most likely not understanding what we say to him."

Abe waved a hand at the prof. "But always with the numbers—why?"

"Ah, that is most interesting." Gupta seemed excited beneath his blasé surface. "What numbers has he spoken to you?"

"Forty-nine just before you came in," Jack said.

Gupta jotted something on the chart cover.

Abe added, "One-sixty-one and three-twenty-nine before that."

More scribbling as he muttered, "Fascinating . . . *fascinating.*"

"Not so fascinating," Abe said, his face darkening. "More like tragic."

"Ask him something."

Abe shook his head, so Jack leaned over the man and touched his hand.

"Doctor Buhmann—where's the *Compendium*? It's not in your office. Did you hide it somewhere?"

The prof looked up at him. "Ninety-one."

"Yes!" Gupta muttered as he scribbled.

Abe's fury seemed to be growing.

Jack pulled out the Xerox of the Kicker Man and held it up.

"Why did you copy this?"

The prof's eyes widened. He raised his shaky left hand and pointed at the figure.

"Six-five-fifty-nine! Two-seventeen!" He snatched the sheet from Jack's hand and stared at it adoringly. "Seven-ninety-one!"

More scribbling by Gupta. "Amazing!"

Abe took a step toward him. He had mayhem in his eyes.

"Enough already! What's going on?"

"Multiples of seven! Every number he says is a multiple of seven! Seven-ninety-one is one-thirteen times seven. Two-seventeen is thirty-one times seven. One-sixty-one is twenty-three times seven. Six-five—"

"We get it," Jack said. "So what?"

Gupta looked up with bright eyes. "I have never heard of such a thing. I'll have to do a search to see if it's ever occurred before."

Jack could see visions of publishing a paper dancing in his head.

"But what are you *doing* about it?" Abe said.

"We have excellent speech pathologists on staff. I've already ordered a consult."

"What's that going to do for his cancer?"

"I have an oncologist coming in later, but renal cancer at this stage . . ." He shook his head.

Abe looked heartbroken.

Gupta said, "Tell me, he is a professor, yes?"

Abe nodded.

"Of mathematics?"

"No. Linguistics."

Gupta frowned. "Odder. One would expect—"

"Odd you want? Try this: All those numbers he's multiplying by seven are prime."

Gupta stared. "You are sure?" He looked down at the chart cover and checked through the list. "Yes, I believe you are right! Oh, this is marvelous, simply marvelous!"

He turned and hurried from the room, leaving Jack and Abe staring at each other.

"All prime numbers?"

Abe nodded. "And all multiplied by another prime."

The creep factor had just doubled.

They stood and watched the prof stare adoringly at the Kicker Man. His eyes shone like Gawain contemplating the Holy Grail.

5

Jack pulled his big black Crown Victoria out of the Upper West Side garage where he kept it for a monthly fee that equaled a mortgage payment in some states. He headed east through the fading light.

Three messages left with Michael Gerhard's office voice mail had sparked no callback. Half a dozen calls to his house had gone unanswered as well. Add to that the stuffed mailbox and maybe Mr. Gerhard was on vacation.

And maybe not.

Whatever the reason, a knock on his door was called for, which meant a trek out to Flatlands.

Swell.

The Flatlands section lay on the far side of Brooklyn. Not even a subway stop out there. He had to drive. And driving anywhere in the city lately made him crazy.

Ten miles and forty minutes later he was driving past Gerhard's house on Avenue M. It stood midway along a line of detached, two-story, cookie-cutter houses that must have been depressingly identical when built half a century before, but changes in siding and different plantings over the years afforded them a modicum of individuality. The area had been farmland in the old-old days but was purely residential now.

Jack slowed as he passed . . .

The place looked dark and empty except for one lighted upstairs window. Maybe a security light, but Jack would have expected one downstairs as well.

He found a parking space two blocks past and walked back. He'd dressed in construction-worker casual for the trip: flannel shirt, jeans, and six-inch, steel-toed Thorogrip Commando Deuces.

He skirted a puddle on the front walk and stopped on the steps before the door. The place looked like it once had sported a front porch, but that had been enclosed for extra living space. He was raising his hand to knock when he noticed the steps were wet. Hadn't rained in days. He bent and touched the weather stripping along the bottom of the door . . . worn . . . with water leaking through from inside.

Something wrong here.

Ya think?

His instincts urged him to turn and run—not walk, *run*—back to his car and get the hell out of here. But a need to know made him stay. He promised himself if he could find an easy way in, he'd take a quick look and then be on his way. If a break-in was necessary, he'd skip it and go home.

He pressed the doorbell button and heard it ring inside. He didn't expect an answer but you never knew. As he rang it again he turned the doorknob and gave a push.

Locked.

He looked around. Nobody about, and he was pretty well hidden in the shadow of the door's overhang.

He slipped around the side and found a basement window behind some bushes. He pulled out his little key-chain penlight and briefly flashed it a few times through the dirty window. The beam reflected off a pool of water within.

Whatever was leaking had been doing so for a while.

Jack saw no sign that the window was wired, so he tested it—not that he wanted to wade through that water, but he felt obliged to check.

No luck.

He could have taken off his jacket, wrapped it around his fist, and broken the window, but he'd promised himself no break-in. So he rose and walked around to the back door. No water leaking out here. He turned the knob and pushed.

It swung inward with a melodramatic creak.

Jack pulled his Glock from the nylon holster at the small of his back and stepped inside.

"Hello? Mister Gerhard? This is Jack Prince. I've been trying to reach you all day. Anybody home?"

No answer.

He closed the door behind him and started through the kitchen toward the front. The inside of the house was a moonless night. The floor stayed dry until he reached the living room. There the carpet began to squish under his boots. When he reached the stairs he risked a quick flash of the penlight. The runner was saturated. Water dripped off the uncarpeted edges of the treads. He touched it—cold.

From somewhere above, the light he'd seen from outside threw just enough illumination to silhouette the banister and newel post on the upper floor.

He called out again but received no answer.

Okay. Time to go see what's what.

Keeping the Glock ahead of him and pointed up, he took the steps two at a time, squishing and creaking all the way. So much for stealth. When he reached the top he stopped and listened.

There . . . to his right . . . light and water running under a closed door, the faint splash and gurgle of running water within. Three strides took him to the threshold where he pushed the door open.

Jack's stomach lurched at the sight of a fully dressed man crouched face-down in an old-fashioned pawfoot tub. Underwater. The bloated condition of the corpse and the attendant stink said he'd been there awhile. Probably be stinking worse if not for the continuous flow of cold water.

Mr. Gerhard, I presume.

Jack stepped into the tiny room and did a quick check to make sure he was alone. Then, keeping his pistol trained toward the door, he squatted next to the tub for a closer look.

The back of the guy's head and a stretch of his lower back were the only parts above water. Jack was glad he couldn't see the face. He didn't know what Gerhard looked like and probably wouldn't recognize him if he did. The cold tap was running at maybe half speed, keeping the tub overflowing.

He groaned aloud when he spotted the bungee cord knotted around the corpse's swollen neck.

Swell. A murder. How much trace evidence had he left already?

Another look revealed handcuffs around the wrists; the cord from the neck fed through the eye of a bolt fastened to the bottom of the tub. No, not fastened—drilled through a hole in the bottom of the tub and screwed into the flooring beneath. Another look at the corpse showed the legs bound together at the thighs, knees, and ankles.

Not just murder . . . some form of ritual. Or torture.

This was no place to be hanging out. Past time to get out. But as long as he was here . . . why not see if Gerhard had any notes on Jerry Bethlehem?

Toward the front he found a bedroom with an unmade bed, clothes on the floor, and open dresser drawers. Tossed or just a sloppy guy? Jack checked the closet and under the bed, then grabbed a T-shirt from the floor and headed rearward.

There he found a guest bedroom. He made sure it was empty and moved on to another bedroom Gerhard had converted into an office.

After pulling the shades on the two windows, Jack flashed his light around and found the usual: desk, filing cabinets, and a computer with a dark screen but a glowing power light.

He turned off the flash and stood listening. He was ninety-nine percent sure he was alone in the house and one hundred percent sure he had the second floor to himself. As for anyone sneaking up those noisy stairs—no way.

He stowed the Glock and began searching the office.

The filing cabinets came first. A quick search showed no Bethlehem or Pickering file. He wiped down the drawer handles with the T-shirt and moved to the desk. No help there. He sat before the monitor and wiggled the mouse with a T-shirt-wrapped hand. The computer awoke and the screen came to life with Explorer up and running.

The current page was an article on the assassination of abortion doctors in Atlanta. Jack frowned. When was this? The story was dated nearly twenty years ago. It came back to him. Big deal at the time. Someone had shot down a couple of abortionists within a week of each other. The whole country had been buzzing, cops posted at all the clinics and outside doctors' homes. They'd finally caught the guy and put him away, but it had been all anyone had talked about at the time.

Just in case, Jack scanned the article for the name Jerry Bethlehem but found no mention.

He clicked the BACK button. He'd learned a few simple computer tricks—ways to hide his browsing history and locate others'—but didn't need them here. He found a page of Google search results for "atlanta abortion assassination." He checked out a few but found no mention of Bethlehem. Maybe related to another case Gerhard was working on? Had he stumbled onto something he shouldn't have? Was that why he'd been killed?

Going further back he found searches for "aaron levy md" and "creighton institute," and finally "gerald bethlehem." Jack clicked that and was rewarded with half a million hits ranging anywhere from people named Gerald living in Bethlehem, PA, to articles on Jesus or Christmas by guys named Gerald.

Forget it.

He found a pen, then a pad with *oDNA?* written on the top sheet. Huh. He tore it off and shoved it into a pocket. He copied down the search strings, then searched Gerhard's computer for "Bethlehem." A folder popped up in the search results window. He opened it and found a list of .jpg files. Clicking through them revealed a series of photos of a man with a neat beard walking with his arm across the shoulders of a young blonde. The flattened perspective indicated they were surveillance photos taken with a telephoto lens.

He checked out the girl. Had to be Dawn Pickering. Had her mother's eyes, but a round, pug face and a body bordering pudgy. Not exactly a traffic stopper. What attracted Bethlehem to her? They say there's someone for everyone. Was that it? Was this the girl of his dreams? Maybe he just had a thing for young stuff. Or was it, like her mother suspected, something else?

Jack printed out a couple of the shots. The old laser printer turned the color originals into grainy black and white, but at least they gave him an idea what this guy looked like.

The Bethlehem folder also contained a Word file labeled "Levy." He opened that and found a telephone number with a 914 area code and an address in Rathburg, New York. Jack had heard of it—someplace north of the city, he thought, but wasn't sure. He printed out a copy of that too. When he'd folded the printouts and stuffed them in a pocket, he wiped down whatever he'd touched and returned to the bathroom.

He used the shirt to turn off the water, then squatted next to the tub and tried to piece together what had gone down here.

The long bungee cord was tied to the rope that bound Gerhard's knees. It ran forward to and through the eyebolt under the head. From there it stretched up and wrapped around the neck three times before tying into a knot at the nape.

The links between the handcuffs ran through the eyebolt as well.

What the hell . . . ?

And then Jack saw it. Gerhard must have been unconscious when he was hog-tied like this. The cuffs prevented his hands from reaching the knots. The bungee pulled his head down. With the tub filled Gerhard would have to strain against the cord to keep his head above water. Couldn't strain too hard or the bungee would tighten around his neck.

He'd probably screamed for help until his throat went raw and his voice failed, but no one heard him.

Keeping his head above the surface wouldn't be too difficult at first, but as the cold water lowered his body temperature and his muscles fatigued, he'd be forced to let his head sink to give them a rest. Then he'd lift his head for a breath before letting it sink again. Bobbing for air instead of apples.

Inevitably, when the muscles became too weak to raise his nostrils above sea level—depending on his strength, that might have taken a day or so—he'd drown.

Jack shook his head, chilled. Some sick bastard with a major hard-on for Gerhard had spent a lot of time dreaming this up.

The PI might have been a good guy, might have been a sleazeball, but nobody deserved this. Well, maybe not *nobody*—Jack had met a few folks who'd easily qualify—but most likely not Gerhard.

His last moments must have been awful.

Big question: Was the sicko who'd dreamed this up Jerry Bethlehem?

Could be, but Jack could think of other possibilities.

Private dicks make enemies. With guys like Gerhard who specialize in divorce work—"getting the goods on cheating spouses," as Christy had put it—

it went with the territory. Could be one of his pigeons had been taken to the cleaners in a divorce settlement and come by for major payback.

Or it could have something to do with the Atlanta abortion killings. No question Gerhard was researching them. Why, after almost two decades? That bothered Jack. Not as if it was an ongoing case. As far as Jack knew, it was closed—the killer caught and punished. Had Gerhard stumbled upon something that would get it reopened? And was somebody willing to kill to prevent that?

Again, maybe. But this seemed too personal.

Which brought Jack back to the enraged cheating husband scenario as the most probable.

But it didn't let Bethlehem entirely off the hook. Gerhard could have found some dirt on Bethlehem—maybe something incriminating—and tried to blackmail him.

Jack shook his head. Whatever had gone down, this was not the place to ponder it. He had a couple of surfaces and doorknobs to wipe down and then he was out of here.

6

Christy cruised the Queens Boulevard outer road, slowing as she passed in front of the bar. She spotted that damned Jerry Bethlehem's Harley out front. She'd learned this was his hang when he wasn't eating at Dawn's table at the Tower or home working on his latest video game.

She parked her Mercedes half a block down the street, facing the place. She'd used this spot a number of times before; the perfect vantage point because it offered a clear view of the front entrance.

She turned off the engine and checked her watch as she settled in for her vigil. Dawnie's shift at the Tower didn't end for another hour. She'd most likely be hooking up with Jerry after work. The question was: What would Jerry be up to until then?

The place was called Work. Ha ha. Very funny. *Honey, I'm really busy at Work and won't be home till late.*

She'd peeked in there a while back. It was a sort of eatery-bar–pool hall. Not the sort of place she'd expect a well-heeled guy like Jerry to hang out. His expensive clothes didn't exactly match the décor—or the other patrons for that matter. She couldn't imagine any of them going home to a Rego Park condo a tenth as luxurious as his. Christy had never been inside, but she knew the complex—very tony—and Dawn had gushed about all the state-of-the-art electronics it housed.

Bethlehem ate lunch at Work almost every day and hung out at the bar when he wasn't stalking Dawn at the Tower.

But every once in a while he'd disappear. Like yesterday. Where did he go? That was what Christy intended to learn.

This was what they called a stakeout, right? Mike Gerhard should be here, doing this. Or that new guy, Jack. Maybe she could convince him to take over after he located Gerhard.

She had a good feeling about Jack—never did get his last name. How had she let that slip by? His reluctance to get too involved inspired a strange sort of trust. He didn't seem to be money motivated. None of that grubbing attitude: Sure-sure, I'll do—or pretend to do—anything you want, just pay me. Oh, he wanted to get paid, but she sensed it was as much to set a value on his efforts as to make a living.

The thing was, *someone* had to watch Bethlehem. Someone had to catch him in the act.

What act, she didn't know, but he was hiding something. Had to be. As soon as she'd set eyes on him, standing in her living room, she'd sensed something wrong. Maybe it was the strange way he'd stared at her when he walked in. Whatever it was had sent ripples of revulsion through her . . .

. . . and yet, he was sexy in a way. The lazy Southern drawl, the longish hair, the long, lean frame, the mystery of what lay behind that beard, the mesmerizing blue eyes that seemed to pierce you . . .

Maybe it was that bad-boy thing. He had a certain sense of danger about him that, in another time, another place, might have attracted her. But to know that it was aimed at her daughter, attracting *her* . . . well, that was too much to bear.

Maybe because he'd been with her little girl—not yet with her in *that* sense back then—just . . . with her. She'd wanted him gone, wanted to kick him out on his ass, but she couldn't. They'd only go elsewhere, and she wanted him where she could keep an eye on him.

Finally they did go elsewhere. To his place. And once they got there she knew they wouldn't limit their relationship to working on video games. At least not for long.

The thought sickened her.

Not that she was a prude. Anything but. She'd lost her virginity at sixteen and had got it on with half a dozen different boyfriends in high school before . . . never mind. She didn't want to think about that. But the operative word was the *boy* in boyfriend. They were *boys*—her age or maybe a year older. They were all growing and learning the sexual ropes together. This Bethlehem creep had the benefit of a whole extra lifetime of experience beyond Dawn's. What was he into? What was he teaching her? What was he making her do?

Don't you hurt my little girl.

And she *knew* he was going to hurt her. Not emotionally, by dumping her after he'd used her up. Christy could help Dawn through that. No, worse. He wanted something from her. But what? And why Dawn?

Dawnie . . . how could an Ivy League–bound girl act so dumb? And *sound* dumb too. Despite all her reading and all her A's in English, she'd fallen into the "like" and "totally" habit of her peers. Really, with laws about everything else, why couldn't they pass a law about the number of times someone could use "like" per day?

So she'd started fining Dawn—twenty-five cents for every time she misused "like." It had worked, making her conscious of it, and her use trailed off. Christy had just instituted a similar program to wipe out "totally" when that man came along.

Did he care about Dawnie—at all?

She couldn't believe that, and so she needed something on this cradle-robbing bastard.

She hoped tonight would be the night he'd make a mistake. She'd follow—

There he was, sauntering out of the bar, talking on his cell phone as if he didn't have a care in the world—and all the while making a wreck of Dawnie's.

And yet, watching the sinuous way he moved, the swing of his shoulders, the twist of his narrow waist, she couldn't help feel a pull. She understood why Dawn was so gaga over him. He was sexy—no other word for it. He could have just about any woman he wanted.

So why on Earth did he want Dawn?

Unlike so many other mothers, Christy had never kidded herself about her daughter's looks. Dawnie was plain. Those words would never leave her lips. In fact she'd always told Dawn she was beautiful. And inside she was. But the girl wasn't stupid. She had a mirror. And knowing she wasn't pretty had had its effect, pushing her into academics instead of boys. Which was wonderful. Plenty of time for guys later.

All of which made her a sitting duck for a magnetic guy like Jerry Bethlehem.

Again the question: Why Dawn?

Not knowing the answer made Christy's skin crawl.

She watched him hop on his Harley. He had a sporty little Miata too, but tonight he was using the bike. She watched him adjust his helmet and wished he didn't wear one. Then she could pray he got hit by a car and wound up brain dead. Or maybe she'd run him off the road and—

The thought shocked her. Where had that come from?

From deep in her gut. If push came to shove, she'd do anything to keep Dawnie safe from him. A mother protected her own.

She remembered her pregnancy. She'd been single and scared, with her mother royally pissed that she was knocked up. She'd planned to give up the baby, but the instant she'd held her little girl in her arms she felt herself change. She was going to find a direction, make a life for herself and this baby. It was the beginning of a new day, a new life for her, and so she'd named the baby Dawn.

Trite, yes. But she'd been Dawn's age at the time and it had seemed like the right thing to do.

Up ahead, Bethlehem revved his engine and took off with a roar. Christy followed and cursed as she saw him head toward Queens Boulevard.

She followed him to Rego Park and, sure enough, he was heading for the Tower. She slowed as he pulled into a narrow spot at the curb. Dawn ran out to meet him and give him a big hug and a long kiss. Christy's stomach turned as she watched him fondle her buttocks.

She *had* to get something on this son of a bitch.

God, she wished she could follow him some night to a house where he visited a wife and kids. Wouldn't that be great? Threaten him with exposure if he didn't leave Dawn alone. Show her proof if he didn't heed the warning.

Yes, the truth would hurt her little girl, but the truth was the truth, and shouldn't be hidden.

Except in my case, she thought.

That was the danger in hiring a detective. He might broaden the investigation, uncover things better left hidden, start asking questions she didn't want to answer.

7

Jack sat in his idling car, cell phone in one hand, Dr. Levy's number in the other.

To call or not to call.

He'd just come from the scene of a torture-murder. It might not have anything to do with what he'd been hired for. In fact, odds were high against it, but not in the sure-thing range.

Did he want to get involved in this? Did he want to touch anything the late Michael Gerhard had touched?

Not really. But he'd accepted a fee to find out what Gerhard had learned about Jerry Bethlehem, and since Gerhard wasn't talking, Jack felt obligated to speak to at least one person the PI had contacted.

What the hell.

He punched in the number. After three rings, a man answered.

"Yes?" His voice sounded a little strange . . . tentative.

"Is this Doctor Aaron Levy?"

"Who's calling?"

"I'd like to ask the doctor a few questions about a man named Jerry Bethlehem."

"Who?"

"Jerry Bethlehem. I—"

"Never heard of him!" he said, but his tone said otherwise.

"Are you sure? I was given to understand—"

"Who is this?" A sharp jump in pitch and volume. "Are you the one who just called and hung up?"

"No, I—"

"You are, aren't you. I don't know what your problem is, but I want you to stop it."

"But I'm not—"

"Are you listening? Stop this or I'll have you found out and stopped. And

I'm not talking about calling the police. I'll be going much higher up. So stop this if you know what's good for you."

And then he hung up.

Whoa. That was one rattled man. He'd mistaken Jack for someone making harassing phone calls. Gerhard? Unlikely if Levy'd had a hang-up tonight.

Looked like he was going to have to arrange a face-to-face with Dr. Levy.

He put the car in gear, powered up his officialdom phone, and dialed 911. He told the operator he was a neighbor of Gerhard's and that water was leaking out his front door. He said he'd knocked but no one answered and he was afraid something was wrong inside. He broke the connection without leaving a name.

Not the sort of message to spark EMTs to race to the scene, but eventually someone would get around to checking it out.

He turned off the phone. He reserved it exclusively for calls that had the remotest chance of being traced. Those were the only times he powered it up.

He had no sources in officialdom and no way of knowing what kind of tracking capabilities the emergency services center had. Even though the number was untraceable to him, they might be able to pick up some sort of identifier code from his phone and track it. And they might not. But he did know they couldn't trace a powered-down phone. So he kept it off.

Was this any way to live?

Yeah. A major pain in the ass at times. A constant battle of wits. But he found it hard to imagine life any other way.

THURSDAY

1

"You're going to buy a map?" Abe said. "What for a map when you've got Mapquest?" He turned to his computer. "I'll look it up for you right now."

An hour after a simple breakfast of plain old Entenmann's crumb cake and newspaper skimming at Abe's rear counter—no story on finding Gerhard's body yet—Jack was readying to wander off in search of a New York state map. The one he had was falling apart.

"Don't bother. I've already got driving directions from Mapquest, but I like a map I can fold and unfold. I like to see the big picture."

"You want a big picture, I can get you a satellite photo of where you're going."

"No thanks. But you can do a reverse look-up on Doctor Levy's phone number for me."

"I thought you had an address already."

"I do, but I just want to check."

"You mean you want *me* to check."

"Okay, I want you to check. Please?"

Jack had been into computers from his early teens through his college years. But after he'd dropped out—of everything—he lost touch with the cyber world. His early years in the city had been a catch-as-catch-can existence, with no permanency, no way to stay wired in. Only in the past few years had he begun exploring the World Wide Web. A lot had changed in the years he'd been disconnected. He was still in an acclimation stage.

Abe, on the other hand, with his international connections and dealings, was a whiz—or as he'd say, a maven.

He watched Abe do some mousing and keyboard tapping, frown, do some more, then come up with . . .

"Nothing. The name and address connected to that number are restricted."

Jack shrugged. "I'll go with what I have then. How's the professor, by the way?"

Abe shook his head. "Again I dropped in on him last night. No change. His mind . . . I don't know. Still with the numbers."

"Shame. Okay, I'm off on my map quest."

"Wait. I just thought of something. Let me try a straightforward lookup." More tapping. "Ha! Here's an Aaron Levy, M.D., at twenty-six-eighty-one Riverview Road in Rathburg, New York."

"That's the address I have. Okay, we've found him. What can you tell me about him?"

Abe did his click-click-tap-tap thing and then smiled.

"Here's something mentioning him as an attendee at a fund-raiser for the Rathburg Public Library."

"Got a picture?"

"What for you want a picture?"

"Because I've got a lawyer's chance of heaven of getting through the front door to see this guy. I'll have to use some backdoor tactics. And to do that I need to know what he looks like."

"Here we go: *'Doctor Aaron Levy, associate director of patient care at the Creighton Institute, with his wife, Marie, and daughter, Mollie'* at the same fund-raiser."

Abe turned the monitor toward Jack. He saw a smiling dark-haired man in his early fifties with a dark-haired woman of the same age, flanking a dark-haired girl who looked about twelve or so. The article, from the *Rathburg-on-Hudson Review,* had appeared two years ago.

"Perfect. Print that out for me, will you?"

"It's printing already."

"Great. And while we're waiting, see where I can find this Creighton Institute. I saw that mentioned on Gerhard's computer. Sounds like a hospital or something."

"Here it is: The Creighton Institute. And you'll never guess the address."

"Twenty-six-eighty-one Riverview Road in Rathburg?"

"You got it."

"Okay. That's where he works. But where does he live? There's gotta be a way—"

"Tax records, maybe. No, wait. Let me Google this." Abe started tapping again. "New . . . York . . . property . . . search . . ." He hit ENTER. "*Gevalt!* Let me fill in these boxes. County . . . Westchester. Town . . . Rathburg. Name . . . Aaron Levy. Enter." A pause, then, "Here it is: Nine-oh-three Argent Drive."

Jack felt a little queasy as he said, "Print that out for me too."

Abe shook his head as he hit PRINT. "This is terrible."

Jack knew exactly what he was feeling.

"Because it's so easy?"

"Frighteningly so."

"Makes me glad I rent, Abe. Go back to that Creighton Institute. What else can we find out about it?"

"Let's see." After a few more clicks Abe leaned back and looked at him. "Oy. The full name is the Creighton Institute for the Criminally Insane."

Jack shook his head. "Swell."

2

Broadway seemed like a good place to find a map, so Jack ambled west.

Broadway ran north-south up here. A few blocks downtown, at 79th Street, it broke from the grid and started angling east, crossing the city on a diagonal all the way down to the East Village where it headed due south again.

He spotted a Barnes & Noble and saw a display of *Kick* in its front window. The cover was hard to miss with its bold black type and stick-figure drawing against a neon-yellow background.

He stared at the Kicker Man, feeling that same odd sensation.

Enough of this wondering. He needed to find out why that figure looked so . . . what? Familiar?

A placard with a similar color scheme posted behind the display read:

JOIN THE KICKER EVOLUTION!

Evolution?

He went inside, picked up a trade paperback, and flipped through it. Large type and a little Kicker Man in each of the breaks.

"Save your money, man."

Jack looked up and saw a long-haired guy in jeans and a tie-dyed shirt giving him a sidelong look.

"Say what?"

"That book." He spoke in a conspiratorial whisper from the corner of his mouth. "It's a load of crap, man."

Nodding knowingly, he moved off.

Well, well. A reader review. But not a helpful one. Jack expected a load of crap. He simply wanted to know how Hank Thompson had come up with that four-armed man.

He found a New York State map and headed for the checkout counter. On the way he passed a "New Paperback Fiction" rack where a cover caught his eye: cobalt blue with a pair of glowing yellow eyes—definitely not human—staring out above a pile of pills. He stopped when saw the title: *Berzerk!*

Those eyes were startlingly close to a rakosh's. And the pills . . . last spring he'd run up against a drug with a lot of street names, one of which was Berzerk—misspelled just as it was on the cover.

And then his heart stuttered a beat when he read that it was "a Jake Fixx novel" and "sequel to *Rakshasa!*" by P. Frank Winslow.

He snatched it from its rack and grabbed a passing employee—a twenty-something guy with thin hair and thick sideburns.

"What is this?"

The guy looked at Jack, then the novel, then Jack. "We call that a book."

A comedian. Yay.

"I know that. But who's this guy Winslow? How many of these has he written?"

The guy shrugged. "I dunno. You'll have to check with Information."

"But you work here."

"Yeah, but I just put them on the shelves. I don't read them. Sorry. Check with Information."

Jack did, but the kiosk was empty. He found the fiction section and searched through the *W* authors where he found one copy of *Rakshasa*. He checked out the cover and found the same cobalt blue, same glowing eyes, but instead of pills, a freighter floated in the foreground.

"Christ!"

He didn't know what was inside, but from the look of the covers it seemed like someone was peeking into his life.

The information kiosk was still empty so he headed for the checkout area. With no line he walked up to the only cashier, a guy with a shaved head and a black soul patch.

Jack slapped the novels on the counter and pushed them forward.

"What do you know about these?"

He shook his head. "Nothing." He pointed to the copy of *Kick*. "But I know a lot about that."

Jack noticed a tiny Kicker Man tattoo in the web between his thumb and forefinger.

"Fine, but—"

"You'll love it, I can tell. It'll be like a wire into your brain. I've read my copy so many times it's damn near worn out."

Jack pointed to the tattoo. "Who'da thunk."

The guy held up his hand. "That lets the world know I've dissimilated and evolved. I'm a Kicker and proud of it."

He scanned and bagged, then said, "That comes to twenty-four-seventy-one."

Jack reached for his wallet. "Comes to more than that, I think."

The guy smiled and lowered his voice. "The *Kick* is on the house."

"Yeah? Where does it say that?"

"I'm giving you a special discount. You know, Kicker to a soon-to-be Kicker."

"No thanks. I'll pay."

The guy spoke through his teeth as he pushed the bag toward Jack. "Take it."

"I'll pay my own way, if you don't mind." He pushed the bag back. "Scan the book. Now."

The guy glared at him as he snatched the book from the bag, scanned it, then shoved it back in.

"Forty-two-oh-seven."

Jack handed him a MasterCard. The John Tyleski identity was still good. Barring a glitch he'd probably keep it until fall.

After he signed and pocketed his receipt, he picked up the bag and started to turn away.

"I see you at the rally, I'll kick your ass."

"That a pun?"

The guy looked confused. "Huh?"

"Never mind. What rally?"

"The Kicker rally at the Garden next month. Don't you know nothin'?"

"I know I won't be there."

The guy nodded and sneered. "Oh, you'll be there. Once you read that book you won't be able to stay away."

"No, really. I won't. I might've gone, but now you've scared me off. I don't want to get my ass kicked. Get it? *Kick*ed?"

The guy's expression said he didn't. Jack waved and left.

Quality folk, these Kickers.

As he stepped onto the sidewalk he thought of the *Compendium of Srem*: No word yet on whether security had followed up on the Kicker janitor. Petty theft was probably low on their list of priorities. Looked like Jack was going to have to resolve this on his own.

3

As Jack waited in line at the Thruway's Yonkers toll plaza, he watched with envy as the E-ZPass cars zipped past without stopping. He didn't leave the city often enough to make an E-ZPass account useful, but even if he did he probably wouldn't open one. Maybe he was paranoid, but who knew what was really in the transponders clipped to all those windshields? GPS technology being what it was, or soon would be, he couldn't risk the possibility of someone being able to pinpoint his car at any time.

Call me crazy, but a few extra minutes in line ain't such a bad price for a little peace of mind.

After paying he continued north to the Tarrytown exit where he followed 9 north. The directions led him through greening hills and valleys toward Rathburg, New York, but he was only dimly aware of the scenery.

Other images—book cover images—kept him distracted. One was the Kicker Man and the question of how a figure from the *Compendium* had wound up on the cover of Hank Thompson's book. The other was the eyes on the cover of the Jake Fixx novels.

Back to back he'd encountered two authors who knew things they shouldn't. Coincidence? He'd been told no more coincidences in his life and he'd come to believe it. But where was the connection?

He'd wanted to hole up in his apartment and read the novels, but hadn't had time—not with this Rathburg jaunt looming. He'd got a look at the back covers, however, where he learned that the hero, Jake Fixx, was an ex-Navy SEAL and former CIA black-ops expert. Usually these characters are one or the other, but this guy was both. He'd been betrayed by his superiors—weren't they all?—and had gone underground. He now lived in secret, helping those who couldn't help themselves. A rogue Robin Hood, sticking it to the Man at every chance.

Hoo-boy. Cliché piled on cliché.

Many times Jack wished he'd had SEAL training or its equivalent. To learn about weapons and ammo and demolition in an organized setting instead of piecemeal on and off the street—wouldn't that have been a treat. And having an FBI or CIA connection would be beyond cool. Want to know about this Jerry Bethlehem? All he'd have to do was get a fingerprint and have his contact run it through the databases. Probably wind up with a whole file on him.

But not for Jack. He had to do it the old-fashioned, low-tech—damn near no-tech—way.

So, the Jake Fixx character was far off the mark, but the *Rakshasa!* and *Berzerk!* story lines weren't. Especially the first, involving a ship full of flesh-eating demons—the rakshasa of Indian mythology—controlled by a Hindu madman who was going to set them loose on Manhattan if a magic jewel was not returned to him. Much more lurid and melodramatic than the reality Jack had survived a couple of years ago, but uncomfortably close to the mark. In *Berzerk!* the blood of one of the surviving rakshasa was the source of a drug that drove people into murderous rages—*way* too close to the truth.

Jack shivered. It was like this writer, this P. Frank Winslow, had been peeking over his shoulder the past two years.

He shook it off as he cruised into Rathburg. Had to concentrate on getting a little face time with Dr. Aaron Levy.

Rathburg proved to be an old, rustic, Sleepy Hollowesque town, like so many others along this stretch of the Hudson's east bank. Washington Irving could have slept here. Probably had. Tudor-style buildings with cracked stucco and peeling beams leaned over the narrow streets as Jack followed his directions to Riverview Road. Once there he didn't have to check the street numbers to find 2681: Had to be the huge mansionlike structure that dominated the rise overlooking the river.

Sunlight glinted off the concertina wire that crowned the stone wall along its perimeter. The arched front checkpoint—maybe the only entrance—had a heavy, wrought-iron gate and a uniformed guard visible through the window of a stone gatehouse. The plaque on one of the columns read CREIGHTON and no more. No mention of it being an institute or place for the criminally insane. Just the name.

Jack was set to turn into the drive and try to bluff his way in when he saw the security camera atop the gatehouse. He didn't want his face recorded if he could avoid it.

As he drove past he checked out the sprawling building standing a good five hundred yards from the street. It looked just right for the criminally insane because it appeared to have been designed by a schizophrenic. The central section looked like a French stone chateau. If Jack had to guess, that was probably the original structure because it looked all of a piece. But whoever had added the wings—a graduate of the Berlin Wall school of architecture, from the look—hadn't bothered to continue the same design. And yet a third wing that didn't match any of the others had been added on the left.

Not exactly maximum security. Concertina wire was mean, but hardly impassable.

He drove back to town and parked. He'd looked up the Creighton Institute's number earlier. First he'd try to get to Levy through channels. His office was the best bet—if phone calls were making him paranoid, he'd feel less vulnerable there than at home.

Since he did not know Levy's extension, he was shunted into a phone tree. He hated goddamn phone trees so he kept pressing 0 until he reached a human. He told her who he was looking for and she switched him to a line where a female receptionist or secretary or whatever picked up and announced that he'd reached Dr. Levy's office.

"Is the doctor in?"

"Who's calling, please?"

"Name's John Robertson. I'm a private investigator."

He'd met the real Robertson a few years before his death. A sharp old dude who'd liked to wear a Stetson. Jack had kept his card and made duplicates, adopting his identity now and again but not his sartorial taste. He'd changed Robertson's address to one of his mail drops and kept renewing his investigator's license. Anyone checking with the New York Department of State would learn that John Robertson was the real deal.

The identity had proven handy over the years.

"And what do you wish to speak to the doctor about?"

"That would be between him and me."

Jack sensed a sudden drop in temperature on the other end of the line.

"I'll see if he's in."

After a full minute's wait—she probably had her answer in ten seconds—she came back on the line.

"I'm sorry, but Doctor Levy will be in meetings for the rest of the day."

"Okay. How about tomorrow?"

"He's booked all day then too."

"And the next day?"

"I'm sorry, but Doctor Levy is a very busy man. Perhaps you could send him a letter?"

"Perhaps I could."

Jack broke the connection.

Okay. After his brief conversation with Levy last night, he'd pretty much expected that. He'd have to follow him after work and look for an opening for an ambush conversation.

He checked his watch. Still hours to go before quitting time.

Time to go exploring.

4

He wound up in the Rathburg Public Library. A computer search had yielded nothing—the Creighton Institute did not have a Web site and other hits yielded nothing useful. So he'd started searching through the microfilm files of the *Rathburg-on-Hudson Review* and again came up empty. Lots of passing mentions, but no background. Maybe a local paper was the wrong place to look. It seemed to take for granted that its readers knew all about Creighton.

He gathered up the microfilm rolls and returned them to the desk.

"Find what you need?" said the withered, blue-haired lady behind the counter.

"No, unfortunately."

He studied her. She had a Miss Hathaway voice, rickety limbs, a slightly frayed dark blue skirt and jacket with a white silk scarf loosely tied around her neck—to hide the wrinkles? A cloud of gardenia perfume enveloped her. She looked old enough to have dated Ichabod Crane. If she'd spent most of her days around here . . .

"Are you a native of this area?"

"Born and bred."

"Then maybe you can help me. I'm doing some research on the Creighton Institute but I can't seem to find much on it."

"I'm not surprised. There's not been much written about it." She raised a gnarled finger and tapped her right temple. "But there's a lot stored right up here."

"Would you care to share some of that? I'd be willing to compensate you for your time."

She frowned. "Pay me for letting me ramble on about the old days? Don't be silly."

"Well then, why don't we find someplace where we can sit and have some coffee. I'll buy."

She winked. "Make that a Manhattan and you've got yourself a deal."

This lady was all right.

"Deal. When do you get off?"

"Any time I want. I'm a volunteer." She turned toward a small office behind the counter. "Claire, watch the front desk. I have to go out."

Within seconds she'd shrugged into a long cloth coat and was heading for the door.

"Time's a-wasting and I've only got so much of it left. Let's go."

Jack followed her outside. The sky had gone from clear blue to overcast while his nose had been stuck in the microfilm viewer.

She stopped at the foot of the front steps and thrust out her hand.

"I'm Cilla Groot, by the way."

Jack shook her frail hand. "And I'm Jack." He looked up and down the street and spotted a pub sign hanging over the sidewalk. "What about that place?"

"Van Dyck's? I've been in there once or twice. I suppose it will do."

As they started toward the pub Jack had to ask: "Do you have a dog?"

She looked at him with concern, then down at her coat. "Why? Do I have hair—?"

"No, just curious."

"What an odd question. No, no dog. Three cats though."

Good. Ladies with dogs had been popping up in his life for the past year or so. They all seemed to know more about his life than anyone should. He'd seen one of them right after the accident, but none since. He wouldn't mind sitting down with one—he had endless questions—but he didn't like them sneaking up on him.

He held the door to Van Dyck's and followed her in. Her arrival was greeted by calls of "Hi, Cilla" from the half dozen or so men around the bar.

She waved, then turned to Jack and said, "Let's take that table by the window where we can have some peace."

Fine with Jack.

He helped her out of her coat and they were just seating themselves on opposite sides of the table when the bartender arrived carrying a straight-up Manhattan with two cherries. He placed it before Cilla with a flourish.

"There you go, my dear."

"Thank you, Faas."

Jack smiled. Only been here once or twice, ay?

Faas—was that a first or last name?—turned to Jack. "And what can I get you, sir?"

Jack asked what was on tap and Faas recited a depressing list of Buds and Michelobs and various lights that ended on an up note with the Holland Holy Trinity: Heineken, Grolsch, and Amstel. Jack took a pint of Grolsch.

"So, what can you tell me about the Creighton Institute?"

She took a sip of her drink and closed her eyes. "Nothing so perfect as a perfect Manhattan." Then she looked at Jack. "It didn't start out as an institute of any sort. The original building, with its French chateau design, marble terraces, and classical revival gardens, was built in 1897 by financier Horace Creighton as a summer cottage."

"Cottage?"

"Yes. The Creightons lived there only during the summer months when it was too hot in the city. He said that he chose Rathburg rather than Newport because he liked the climate better and it was more convenient to his business in New York, but I suspect he avoided Newport so as not to have to compete with the Vanderbilts and Astors. Here he could be quite literally king of the hill."

"But I take it there are no more Creightons there now."

"Correct. He lost everything in the stock market crash of twenty-nine. The state government took it over for back taxes and it remained abandoned and boarded up for years. That didn't stop children—yours truly was one of them—from breaking in and using it as a playground. After the war the federal government took it over and turned it into the Creighton Hospital for Disabled Veterans."

"And that's when it was expanded, I take it?"

"Correct." She made a face. "Have you seen those wings they added? Abominations! What an awful, terrible, wretched thing to do to such a grand old house."

She tossed off the rest of her Manhattan and held up her empty glass. In less than a minute Faas appeared with a full replacement. He pointed to Jack's half-finished pint. Jack shook his head.

"When did it become a booby hatch?"

Her brief glare told Jack what he'd hoped to learn from the remark: The locals weren't happy with having an institute for the criminally insane in town.

"In nineteen-eighty-one it passed from the Veterans Administration to another federal entity. That was when it was renamed the Creighton Institute."

Jack finished it for her: "—for the Criminally Insane."

"That was never an official designation," she huffed. "I don't know how that got about, but it's not accurate."

"Okay. But they do house nutcases there, correct?"

"It's a mental research institute. There's never been a lick of trouble since its conversion, not a single incident. The barbed wire is an eyesore, yes, but they mind their business, pay their taxes, and some of the staff have joined the community and become active in local affairs."

"Like Doctor Aaron Levy?"

Her eyebrows lifted. "If you know him, why do you need me for this information. He certainly knows more than I do."

"I know *of* him. We'll be having a meeting in the near future, and I wanted to have some background on the place before then."

"Yes, well, he's a nice man, devoted husband and father, and gives generously to local causes, especially the library."

"But as a doctor at the institute, that makes him an employee of the federal government. What branch? Department of Entropy?"

Cilla gave him a tolerant smile. "No one knows. Lord knows I've tried to find out—"

"Why would you want to know?"

"Because someone wants to keep it secret." She smiled. "Why else?"

"Why else indeed?" Jack liked this old biddy. "So no one knows who's running the show? Don't people find that suspicious?"

"Some of us do. I'm one of them. I've been watching and listening and snooping for years, and you know what I think?" She leaned across the table and lowered her voice to a whisper. "Department of Defense."

"But what would the Depart—?"

She held up a finger. "You didn't hear it here. And I'll say no more. But maybe when you meet with Doctor Levy you can wheedle it out of him."

He'd try.

"Odd that that particular branch of the government in question would be funding a mental institution, don't you think?"

She finished her second drink and held up the glass. She weighed all of a hundred pounds, if that, and had downed two Manhattans before Jack had finished his first beer, yet her eyes and speech were as clear as when they'd first sat down.

"Odd and bothersome. If you find out why, let me know. I have an insatiable curiosity."

And one hell of an efficient liver, he thought as he watched Faas approach with a fresh drink.

5

Jack swung by 903 Argent Drive to get a look at the Levy house. The property out here appeared to be zoned for at least an acre and it looked like all the lots had been wooded to start with. A lot of the residents had left a fair number of trees as buffers between the houses, which tended to be of the brick-fronted, high-foyered McMansion design. The house at 903 sported Taraesque columns.

Probably considered a premiere location, what with some sort of forest preserve across the street. That made for enviable privacy. The owners could stand on their front porches and know that they'd never see another house looking back at them.

The Levy place sported a two-car garage which they probably used. That meant no telltale auto in the driveway to signal when the doc was home.

Jack drove past a couple of times, looking for a spot where he could park and watch for Levy's arrival. No such place in daylight—at least none where he wouldn't attract attention, and maybe even earn a call to the police. In the dark, with all these trees, a different story. He'd have to try something else.

He cruised the area looking for a watch post. His problem was he didn't know what kind of car Levy would be driving, so he needed a spot where he could get a look at the drivers as they passed.

Argent Drive had only one access point from the direction of the Creighton Institute. Jack found an empty-looking house—overgrown yard, no curtains on the windows—with a FOR SALE sign out front. He backed into its driveway, left his car running, and waited. The good news was that daylight saving time was in effect and the sun wouldn't set until around seven. He wished the overcast would clear. He'd need all the light he could get to recognize Levy as he passed.

And so he waited and watched, studying the Levy photo between cars. Around four-thirty traffic picked up. His eyes burned and a dull headache started in his temples as he strained to catch the faces in all the westbound vehicles.

The guy was a doctor with a big house. He wouldn't be driving a Taurus or a pickup. Or would he? Jack knew next to nothing about the man.

A little after five Jack saw a Infiniti M35 go by, driven by a guy who looked a lot like Levy, but he couldn't be sure. Decision time: follow or not follow? He chose follow.

Turned out to be the right decision. Jack stayed a quarter mile behind and eventually saw the Infiniti turn into Levy's driveway. The garage door began to rise as the car eased toward it.

Jack kept going. He'd been debating his next step after locating Levy—knock on his door right away, or wait till he'd relaxed and had a drink? Jack chose now.

He made a U-turn and headed back. He was almost to the house when he saw the Infiniti pull out of the driveway and race off.

Levy wasn't driving. A bearded man who looked an awful lot like the guy in Gerhard's surveillance photos had the wheel.

Bethlehem?

What the hell—?

When Jack saw the guy steer the Infiniti onto the southbound lanes of the Thruway, he knew following had been the right decision. Levy was somewhere in that car. Had to be.

But just to be sure, Jack called the house. A woman answered.

Jack said, "Hi, this is Doctor Bates. Is Aaron there?"

"Doctor Bates?"

"Yes, I'm new at the institute and I need to verify something with him before I go home."

"Well . . . he's not here right now. He pulled into the garage a few moments ago but then he pulled right out again. He must have forgotten something at work. Have him call me if you see him."

"Will do. Thanks."

Well, that confirmed that. Levy was in the car. Bethlehem—he was going to assume that's who he was—hadn't had enough time to overcome him and truss him up, so he must have bopped him and tossed him into the trunk.

What the hell was the connection here? And what would make Bethlehem so desperate that he'd abduct the man in his own garage?

A vision of Levy bungeed facedown in a tub flashed through Jack's head. Even though he hated to resort to cops, the best thing to do here was call the staties and report a stolen car on the Thruway. He'd take care of this himself if he'd been hired by Levy, but he hadn't. So make the highway smokies stop hassling honest, hardworking dudes who just happened to be going too fast, and stop a real bad guy.

Let them pull Bethlehem over and find the good Dr. Levy in the trunk. Not only would the doc be safe, but Bethlehem would end up in the slammer for assault and battery, kidnapping, and whatever other charges the prosecutors could come up with. All of which would solve Christy Pickering's problem as well.

Perfectomundo.

As Jack was reaching for the officialdom phone he saw the Infiniti veer into the Ardsley rest stop. Curious, he followed.

The sun was almost down, casting the long shadow of the barnlike stone-and-stucco food court across the parking area. He saw Bethlehem back the Infiniti into a spot in a far corner that he had all to himself. Jack parked in a more crowded area, then hunkered down to watch.

The driver—definitely Bethlehem, wearing a work shirt, jeans, and cowboy boots—jumped out, trotted over to an old maroon Buick Riviera which he maneuvered around until it was parked next to the Infiniti.

So . . . this wasn't some spur-of-the-moment deal. He'd planned this out in advance. Jack could see what was coming.

Bethlehem opened the Buick trunk and pulled something from his pocket. Sunlight flashed off the blade that unfolded. Then he opened the Infiniti's trunk. Nothing happened for a moment, and then a man was yanked from one trunk and shoved into the other. It happened so fast that if Jack hadn't been watching for it, he would have missed it.

Bethlehem closed the Riv's trunk, then the Infiniti's. But instead of getting into one or the other, he started toward the restaurant area. Jack watched in confusion.

What the—?

And then he realized that Bethlehem might have a dire need for a pit stop. He'd probably been hiding in Levy's garage for hours. Couldn't relieve himself there without leaving damning evidence. This rest stop was probably his first opportunity.

And gave Jack an opportunity too.

Pulling on a pair of driving gloves, he watched Bethlehem enter the food

court, then eased his car toward the Riviera, backing in next to it. He popped
his trunk and raced around to the rear. He kept a collection of burglar tools in
the spare tire well. He could hear Levy banging and shouting within the neighboring trunk. No one but Jack was near enough to hear. He pulled an eighteen-
inch gad pry bar from the kit, jammed the flat end under the lip of the Buick's
trunk lid, and threw his weight down on it.

The lid popped up revealing a disheveled, frightened-looking man with
his hands raised before him as if to ward off a blow. Aaron Levy's hair was
longer now than in the online photo, and he had heavy five-o'clock shadow, but
it was him.

"Get out of there!" Jack said, reaching a hand toward him. "We haven't
much time!"

Levy grabbed Jack's hand and levered himself out.

"Who—?"

"The guy who's saving your ass." He pointed to the Crown Vic. "Into the
passenger seat. Move!"

Levy hesitated a second, then leaped toward the door. Jack memorized the
Riv's license plate as he closed the trunk, then ran around to the driver seat.
As soon as he was in he threw the Vic into gear and roared off.

He was a hundred yards away from the other cars when he saw Bethlehem
step out of the food court.

"Down!"

Levy ducked as they raced past. Bethlehem didn't so much as glance in
their direction as he hurried back toward his car.

As Jack pulled into the southbound traffic, he said, "Okay, we're clear now."

Levy straightened and stared at him. "Who are you?"

"Never mind that. What's Jerry Bethlehem have against you?"

"Jerry Bethlehem? That wasn't—" And then suddenly he clammed.

Wasn't Bethlehem? That meant Levy knew his attacker and knew him as
someone else.

Will the real Jerry Bethlehem please stand up?

"Well, if he wasn't Jerry Bethlehem, who was he?"

Levy ran a shaking hand over his face. "I don't know."

"You're a lousy liar. Do you or don't you know Jerry Bethlehem?"

"Never heard of him."

Another lie.

Levy turned toward him. "But never mind this Bethlehem or whoever he
is. Who are you and why did you—?"

"Pluck you from the slavering jaws of death? Name's John Robertson. I'm
a private investigator. I've been trying to talk to you for two days now but you
keep ducking me. Why is that, Doctor Levy?"

"I remember. You called my office today. Look, I'm sorry, but I'm very busy lately and—"

"I also called your house last night—and no, I'm not the guy who's been hanging up on you. That was most likely your friend Bethlehem."

"He's not my friend! I—"

Jack watched out of the corner of his eye as he asked, "Ever hear of a guy named Gerhard—Michael Gerhard?"

"No. Never."

The sudden stiffening of Levy's posture said otherwise.

"He's dead. Murdered."

Further stiffening. His voice dropped to a whisper. "My God! That's . . . awful. I mean, it's awful for anyone to be murdered, but what's this got to do with me?"

"Because there's a chance Bethlehem did it and I think you were going to end up the same way."

Jack then proceeded to describe the scene in Gerhard's bathroom and the man's ordeal before he drowned.

"But-but what makes you think it was him—this Bethlehem?"

"Because Gerhard was hired—just as I was—to investigate him. And I found your name connected to Bethlehem in Gerhard's files. It doesn't take a rocket scientist to add that up."

Levy slumped in his seat. "What . . . what did I ever do to him to make him want to . . . ?"

For once he seemed sincere. Question was: Who was the *him* he was referring to?

"Only he knows that—and maybe you do too. But I think you'd better do something to keep him from trying again."

"What?"

"I don't suppose you've got your cell phone."

"No. He took it."

Jack pulled his out and handed it across.

"Use mine. Call the cops. Tell them you were abducted and escaped from an old-model Buick Riviera car headed south on the Thruway."

"But surely he'll have ditched the car by now."

"Why? There's a pretty damn good chance he thinks you're still in the trunk and he's finalizing his plans for you as he drives."

Levy took the phone, then handed it back.

"No. Thanks, but no."

"You've gotta be kidding!"

"Sorry. I can't."

"Why the hell not?"

"I'm . . ."

He paused and Jack could hear the falsificator start to bubble.

"You're what?"

"I'm involved in some sensitive research—federally funded research. I can't have police involved in my activities."

"So instead of pressing charges you're just going to sit back and wait for him to try again?"

"No, I'll have federal authorities look into the matter. They'll take care of it."

"By federal you mean the DoD?"

Levy's head snapped around. "What did you say?"

"You heard me."

He turned and stared out the side window. "Please take me back to my car. Or if you can't do that—"

"I'll take you back."

The Bronxville exit was coming up. Jack could get off there and swing onto the northbound side.

Or he could pull off onto a deserted country road—no shortage of those near Rathburg—and put the screws to Levy until he came across with something straight about Bethlehem.

Because that guy was a bad actor. Jack was now ninety-nine percent sure he'd killed Gerhard. He hoped when the cops worked the murder scene they'd come up with something to connect him. If not, maybe Jack would drop a dime and help them along.

One thing he knew, this was no guy to be messing around with an eighteen-year-old girl. Jack had never met Dawn Pickering but he'd decided to help Christy build a wall between her daughter and Bethlehem.

As for the doc . . . he'd take him to his car. That would create another deposit to his good-will account in the Bank of Levy. He might need to draw on that someday.

On the ride back he let Levy use the phone to call his wife to reassure her that he was fine and would be home soon. After that he pressed the guy for more information but could pry loose nothing about Bethlehem.

On the subject of his research, however, Levy was a little more forthcoming. But not much.

"It involves genetics."

"Looking for an insanity gene?" Jack couldn't resist: "Or creating *mutants*?"

"Don't be silly. They're not insane—at least not most of them. We're not altering genes or rearranging them or doing anything but studying them—lots of looking but no touching. Our findings, when we finally publish them, will have global repercussions."

Oh, no. Another one like Hank Thompson and his *Kick*.

"Don't tell me: You're gonna change the world."

Levy shook his head. "Not the world, just the way people see themselves and others. I'm talking a paradigm shift."

"Fine. But how does that prevent you from calling in the locals to take care of Bethlehem."

"It does. Trust me, it just does."

That was just it though: Jack didn't trust him.

Levy wouldn't say much else for the rest of the trip. Jack eventually dropped him at the rest stop. Levy's car was where he'd left it.

"I'm here," he said, staring at his car as if he'd never expected to see it again. "I'm really here." He turned to Jack and extended his hand. "I don't know how to thank you, Mister Robertson."

"It's John, but most people call me Jack." He pressed one of his cards into Levy's hand. "You take that, and you call me if you ever want to talk about Jerry Bethlehem."

The number connected to one of Jack's voice mail accounts.

"I will."

They both knew that was a lie, but Jack was doing a bread-upon-the-water thing here.

He pulled his Glock and Levy shrank back against the door.

"Wh-what are you doing?"

"Making sure there are no surprises waiting for you in the back seat."

He got out and checked the Infiniti—unlocked and empty. A set of keys and a cell phone lay on the front seat. He motioned Levy over.

"Pop the trunk for me."

Levy reached inside and hit a button. The lid popped open—empty.

"Okay, doc. I guess you're home free. Your guy is probably still headed south, blissfully unaware he's got an empty trunk. But just to be safe, be sure to keep your doors locked and give your garage a good once-over before you get out of your car."

Levy nodded. "I'll do that. And thanks again."

"Yeah."

He watched Levy drive out of the rest stop to make sure no one was following him, then he headed back toward the city.

One strange night.

Lots of questions raised, few answered. But the question was what to say to Christy.

He could scare the hell out of her by telling her about Gerhard's murder and Levy's abduction. But without proof, what would that do to drive a wedge between Dawn and Bethlehem? Might have the opposite effect. If Dawn couldn't or wouldn't believe her snookums capable of such things, it might push her closer than ever to Bethlehem and drive the wedge between her and her mother instead.

Still, Christy had a right to know that her instincts had been dead on the money. But if Levy wasn't pressing charges, and if the police found nothing to connect Bethlehem to Gerhard, she'd have nothing to back up her claims. She'd sound like an overprotective, possessive, paranoid madwoman. Hell, the cops hadn't even released news of Gerhard's death yet. Jack wondered about that, but figured they might want to notify his next of kin first.

He'd set up a meet with her, tell her what he knew, and let her take it from there.

7

As soon as he was on the move, Aaron speed-dialed Julia's cell phone.

"It's me," he said when she answered. "You home?"

"I'm just leaving the office. Why? Something wrong?"

"Damn right it is. The therapy is a bust. He's on a rampage."

She said nothing for a while, then, "Meet me at home."

He cut the connection and upped his speed, yet his thoughts raced ahead of him. And his heart raced ahead of his thoughts. He'd finally stopped shaking, but a soaked undershirt lay plastered against his skin.

He'd been as good as dead tonight. The shock of finding Bolton in his garage had paralyzed him. The look of death in those cold blue eyes, the point of the knife against his throat . . . he'd almost passed out. The suffocating ride in the trunk and then . . . salvation.

But the things that stranger, Robertson, had told him . . . about Gerhard's torture-murder . . . they had to be true. It made no sense for Robertson to save him, drive him back to his car, and let him go, just to lie to him.

Gerhard dead! It had to be Bolton. He'd found out the detective was investigating him and killed him. And *how* he'd killed him. Aaron shuddered. That might have been him.

But why me?

He posed no threat to Bolton. Of course, he didn't have to. Bolton merely had to perceive him as a threat. But why would—?

Julia. Had Julia set him up? Had she sicced Bolton on Gerhard and then on him? But why would she do that? Sure, he'd been a reluctant partner in this experiment, but he'd gone along with all her risky plans.

None of this made any sense!

He called Marie next and told her he'd be stuck at the institute for a few more hours. Good wife that she was, she said she'd keep some dinner warm for him.

He got off at Tarrytown and went straight up 9 to Julia's house.

His superior at the Creighton Institute, Julia Vecca, M.D., M.S., Ph.D., was single, ascetic, politically connected, and intensely, relentlessly devoted to her job as medical director. Aaron had been there a couple of years longer but was not so driven—he had a life outside the institute, after all—and not the least bit connected. Hence her position as director. Which was fine with Aaron. He wouldn't have minded the extra money—something Julia didn't seem to care about—but didn't want the administrative headaches. He shared Julia's commitment to the project, but not her zeal.

He pulled into the parking lot of her condo complex and parked next to a grime-caked Jetta—Julia's car. Always easy to find. Just look for the dirtiest car on the lot and that would be Julia's. She didn't believe in washing cars. They'd only get dirty again.

He sat waiting and watching, afraid to leave the locked womb of his Infiniti. No sign of Bolton but that meant nothing. He could be hiding anywhere.

Aaron stared across the small expanse of pavement and lawn to Julia's front door. So near, and yet . . .

He called her again. When she answered he said, "I'm outside."

"Really? I didn't hear you knock."

"I didn't. Open the door and wait for me."

"I don't—"

"Just do it." He added, "Please."

After all, she was his boss.

He saw a rectangle of light appear, silhouetting a vaguely female figure. With his heart pounding he leaped from the car and dashed toward it. Julia backed away, her expression alarmed, as he charged in and slammed the door behind him.

"Aaron, what the hell is going on?"

Julia almost never cursed.

He noticed that she'd let her hair down, an act that made many women more attractive. Julia, however, proved an exception. Her barely shoulder-length mouse-brown hair—just long enough to tie back with an elastic band—was stringy and in need of a good shampooing. Her makeup-free face was pale and shiny as her wide dark eyes regarded him through thick glasses. She'd traded her usual blouse and slacks for a baggy gray NYU sweatsuit that softened the sharp angles of her thin frame.

Aaron locked the door, then turned to her.

"Bolton kidnapped me."

Her eyes widened further, growing huge through her lenses. "Are you crazy?"

"No. *He's* the crazy one, remember?"

He peeked through one of the door's sidelights, looking for movement outside. God, he was still shaking inside.

"But why would he—?"

He whirled toward her. "Exactly what I want to know. If some detective hadn't seen it and set me free—"

She stiffened. "Detective? Are the police—?"

"No, this one's private. I never got around to asking who hired him, but I assume it was the same woman who hired Gerhard."

"Why would she hire two detectives?"

Aaron steadied his jangling nerves as best he could and watched her closely, gauging her reaction.

"Because the first one is dead. Murdered."

Her hand flew to her mouth. "What?"

Aaron knew Julia was no actress—a strictly what-you-see-is-what-you-get type—and her shock seemed genuine.

He nodded. "The new detective found Gerhard's body. He'd been put through some bizarre sort of water torture before he drowned."

Julia dropped onto a couch and began picking her nose as she stared at a wall—a blank wall, just like all the others in her townhouse.

Aaron had asked her once why she didn't hang a picture or two; she'd seemed genuinely puzzled by the concept: *Why? Once I've seen a picture or a painting, I've seen it. Why would I want to look at it again?*

She made a good salary but Aaron had no idea what she did with it. Certainly didn't spend it on furniture. Most of hers was mismatched and second-hand. She was the least materialistic person he'd ever met. All that mattered to Julia Vecca was her work.

And now her work had murdered a man.

She extracted her finger from her nose, stared at the tip, then wiped it on her sweatsuit pants.

Aaron kept close watch on her face as he said, "How did Bolton know about Gerhard?"

She didn't blink, didn't shift her gaze from the wall as she said, "I told him."

Aaron had suspected that, but it was a jolt to hear it put so matter-of-factly. Now came his turn to drop into a chair.

Private investigator Michael Gerhard had shown up at Julia's office one day and rocked them with a question neither of them had expected to hear: Why was a murderous psychopath like Jeremy Bolton out on the street?

The detective had been hired by the mother of some young thing Bolton was diddling. He'd snagged a glass with Bolton's fingerprints from some restaurant, run it through various databases, and come up with a hit in ViCAP.

Julia had explained that it was all legal, a government-funded-and-sanctioned pilot program, and how secrecy was crucial to its success. The new identity they'd created for Bolton must not be compromised.

Gerhard had said his client had a right to know what sort of man her daughter was dating. He'd been hired to find something on the man and he had. He was going to tell his client.

Julia offered him twice what the client was paying, and to put him on permanent retainer with the institute if he'd keep what he'd learned to himself. Gerhard had taken the money and kept his mouth shut. But he hadn't stopped snooping.

"Why . . . why on earth would you tell Bolton?"

"I thought he should know. Dating a teenager is risky behavior. I couldn't tell him not to, but I thought if he knew the mother was looking into his past he might decide to break it off."

Aaron guessed that was only part of the truth.

"You were testing him, weren't you."

Finally she looked at him. "Yes . . . yes, I suppose I was. Provocation would test the therapy."

"You sicced him on Gerhard."

"I did no such thing!"

"He's a mad dog! You pointed to Gerhard and said, 'That man's a threat.' What did you expect him to do?"

"I expected him to alter his behavior to avoid the threat, not kill it!"

"Well, kill it he did, and now we've got to reel him in."

She shook her head. "Absolutely not. We simply need to increase his dosage."

"It's time you faced the hard cold fact that two-eight-seven isn't working. It's not suppressing the gene set."

"And you're glad of that, aren't you. You've been against this trial from the start—"

"Is that why you sicced him on me?"

She leaped to her feet. "Don't talk like a fool! I'd never do such a thing. It had to be Gerhard. He sniffed out your negativity the first day we met with him. That was why he kept pestering you for more information. He knew we'd given him only part of the story and he sensed you were the weak link. He must have told Jeremy while . . ." Her voice drifted off.

"While he was being tortured. Proud of yourself, Julia?"

She didn't seem to hear. She began to pace her living room.

Aaron rose and stepped to her front window. He peeked out and froze as he caught a flash of movement by the bushes. He held his breath and watched. No. Nothing. Just the wind blowing the branches about.

"It's not his fault," Julia was saying. "It's ours. We simply haven't suppressed the trigger gene enough. We'll have to up his dose." She stopped and glanced at him. "What do you think—jump it fifty percent?"

"No. Jump *him* and drag him into a cell and throw away the key, that's what I think."

She stared at him. "You're serious, aren't you."

"Damn right."

"How can you say that after all the years we've worked on this?"

"*You* get forced into your car trunk at knife point by a madman, then come back and we'll discuss how I can say that."

She held up her hand in a peace gesture. "Point taken. I'll talk to him. When I explain that he's got it all wrong, he'll be sorry. He'll apologize. And then we'll put this behind us."

"Easy for you to say. And no apology is going to mean anything. Bolton's an expert at saying whatever anyone wants to hear. Besides, I don't want an apology, I want him locked up."

Her expression turned fierce. "That's not going to happen and you know it! The agency has too much invested in this. Not just money—they've got *plans*. You know that. And you know they're not going to change them just because you've developed cold feet."

"I damn near developed cold *everything*! I won't be able to sleep or eat or even *think* knowing he's out there looking for me."

She stared at him a moment, then turned and left the room. She returned with her cell phone.

"I'll call him right now and get this settled."

"No, don't."

Aaron didn't know why he said it. It made no sense, but he quailed at the thought of any sort of contact with that madman.

"We're going to get past this," she said, punching buttons, "put it behind us, and move on. I'm not about to let a little setback derail this project."

"Little setback? A man is dead!"

She ignored him as she listened to her phone. After a slew of rapid heartbeats she spoke.

"Hello, Jeremy. You know who this is. I've been speaking with my colleague and he's told me some very disturbing things . . . yes, well, you were misinformed. Terribly misinformed. Where are you? . . . Is that so? Well, then, let's settle this right now."

She lowered her phone and stepped to the door.

Aaron stood paralyzed with shock.

"What—what are you doing?"

"He's right outside."

8

Julia heard Aaron's cry of alarm but ignored him and opened the door.

Jeremy Bolton stood outside. His usually neatly combed hair was wind tossed and his normally handsome features were distorted by a scowl. He looked distressed. Julia knew Jeremy could be difficult when distressed.

But God help her, he was attractive. She'd never had much of a sex drive, and was glad for that—sexual entanglements were notoriously distracting. But Jeremy Bolton had an air about him. She'd always pooh-poohed the idea of animal magnetism, but this man had *something* going on. Maybe he secreted a pheromone. Whatever it was, she'd met only a few men in her life who could affect her this way . . . make her almost . . . impulsive. Make her want to feel those bearded cheeks rubbing against her nipples—

Stop.

Impulses be damned. Giving in would be counterproductive in the extreme. She could not jeopardize her neutrality, her scientific objectivity.

"Come in, Jeremy."

He paused for a second, then stepped inside. His scowl hardened when he spotted Aaron.

"I think you owe Doctor Levy an apology," she said quickly.

She noticed Aaron had retreated to a spot behind one of the chairs. His face had turned a cadaverous shade of white.

Jeremy continued to stare at Aaron. "How'd you get out of my trunk?"

Aaron only shook his head. He seemed too frightened to speak.

Julia said, "The apology, Jeremy. We're waiting."

His gaze remained locked on Aaron. "He wants to cancel the trial, lock me up again."

"He wants nothing of the sort."

"I was told—"

"You were misinformed. And for your information, the surest way to get the trial canceled is for Doctor Levy to disappear. That would be the end for you. You'll never see daylight again."

Without a word, he shot her a look, then went back to staring at Levy.

Julie pressed on. "And don't think for a minute you could elude capture. Your clinical trial is under the aegis of a government agency that has vast resources and a long reach—one that can be just as ruthless as you. They will track you down, and when they find you they will not be kind. Look at me, Jeremy."

After a few seconds he turned his smoldering blue gaze on her.

"Listen carefully to what I say. This experiment is very important to a number of highly placed people in this country's intelligence and defense communities. If you disrupt it they will be very angry. They will take out that anger on you in ways not sanctioned by the Geneva Conventions."

She hoped he didn't think she was overstating the case. She wasn't.

"I want to tell you right now, right to your face, that Doctor Levy is one hundred percent behind this trial. He is one of the developers of D-two-eight-seven. He has a vested interest in its success. *He wants you to succeed.* Can I make it any clearer than that?"

She sensed an easing of some of Jeremy's coiled tension. She pushed further.

"Have I ever lied to you, Jeremy?"

After a pause, he shook his head. "No. Least not that I know of."

"Well, I haven't. And since that's the case, I believe you owe Doctor Levy an apology."

He looked at Aaron again, then shrugged. "Sorry, Doc."

Aaron looked stunned. His mouth worked a few times before he managed to speak.

"*Sorry?* That's it? You were going to kill me!"

Jeremy grinned through his beard. "Nah. Just takin you for a little ride. I got some bogus info on you, that's all. I heard if anyone was gonna rat me out it was you. If Doc Vecca says that's wrong, well then, I guess it's wrong. My bad. No hard feelings, 'kay?"

As Aaron stood there, stone faced, Julia prompted him.

"Aaron, we need to put this behind us and move on."

Finally he raised his hands in a gesture of defeat, acceptance, and capitulation. "All right, all right."

Julia clapped once. "Wonderful! Now I want to see the two of you shake hands."

"I don't see why that's necessary. If we—"

"Come on, come on. It's what men do, isn't it. A sign of peace, right? I want peace between you."

Jeremy too looked reluctant, but finally he stepped forward and thrust out his hand.

"Sorry for the misunderstandin, doc."

Aaron hesitated briefly, then grasped it and shook. But before he released Bolton's hand he raised it for a closer look.

"What's that? A tattoo?"

Jeremy pulled his hand free and held it up. "Yep. Got 'er done a couple weeks ago."

Julia stared at the odd little stick figure in the web between his thumb and index finger. It had a diamond-shaped head and—

"It looks like it has four arms."

Jeremy grinned. "It does. That's the Kicker Man."

"Why the extra arms?"

The smile faltered. "Don't rightly know. Never thought to ask. It is what it is, I guess."

Tattoos. Julia had never understood them. Permanent drawings on your skin . . . what for? But then, she didn't understand jewelry either. Who could be bothered?

"Well, whatever. Now that we're all friends again we can get back to business and refocus on the project as—"

"Aren't we forgetting something?" Aaron said. "Like a body tied facedown in a tub in Brooklyn?"

Jeremy put on a sheepish look. "I think I sorta kinda got carried away."

Julia stared at him. "Why did you do it, Jeremy?"

"You told me he was tryin to split me and Dawn. I know it was her mother's idea, so one of them had to be stopped. I couldn't take out her momma without gettin Dawn all messed up, so he had to go."

Julia had known deadly violence might result from telling Jeremy about

Gerhard and what he knew. But she couldn't resist. Call it an experiment within an experiment. Jeremy seemed to be doing well on the D-287 therapy, but without something to provoke him, how would they know if it was having any real effect? Gerhard had provided an opportunity to inject an external stimulus. She'd hoped Jeremy would find a rational course—thus confirming the success of the therapy—but if he resorted to violence, that too would provide them with valuable data. She was glad he'd chosen Gerhard as the target for his rage. The man had known too much.

Jeremy gave another shrug. "Don't see how I had a choice."

"Of course you had a choice!" Aaron cried. "You could have stopped seeing the girl!"

Jeremy's eyes narrowed as his forehead darkened. "That ain't in the cards, doc. Nobody comes between me and Dawn."

"Oh, come on! There must be dozens, hundreds of women—"

"No! Only Dawn. She's my one and only."

"Your one and only what?" Aaron said.

Julia raised a hand. "We're getting sidetracked here. What's done is done. What I don't understand is why you did something so reckless."

"I wanted the answers to certain questions."

"You didn't have to kill him."

"Did too. Told you: He was gonna come between me and Dawn, and I wanted to know what he'd found out and what he'd told her momma."

"And then you compounded it by leaving the body where it could be found. Why?"

Aaron said, "You wanted to show off your elaborate torture handiwork, didn't you."

Jeremy said nothing at first, but his expression told Julia that Aaron had hit this particular nail square on the head. Then Jeremy took a step toward him.

"Where'd you hear about—?"

"Stop this right now!" Julia said, jumping in before things escalated out of control. "It was a foolish thing to do but we'll have it taken care of."

Jeremy turned toward her. "'We'?"

"Our people. The ones you want to stay on the right side of. They're experts in crime-scene cleanup." She'd call them as soon as Jeremy left. "Meanwhile, you will report to my office tomorrow for a booster dose."

Jeremy's eyes narrowed. "What's that gonna do to me?"

"Nothing you'll notice."

"Better not. I been feelin pretty good lately and I want to stay that way. Don't want nothin comin between me and Dawn. That's my *numero-uno* priority."

Aaron said, "Your '*numero-uno* priority' is the therapy."

Jeremy shook his head. "You got that wrong, doc. I'm goin along with the therapy just so's me and Dawn can be together. Me and Dawn—that's all that matters. Anybody who gets between us goes down. 'Cause me and Dawn . . ." He grinned like a man who knew the world's greatest secret. ". . . we're gonna change *everything*."

9

"What on Earth is so interesting?"

Jack looked up from his copy of Hank Thompson's *Kick*. He was propped up in bed by two pillows, reading in a pool of light from a goosenecked lamp attached to the headboard. The rest of the bedroom lay dark around him.

He glanced at Gia where she lay beside him. She'd turned over to face him. Her eyelids were at half mast. She looked ready to drop off any minute.

"Is the light keeping you up?"

"Nothing keeps me up when I get tired, you know that. But what've you got there? You never read in bed."

Jack didn't know how to explain it. He'd returned from Rathburg feeling restless and uneasy. He sensed he was being drawn into something he should avoid, dragged into a place he didn't want to go. Christy Pickering seemed to be at the heart of it. Since talking to her he'd had a priceless book stolen from a stroked-out old man, found a dead body, and witnessed—and foiled—an abduction.

Or was it all coincidence?

Yeah, he'd been told no more coincidences for him, but surely that didn't apply to *everything* in his life. Coincidences did happen in the normal course of events. He couldn't buy that something was *preventing* everyday coincidences.

He couldn't see how the loss of the *Compendium* could be connected to the Pickering problem. But he most certainly saw a connection between the *Compendium* and the book in his hands: the four-armed stick figure.

Jack had a pretty good idea of how the theft had gone down: the Kicker janitor—they still hadn't found him—had seen the prof at the Xerox machine copying the drawing of the Kicker man. He'd recognized it and decided he wanted it.

Why?

Then again, why not? Judging from today's experience at the bookstore, "mine" and "not-mine" appeared to be concepts either unappreciated or not easily grasped by Kickers—especially when it came to books.

The janitor had been around the museum. One look at the *Compendium* and he had to know or at least guess it was worth a fortune. Which was why he'd disappeared. Probably trying to fence it now.

The idea of the *Compendium* in the wrong hands bothered Jack. He didn't know to what uses it could be put, but he had a feeling they weren't all good.

Tomorrow he'd see if he could get the guy's name and do a little tracking on his own. He doubted the cops would tell him—too bad he wasn't Jake Fixx with all those law enforcement contacts. He'd have to look elsewhere. Maybe the museum staff . . .

But right now he wanted to see if Hank Thompson gave any clue as to how an ancient symbol—of what, he wished he knew—from an equally ancient one-of-a-kind tome had ended up on the cover of his book.

He held it up for Gia.

"I was intending just to skim through it, but the first part of the book is a memoir and I sort of got caught up in this guy's personal story."

Hank Thompson hadn't had it easy growing up. Far from it. Born in Arkansas in poverty to a single mother who died young, his unnamed absentee father would visit him now and again, but never helped him off the foster-home merry-go-round he rode into his teens. Yet Thompson didn't seem to bear him any animus. Seemed to revere him instead.

"How far along are you?"

"He's just coming out of his teens and surprisingly up front about the petty crimes he committed."

Gia yawned. "You think he really committed them or is just looking for street cred?"

"It rings true."

Gia looked at him. "You'd know, I guess."

"Unfortunately, yes."

Thompson's account reminded Jack a little of the time he spent on the street when he first arrived in the city. He'd wanted to stay below the radar, and that meant working off the books for cash and hustling for every buck. He wasn't proud of some of the moves he'd made back then.

Gia yawned again, then lifted her head and kissed him on the cheek.

"Have fun. I'm outta here."

As she rolled over and tugged the blanket up over her head, Jack returned to *Kick*.

Thompson had just turned nineteen in the story when he started stealing cars in Columbus, Georgia, and driving them into Alabama where he got top dollar from a chop shop in Opelika.

Maybe this was why so many Kickers had criminal records—they identified with Thompson.

He read on . . .

Then came a major turning point in my life. One bright hot summer day I wheeled a Lexus LS 400 into one of Jesse Ed's bays. The Lexus was still the new kid on the automobile block back then and damn hard to find in the South. This was a primo grab and I was expecting a big payday. What I got instead was trouble. Instead of finding a grinning Jesse Ed waiting with his acetylene torch, I found a gang of Alabama state troopers who'd raided the place about an hour before I got there.

Well, let me tell you, I smoked that Lexus's tires backing out of there and led those troopers on a merry old chase back to the state line. Beat them too. But I ran into a Georgia state cop roadblock where they shotgunned my tires.

I was so royally pissed at getting caught that I guess you could say I went a little bit nuts. It took four of those boys to take me down. And take me down they did. If someone had been around with a video camera, I could have been the white Rodney King.

I woke up the next day battered and bloody and facing not just a local GTA rap, but federal charges for ITSMV. (For those of you who've never been on the wrong side of jail bars, that's grand theft auto and interstate transportation of stolen motor vehicles, respectively.)

Jack had to smile. Yeah, he could see where getting busted simultaneously for both state and federal raps could be a life-changing experience.

He read on with amusement about Thompson's troubles with incompetent—at least according to him—public defenders and drunken judges and crooked prosecuting attorneys, but the chapter's last paragraph stopped him cold.

Well, no question the Lexus was stolen, but they couldn't prove I did the actual stealing, so I skated on the GTA charge. But I couldn't dodge the ITSMV. Not with all those pursuing Alabama smokies as witnesses to my crossing the state line in a stolen car. So I was looking at federal time, and not in some country club either. They had me slated for the Jesup medium security FCI when out of the blue came a reprieve. Oh, not that kind of reprieve. I was still going to do time, but in much cushier surroundings. Don't ask me why, but for some reason the fed-

eral government, in all its wisdom, had decided to ship me to the East
Coast, to a place in New York I'd never heard of. I didn't know it then,
but the Creighton Institute would change my life.

Jack stared at the page in shock. This was too much of a coincidence to be
a simple coincidence. It was happening again: Something was pulling his
strings.

But the question remained: Why had a nobody car thief like Hank Thompson been shipped across the country to a federal facility?

Jack had a feeling that, whether he wanted to or not, he'd be searching for
the answer.

FRIDAY

1

"You'd like to talk to Hank Thompson?" Abe said. "Want I should arrange a meeting?"

Jack smiled. "Why don't you do just that."

He took a bite of one of the bagels with fat-free cream cheese he'd brought along. Time to get serious about Abe's waistline again.

He thought Abe was kidding when he picked up the phone, but then listened as he got the number of Vector Publications from information. He dialed that and asked for publicity. As he waited he put his hand over the mouthpiece and turned to Jack.

"Who do you want to be and what paper are you from?"

"You think you can pull this off?"

"Of course. Such a publicity hound I've rarely seen. Been on every radio station in town already. Probably be on WFAN if he could work in a sports angle. This rally of his he's pushing like there's no tomorrow."

This might work. Jack had some questions for Thompson—details he hadn't shared in the book. Like what had really gone on at Creighton. He'd made vague mention of counseling and psychological testing, but no mention of why the long arm of the federal government had reached across the country to pluck him out of the county jail in Columbia. And did he know a certain Dr. Levy.

"Okay. I'll be John Tyleski." Why not? "And I'll be from . . ." He didn't want a New York City paper—the publicity people would be familiar with the names on the local book beat. He thought back to his boyhood when the city papers near home were in Philadelphia and Trenton. "Say I'm with the *Trenton Times*."

Abe nodded as he started to speak again—with no accent. "Hello, publicity? Who there is handling Hank Thompson? Oh, you are. Excellent. I'm Moishe Horowitz, features editor for the *Trenton Times*."

Jack mouthed, *Moishe Horowitz?* Abe shrugged.

"Yes, well, one of my reporters happens to be in New York today and we're wondering if Hank Thompson would be available for an interview. We'd like a face-to-face if possible. Yes, of course." He fumbled for a pen and handed it to Jack. "Let me give you my reporter's cell number. His name is John Tyleski and his number is . . ."

Jack scribbled it down on the back of an envelope and Abe read it off. Abe closed with a few stroking pleasantries about the success of the book and what a wonderful job they were doing promoting it.

"There," he said as he hung up. "What could be simpler? Her name is Susan Abrams and she'll call after she talks to Thompson."

"Great." Jack took a sip of his coffee. "What do you think about all this? The Kicker Man links the *Compendium* to Thompson, and Thompson's linked to the Creighton place. Christy Pickering is linked to Jerry Bethlehem—whoever he really is—who's linked to Doctor Levy who works at Creighton."

"Bethlehem is linked to a dead man as well, don't forget."

"I'm not. But I wonder why there's been no mention of Gerhard's death. You sure you haven't seen anything?"

"Not a word."

If Abe hadn't read it, then it hadn't been published. He pored over every inch of his papers.

"Why are they keeping it under wraps?"

"Maybe he was more than he pretended to be. Maybe he worked for this group you mentioned already that runs Creighton. Your instincts say what?"

"That the Creighton Institute is the key."

"I agree. Might be something going on there that connects everything. Then again, maybe not."

"Well, I know someone on the inside at Creighton, and he owes me—big time. But I've got a feeling that's not going to be enough to make him open up." Jack checked his watch. "Gotta run. I'm meeting Christy Pickering in an hour."

"Go already. I'll do searches on Creighton. Such fun I'll have."

"See if you can get me an interview with Winslow while you're at it."

If he was going to go to the trouble of printing up some business cards, might as well multitask them.

2

Jack rode the R out to Forest Hills. He did not want what he had to tell Christy floating along over a phone—land line or cell, no telling who was listening these days. Christy had begged him to meet her outside the city. He'd agreed. She'd hired a block of his time, so why not?

He'd opted for the subway over his car. Rush hour had passed, and even if it hadn't, he was headed against the morning flow. It was a local but he had time.

He plowed further into *Kick*. According to Thompson, his stint at Creighton didn't put him on the straight and narrow so much as make him more choosy about his activities, opting for the dubiously legal over the blatantly illegal. He worked various scams and cons that Jack found uncomfortably familiar.

Been there, done that.

He closed the book and glanced down at the rumpled copy of this morning's *Post* on the seat next to him. He'd already been through the paper looking for news of Gerhard's death. Strange that it hadn't been announced.

Maybe he should try another call . . .

He looked around. Less than a dozen other people on the car in various states of age, quality of clothing, and consciousness, either dozing, walled off behind headphones, staring at the ads or at the floor. His gaze came to rest on one of the sliding doors. He hadn't noticed it when he came in, but someone had spray-painted an all-too-familiar figure on its lower half . . .

Couldn't get away from the Kicker Man, it seemed.

Okay. Nobody within earshot. He pulled out his officialdom phone, powered it up, and gave 911 another try.

"Emergency Services," said a woman's voice.

"Yes, I called the night before last about a problem with a house in my neighborhood and nothing's been done about it."

"What house was that, sir?"

Jack gave Gerhard's address. "There was water running out the door and I was afraid maybe someone had left the water on or, God forbid, died while running the sink."

"Let me look that up for you, sir." After a pause, she said, "We sent someone out there this morning and—"

Jack put a huff into his tone. "This morning? What took you so long? I called you two days ago."

"Yessir, but things have been extremely hectic lately, and we must prioritize. I'm sure you can understand that when we have to choose between, say, a missing child or someone found unconscious in an alley, and a water leak, we put off the water leak. I assure you, we got there as soon as our schedule allowed."

Jack couldn't argue with that.

"So you were there this morning. What did you find? Was everybody okay inside?"

"Well, they went in and . . . let's see . . . it says here they found extensive water damage—apparently an upstairs tub had overflowed—but the house was empty."

Empty! How . . . ?

"Mister Gerhard wasn't home?"

"It says no one was home."

Jack sat in silent shock. What the hell? He wasn't crazy. He'd seen Gerhard's bungeed-up body.

"Is there anything else I can help you with, sir?"

"No . . . thank you very much."

He hung up and turned off the phone. Someone had gone in and removed Gerhard's body. Who? Bethlehem? Someone had left him there with the water running. Why go back?

None of this made sense.

His other phone rang: Susan Abrams of Vector Publications calling. It just so happened that Hank Thompson was going to be visiting their offices this afternoon. If Jack could be there at two thirty, he could interview Hank in their conference room.

Jack said he'd be there and she gave him the address.

He reopened *Kick* and began skimming so he'd be up to speed when he faced Thompson. But images of Gerhard's corpse kept flashing between him and the pages.

The car pretty much emptied out at Woodhaven Boulevard—everyone going to Queens Center Mall, he guessed. He watched a pregnant woman, a brunette six months or better along, get on and take a seat. She carried a *bebe* shopping bag. She glanced around, flashed him a quick, shy smile, then pulled a magazine from the bag.

Gia had been just about that far into her pregnancy before . . .

Before it was ended.

He felt his mood darken. The lights seemed to darken too. He'd been in a decent mood, hadn't thought about Emma for a whole couple of hours, and then this lady had to show up and ruin it.

Not her fault, of course.

He tried not to look at her as the train moved on.

As the train was pulling out of the 67th Avenue station, the car's forward door opened and a couple of hip-hop zoolanders swaggered in. Could have been sixteen, could have been eighteen. Hard to tell. Ghetto manqué white kids—headed for Forest Hills, no less—regurgitating the clichés of the sideways Amahzan baseball cap, the way-too-big basketball jersey, and the baggy, falling-off jeans. These guys had added some gang accessories, like blue stubby do-rags under the caps and blue-and-white bead necklaces along with the gold.

Crip never-bes.

The shorter one snatched the paper from the old dude near the front and tossed it across the car.

"What you readin that fuckin shit for, asshole? It's all lies!"

His buddy laughed as they moved on, leaving the old guy scrabbling to reassemble his paper. They passed Jack, giving him a don't-mess-with-us look. Jack looked back down at his book.

Trouble today? No thanks.

After they'd passed he glanced up in time to see the taller one stomp on one of the pregnant girl's feet as he went by. The kid was wearing sneakers, but Jack bet it hurt.

She winced, then said, "Don't you say 'Excuse me'?"

They both swung on her.

Tall got in her face and said, "Shut the fuck up, bitch, 'cause I got my balls in your mouth!"

Shock flattened her features. "You've got *what*?"

Short said, "Aww, bitch, you better shut the fuck up because he's got his balls in your mouth!"

Jack felt a switch close inside. He knew that on another day, in different company, he might have laughed at how pathetic they were. But they'd picked the wrong moment and the wrong lady.

He laid the book on the seat beside him. "I think you owe her an apology."

They turned as one and stared at him.

Short shot him a hard look. "The fuck you say?"

Tall held out his right hand. Looked like he'd used a black Sharpie to decorate his palm with a crude version of the same stick figure as on the door.

"Don't even *think* about fuckin with us, man! We're dissimilated!"

"I'm sure you are—whatever that means—but why don't you be good boys and say you're sorry to the nice lady."

"Or what?"

"Or I'll have to unfriend you on MySpace."

Short jabbed a finger at him. "*My* balls in *your* mouth!"

Jack gripped the pole at the left end of his seat, then cupped a hand around his right ear as he leaned forward.

"Sorry? What did you say?"

An old, old trick. He wondered if the jerk would fall for it.

He did. He bent and leaned toward Jack. Got within two feet.

"You fuckin deaf? I said, my balls—"

Jack's hand was already raised, its blade edge angled toward Short. All he had to do was snap his arm straight to deliver a sharp chop to the chain-layered throat.

Which he did.

Not a larynx crusher, but hard enough to crack some cartilage and send the kid tumbling backward onto the floor, kicking and gagging as he clutched his throat.

Someone screamed—the pregnant girl. She had a hand over her mouth, her wide eyes bulging.

Jack was already up and pivoting to ram his right heel into the shocked Tall's knee. He felt it give and bend the wrong way—just a little, but enough to guarantee a payment or two on an orthopedist's Porsche. Tall screamed as he fell toward the floor, and Jack took that opportunity to land a second kick, this one square into his family jewels. Another turn, another good shot to the presumed location of Short's berries. The hoarse wails climbed to tenor. Bull's-eye.

"Now, gentlemen, your balls are in *your* mouths."

The pregnant girl's gaze was shifting between Jack and the writhing not-so toughies.

"W-w-what did you just do?"

"Hurt them."

And loved every second of it.

How many seconds? Four? Five, tops. That was all it had taken.

Amazing how much better a few seconds could make you feel.

He noticed movement to his right and saw the old man pulling a cell phone from his pocket. He pointed at him.

"And you think you're doing what with that?"

"Calling nine-one-one."

"On *me*?"

"No, of course not. On them."

"You will put that away. Now." He looked around at the two passengers at the rear end of the car. "I don't want to see anyone with a phone. No calls until Elvis has left the building. Got it?"

They nodded. The man at the front end tucked his phone away.

Jack looked back at the pregnant gal. "Got it?"

She nodded.

"By the way," he said, jerking a thumb at the pair of writhing, groaning losers. "They're sorry."

The train began to slow then. When it stopped at the Forest Hills station Jack stepped out and quick-walked toward the exit. When he looked back, the rest of the able-bodied passengers were leaving the car as well.

No one was talking on a phone.

3

The R line terminated in Forest Hills. When Jack trotted up to street level he looked around for Christy Pickering.

That name . . . he still couldn't nail down why it struck such a familiar chord . . . something from way back in his past.

He heard a toot and saw her waving from a big black Mercedes. As he slipped into the passenger seat, she stuck a twenty-ounce bottle of Diet Pepsi into a cup holder and offered her hand.

"Well, Mister Jack, should we drive or just sit here?"

She wore dark blue slacks, a red-and-white-checked blouse, and looked nervous. Her palm was damp when Jack shook her hand.

"Let's drive."

He didn't want to hang around the station. Sooner or later someone would find those two and call an ambulance. Cops would tag along.

"Okay." She put the car in gear. "Where?"

Jack could have taken her on a tour of all the gardens he helped plant a dozen years ago when he'd worked for a landscaper. Giovanni had been based in Brooklyn but he'd built up quite a following in the patrician enclaves out here. Hot, hard work, but Jack had always enjoyed it. He'd done it as a summer job in college so he didn't come to Giovanni as a complete newbie. The major benefit was getting paid off the books. The major drawback was finding something else to do in the winter. He'd been the only American in Giovanni's crew and had learned along the way to swear fluently in Spanish.

"How about past the tennis club, then you can take me to the station on Sixty-third. I've got to get back on the train pretty soon and that'll put me two stops closer to the city."

And two stops away from this one.

"You into tennis?"

Jack had done some landscaping at the famous West Side Tennis Club, but that wasn't the reason.

"When I was a kid my dad used to sit me down in front of the TV and we'd watch the US Open when it was played here." A mantle of melancholy settled over him. "He really loved tennis."

She pulled into the traffic.

"He's gone?"

"Yeah."

"Sorry."

"So am I."

All those years spent ducking his calls, and now he'd never call again.

Christy sighed and ran a quick hand through her ash blond hair. "Never knew my father."

Jack glanced into the back seat and saw a stack of sheet music.

"You're into musicals?"

"Literally—but strictly community-theater level."

"And *Promises! Promises!* is the latest?"

She smiled and nodded. "I landed the part of Jill."

"Ever dream of Broadway?"

"When I was young." Her eyes shone. "And who knows? After Dawn's off in college I might give it a try. But right now I'm delighted to get the lead in this little show. I love the music, but the musicians are having trouble with the shifting time signatures."

"Especially the title song, I'll bet."

She was staring at him. "You know musical theater?"

"Some."

"More than some. Not many people remember that kind of detail from *Promises! Promises!*"

Jack shrugged. "I don't know if it's much of a detail, but I do know I never liked the late, great Jerry Orbach's voice."

She smiled. "Do you mind my asking if you're gay—not that it matters."

He laughed. "No. Why?"

"Just wondering." She gave him a sidelong glance. "Let's talk about another Jerry. What have you got for me?"

"Let's wait till we're at the other station."

She gave him a strange look but he said nothing. He had a reason: He didn't think it was a good idea for her foot to be on the gas pedal when she heard what he had to tell her.

They passed the huge Tudor-style tennis club, set on the edge of one of the nicest neighborhoods in all of Queens.

"You live in one of these?" he asked as they cruised Exeter Street.

"I wish. But I've got a nice place on the other side of the boulevard in the upper Sixties near Peartree."

A few minutes later they pulled into a parking spot near the station. She turned off the engine and angled to face him. Her smile looked forced.

"Okay. Shoot. Don't forget—bad news can be considered good news in this case."

"Don't count on that."

The smiled faded. "Okay. Hit me."

"I'll tell you what I know for sure. First off, Gerhard is dead. Murdered."

She paled. "What? You're sure?"

He told her what he'd found.

"Oh, my God! Do you think Jerry did it?"

"I don't know, but even if he did I doubt there's a shred of evidence to prove it. Not even a body."

He went on to explain his 911 calls.

"But he *might* be involved?"

She'd wanted bad news about Bethlehem, but Jack could tell by her expression that she hadn't wanted it to be *this* bad.

"Yeah. Because he's violent."

Without mentioning Levy's name, he told her about witnessing his abduction.

"And this guy's not pressing charges?"

"He refused."

"For God's sake, why?"

"Not sure. He gave some lame excuse about working on a sensitive government project, but there's got to be more to it than that. He knows Bethlehem . . . but seems to know him by another name."

"Jerry's leading a double life? Poor Dawnie!" Christy slumped against the seat, head back, staring to the roof. "I had a feeling something was off with him, but never in my wildest dreams . . . I've got to get her away from him."

"Tread carefully here. Again, I can't be sure, but his MO for dealing with threats might be to eliminate them."

She looked at Jack, fear alive in her eyes. "You don't think he'd do anything to me, do you?"

"I don't think so—at least not as long as he wants to stay on Dawn's good side—but I'd play it cool for now anyway. Instead of you trying to break them up, let me see if I can arrange for the legal system to do the job for you."

"What do you mean?"

"During my first twenty-four hours of digging into this clown I found one man murdered and witnessed the abduction of another. I don't know if Bethlehem did the former, but there's no doubt about the latter, which I doubt very much was an aberrant event in an otherwise blemish-free life. Jerry Bethlehem—or whoever he really is—probably has a closet crammed with skeletons. I'll try to sniff out one of them. When I find one, I'll drop a dime. And then, as he's cuffed and led away to the hoosegow, you can be on hand to comfort Dawn."

"I don't think I can handle knowing she's with that kind of man . . . monster."

"Remember, we don't *know* he's a monster. And so far he's done nothing to harm her. So just hang in there. Come on too strong with nothing to back you up and you may only push her closer to him."

Listen to me: Family Counselor Jack.

"But—"

"Give me a chance to take care of this without wrecking your relationship with Dawn."

She stared at him. "I could bear Dawnie never speaking to me again if I knew she'd never speak to Jerry Bethlehem again either."

Jack nodded. A mother's love. Christy didn't look tough but he sensed a lioness beneath her skin . . . one whose cub was threatened.

"A couple of days . . . can you keep mum for a couple of days?"

"It won't be easy, but yes, I can give you a couple of days."

Jack hoped she could hold to that.

4

"Tell me about that cute little stick man on the cover of your book," Jack said.

Hank Thompson smiled. "I wouldn't exactly call the Kicker Man cute."

After returning from Queens, Jack had made a quick stop home for a tape recorder, notepad, and pens to help him look reporterish, then headed for Fifth Avenue.

Vector Publications occupied the fourth floor of an office building in the upper Thirties. He'd stepped out of the elevator and found himself in a bare, nondescript hallway painted a sickly green. To his left he spotted a pair of glass doors etched with VECTOR PUBLICATIONS, LLC. On the far side of those he found a book-lined reception area. The guy at the desk had paged Susan Abrams and she'd led him to the author.

"Hank gives a great interview," she'd gushed. "You're going to love him."

Apparently Ms. Abrams—black hair, black dress, and bare arms as pale and thin as dental floss—already did.

She'd ushered him into the conference room and introduced him as John Tyleski of the *Trenton Times* to a rangy six-footer leaning against an oval mahogany table. With obvious reluctance, Susan left them to get down to business.

Most of Thompson's responses so far had been virtually word for word the same as Jack had read in the first article. Thompson seemed to have memorized them. When pressed on how the world would be changed, he'd offered only vague platitudes.

The guy had charisma, Jack had to grant him that. An easy smile and a comfortable, confident way about him. In person he looked even more like a mid-thirties Jim Morrison than in his photo, except for the eyes—his were blue.

They sat facing each other across the conference table, the recorder midway between them. Jack had opened with a few typical questions he'd read in dozens of author interviews: Where did he get his ideas, how had the book's success changed his life, blah-blah-blah.

Then came the time to home in on the Kicker Man. He'd undoubtedly been asked about it before, but Jack hadn't seen the answer.

"No, *Hank*"—Thompson had quickly established a first-name relationship—"I don't suppose he is. Not with four arms. Why four?"

"I don't know. The figure kept recurring in my dreams. I figured that meant it was important so I began to draw it on all my things. And every time I looked at it I had this strange feeling inside."

Jack swallowed. Like what he'd felt when he'd first seen it?

Thompson added, "And later I found out I wasn't alone. A lot of people have told me they feel something when they look at it." His gaze locked on Jack. "How about you? Get a little chill when you first saw it?"

Jack shook his head. "Afraid not."

He hoped he was convincing.

"Well, it still does something to me. So much so that I even put it on the cover of my book."

Time now for a little probing.

"I've heard it's an ancient symbol."

His eyebrows shot up. "Really? Of what? I'd love to know."

He seemed sincere on that point.

"I don't know, but I read somewhere that it appeared in an ancient book."

Jack noticed a slight lessening of Hank's easygoing manner, a minor tightening of his tone.

"What ancient book?"

Jack frowned and put on a puzzled expression. "I wish I could remember the title. But I recall something about it having a metal cover. You ever see a book like that, Hank?"

He sensed Thompson stiffen in his chair. "No, I don't believe I ever have. How about you?"

Jack kept his tone innocently blasé. "I believe I heard that it once belonged to Luther Brady."

"The Dormentalist guy?"

"Yes. Did you ever meet him?"

"No. And if what he's accused of is true, I don't want to." Thompson's eyes narrowed. "You're not one of them, are you?"

"One of whom?"

"A Dormentalist?"

If you only knew . . .

"No. But if I were . . . ?"

"Check out their Web site. See what lies they're spreading about me. Scientologists too."

"Why would they do that?"

"Because lots of their members are leaving to become Kickers. They're losing dues to my clubs and it's driving them crazy."

"Interesting. But back to the book: I think I saw it in a museum once, but I can't remember which one. I'll let you know if it comes to me."

"You do that."

A definite cooling on the far side of the table.

"Let's move on to another topic. Tell me about your stay at the Creighton Institute."

Thompson fixed him with his blue gaze. "Why do you want to know about that?"

"Well, Hank, as I told you, I read your book to prepare for this, but I also read a lot of your other interviews as well."

He smiled but it had lost some of its previous warmth. "Doing your homework. I like that."

"Well, I wanted my piece to be a little different. You've earned yourself a lot of column inches lately and I'm looking to cover some new ground, if possible. So . . . about Creighton . . ."

"If you want to cover new ground, that's fine with me. But why the Creighton Institute?"

"Well, it struck me as odd that after your conviction—and I must say, I was impressed with your candor—the federal government shipped you from Georgia all the way across the country to New York. I don't know a lot about the federal penal system, but I doubt that happens very often." Jack put on a smile. "I mean, ITSV hardly makes you public enemy number one. You must have wondered at that yourself."

"I sure did."

"Did you ever find out why?"

"Nope."

"Not even from the Creighton people?"

"Not a hint. Can we move on?"

Jack was far from finished. "Did you know that the Creighton Institute is listed as an incarceration facility for the criminally insane?"

A semi-strangled laugh, then, "I'm a little crazy, but I'm not that crazy. Seriously, though, they had two separate populations: the violent types in the lockdown wing, and the nonviolent sort in the medium-security area."

Violent types . . . lockdown wing . . . could Jerry Bethlehem have been one of Levy's patients at Creighton? Could they be connected?

"Did you make any friends there?"

"I suppose."

"Have you kept in contact with any of them?"

"One of the conditions of parole is that you avoid contact with any other criminals—and anyone I knew inside was a criminal."

"How about the staff?"

"Look," he said, his annoyance clear, "when I got out they shipped me back to Georgia."

"But now you've returned to New York. Do you like it here?"

He relaxed a smidge. "Yeah. A lot. I'm thinking of setting up the Kicker HQ here. The city's already got the biggest number of Kicker clubs in the country. Seems like a logical choice."

"Indeed it does. Does that mean we can expect to see a lot more Kicker graffiti around town?"

He frowned. "That's not approved nor encouraged, but it is an indicator of the level of enthusiasm for the evolution."

"You keep calling it 'evolution.' Why is that?"

"It's like when an ugly caterpillar makes a cocoon and then comes out as a big, kick-ass butterfly—it's kicked off its lower form and evolved into a higher one."

Jack wondered whether this would be a good time to tell him that he wasn't describing evolution at all.

Nah.

"Speaking of the Creighton staff—"

"We weren't speaking of the staff."

"—did they do any testing on you?"

"Sure. Blood tests, x-rays, psychological tests up the wazoo. Where's this going?"

"Did they perform any experiments on you?"

"What do you think I was living—a grade-Z horror movie?" He glanced at his watch. "Sorry. Gotta run. More interviews scheduled."

Yeah, right.

Jack rose and retrieved his recorder. "Same here. Gotta get back to Trenton and type this up. By the way, got a title for your next project?"

Like, maybe, *Punt*?

"Haven't decided what to write next, but I'm sure it will come to me."

They shook hands, assured each other it had been a pleasure, then Jack headed back to the street.

Not a wasted trip. He'd learned a few things about Hank Thompson.

First off, he was a little scary. A hint of Manson lurking beneath the Morrison.

Second, he'd seen the *Compendium*. Jack didn't know if he'd come up with the Kicker Man figure on his own, or from an earlier peek at the *Compendium*, but the look in his eyes when Jack mentioned the metallic cover . . . he'd seen it . . . maybe even had it now.

Third, he was defensive about the Creighton Institute. Maybe it was the "for the Criminally Insane" part that bothered him, but Jack had a feeling it might be something else. Something he didn't want made public.

Jack saw another trip to Rathburg in his future. The very near future.

5

"Who was that son of a bitch?" Hank said as he barged into Susan Abrams's office without knocking.

She jumped in her seat and looked up at him.

"Who? That reporter?"

"Who else would I mean? Did you check him out?"

"Well, no—"

He felt like strangling her.

"Damn it, isn't that part of your job?"

She blinked. "We—we don't vet every reporter who requests an interview. What happened?"

"Never mind that. Just call his paper—the Trenton whatever it is—and check on him."

"But—"

"*Now!*"

He paced back and forth outside her door—no room for it in her tiny office—as she fumbled with this and that trying to get in touch with the paper.

John Tyleski . . . he'd bet his next six months of royalties that guy was no reporter. Because a simple everyday reporter from a hick paper in Trenton wouldn't know about the *Compendium of Srem*. Hank had known about it for only a couple of days himself.

What a find!

And all because one Marty Pinter, a janitor at the museum, just happened to notice the Kicker Man in an ancient book on the desk of a professor who just happened to have had a stroke; and Marty, who just happened to be a

Kicker himself, decided that the old book belonged in the hands of the Alpha Kicker.

Almost as if Fate had been pulling a few strings . . .

Hank had known at first sight it was a hell of a find—especially with the Kicker Man big as life inside. The book called the figure something else, something unpronounceable beginning with a Q, but no matter. Hank was itching to go through that *Compendium* with a fine-tooth comb and learn all he could from it, but he had no time, damn it. He'd had it almost three days now and he'd only been able to skim the surface. If he wasn't doing interviews and radio and TV, he was speaking at Kicker rallies. He didn't have a life of his own anymore.

Well, he'd make time. He had a feeling it was going to be very important to his future, and the future of the Kickers.

Maybe it would give him a hint of where they were going. He wanted to know because he had no idea where this movement he'd started was headed.

No way he'd ever admit that, but it was true. Sometimes he'd wake up at night bathed in sweat, scared by the numbers of people responding to his words, to his book—joining Kicker clubs all over the country, paying dues, donating money.

Every few days, for maybe a few seconds, he missed his old life before he got inspired to write the book. His job in the slaughterhouse had alternated between being a "knocker"—shooting the steel bolt into the cow's head to knock it out—and a sticker—slitting the cow's throat after it was hung upside down by a leg from the overhead rail.

Hot bloody work, dressed head to foot in a yellow rubber suit that was red after the first ten minutes of the shift, but very satisfying in some ways. At least he'd known what he was doing. Now . . .

He had to trust in whatever had brought him this far. He felt like a human antenna, receiving signals from someplace far off in the universe. He sensed it most when he was speaking. The words, the rising and falling in volume, the gestures, they just came to him. And as for writing the book . . . he'd never been much of a reader, but the words had just flowed from him through his pen and onto the backs of flyers or envelopes until he'd graduated to yellow pads.

He hoped to hell whatever had inspired and guided him this far would take him to the next step.

The question that nagged him the most was, *Why me?*

He made a point of coming on strong and confident in public, but in private he hadn't the vaguest clue what he'd tapped into. He knew it was powerful, and he knew his words were appealing to others like him, sending out some sort of vibe that was picked up by their own antennas. They all seemed tuned to the same wavelength, but was his the most sensitive? Was he the alpha antenna who broadcast to the rest?

He wished he knew.

But what he did know was that this was the greatest high he'd ever experienced. Pot, coke, crank—he'd tried them all, but nothing compared to bringing a crowd to its feet and hearing them clap and yell and whistle and stomp their feet. He'd thrown out the drugs, vowing never to touch them again—not because he was no longer interested, but because a bust could land him in the slammer, cutting him off from his audience, his *people*.

The money was rolling in and the women were rolling over—as long as they liked it rough, that was fine. He felt like a goddamn rock star. The sky was the limit.

This reporter, though . . . this John Tyleski . . . he'd become a little cloud in that sky.

He turned back to the publicity bitch just as she was hanging up.

"Well?"

Susan Abrams chewed her upper lip and looked miserable. "That was the managing editor of the *Trenton Times*."

"And?"

She cringed. "There is no John Tyleski on their staff."

"*What?*"

He'd sensed it, suspected it, but to hear it from this stupid bitch's mouth . . .

"You've got to understand," she said, "this was an interview conducted in our own offices. We wouldn't normally—"

"What if he'd been some nut with a knife or a gun?"

"I'm terribly sorry about—" she began as she started to rise.

Hank shoved her back into her seat. "Damn right you are, you stupid, useless bitch! You're finished. I'm getting someone else for PR—someone who knows what she's doing."

She began to cry and that only made him want to smash a fist into her blubbering face. But he held back—last thing he needed was an A-and-B charge. He stomped out, leaving her sobbing at her desk.

Count yourself lucky, honey.

He went back to the conference room and slammed the door behind him. He stood there until his anger faded a little.

What had happened in here?

Pretending to be a journalist was a good way to get close to a celebrity or someone with notoriety, into places other folks weren't allowed. Hank should know—he'd been playing that card for years.

Hank knew why *he'd* done it, but what had Tyleski—bet the ranch that wasn't his name—wanted? Was he looking for that old book—to get it back for the professor? No biggy then. He'd never find it. And with Pinter hidden away in the Lodge downtown, he'd never find the thief either.

But the questions about Creighton bothered him. In all his interviews, lots of folks had asked about the events leading up to getting sent to Creighton, but this was the first time anyone had asked about what had gone on inside. This guy had asked about tests and, worse, about keeping in touch with anyone he'd met inside. What had made him ask *that*? If he knew something he shouldn't, could be big trouble brewing.

Did a piss-poor job of handling that, Hank, he told himself. Let him get under your skin. Most likely gave something away.

The worst part was realizing someone knew too much about him. Someone was gunning for him, and Hank had no idea why.

Unless . . . the Enemy?

He clenched his jaw. Keep your distance, asshole. I see you again, I'm taking you out.

6

Christy sat before her computer in her home office, staring at the screen but only dimly aware of the numbers scrolling past.

She wandered out into the living room and looked around at the antique furnishings, the paintings she'd picked up at various galleries in SoHo. A nice home—part of the life she'd built for Dawn and herself. All from nothing.

She remembered arriving in New York City all those years ago with a few hundred dollars in her pocket, a suitcase in one hand, and a baby in the other.

Now look at me.

She could buy pretty much anything she wanted without a second thought. But she usually did give it a second thought. And sometimes a third. And very often she said no. Better to save it for the inevitable rainy day. She'd spent too many years counting pennies to feel comfortable with careless spending. Old habits died hard.

She'd done it for Dawnie. Not all of it, of course. Some had been for her own sake, but the driving force had been building a secure life for her daughter to give her the kind of home she'd never had. And now everything seemed ready to go up in smoke.

Because she'd really blown it with Dawn today.

Why on Earth hadn't she listened to Jack and kept her mouth shut? She'd planned on doing just that, and when she'd come home and found Dawn doodling on the computer, everything had been fine. If nothing else, this relationship with Jerry had made her start taking better care of herself. She'd slimmed down some, started wearing a little makeup. She seemed to glow with happiness. Soon—not today, but *soon*—Christy would be forced to douse that glow. It would hurt, but it would be for the best.

They'd made small talk, then Dawnie announced that she had to get changed to spend the rest of the afternoon at that man's place. That was when Christy lost it.

She'd told her about hiring Mike Gerhard to investigate Jerry and how Gerhard was found murdered, and how the detective she'd hired to find Gerhard had witnessed Jerry kidnap someone.

Christy had seen the look of horror growing on Dawn's face and that had spurred her on. But then she realized that the horror wasn't at what her beau had done, but at her mother hiring a detective and then making up these awful stories.

She'd run out of the house before Christy could stop her. She prayed she hadn't caused an irreparable breach. If only—

She jumped as she heard the front door open. She always kept it locked.

"It's me."

Dawnie's voice. Thank God!

She rushed into the living room only to stop cold at the sight of that man.

"This is so not my idea," Dawnie said, glaring at her. "If it was up to me, I'd never come back here again. But Jerry wanted to talk to you."

Christy looked at him and shivered at the cold menace in his eyes. But his voice was calm and measured.

"I'm not sure what to say about all this," he drawled as he rubbed a hand through that short, neat beard. "But, unbelievable as your accusations sound, I can't let them go without sayin somethin."

That drawl . . . how could a cracker like this develop video games? Then again, you didn't need a degree from Harvard or even Queensborough Community College for that. You just needed cunning, and Christy sensed he had plenty of that.

But she was damned if she was going to back down. "Everything I said is true!"

"I'm sure you believe that, but you been lied to."

"I have not! I—"

"You say you hired a detective and that he was murdered. What was his name?"

His name? He had to know his name—if he'd killed him.

"Michael Gerhard—as you well know."

"And you say he's dead. Murdered."

"I have a witness."

"Who?"

Christy didn't think it wise to identify Jack.

"I'm not telling you that."

"And why not?"

"Because I don't want him to end up dead too."

She thought she caught a hint of a smirk, but couldn't be sure through the beard.

Dawn said, "That's it, Jerry! I told you this was totally a waste of time! We're going!"

"No-no. Just a second, darlin. This is your mother and she's got some bad ideas about me. I don't know why and I don't know who, but someone's been feedin her lies and I need to set her straight. I can't have her or anyone else believin this about me."

So calm and reasoned . . . an excellent portrayal of an innocent man confronting his accuser. If it weren't for those eyes, Christy could almost believe . . .

"Just get out of Dawn's life and I won't say a word about this."

He smiled sweetly and put his arm around Dawn. "But I want to be a part of her life. She's become very important to me. So let's get back to this man I supposedly murdered—Gephardt, was it?"

"Gerhard. Michael Gerhard."

"I haven't read or heard anything about this. Where did it happen and what was the time of his death?"

Dawnie tugged on his arm. "Come on, Jerry. This is total bullshit."

"Just give me a minute, darlin. If he was killed while you and I were together, that'll prove I had nothin to do with it." He turned back to Christy. "If you'll show me the news article, we can probably settle this here and now."

Oh, hell.

"There is no article."

"Well then, a police report."

"I don't have that."

His expression turned puzzled. "Then . . . what *do* you have?"

"The man who found the body."

"The man you can't name. Well, if he reported the crime—"

"He did, but by the time the police got there the body was gone."

"What?" He laughed. "Somebody tells you a man was murdered but there's no body? How do we know this Gerhard ain't sittin in some bar in Florida drinkin up the money you paid him? I think you've been sold a bill of goods, Mrs. P."

For an instant, Christy floundered, at a loss for a response. Without a body, she looked like a fool. Then she remembered—

"Where were you last night?"

"Was that when he was murdered?"

"No, that's when you kidnapped a man."

"Really? Let's see . . . I was eating dinner at Peter Luger's with a game producer from Konami." He looked at Dawn. "I told you about that, right?"

She nodded. "He was pitching our game concept."

He turned back to Christy. "Now, I wish I could show you the receipt from the restaurant, but I didn't pay for dinner. I *can* have the producer back up my presence."

"You do that."

"I will. Meanwhile, where am I keepin this person I supposedly kidnapped?"

"He escaped."

"Well then, he must have pressed charges against me. How come I ain't been arrested?"

"He won't press charges and you know it."

"I know no such thing. When this man reported the crime, did he at least say when it happened?" He grinned. "I mean, what's the point of havin an alibi if we don't know the time of the crime."

Christy knew then that she was beaten. He'd played her like the proverbial fiddle, coming on all calm and rational while making her look like a scatterbrained paranoid.

Just what Jack had said would happen.

He raised his eyebrows. "Don't tell me there's no police report of this crime either."

"You know damn well there isn't."

He spread his hands in a gesture of supplication. "Mrs. P, do you hear yourself? You've been accusin me of two terrible crimes that never happened."

Christy wanted to shout that they damn well did happen but knew that would make her look more unbalanced than she already did.

"Look," he said. "Because of my feelings for Dawn, and because you're her mother, I'm gonna forget this ever happened—"

"Don't you—"

"—because I know you're upset about the difference in our ages."

"She's still in *high school*, damn it!"

"I'm aware of that. And I know I'd be just as upset if positions was reversed. But she's a woman now, and we have feelins for each other that won't be denied. I hope that you'll eventually find it in your heart to accept our relationship and give up usin these outrageous accusations to try to break us up. It ain't gonna work." He hugged Dawn against him. "We're in this together for the long run." He turned her toward the door. "Come on, Dawn. Let's go."

As she stepped through the door Dawnie looked over her shoulder and said, "Really, Mom, that was totally pathetic."

Christy stood frozen, paralyzed. She wanted to run to the door and scream for Dawn to come back. But that wouldn't work.

She's right: I am pathetic.

The very thing Jack had warned her about had happened. That man had driven a wedge between her and Dawnie—and she'd provided the hammer. He'd been so convincing, made such a good case for his innocence, that she'd almost started to doubt his guilt herself.

His guilt . . .

A wave of dizziness swept over her and she dropped into a chair.

What proof *did* she have of his guilt? Nothing. Just Jack's opinions. What if he was conning her? Without police reports, who could say a crime had been committed. What if—?

Wait. What was she thinking? She had to trust someone, and the same instinct that warned her against that man told her she could trust Jack.

She hoped she was right about him, and prayed he was having some luck finding hard evidence against this son of a bitch.

7

"Sounds to me like you shouldn't be expecting to ask him any follow-up questions," Abe said after Jack finished telling him about his Hank Thompson interview.

"Not likely."

Holding a chip laden with green glop before his mouth, Abe said, "Looks awful, tastes wonderful," then made it disappear.

Jack had brought tortilla chips and a container of Gia's homemade guacamole.

"I can't believe you've never had guacamole before."

"I was raised kosher. What do I know from Mexican food?"

"You haven't been kosher since the Roosevelt administration—Teddy's."

Abe sighed. "I should get out more already."

He dipped another chip, but on the way to his mouth some of the guacamole slipped off and landed on the cover of *Rakshasa*.

"Oy. Sorry."

Yesterday he'd dropped off the pair of Jake Fixx novels and asked Abe to give them a look while Jack concentrated on *Kick*.

"Did you get to read it?"

A stubby finger transferred the green dollop from the cover to his mouth.

"Skimmed is more like it. A novel maven I'm not. I prefer my fiction to pretend to be true."

"Like histories and biographies and newspapers?"

"Exactly. I need that pretense already. Take that away and my mind wanders."

"Did it stay on track enough to finish the book?"

"Barely."

"And?"

"As I said, I'm no maven of the novel, but for a Pulitzer Prize I don't think this P. Frank Winslow should be holding his breath."

"I don't care if he's any good. How close is he to what really happened?"

"Very. Too."

"Should I be creeped out?"

"Like a thousand hairy spiders crawling all over you."

"Swell." Jack shook off the sensation. "How the hell—?"

"The little details, they're different, but the big ones he's got: the ship, the big blue *breeyes* from India—maybe you should have been interviewing him instead of Thompson."

"Maybe I will." No, he definitely would. Had to. He could not let this go. But later. Now . . . "What do you remember about the Atlanta abortionist murders?"

Abe slapped a hand to his head. "Oy, the head spins from the change of subject. Whiplash I've got. Call a lawyer."

"Sorry. That was what I was about to ask you when you glopped on the book."

"Atlanta abortionist murders?" Abe drummed his fingers on the counter. "About twenty years ago, no?"

"Almost. It was all anyone was talking about for months."

"And this sudden interest comes whence?"

He told Abe about finding the Google search on Gerhard's computer.

"It's been bugging me, wondering if Gerhard had found a connection between Bethlehem and the killings."

"You did your own search, I assume?"

Jack nodded. "Yeah. 'Jerry Bethlehem' plus 'Atlanta abortionist murders' got no hits. Couldn't connect him to the Creighton Institute either."

"Well, if you say he's in his mid-thirties, he would have been a teenager back then."

A little gong sounded somewhere in Jack's brain. Teenager . . .

"It's coming back," Abe was saying. "Two abortionists in two centers in the same week. Two dead doctors, correct?"

"Correct." Jack saw where Abe was going. "You think one of the doctors might have been connected with Creighton?"

Abe jerked a thumb at his computer. "One way to find out." He wiped his hands on his shirt, leaving green streaks. "You remember their names?"

"No way. Too long ago. You'll have to pull up an article."

"Such a help you are."

Abe attacked the keyboard and after some vigorous tapping and clicking, he pulled out a pen and scribbled on a pad.

"Horace Golden and Elmer Dalton. Let's see if either one of those ever worked at Creighton." After more tapping Abe shook his head. "No connection— at least online."

"What about the killer? What was his name?"

Abe said, "I just saw it: Jeremy Bolton."

As Abe began to type, a connection hit Jack with the force of a blow.

"Oh, shit!"

"What?"

"Jeremy Bolton . . . Jerry Bethlehem: J-B . . . J-B. It can't possibly be, can it?"

"Let's find out."

Jack already knew the answer. Because he recalled now that the biggest shocker of the story, what had kept it in the news for months, was the discovery that the killer turned out to be a teenager, an eighteen-year-old. Jack remembered because he had been about the same age. He'd wondered what it took to kill someone in cold blood.

He no longer wondered.

Abe slapped a hand on his counter. "It says here Jeremy Bolton is serving two consecutive life sentences at the Creighton Institute." He frowned. "How did he go from an Atlanta courthouse to a New York funny farm?"

"Probably some federal civil rights charges got filed somewhere along the way. What's he look like? Any photos?"

Abe clicked around, then turned the monitor toward Jack.

"This is all I can find."

Jack saw an old black-and-white newspaper photo of a pimply, baby-faced kid facing the camera but staring past it. He looked nothing like Jerry Bethlehem.

But that didn't mean a thing. Jack figured if he had a beard himself now, no one would be able to look at him and recognize the kid in his high school yearbook. Be pretty hard even without a beard.

"It can't be him," Abe said. "Two consecutive life sentences already. A thirty-inch waist I'll have before he's free."

"Maybe he escaped."

"We would have heard. News like that would be all over."

Jack grabbed the mouse and clicked through a couple of the hits from Abe's search. As he read the articles it all started coming back.

Eighteen-year-old Jeremy Bolton had had nothing in his background to in-dicate the slightest interest in fundamentalist religion—or religion of any sort, for that matter—and no one found a connection to a single anti-abortion group. But the most bizarre aspect had been his refusal to talk—to anyone about any-thing. He wouldn't even speak to the attorney the court assigned him. Not a word in his own defense.

His attorney tried to go the insanity route but that didn't fly because up until the murders he'd had a reputation as a loquacious charmer.

"Check it out: the Creighton connection, the initials, the fact that Jeremy Bolton would be in his mid-thirties now . . . just like Jerry Bethlehem. It's too good a fit."

Abe was shaking his head. "It's no kind of fit. How can they be the same? We'd have heard of an escape. And he can't be on parole—such an uproar that would have caused from the pro-abortion crowd already. So how can he be dat-ing this Forest Hills *maidel*?"

"I don't know. But I'll bet it has something to do with Levy not want-ing to report his abduction." He pounded the table. "If I had a connection in the PD I could run Bethlehem's fingerprints and see if they match Bolton's."

"And you'd get these fingerprints where?"

"Easy. Christy says he eats at a certain diner a lot. I just snag a glass or coffee cup from his table after he leaves." He shook his head. "I bet Jake Fixx would have no problem IDing him."

"Being an ex–Navy SEAL who used to work for the CIA, none at all. But a shlub like you . . ."

". . . has got to do it the hard way. Which means a more pointed conversation with a certain Doctor Levy."

8

Dawn sprawled naked on the bed beneath Jerry, panting in the afterglow of her fifth and final orgasm, the biggest and maddest of this bout of lovemaking.

God, sex was great. How had she gone without it for so long? Not that she'd been like a total virgin when she'd met Jerry, but pretty damn close. One drunken, clumsy, fumbling, all-too-brief encounter in the back of a minivan last year hardly made her experienced. Pretty much she'd done it just to do it. Hadn't even liked the guy all that much. Terry had been okay—at least less of a jerk than most of the guys in her school—but so not what she was looking for in a steady. She realized now she'd been totally clueless about what she was looking for until she'd met Jerry.

She watched him as he levered himself up and rolled away. She totally loved every part of his long lean body, especially his beard when it rubbed against her cheek, and her nipples, and the insides of her thighs. But she loved most of all the part that was slipping out of her now.

She almost laughed. God, I've become such a slut. I should get an I ❤ COCK bumper sticker.

As he wiped himself off she felt a flash of concern. They never used protection. She knew she was clean, but what about Jerry? He'd had a lot more years to pick up an STD or two. He swore he was clean, and she believed he believed that, but he might be mistaken. So far, so good. And as always, the flash of concern was just that: a flash.

And as for pregnancy, no worry. He'd told her he'd been "fixed"—a vasectomy ten years ago when he decided he didn't like this world enough to bring a child into it.

She totally agreed with that. Have a child and watch him or her grow up into dorks like she'd gone to school with? No way.

And somehow that made her think of Mom, and like how she'd always been working to make her a better person. Yeah, Mom. Charging her every time she used "like" or "totally." How corny was that?

Like totally—totally-totally-totally.

There. That would have cost $2.50.

Mom loved her—Dawn had no doubt about that. But maybe she loved her too much. So totally too much that she'd started making up stories about Jerry.

Looking at Jerry she wondered for the millionth time what he saw in her. She knew she wasn't pretty—plain and thick-waisted, to tell the total truth. Didn't have like a great ass or the bodacious tatas that tended to bring the opposite sex sniffing around. She'd wound up preferring books to boys because boys had so totally not gotten her, and she'd never really gotten them.

She now knew why: Because they were boys. Jerry was a man.

Vive la différence!

She looked at him and wanted him again. She felt bad taking him away from their work designing the ultimate unisex video game, but every time they sat down and put their heads together to do some design, they started putting their lips together and pretty soon they'd have everything together.

LOL!

She loved this townhouse. A bangin' cool place. All this mad chrome furniture and a home theater with a huge screen and a surround sound system to die for. She totally wanted to move in here but didn't want to push things— Jerry might not be ready for that yet. But he would be. And soon. She could tell.

The only thing she didn't like was the painting Jerry had stuck here on the bedroom wall. She didn't know why the turbulent abstract swirls of black and deep purple bothered her, but she always got the totally crazy feeling it was watching her.

Looking at it now made her pull the sheet over her. Weird. And even weirder, she'd touched it once and it felt wet. Ugh.

But Jerry loved it. Said it "spoke" to him. He'd found it in a secondhand store in Monroe. He was always on the lookout for others by the same artist— Melanie Ehler or something like that—but never found any. Dawn was glad for that.

As she was deciding whether or not to reach up and grab his joy stick, the phone rang. Jerry stepped over to it, stared down at the caller ID readout, and frowned.

"Hey, it's your momma."

Dawn felt all the heat rush out of her.

"Don't answer."

He looked at her. "Maybe I should. Maybe it's important."

"Nothing she has to say can be important. Let her leave a message."

"I'm gonna see what's on her mind." He picked up the receiver and said, "Hello, Mrs. P. What can I do for you?"

Always such a gentleman. Even to her. Dawn couldn't believe she'd cooked up those things about Jerry. If she were him she'd so tell her to go to hell.

What had come over Mom anyway? Maybe it was more than love. Maybe it was crazy-mad possessiveness. Yeah, Jerry was twice her age, sure, but so what? It was only eighteen years. So okay, get a little upset, but don't go around accusing him of murder!

And if you are going to make some total bullshit charge, at least make sure whoever he was supposed to have killed is dead.

That wasn't like Mom either. She was usually pretty together and well thought out. If she so wanted to bust them up, you'd think she could come up with something better than that.

Maybe she'd been lied to. Maybe she'd believed because she wanted to believe anything bad about Jerry.

Dawn was so proud of how Jerry had handled it. Yeah, he'd looked like he was going to go totally nuclear at first, but then he'd calmed himself down and wanted to go over and confront his accuser.

She watched Jerry's frown deepen as he listened. What was she saying? Then he glanced at her.

"Without Dawn? I don't know about that."

Without Dawn? She sat up. What was she saying to him?

Finally he said, "Okay. Give me about an hour." Then he hung up.

"What's going on? What did she say?"

He stared at her. "She wants to talk to me. Alone."

"Why alone?"

"She didn't say. Just said we have to talk—without you around. Maybe she thinks if we have a heart to heart she can somehow convince me I'm wrong for you."

Dawn's stomach spasmed at the possibility. She jumped to her feet.

"And you're going?"

"Look at it this way, darlin: It's a chance for me to turn the tables on her and convince her how important you are to me. If I can convince her that I'll never harm you—in fact, I'll protect you with my life—maybe she'll stop seein me as a threat and get off our backs."

Dawn threw her arms around him.

"Don't go. She's gone totally crazy. She's got a gun, you know. For all we know she's going to shoot you."

He stiffened. "Whoa! Didn't know about that. But I wouldn't worry about it. She seemed very calm."

Dawn pleaded with him as he showered and got dressed, but couldn't change his mind.

As he smiled and waved on his way out the door, Dawn prayed he'd return in one piece.

9

Jack pressed the doorbell and waited. A few seconds later he saw Dr. Levy peek out through one of the sidelights, then duck back. The door didn't open right away, so Jack reached for the knocker. The door retracted a few inches just as his fingers touched the brass.

"What are you doing here?" Levy said in a hushed tone.

"We need to talk."

"I have nothing to say."

After the way Levy had clammed up last night, Jack had expected resistance tonight. He'd decided during the trip up that the best approach might be to fire his big gun immediately and see if it hit something.

"Not even about Jeremy Bolton?"

Levy's expression didn't change. He didn't even blink. But the color in his cheeks faded half a shade toward white.

"Doctor-patient privilege prevents me from discussing anyone incarcerated at Creighton."

Jack locked eyes with him. "What if we're talking about a Jeremy Bolton who's *not* incarcerated?"

Now he blinked. And shook his head.

"You don't want to go there. You may think you do, but really, you don't."

"You're probably right. Answer a few questions for me and I might decide to disappear."

"Sorry, no."

He went to close the door but Jack jammed the steel toe of his work boot into the opening first.

"You *owe* me."

"Yes, I do. But you're asking too much."

"Aaron?" said a woman's voice from somewhere in the house. "Is someone at the door?"

"Your wife might think you're being ungrateful. Why don't we ask her?"

"You leave her out of this!" he hissed.

Jack saw an opening and pressed his advantage.

"You mean you didn't tell her about your ride in the trunk of the family car last night? About the stranger who took it upon himself to save your ass? She'll probably have a lot of questions for you after she hears. I'm sure she'll be especially interested in why you didn't tell *her*. Or anyone else, for that matter—not even the police."

Levy's shoulders slumped. He pulled the door open.

"All right. But just for a few minutes." He turned and called up the stairs. "Business, Marie. Papers to be signed. I'll take him to the office."

He ushered Jack into a room off the front foyer—medical texts lining the shelves, a computer and a brass banker's lamp on a cluttered mahogany desk. He shut the door and pulled out a set of keys as he went to his desk.

As Levy unlocked a lower drawer and reached in, Jack pulled his Glock. Levy rose from his stoop with something in his hand—and found the muzzle of Jack's pistol an inch from the bridge of his nose.

He froze.

"What's this?"

"This is a Glock twenty-one. You saw it the other night." Jack gestured to the gizmo in Levy's hand. "What's *that*?"

"An RF detector."

"You think I'm wired?"

"Never can tell. Just let me turn it on and check. Otherwise, I don't say another word."

"Fine with me."

As he watched Levy fire up his little meter he wondered what kind of guy kept an RF detector in his desk drawer. With a start he realized: a guy like me. Jack owned a different model of the same thing. But he didn't keep it within such easy reach. He wasn't that crazy.

The readout indicated background levels, and no increase when Levy moved it closer to Jack.

Okay," he said as he slipped it back into the drawer. "One question. I'll answer *one* question."

Jack intended to ask more, but figured he'd go with the Big One again.

"Why is Jeremy Bolton out of jail?"

Levy seemed prepared for it. His face was as expressionless as a DMV photo, and half as happy.

"Who told you he's out?"

"Your face did a few moments ago."

"Sorry. I'm not responding to that."

"You said you'd answer one question."

"And I will. But I didn't say *any* question."

"If you want to play word games—"

"I hope you're not going to threaten me, because you'll be asking for a world of trouble."

Jack sat down—figured it was time for Levy to start getting used to the fact he was going to be here awhile.

"Really?"

"I did a little background on you, John Robertson, private detective." He flashed a mirthless smile. "You look awfully good for a dead man."

Uh-oh.

Jack smiled. "That happens all the time. There's another detective with the same name . . ."

Levy was shaking his head. "Someone is paying the dead man's annual license fee. And that would be you. So let's have you answer a question for me: Who are you?"

"The man who saved your life."

Levy looked annoyed as he dropped into the chair behind his desk.

"Do you have to keep bringing that up?"

"I will till it works. Now spill: Why's Bolton running free and nobody knows about it? Check that: *I* know about it. And I know he's posing as Jerry Bethlehem."

Levy raised his hands. "For the love of God, keep that to yourself. I don't know who you are, but I do feel a debt to you. So unless you want your life turned into a living hell, forget what you know."

The genuine distress in Levy's voice disturbed Jack.

"Who's going to bring the hell? Bolton?"

He shook his head. "No. Look, this is big—bigger than you can imagine. You're dealing with a powerful government agency with roots in the Pentagon, congress, and ultimately the White House. This is important to them. You interfere with their plans and they'll comb through your life for every little—"

"Got to find me first."

"Oh, they'll find you. You may think you're hiding behind this John Robertson persona, but they'll rip through that like tissue paper. Everybody leaves tracks. They'll find yours and follow them and make you wish you'd never been born."

Jack's stomach turned sour. Yeah, he'd gone to elaborate lengths to insulate himself from scrutiny, but a motivated organization with enough manpower, access to all sorts of databases, the power to twist arms . . . he wouldn't stand a chance. They'd haul him up from underground and hold him to the light. And have a field day with what they'd find.

But he couldn't let Levy see that he'd touched a nerve.

"So that's why you didn't want to call the cops."

He nodded. "I'm not immune from their wrath. Nobody is."

"What if I've got nothing to hide?"

Right.

"Everybody's got something to hide. But just in case you're that rara avis with a spotless life, it won't remain spotless for long. If they can't find something, they'll manufacture it."

Jack knew in his case they—whoever *they* were—wouldn't have to manufacture a thing.

Still, he had to know.

"Heard and understood. Now, back to square one: What's he doing running around free?"

Levy stared at him. "Are you insane?"

"It's sort of the general consensus."

Another long stare, followed by a sigh. "All right then. It's all legal—legal in that the agency in charge of Creighton has designed a closely monitored, special-circumstances release."

"Whoever's in charge of the monitoring sure as hell dropped the ball. Where was his monitor when he drowned Gerhard? Or shoved you into your trunk?"

"Not that kind of monitoring. Nobody's got binoculars on him all the time. And besides, who says he killed Gerhard? When did it happen?"

Jack could only guess. "Tuesday night I'd guess."

Levy gave a quick, nervous smile. "There you go. All day Tuesday—day and night—he was at Creighton for testing. It's his blood we monitor."

"I don't get it."

Levy hesitated, then said, "Considering what you already know, I can't see what difference it makes to tell you. This release program is a clinical trial of sorts. We're testing a special medical therapy developed for a certain subset of violent criminals."

"What kind of therapy?"

"That is off-limits. All I can say is that it is designed to suppress violent tendencies. The subject shows up for a weekly injection and blood tests to monitor the level of the drug in his system."

"Got a medical bulletin for you: It's not working."

"It's a clinical trial. We don't know the proper dose yet. We expect a setback or two in the early—"

"*Setback*? Torture and murder—"

"I can assure you he did not lay a finger on Gerhard."

Jack would need more than just Levy's word.

"What about kidnapping? Just a 'setback'?"

"You keep blaming him without proof. And he has an alibi. The attempted abduction was . . . unfortunate. But it doesn't mean the trial is a failure, it simply means we need to adjust the dosage. Which we have. I'm sure nothing like that will ever happen again."

Jack stared at him. "You're not sure at all."

Levy looked away—confirmation enough.

"We'll make you the same offer we made Gerhard."

"Who's 'we'?"

"Why . . ." He seemed flustered for a second. "Why, Creighton, of course. We'll pay you whatever you might have received from Mrs. Pickering and—"

"Gerhard took your offer?"

A nod.

Crook.

"And true to his word, he said nothing to the Pickering woman. So you can see there was no need for Jeremy to even talk to him, let alone kill him."

"Speaking of Mrs. Pickering, what's the story with Bolton and her daughter?"

"Well, he's a hetero male, she's a female the same age he was when he was locked up. What more story do you need?"

Keeping in character, Jack said, "Yeah, I suppose the first thing I'd do once I got out of stir was hook up with some poontang."

"Well, it wasn't the first thing. The very first thing he did was get himself tattooed." He held up his hand and pointed to the web between his thumb and forefinger. "Right here, of all places."

Jack remembered the Kicker in the bookstore yesterday.

"Tattoo of what?"

"Some ridiculous little stick figure."

Jack felt a chill ripple across his back.

"With a diamond-shaped head?"

"Why, yes. How did you know? You've never been that close to Bolton." His eyes narrowed. "Or have you?"

Jack didn't answer immediately. His brain was too wrapped up in all the unfolding connections. Connections . . . not coincidences.

Jeremy Bolton was a Kicker.

"Excuse me?" Levy said, waving a hand. "Are you there? How did you know?"

Jack shook himself. "That figure is all over Manhattan. Followers of a book called *Kick*."

Levy snapped his fingers. "Right. Bolton once had a book with that figure on its cover. What's it mean?" He grimaced. "Working at Creighton tends to insulate you from the zeitgeist."

Jack wished he could escape the zeitgeist. He didn't know what the figure meant, but knew he had to find the connection.

"The author, Hank Thompson—"

"Did you say Hank Thompson? That's the author who's been interviewing Bolton."

Jack felt as if he'd been kicked.

"What? Why? How?"

"Research. His next book is going to be on the Atlanta abortionist killings."

Funny . . . just a few hours ago he'd said he hadn't decided yet. But he might simply be keeping the topic under wraps.

That didn't bother Jack anywhere near as much as the way two supposedly separate parts of his present-day life were intersecting.

"I'm kind of surprised you let anyone get near Bolton."

"The last thing we wanted, believe me. We turned him away but Thompson threatened to take us to court. We feared he might win—freedom of the press and all that crap—so we granted him access. But we've limited it as much as possible."

"How limited?"

"Thompson had one hour access a week."

"He did time at Creighton back in the nineties, you know."

"Of course I know. Our security had him fully vetted before we let him in. Unfortunately he turned out to be just what he said he was: a former inmate and a bestselling author." He smiled. "I never knew he was the author of *Kick*. I'll have to read it sometime."

"Their stays at Creighton overlapped. Any chance they could have met there?"

He shook his head. "Highly unlikely. Prisoners in the maximum security wing have no contact with the other residents. He told us it was the Creighton connection that inspired him to write Bolton's story."

All very probable. Maybe even explained Thompson's reluctance to talk about Creighton, but a part of Jack wasn't buying it.

Damn, he wished he'd known this before interviewing Thompson. Could have asked some interesting follow-up questions when he said he hadn't decided what to write next.

"Would you believe," Levy was saying, "Thompson says he thinks Bolton is innocent, that he was framed by the real killers?"

"Who were . . . ?"

"Who else? Radical Christian extremists."

"Any chance that's true?"

"Are you kidding? Not in a million years. I've seen the case files—we check out every inmate exhaustively—and the evidence against Jeremy Bolton was overwhelming. After what he did to me, can you doubt his impulsive violence?"

No, Jack couldn't.

"What did you tell Thompson when you let Bolton out?"

"Nothing. Didn't need to. He'd completed his interviews before the start of the trial."

"A convenient coincidence. Could they possibly be meeting outside?"

Levy shook his head. "Bolton is violent but he's not stupid. If Thompson exposes him—accidentally, or deliberately for the publicity—the clinical trial is over and Bolton is back behind bars."

Jack had a strong sense that that was just where this man wanted him.

Levy waved Thompson away.

"Anyway, back to this Pickering girl. I just wish she were a few years older, then we wouldn't have her overprotective mother in the picture."

"How did you sneak him back into civilization?"

"We put him through the witness protection program—even the FBI didn't know his real identity."

"So you Earl Scheibed him into a law-abiding citizen. Why put him in Queens?"

"He wanted Rego Park and he persuaded the Bureau to put him there."

"Wait-wait-wait. He *wanted* Rego Park? Why?"

"I have no idea. I remember thinking it odd—born and raised in Mississippi, and he insists on Rego Park, Queens. Go figure."

"Yeah. Go figure."

Something about that bothered Jack, but he couldn't say why.

"The other odd thing is his money. He was set up with an apartment and a stipend to provide him with the essentials, but not enough to be comfortable. The idea was to spur him to get a job. He's been locked up since his teens. We gave him some training, but we wanted to see how he functioned as an adult in the real world."

"He's telling people he designs video games."

"Yes, I know. He's obsessed with them—structure, design, gameplay. He probably could design one."

"But he doesn't. He doesn't do much of anything according to Mrs. Pickering. Yet she told me he's got a beautiful townhouse with state-of-the-art computer and AV setups. How's he afford that?"

"We don't know. He goes out and buys these things for cash. When we ask he won't tell. When we threaten he says what's the difference where he gets his money as long as it's not jeopardizing the clinical trial?"

Jack wondered if Thompson might be the source—paying him for an exclusive story.

Thompson's reticence about Creighton was becoming more and more understandable.

"So, you tell him to 'fess up or you'll haul his ass back behind bars, but he blows you off. Seems to know you don't mean it. He indispensable?"

Levy looked at him. "Let me put it this way: If we can succeed in taming and making an upstanding citizen of Jeremy Bolton, we can succeed with anyone."

10

Christy paced her living room, wringing her hands as she waited for that man to arrive.

Even though she'd been expecting it, she jumped at the sound of the doorbell. Instead of moving toward it she stood frozen, frightened.

She'd asked a possible murderer to meet her. Alone. In her home.

Am I crazy?

As a precaution she'd hidden her little semiautomatic within easy reach under a cushion, but she doubted she'd need it. That man seemed obsessed with her daughter. Possessive. He wouldn't do anything that would cause him to lose her. One sure way of doing that was to harm her mother.

At least Christy prayed it would be that way. What if he was some sort of Svengali who could force Dawnie to stay with him even after he'd harmed her mother?

All right. Enough of that. Be calm. This is going to work. He's not going to hurt you because you're not going to threaten him or accuse him of anything. What was the point anyway? She'd toyed with the idea of calling the police and telling them what she knew about Michael Gerhard, but without proof—with no body even to indicate there had been a crime—she'd wind up right where she was now.

So she'd come up with another way.

The bell rang again. She moved to the door and opened it. There he was, standing on the front steps. He wore jeans and a fitted black western shirt that clung to his frame. Christy couldn't deny his aura of raw-boned animalism. Once again she could see why Dawnie was so taken with him.

"May I come in?" he said, his tone and expression neutral.

Well, at least it was a cordial start. She stood aside and motioned him into the room.

"Please."

Before closing the door she sneaked a peek to see if Dawn had tagged along, but saw no sign of her. She decided to address him with the same level of cordiality.

"Forgive me for not offering you a drink or a seat, but I don't think our business here will last all that long."

"Business?"

Might as well get to it.

"Yes. I have a business proposition for you."

"Really." He drew out the word. "Okay. I'm listenin."

She picked up a Talbot's shopping bag from the coffee table and handed it to him.

"That's yours if you agree to certain conditions."

Frowning, he took it and glanced inside. Then he looked up at her.

"Cash?"

"A quarter of a million dollars."

After her confrontation with Dawnie and this man, she'd run out and withdrawn it from the money-market account she used to hold her cash between trades. The bank had given her a hard time but she'd insisted. This was worth every penny if it worked.

"What?"

"It can be yours. All you have to do to earn it is say good night to Dawn tonight as usual, and then drop out of her life forever."

His blue gaze bored into her, through her. "You must think I'm the worst sort of lowlife."

She stepped back, closer to the pistol. Remember: no threats, no accusations.

"My only thought is that you are the wrong man for Dawn."

He shook his head. "You got it all wrong. I'm the *right* man for Dawn, the rightest man in the world. Our destinies are twined. Together we're gonna change this big ol' world."

Christy wanted to scream but kept her tone level. "I want you out of her life and I'm willing to put my money where my mouth is. Take it."

Of course he could take the cash and stay with Dawn, but that would cause a fall from grace in her eyes. Dawn would want him to give it back, and if he refused . . .

"You don't get it, do you. We was made for each other. I'll fight to keep her and I'll fight anyone who tries to come between us. But more"—he pointed a finger at her—"and you as a mother ought to appreciate this—I will protect her from all harm. I will trade my life for hers if it comes down to that."

The words stunned her. Not so much because she hadn't expected them, but because of the undeniable sincerity behind them. This man would indeed die for Dawnie.

Why? He'd known her only a few months.

This was crazy.

He stepped to the side and dumped the stacks of bills onto the coffee table.

"What are you doing?"

He said nothing as he pulled out his cell phone. She watched as he opened it and started pressing buttons.

Calling Dawn? Oh, no!

"What are you doing? Who are you calling?"

"Nobody." He aimed the flip top of the phone at the pile of bills and pressed a button. "Just gettin proof."

"Proof of what?"

And then she knew. Her heart twisted in her chest when she realized what he was up to.

"No, please. Let's forget this ever happened! Please?"

He smiled as he slipped past her, opened the door, and stepped out into the night.

Christy stood there, numb, bloodless.

What would make a thirty-something man turn down a quarter of a million dollars to stay with a naïve eighteen-year-old? Most people would say it had to be love, but Christy couldn't buy that.

It was something else. He talked about entwined—"twined"—destinies and changing the world . . . what was going on in that man's head?

But worse than that . . . she had a feeling she'd just made an awful mistake.

She had to call Dawnie, reach her before that man did. Find some way to explain.

She ran for her phone.

11

"What I don't get," Jack said, eyeing Levy, "is why you'd even think of letting a psycho killer like Bolton loose."

Levy smiled. "He's not a 'psycho.' He's just . . . different."

"What kind of a guy doesn't say word one to anyone—not even his lawyer—during his entire trial? Doesn't that fit with psycho?"

The smile turned condescending. "It's not a term we use in the medical field, but yes, that sort of behavior would certainly be considered aberrant. In Bolton's case, however, it was aberrant like a fox. As soon as he arrived at Creighton he began talking. He's never explained his silence. He might have been looking for a verdict of not guilty by reason of insanity, but it didn't work."

"All right then, but psycho or not, he's still a stone killer. Why can't you test this drug on him behind bars?"

"Because that's not the real world. He's been a model prisoner, but it's a rigidly controlled environment. We couldn't gather worthwhile clinical data while he was locked up. It simply wasn't possible. We had to test him 'in the wild,' as it were."

"He's wild, all right."

Levy cleared his throat. "I'm not going to discuss experimental protocols with you. We'll make you the same offer we made Gerhard: We'll match what the Pickering woman is paying you."

Levy obviously figured he was talking to a sleazeball. Why disappoint him?

"Some offer. I'll be pocketing the same either way. Where's the benefit to me?"

"No, you misunderstand. *We'll* pay you while *she's* paying you. We want you to keep working for her—*pretend* to be working for her—so she won't hire a third detective. That way you'll be getting double your fee for nothing. Because that's what you'll be doing: Pretending to be conducting an ongoing investigation but coming up empty-handed."

Jack leaned back and thought about how he could make this work.

A crummy, complicated situation. Christy had hired him to come up with some way to split up Dawn and her older guy. Jack had that. All he had to do was go online to the FBI site and find a white male in his thirties on their most-wanted list, then drop a dime and identify Bethlehem as the guy. The feds would investigate, check his prints, and *voilà,* back behind bars.

But would that trigger another sort of investigation? Would the agency Levy had spoken of figure John Robertson for the finger man and come after him? Might. Might not. But Jack couldn't afford to take the risk.

Especially if Bolton had nothing to do with Gerhard's death.

He'd have to find another way to fix this. Come at it from an entirely different angle. And it wouldn't hurt to maintain ties with Levy and Creighton while he was looking.

But he didn't want to sell himself too cheaply.

"Give me double what the lady's paying and it's a deal."

Levy nodded. "I believe we can handle that—as long as you hold up your end of the bargain."

"No problem there." But Jack saw a major hitch. "Might have a little problem taking back what I already told her."

Levy stiffened. "What's that?"

"That Gerhard's dead and Bethlehem could be the perp."

Did that sound detectivey enough?

"You didn't!" he said, bolting from his chair. "How could you be so stupid?"

Jack gave him an angry look. "Hey, watch it. I was doing what she was paying me to do. And now I'll do what you're paying me to do."

"Which is?"

"I'll tell her I checked out where Bethlehem was at the time of Gerhard's death and that he has an alibi."

Jack hadn't bought the alibi yet, but, not a bad plan. It might allay Christy's fears while saving her life.

"Just do whatever is necessary to keep her from exposing Bolton—for her sake as well as yours."

"When do I get paid?"

"I'll mail you a check tomorrow."

Jack shook his head. "Uh-uh. No way I want a paper trail between us. Cash."

"We can't do cash. We have to account for expenses."

"Cash or I walk away from this whole thing. Then you'll have to deal with the next dick Pickering hires."

"All right, all right! Cash it is. Now leave me alone. I've said too much already."

"Not nearly, but I can take a hint." He rose from his seat. "I'll be back to pick it up tomorrow."

"Not here! I don't want you near my home ever again."

"Your office then. Makes no difference to me."

"Not my office either."

Jack hid his disappointment. He'd wanted a look inside Creighton.

"Why not?"

"It's not a good place for private transactions."

Private . . . Jack realized that Creighton was probably lousy with bugs and security cameras. He remembered Levy's RF detector and figured he was worried his own place might be bugged.

"Where then?"

Levy thought a few seconds. "The shopping mall. We can meet in front of the A&P, say, around five-thirty."

Jack had one more question, so he pulled a Columbo—started for the foyer, then turned at the door to face Levy again.

"What makes Bolton so special?"

"Whatever do you mean?"

"Why's he still out there after kidnapping one of his handlers?"

"He's unique, and that's all I can say."

"Is it in his blood?"

Levy frowned. "Blood?"

"You know—his genes?"

"The nature-versus-nurture argument in regard to criminal behavior has been going on since before Darwin's day."

"Who's winning?"

"The nature argument—as it should. I am a geneticist, after all."

"So you believe people are born bad."

That condescending smile again. "We're all born bad—some just badder than others."

Helluva worldview.

Genetics, ay? Jack remembered what he'd seen on the notepad in Gerhard's office and decided to see if his next question would wipe that smile off Levy's face.

"So as a geneticist you've probably heard of oDNA."

The smile vanished. "Wh-what? What did you say?"

"Little-oh, big D, big N, big A—oDNA."

"Where did you hear of that—of such a thing?"

Jack winked. "I'm a crack detective."

Levy recovered a little. "You must mean crack-*head* detective. There is no such thing. Forget about it."

"You mean if I do some heavy research I'll come up empty?"

"Exactly. But if you do stumble upon anything, let me know. I'd be very interested to read whatever you find. Now if you'll excuse me . . ." He guided Jack toward the door. "I have other matters to attend to."

Jack noticed how Levy's hand shook when he reached for the knob.

"Sure thing. Be seeing you."

Oh yeah, doc. Count on that.

12

Aaron closed the door and leaned against it, exhausted. The stress of this project alone was wearing him out, and this detective, this man calling himself John Robertson, was making it worse.

Where the hell had he heard of oDNA? Only a handful of people besides him and Julia, all with top security clearances, were privy to it. Every mention of it—and there hadn't been many—had been expunged from public and private records.

So where had . . . ?

Gerhard must have told him.

But he'd said Gerhard was dead when he found him . . .

Just last night, Aaron had concluded that someone had tapped into his home computer. He assumed it had been Gerhard. His own damn fault, really. Last year he'd succumbed to the alluring convenience of a home wireless network. His daughter wanted it—everybody was doing it—and after a while the idea of sitting down with his laptop and surfing the Internet from any room in the house had proven too seductive.

He'd been able to set up the network—firewall and all—in a matter of hours, and it had been a great convenience. But last night he'd discovered that a few old documents on his hard drive had been recently accessed. It hadn't been him, and he was sure it wasn't his wife or daughter.

That left someone from outside. If Gerhard had the means to breach the firewall, all he'd have had to do was sneak to the side of the house with a wireless-enabled laptop and tap into the network.

The good news was that Aaron had a habit of turning off his computer before turning in, otherwise Gerhard would have had all night to wander through his files.

That had been the end of the Levy wireless network.

As for this detective, he'd worry later about how he'd heard of oDNA.

He peeked out the sidelight and watched Robertson get into his car. Had he bought the story about Bolton's alibi? Flimsy at best, but no way to disprove it. As he drove off Aaron tried to get a look at his license plate but couldn't make out the numbers. He remained at the sidelight, watching the yard after Robertson's taillights disappeared.

Bolton could be out there. He shuddered at the thought. Damn it, he wished the man were back behind bars. He didn't care what Julia said, or what warnings or threats she'd issued to Bolton, he was a loose cannon, primed and ready to fire.

Aaron wanted to see the therapy succeed as much as Julia did. Well, almost as much. Nobody had more invested in D-287, time and careerwise, than Julia. But he wanted someone other than Jeremy Bolton to be the guinea pig. He'd been overruled, however, and he couldn't risk doing anything to jeopardize the clinical trial. At least not directly.

But indirectly . . .

Robertson or whoever he really was . . . he struck him as someone as foolish as Gerhard, someone who would keep poking his nose where it didn't belong.

Which wouldn't be a bad thing if Aaron could guide him in a useful direction, one that would trip him into exposing Bolton's identity and ending the trial. Robertson could act as a stalking horse of sorts. And if he wound up exposing Bolton, the resultant shit storm would focus on him, leaving Aaron watching safely from the sidelines.

Yes . . . this had possibilities.

13

As Jeremy Bolton reached for the front doorknob on his townhouse, he knew he'd have to play this very carefully—just the right combo of hurt pride and indignation. Strike a single clinker and Dawn might start to wonder. Couldn't allow any doubt in that little girl's head. She had to believe him like his momma had believed in Jesus on her deathbed. Before that, she hadn't believed in nothin except maybe a snootful of hooch before she bedded down with the latest truck driver stopping over on his way to Shreveport, but she became a major Bible thumper after she heard she had the cancer.

Yeah, Dawn damn well better believe, because turning away from those stacks of C-notes had been just about the hardest thing he'd ever done. All those zeroes . . . damn! His fingers had fought like they'd had a life of their own.

He shook his head. He could have taken off with that envelope and had a real good time—maybe even started a new life.

But no go. He had to keep his eye on the prize and stay on course. Plenty of time—all of time—for fun and games afterward.

He patted his pocket. He'd left the money behind but the photo was about to come in very handy.

He stepped inside and found Dawn sitting on the couch in a sweatshirt and a thong. His groin stirred at the sight of her smooth, firm, young flesh. Not a pretty face and not a fantasy body, but no flab, no sag, no wrinkles, no lumps—the freshness of her flesh made up for whatever flaws she might have.

God, he'd been horny when he got out of Creighton, so horny that he couldn't wait till he'd sweet-talked Dawn out of her clothes. He didn't know how experienced she was—not too very, from the look of her—but he knew he wasn't. Damn near all his adult life without a woman. He wanted to come on as more experienced than her, but to do that he had to get some experience. So he'd hired hookers and had them teach him ways to make Dawn forget she'd ever had anyone else.

And it had worked.

He noticed she had her damn iPod buds plugged into her ears and didn't even know he'd come home.

These iPods drove him crazy. Every damn kid her age or younger didn't seem to be able to exist without them. Earlier today he'd watched a clump of five teen girls shuffling through the Queens Center Mall, two on cell phones and the other three plugged into their iPods. Why go out together if you've got nothing to say to the people you're with?

I'm showing my age.

Couldn't come across as an old fart with Dawn. She had to see him as cool and very much of the moment.

But this illusion of connectedness had to go. Technology—especially the Internet—gave the illusion of bringing people together when actually it was isolating them. They "met" in chat rooms, IM'd and TM'd people who were fifty yards away, and used smilies to overcome the physical and emotional distance that separated them.

That had to change. And it would. Oh, yes, it would.

Finally Dawn spotted him. She disconnected herself from her iPod and ran across the room to throw herself into his arms.

"What happened? What did she say?"

He hugged her, gave her a kiss, then broke free.

"I called you on the way back but you didn't answer."

She pointed to her iPod and shrugged. "Sorry. Didn't hear you, I guess. But what did she *say*?"

He turned away, stepped to the window, and stared out at the night sky.

"I'm not sure I know how to tell you this."

"Oh, God, what?" She was close behind him, breathing on his neck. "Tell me what?"

Without looking around he removed his phone from his pocket, called up the photo, and handed it over his shoulder.

"Take a look."

He felt it snatched from hand, and waited as he heard Dawn fumbling with it. Any second now . . .

A gasp and then, "What is this?"

"Money."

"I can see that, but—"

"Two hundred and fifty thousand dollars, to be exact."

"Ohmigod! I don't get it."

He figured it was time to face her now. After a slow turn he gripped her by the shoulders and stared into her blue eyes.

"Your mother offered it to me."

Her eyes widened. "Why would she—oh no!"

He nodded. "Yeah. All mine if I took it, got in my car, and never saw you again."

She backed away a step, her gaze shifting between him and the phone. "I totally can't believe she'd do this!"

"The proof's right in your hands. And the fact that I'm here is the proof of my answer."

"I still can't believe—!"

He put on a hurt expression. "You think I'm lying?"

"No. No, of course not, but this . . . this is so totally unlike her."

"Call her then. Ask her. See what she says."

She looked at him. "You won't be hurt? It's not that I don't trust you but—"

He pointed to the phone in her hand. "Do it. What are you waiting for? Let's settle this once and for all."

"Okay."

She sounded frightened and looked terrified, touching the keys as if they were red hot. Finally she put it to her ear. Jeremy sat and pulled her down beside him, then angled the phone so that he could listen along with her.

His gut tightened. This was a gamble. He hoped it worked.

Moonglow's voice: *"Hello?"*

"Mom? It's me. I think you know what I'm calling about."

"Oh, Dawn, I—"

"Is it true? That's all I want to know. Did you offer Jerry money to leave me?"

"It's not like you think."

"Did you or didn't you?"

"Yes, but—"

Dawn screamed and hurled the phone across the room. It slid along the flood and bounced off the far wall as she buried her face in her hands.

"It's true! I can't believe it."

"Sad, isn't it," Jeremy said.

Dawn lowered her hands and looked at him with a tear-smeared face. "What?"

"That that's all she thinks you're worth."

"I think it's plenty. But you . . . you turned down all that money for me?"

He'd known she'd ask that, and he'd come up with a perfect response—if he could keep from gagging.

"There's lots of money out there, darlin, but there's only one you."

She fairly flew into his arms and sobbed against his chest.

"Oh God, thank you! I knew you were for real! No matter what she said I totally knew you were the best thing to ever happen to me!" She leaned back and looked up at him. "I can't go back there. I mean like no way I can live with her anymore." She looked at him with pleading eyes. "Can I move in with you? Please?"

Yes!

He couldn't help smiling. "Of course you can. What's mine is yours. But are you sure? That's a big step."

Her eyes glowed as she wrapped her arms around him and squeezed.

"Totally sure. I don't think I've ever been so sure of anything in my life."

He held her and kissed the top of her head and stroked her hair. Across the room he could see his reflection in the mirror. He grinned at it.

You did it, Jerry. She's right where you've always wanted her.

It was all coming together.

Like fate.

SATURDAY

1

Jack stood behind Gia in the first-floor study and stared over her shoulder at the computer screen.

He'd tried every search engine he knew but hadn't come up with a single hit for "oDNA." They'd all produced hits for "odna" but none of those had anything to do with genetics. No problem finding rDNA and mDNA, but that wasn't what he was looking for. So he'd asked Gia to try. She hadn't fared any better, but he'd been buoyed by the way her fingers flew across the keys. Those physical therapy sessions seemed to be paying off.

He noticed specks of dark pigment on her fingers. He touched one.

"You've been painting?"

She shrugged. "If you can call it that."

"That's great. Can I see?"

She shook her head. "These aren't for showing."

"Not a show—just me."

"I'd rather not."

"Why not?"

"Because . . . because they're not mine."

"I don't get it."

"Neither do I. They're too . . . *off*, if that makes any sense. Not ending up the way I'd intended when I started them."

"But at least you're painting."

She sighed. "If you can call it that." She nodded toward the screen. "I'm not having any better luck than you did."

"I thought it was just me."

"No, there's no oDNA on the Internet, which means it's probably safe to assume that it doesn't exist."

"I disagree. Just because it's not on the Internet doesn't mean there's no such thing."

She swiveled in her chair to face him. "The net is chock full of fantasies, delusions, wishful thinking, and outright lies—all sorts of things that *don't* exist. Doesn't it follow that there'd be at least one mention if something *did* exist?"

He looked at the crumpled sheet from Gerhard's pad: *oDNA?* What did the question mark indicate? That Gerhard hadn't been sure about it either?

But Levy's reaction was a clear indicator that he was on to something. So why didn't it show up? And why didn't Levy want to admit that it existed?

Jack had a feeling that oDNA held the key to Jeremy Bolton's value to the Creighton Institute and whoever was funding them. Might even be the key to getting him off the street and out of Dawn Pickering's life—without screwing up Jack's.

But who else besides Levy and others at Creighton would know anything about it?

He'd have to keep hammering Levy.

"What if some super agency cleaned up all mention of it?"

Gia shook her head. "I don't see how that's possible."

Neither did Jack. Unless . . .

"What if they started early—at the first mention of it?"

She looked up at him. "You really think there's some secret government agency doing that?"

Levy had mentioned one, and he believed him. But Jack had given Gia only the sketchiest outline of what he'd uncovered.

She reached out and squeezed his hand.

"Are you sure you want to be involved in this? It started off as helping this woman find her private detective, then it moved into helping her get her daughter out of the clutches of an older man, and now . . . what's it now? This seems to be escalating every day."

No argument there. He hadn't told her about Gerhard's murder or the abduction—she'd only worry.

"I said I'd help her and I can't very well back out now. Her daughter's involved with a bad apple"—though maybe not so bad if the therapy was working—"and I wouldn't feel right leaving her in the lurch. Don't worry, I'm being careful."

All that was certainly true.

"But government agencies and some sort of DNA . . . what's that got to do with her daughter?"

"Not so much the daughter as the guy she's seeing. This oDNA could be something the mother can use to split them up."

She squeezed harder.

"Be careful, Jack."

"You know me." He offered his most reassuring smile. "Careful is my middle name."

Gia rolled her eyes. "If it were, you wouldn't do what you do."

"But I do take every possible precaution."

"And things still go wrong, don't they."

No argument there, either.

The risks involved in this fix-it had quickly escalated. And he was about to take them to a higher level.

But first he had to have a sit-down with another writer. Abe had left a message that he'd made contact with Winslow directly via e-mail through his Web site, pfrankwinslow.com. Winslow had e-mailed him back with a phone number, saying he lived on the Lower East Side and to call anytime.

Sounded like a man looking for all the publicity he could get.

"Any relation to Don?" Jack said with a smile as they seated themselves on opposite sides of a window table at Moishe's on Second Avenue.

Winslow gave him a blank, hazel stare. "Don?" He shook his head. "No Don in my family."

He was skinny and looked about thirty. He had wavy blond hair, a thin face, and what might politely be called a generous nose. Physically unimposing—a far, far cry from the brawny ex–Navy SEAL he wrote about.

"You're sure? Lieutenant Commander Don Winslow—he was a Navy hero during World War Two."

Another shake of his head. "Nope. Nobody ever in the Navy as far as I know."

How soon we forget, Jack thought.

He'd called the writer from Gia's this morning, saying he needed to do the interview ASAP if it was going to make the *Trenton Times* Sunday edition. Winslow said they could meet at a little restaurant near his apartment—that was, if Jack didn't mind coming to the Lower East Side.

Jack didn't mind at all. They had to meet someplace, and it couldn't be Julio's. Winslow's turf was fine. The writer had suggested this kosher deli/coffee shop.

"What'll it be, gents?" said a cracked voice.

An ancient waitress had appeared tableside with two porcelain cups and a pot of coffee. She had bright orange hair, thick blue eye shadow, and a sharp dowager's hump. Her name tag read SALLY.

Winslow ordered eggs over easy with corned beef hash; Jack ordered a bagel and lox, extra capers.

The menu reminded him of the Kosher Nosh, Gia's favorite eatery during her pregnancy. But with the baby gone, she'd lost her cravings. They hadn't been back since. Too painful.

He shook off the melancholy and pulled out his recorder.

"You're amazingly accessible," Jack said. "I interviewed Hank Thompson yesterday and had to go through his publicist and meet him at his publisher's office." He gestured around. "This is much more relaxed."

"Well, as far as being accessible goes, I don't have much choice: I'm available to the press any time, any day."

"That's refreshing."

"No, that's survival. This is off the record, okay?"

Jack had been about to turn on the recorder but stopped.

"I guess so. Sure."

Jack wanted to get to his questions but felt he had to play along.

"I just want you to know my situation. My publisher doesn't do diddly-squat for paperback originals. Like straight-to-video movies. I have to go out on my own and scrabble for every bit of PR I can get. That's the paperback life. As soon as my latest is shipped, my editor and publisher forget I exist."

"Paperback, ay? I'd have thought for sure it would make a million for you overnight."

Jack waited for a rueful smile or some sign of a flash of recognition. Nothing came.

Ah, fame. Fickle be thy name.

"I wish! If I made a million, believe me, I wouldn't be living in a one-bedroom walk-up in Alphabet City."

"Okay. Duly noted." Jack pushed the recorder's ON button. "Now let's go back on the record: Where do—?"

"Right. Okay. And since I know you're going to ask me, I remember the exact moment I knew I had to be a writer."

Jack hadn't intended to ask and didn't give much of a damn, but he couldn't very well tell Winslow that. Probably wouldn't shut him up even if he did.

"It was back in nineteen-ninety-three. I wrote a letter to the editor of a comic book called *The Tomorrow Syndicate*. Just a tongue-in-cheek paragraph with a fake return address poking a little fun at the way the editor—Affable Al—used alliteration. Well, lo and behold, they published it in issue number six. I tell you, it was such a rush seeing my name in print as the author of that letter that I knew then and there I had to be a writer."

"Fascinating." *Not!* "Now, where do you get your ideas?"

Winslow smiled. "I've been told most writers hate that question, but I love it. But then, of course, I'm just happy someone's asking me any sort of question."

Okay, okay. We get the picture: P. Frank Winslow is underpaid and unappreciated.

"The ideas?"

"Dreams."

"Dreams?"

"Yep. They come to me in dreams and I adapt them to the books."

"What was the dream that led to the first book?"

"*Rakshasa!* started off with a real nightmare. I was trapped on a rooftop where I was being chased by a monster or demon of some sort—I can't remember a thing about how it looked, just that it was after me—and no matter what I shot at it, threw at it, cut it with, the thing kept coming."

Jack felt a chill. Winslow had just described what he had gone through on the roof of his own building nearly two years ago.

"When did you have this dream?"

"Summer before last. Early August."

The temperature dropped a little further. The mother rakosh had been chasing Jack in early August.

"I woke up all out of breath, like I'd been doing all that running around and fighting myself. I knew if I could capture that terror and frustration in a story, I could sell it."

"That was it? You got a whole book out of that?"

"Well, no. I had another dream the next night about this cargo ship filled with all these nasty little creatures. So I put the two dreams together and had Jake Fixx come along and clean up the mess. I used real life, too. If you remember, it was right about that time a freighter caught fire and burned in the harbor, so I made that part of the book."

Jack wiped his palms on his jeans. Yeah, he remembered . . . remembered all too well.

"Where's your character Jake come from?"

Winslow lowered his voice and leaned forward, as if about to impart some ancient wisdom.

"Now here's where the art of writing and creating comes in: The character in the dream was this nondescript sort of ne'er-do-well urban mercenary. I mean, you had to pay him to help you out."

"No!"

"I'm not kidding. Well, I hadn't had anything but the letter published back then, but I knew right off that wasn't going to fly."

Jack had an unsettling thought. "Did you get a good look at him in your dream?"

He shook his head. "Just like I didn't get a good look at the monster. The only thing I remember is that he wasn't very memorable. But his looks weren't the only problem. Dreams don't need logic, but novels do. As Mark Twain said, 'The difference between fiction and reality? Fiction has to make sense.' I mean how could a loner like that run license plates and check out fingerprints or call in old debts to get reinforcements or the latest weaponry? The readers weren't going to buy that and neither were the editors. So I created a highly trained professional soldier with tons of survival skills and named him Jake Fixx. Much more realistic."

"Oh, I agree. Especially that name."

Sally arrived with their food. Winslow attacked his eggs and hash as if he hadn't eaten for a week while Jack picked at his salmon. He wasn't nearly as hungry as when he'd come in.

After a few moments of silence, he said, "What about your new book, *Berzerk!*—was that also a dream?"

Winslow wiped some yolk off his chin. "*Berzerk!* was the next book, but not the next dream."

"You skipped? Why?"

He shrugged. "The second didn't come till about Christmas. It was kind of science-fictiony—about a new power source and such. My editor didn't like the idea. Vetoed the next dream as well. That was about all these different conspiracy theories—UFOs and anti-Christs and whatever rolling into one. It ended with this big hole in the Earth swallowing up a house and damn near gulping down our hero. That was probably influenced by that house that disappeared in Monroe last year. Too weird. We settled on the fourth dream I'd had about that drug that was so hot for a while and then disappeared."

Jack's gut knotted. "Berzerk."

"Right—or Eliminator, Predator, Killer-B. It had a bunch of names. In my dream it came from one of the surviving monsters from the first novel. The editor liked that idea because it was a sequel of sorts, so I went with it."

"When was this dream?"

"Last May."

Just when those real-life events were going down.

"How about your next book? Any ideas for that?"

"Way past the idea stage. I just handed in the finished manuscript."

"Already?"

"The publisher's pipeline is long. If I want this one out next spring, it's got to join the queue now. This one's called *Virus!*—and yeah, it's got an exclamation point. Our buddy Jake has to call in some favors from the CDC to stop a mind-controlling bug."

A wave of sadness swept over Jack as he thought of his sister Kate.

"Any more dreams?"

He smiled. "Plenty. I had one about a haunted house last summer that I think will become my next."

This was sick—this guy's dreams connected to Jack's life. He wondered if any of them saw into the future.

"What's the latest nightmare?"

Winslow smiled and winked. "Can't tell you that. Trade secret."

Jack fought the urge to reach across the table and grab him by his chicken neck.

"Just a hint?"

"All I'll say is it involves a stolen book and a stick figure like that Kicker Man you see all over the place. It's still developing. I don't know yet if I'm going to be able to use it."

That just about did it for Jack. As disturbing as all this was, none of it was helpful. And he wanted away from this guy with the creepy dreams. Somehow, some way, he and Winslow shared a circuit. Why? Some cosmic accident? Or did it mean something? He didn't know. Maybe he'd never know. But either way, he hated it. Wanted no one with a periscope on his life, but didn't see how he could stop it.

Who knew? Maybe Winslow would come in handy one day.

He signaled Sally for the check and started gobbling the lox.

"My treat," he said.

Winslow looked up. "Don't you want to know about my childhood?"

"Why would I—?"

"Because anyone who writes weird stuff is assumed to have had some sort of childhood trauma."

"Okay, I'll bite: What was yours?"

He smiled. "Nothing. I had a completely normal childhood."

"So did I."

"Yeah, but nobody thinks you're weird."

Jack didn't comment.

3

Jack arrived at Work about three o'clock and surveyed the spigot handles behind the bar: Coors, Coors Light, Bud, and Bud Light. Depressing. So was Work, kind of. Dark paneling, booths along the wall, scattered tables, pool tables in the better-lit rear section.

Yesterday, as she'd driven him along Queens Boulevard, Christy had pointed out this place, making fun of the name, and saying Bethlehem tended to hang here most afternoons.

Wanting to appear to be a regular schmoe, Jack ordered a draft of the lesser of the four evils from the bleached-blond barmaid and carried the Coors to a nearby table.

He pulled the latest model PSP from his backpack and began to play the brand new 3-D version of DNA Wars. If Bolton was half the gamer Levy had said he was, he might be intrigued by a guy wearing 3-D glasses as he played a game. Intrigued enough to come over and check it out.

Jack wanted him to do the approaching. If Jack wandered in and struck up a conversation at the bar, he might get suspicious. But if Bolton made the first move . . .

After forty minutes and two carefully nursed brews, Jack was beginning to think he'd wasted his time. Maybe Bolton had decided to skip Work today and, oh, say, drown someone.

At least the game was interesting and challenging—different game play and design from the console version—and it made the time go fast.

And then Jeremy Bolton walked in—sauntered was more like it—wearing a denim vest, faded jeans, and light brown cowboy boots. The rustler look. Add a black Stetson he could pass for Kevin Kline in *Silverado*.

Jack peeked at him over the top of the 3-D glasses. Until now he'd seen only photos and long views through a windshield and across a parking lot. Neither had conveyed the man's presence. Here was a guy who was comfortable in his skin. He radiated something. Jack couldn't put his finger on it, but he had a definite aura about him.

The barmaid lit up as she spotted him. She grinned as they shared a few words while she poured him a Bud Light. Beer in hand he turned and leaned against the bar, surveying the room.

Jack focused on the game and let loose a few grunts of frustration as his thumbs pounded the buttons. After a few minutes of this he noticed a pair of booted feet stop next to his table.

"Whatcha playin?" said a voice that dripped the deep South.

Jack gave a little jump, as if startled, then looked up at Bolton through the 3-D glasses. They were the polarized type, rather than the red-blue, but still they made the room look a little strange. He took them off and rubbed his eyes.

"DNA Three-D. Played it?"

"Didn't even know it was out. Thought you had MG Acid-Two. That's three-D too, you know."

"Yeah. But only the cut scenes. This one's three-D all the way through."

"No shit? Tell you what: How's about I buy you a beer and you drink it while I take a look at that."

Jack gave that two seconds of thought, then said, "Deal."

Bolton waved the empty pint glass toward the bar, saying, "Laurie, honey. You wanna get this fellow another on me?"

Just then a sloppily dressed guy, maybe forty, stepped up to the table.

"Need any party supplies?"

Bolton jerked a finger over his shoulder. "Beat it, Danny. You know better."

Danny looked at Jack. "You?"

"Git!" Bolton said.

Danny got.

Jack watched him slouch away. "I assume he's not in the paper-hat and blow-out horn trade."

Bolton smiled. "Not exactly. You just met Dirty Danny. Specializes in E and such. I ain't into that shit. You?"

"Not lately."

Jack figured Bolton wouldn't want to get caught holding if Danny drew heat and got pinched.

He sat opposite Jack and grabbed the PSP. He put on the glasses and attacked the game. He didn't look up as Laurie arrived with Jack's beer. Gave no sign that he noticed. Total immersion.

Jack studied him as he played, watched the Kicker Man tattoo on his left hand dance as his thumbs worked the buttons. He couldn't read Bolton's eyes through the glasses, but he could see the facial muscles twitch under his beard, saw smiles—by turns rueful or delighted—twist his lips now and then.

Didn't look much like a stone killer.

Finally he put it down, pulled off the glasses, and slid everything back toward Jack.

"Totally awesome. Gotta get me one of them."

Totally awesome . . . yeah, he'd been hanging with an eighteen-year-old.

They exchanged names—both lying. Jack wasn't sure how he came up with the name Joe Henry, but that was what he used. They hung out and talked about video games. No question about it, Bolton was a hard-core gamer. They swapped tips and stories about MGS, Halo, Grand Theft Auto, and others. Jack had played them all, but not to the levels Bolton had reached. Then again, Jack had had more to do in his adult life than sit in a cell and push buttons.

And all the while they talked, Jack's gaze kept drifting back to the Kicker Man tattoo. Bolton must have noticed. He held up his hand, palm inward, and stretched his thumb and index finger apart.

"You like this?"

"Been seeing more and more of them. I guess that means you're a Kicker."

"A fully dissimilated Kicker. You know what that means?"

"No, but I'm learning. I'm halfway through the book."

"No shit? Well, you're all right, then. A gamer and a Kicker—"

"Not yet."

He smiled. "Oh, you will be. You'll be dissimilated before you know it."

This was the second time someone had told him that. Not a comforting thought.

"But anyway—a gamer and a Kicker-to-be. Cool."

Jack couldn't resist: "What do you know about the author? Hank Thompson, isn't it? Ever hear of him before?"

Bolton's eyes narrowed. "Why you askin that?"

"Oh, just wondering. One minute nobody's ever heard of him, next he's on TV and his little Kicker Man is everywhere. Pretty amazing."

Bolton eased back. "Yeah. Pretty damn-fuck amazin."

Something in the tone . . . chagrin? A hint of animosity? Jack couldn't peg it.

He let it drop and they moved on to reminiscing about their favorite Atari games in the old days.

"My momma was poor, so I never had a console of my own, but I made sure I hung out with kids who did. Missile Command—I loooooved Missile Command."

Bolton was animated, lively, charming, easy to be with. If Jack hadn't known what he knew, he might have found himself liking the guy. Easy to see why Dawn had fallen under his spell.

He couldn't see this guy doing what had been done to Gerhard. Must have been somebody else. And given that, was it possible he'd been framed for the Atlanta murders as Thompson had said?

Perhaps . . . but his abduction of Levy hinted at what he might be capable of.

Jack needed to know more about this guy. Which was why he was here . . .

"And when I wasn't wearin out an Atari Two Thousand's joystick, I was plunking every quarter I could steal into the arcade."

That reminded Jack of something.

"Hey, there's a place in the city that has all the old arcade games. We could head in and—"

Bolton shook his head. "Maybe someday, but not for a while."

"Hey, if you're short—"

"Hell no, I ain't short. I just got other things to do. I'm what you call a man with a mission. Can't get sidetracked till I done what needs doin. Then I get to the fun stuff."

Jack couldn't help leaning forward. This was what he'd come for. He couldn't believe Bolton was going to tell him.

"What needs doing?"

Bolton got a faraway look. "Workin on a project. Real important. Got to concentrate on that. But when it's rollin, when I done my part, I can coast until the big day."

"What big day?"

He grinned, more to himself than Jack. "Why, the comin of the Key to the future, of course. A new world."

Jack was speechless for a moment, then managed a feeble, "Huh?"

Bolton shook himself. "Just kiddin."

Jack glanced again at the tattoo.

"This wouldn't have anything to do with Kickers, would it?"

Again the narrowed eyes. "What makes you say that?"

"Well, that author's always saying he's out to change the world."

Bolton smiled. "Yeah, he is, ain't he. Well, he's right about one thing: The world's gonna change like it's never changed before. What's up'll be down, and what's down'll be up."

He glanced at the Coors clock on the wall.

"Whoops. Gotta go." He rose and stuck out his hand. "Nice meetin'ya. Maybe we'll work out a two-player arrangement one of these days and see who's top dog."

"Yeah. Let's do that."

He watched him go but didn't follow. Couldn't. Had a date in Rathburg for his payoff. Bolton was most likely heading over to the diner to hook up with Dawn.

Jack stayed where he was, an uncomfortable mix of feelings stewing around him.

A "key to the future" . . . what the hell was that?

But a changing world, up moving down and down moving up . . . it all reeked of the Otherness.

4

Jack pulled into the A&P parking lot half an hour early and set up watch from a shaded corner.

Around a quarter after he saw Levy's Infiniti enter, followed by a battered and dirty old Jetta. They parked in adjoining spaces, then Levy got out and spoke to the driver of the Jetta, a middle-aged woman. After a brief conversation, Levy returned to his car and the Jetta moved two lanes away where the driver had a clear view of the Infiniti.

A little research had revealed that Levy occupied the number two spot at Creighton, right below medical director Julia Vecca. Could the driver be Vecca? Seemed like a long shot. Hard to believe the medical director of a federal facility would drive around in a heap like that.

Whoever she was, what was she doing here?

Jack could think of a couple of ways to find out, but settled on the most direct.

He pulled on a pair of leather driving gloves, stepped out of his car, and walked the perimeter of the lot until he was behind the Jetta. Then he beelined for it.

She jumped and let out a short, sharp screech when he yanked open her door.

"You won't be able to hear a thing from here. Come and join the meeting. I don't want you to miss a word."

She stared up at him through thick lenses. Her gray-streaked brown hair managed to be simultaneously mousy and ratty. Her suit was wrinkled and her white blouse showed ring around the collar. She grabbed for her phone.

"I'm calling the police!"

He took her arm and gently pulled her from the car.

"No need, lady. We're just taking a short walk to your pal Levy's car over there, where we'll sit and get to know each other."

The fear in her eyes turned to annoyance as she allowed herself to be led across the lot.

Levy's eyes fairly bulged through the windshield when he saw Jack and his companion. He jumped out of the car and stepped toward them.

"Julia, I—"

Julia, ay? Thanks for the ID.

Jack waved him back inside. "Nothing's changed, doc. We've got a table for three now, that's all."

Jack opened the front passenger door and ushered Vecca into the seat, then climbed into the rear.

"Comfy," he said as he settled on the soft cushions. He shoved a gloved hand toward Levy. "Now, as they say at the Oscars: the envelope, please."

Without a word, Levy slapped it into his palm. Jack opened it and pretended to count, then stuffed it into a pocket.

"Okay. Now that that's out of the way, why are you here, Doctor Vecca?"

She jumped at the sound of her name, then turned in her seat and focused suspicious eyes on him.

"You know who I am? How? Have I been under surveillance?"

He winked at her. "I'll never tell. But you might consider washing your underwear between wearings."

That had been a guess but, considering her appearance, an easy one. She glared at him.

"I came here to get a look at the man who is blackmailing us. I must say, I'm not impressed."

"Then why didn't you simply arrive with the doc here?" When she didn't answer, he added, "Oh, I get it. You didn't want me to know you were involved. You need deniabilty so you can leave Levy in the lurch should this whole situation head south, right?"

Vecca reddened while Levy's neutral expression said he'd already figured that.

"And as for blackmail," Jack went on, "I didn't ask for this. I was offered."

"That's immaterial. Just make sure you do what you're being paid for— which is nothing."

"Or what? You'll sic Bolton on me like you sicced him on Gerhard?"

He was probing here, looking for a reaction.

"I've heard enough of this." She opened the car door. "Remember what I told you."

She slammed the door and stormed back to her car.

"I do believe I've upset her."

Levy cleared his throat. "The only way to truly upset Doctor Vecca is to threaten her protocol. She's got a lot invested in this clinical trial."

"Enough to want Gerhard dead?"

"She did not 'sic' Bolton on Gerhard. I told you—he was with us the night you say Gerhard was murdered." He cleared his throat. "You mentioned oDNA last night. Tell me honestly: Where did you hear of that?"

"The stuff that doesn't exist?"

"It's obvious that you know it does, so I see no point in denying it. But where—?"

"Let's trade. You tell me about it and I'll tell you where I heard about it."

"You heard about it from Gerhard, didn't you."

"First time I ever laid eyes on him he was dead." Jack wasn't giving anything away. "You first."

Levy looked around the half-full parking lot. Vecca had putt-putted off in her junker.

"Let's move the car."

"Where?"

"I'll show you."

Jack leaned forward for a look over the backrest and saw Levy's RF detector resting on the console.

"Afraid somebody's listening?"

"No, of course not. I'd just like a change of scenery."

The RF detector was reading only background, but Levy could be worried about a laser eavesdropper—bounce a beam off a window and hear everything inside. Then again, he could have something arranged . . .

Jack reached back and pulled out his Glock. He held it low and racked the slide. The cartridge in the chamber popped out and bounced off the rear of the front seat. All for show, but the sound effect brought the desired result.

Levy said, "You brought a *gun*?"

"Of course." He pocketed the ejected cartridge. "Didn't you?"

"No! I don't even own one."

"Probably should. Okay, take us where you want to go."

5

Julia watched Aaron's car pull out of the lot with that private investigator, John Robertson, still in the rear seat.

She'd made a circuit and come back to the A&P to talk to Aaron after the detective left, but apparently they'd made other plans. She wondered where they were going and what they could possibly be talking about. She was tempted to follow but had a better idea.

Before, as she'd driven away, she'd realized she'd seen the investigator get out of his car shortly after she'd pulled into the lot. She hadn't paid it much mind at the time, just a man getting out of a big black car. But that man had turned out to be Robertson.

He was gone but his car remained.

Julia pulled up before it and wrote down the license plate number.

Probably thought he was smart. Aaron had told her about his assuming the identity of a dead investigator. She'd noticed he wore gloves so as not to leave any prints. Probably thought he had all bases covered, that he'd fully insulated his identity.

Well, he'd better think again. He wasn't dealing with the hoi polloi here. He was dealing with another kind of investigator—a scientific investigator used to probing the secrets of life itself. Probing the secrets of one man's miserable life would be a cakewalk.

That remark about her underwear still rankled. How embarrassing. Had he been spying on her? Well, turnabout was fair play.

She'd give the plate number over to the agency and let them run with it. In a matter of hours they'd know everything there was to know about this man. His life would be an open book.

Smiling, she pulled away.

John Robertson, or whoever he really was, had made his last snide remark. He'd rue the day he dared to cross swords with Julia Vecca.

6

After driving in a meandering loop that brought them to a construction site, Levy parked on a dead-end street in the growing development. Apparently the workers had the weekend off.

"Well," Jack said, peering around. "This is intimate."

"I work for suspicious people. Now, tell me where you heard about—"

"Uh-uh. You first, remember?"

Levy sighed. "Very well . . ."

Very well? Who said very well?

"One of the fallouts of the human genome project has been the realization of how much—ninety-eight or ninety-nine percent—of our DNA is noncoding. In other words, junk. Or at least seems like junk. Since we can't find any useful purpose it serves, we call it that. But that doesn't mean it was never useful. Most of us think it's mainly leftovers from viruses and the evolutionary process."

Jack was disappointed. He'd heard of junk DNA. But Levy seemed too interested in oDNA for it to be junk.

"I don't buy oDNA as just junk."

"It is and it isn't. Some junk DNA is oDNA, but not all oDNA is junk."

"Thanks for clearing that up."

"I know it's confusing. Let me go back to the beginning. Back in the eighties I began working on an NIH-funded project that was looking to identify genetic markers for 'antisocial' behavior. This was all very hush-hush because of the controversial nature of the work."

"What's so controversial about that?"

"Politics, my boy. Politics. A number of NIH conferences on the subject were canceled because of protests. They're all afraid that if these markers are identified and confirmed beyond doubt, how will the information be used? Specters of the eugenics movement and the holocaust get invoked and everyone shrinks away. And then come the religious fanatics: it's original sin, not God-given DNA that causes mankind to break the Commandments."

"The good old creationists, sabotaging knowledge wherever it rears its ugly head."

"Recently they've tarted up creationism with some pseudoscientific gobbledygook and are trying to slip it into schools as 'intelligent design,' but it's still creationism." He snorted. "Intelligent design! It's laughable. Look at the cetaceans—creatures that must live, feed, and mate in a medium they can't breathe."

Jack nodded. "Yeah. If that's intelligent design, God must be a blond."

Levy laughed. "Exactly. And has anyone who pushes intelligent design ever looked at the human genome? It's a mess—an absolute mess."

"But it somehow gets the job done."

"That it does, using only one or two percent of what's there. Back in those days, we hadn't yet mapped out the genome. The Human Genome Project was just a dream. But I did find consistent markers in certain violent criminals. Not all of them, but in enough to keep the funding going. Adapting a fluorescent antibody test developed by Julia Vecca allowed me to stain nuclei to show the presence of this DNA variant.

"Once we had that, we needed a criminal population to test. We collected samples from all the federal prisons, and the ones who scored highest were moved to Creighton, which became dedicated to researching the variant."

"Were they all violent?"

"The top scorers, yes, though some white-collar criminals were up there too. But just because they were locked up for nonviolent crimes didn't mean they weren't violent. We could only go on their convictions. We didn't know how they treated their wives or kids or the family dog."

"The closet sadists."

"Right. But with the explosion of knowledge and investigational techniques in the late nineties and early aughts, we found a subset of pseudogenes among the junk."

"Fakes?"

"How do I put this? They're ancient ancestors of functioning genes, but they have no coding ability. They fall under the junk umbrella. But these particular pseudogenes are so unique that you could almost say they indicate a variant strain of humanity . . . another evolutionary line . . . another human race that got pushed aside."

Jack held up a hand. "Just a sec. I don't know a lot about evolution but I do know the evolutionary tree has a lot of dead branches."

"Yes. But this is different. These genes are so distinct that it almost looks as if they were—I hesitate to say this—manipulated."

Jack had two hands up now. He'd heard this kind of talk at the SESOUP convention last year. It had sounded crazy then, and it sounded crazy now.

"Whoa there! You don't happen to be into UFOs, do you? You're not go-ing to start telling me one of those nut-job theories about aliens playing with our DNA."

"Of course not. But I can make a circumstantial case that somewhere along our evolutionary line *something* happened to it. I mean, this stuff's *that different*. So the big question is—where did this DNA come from? It's not found in chimps or any of the apes. It's not found in daffodils or butterflies or sharks—humans share DNA with all of those, believe it or not—or even bac-teria or viruses—and we have tons of viral DNA in our junk. How did it skip every other species since the dawn of time and land in ours and ours alone? If I were an intelligent design dolt I might say it's proof of God's guiding hand in evolution, but it was more likely the devil's. It's completely other. That's why I named it oDNA—other-DNA."

There it was, right out in the open: *other*.

Had the Otherness stirred something of itself into the human gene pool way back when—back in the First Age, when the *Compendium* was suppos-edly written? Or was this unrelated?

No . . . too much of a coincidence. And there'd be no more coincidences for him.

But to what purpose? A cosmic time bomb, set to explode . . . when?

Damn, he wished he still had that book. It might be able to tell him something.

"Why did you pick 'other' rather than 'alien' or something like that?"

"Because when you say 'alien,' people think of flying saucers and little gray men with big black eyes. We've got apes in our genome because we have a common ancestor. The Cro-Magnons live on in our genes, and there's recent evidence that Neanderthals do too. I suspect something happened in our ho-minid past to split off a subspecies from the main line. It developed this 'other' genome, and then was reabsorbed back into the main line, either by cross-breeding or some sort of introgression. I'm guessing about the *how*, but I'm sure of the *what*: We've all got a little oDNA in us."

A tingle ran over Jack's skin.

"All?"

Levy nodded. "To widely varying degrees, but yes. All. Summing up: At some time in the past another human race with altered DNA merged with ours. The DNA of the other race—the 'loser' race—joined the junk pile of the pres-ent human genome. You've heard of 'gone but not forgotten'? This oDNA is for-gotten but not gone—and not necessarily junk."

The Otherness . . . part of the human gene pool . . . the implications stag-gered him.

He wondered if he should tell Levy what he suspected. But that would mean going into all the background he had gleaned over the past year about the ageless, ceaseless cosmic shadow war between two unimaginably huge and unknowable forces—one indifferent, and one, the Otherness, decidedly inimical—waging around them with Earth as one of the many marbles in play.

Yeah, that would go over well. Levy would stamp NUT across Jack's forehead.

So instead he said, "Why hasn't anyone heard of this? It's tailor-made for the tabloids."

"Other people have stumbled upon it, as I did, but the news has been suppressed. All I did was send out a few e-mails on some preliminary findings and suddenly a member of a government agency which I may not name was knocking on my door. And no, they weren't dressed in black suits and fedoras."

"That's good." Jack had dealt with the real men in black and knew they didn't work for any government. "What did they want?"

"My silence. I could A: come work for them; B: keep my mouth shut and direct my research to another area; or C: stay on my present path and find my reputation trashed to the point where the only place I'd ever get published was *Fortean Times*, if there."

"You chose A."

Levy nodded. "Just like a lot of others. It was a win-win offer. I got automatic funding to do the kind of groundbreaking work most researchers only dream of. No filling out reams of application forms or going around begging— just research."

Scary and fascinating, but a connection was missing.

"What's all this got to do with Bolton?"

"Jeremy Bolton is *loaded* with oDNA—the highest score on record."

"Where'd he get it all?"

Levy shrugged. "Who can say? He was born in Louisiana to Elizabeth Bolton. The father is listed as Jonah Stevens but there was no marriage and Elizabeth raised Jeremy alone."

"Could Jonah Stevens be the source of his mystery money?"

Levy shook his head. "He's dead. We traced him because we wanted to see if he was the source of his son's oDNA, but he died in a weird elevator accident."

"Weird how?"

"The police suspected foul play, but nothing was ever proven. Unfortunately for us, his body was cremated, so we never got to check his remains for oDNA."

"What about the mother?"

"Dead too. Cancer. We managed to get an order of exhumation to check her DNA. Elizabeth Bolton carried a significant amount of the o variant, but nowhere near her son's."

"So this Jonah Stevens, whoever he was, must have been a gold mine of the stuff."

Levy nodded. "He was most likely a human monster, because he was also a carrier of the trigger gene."

"What the hell is that?"

"As I said, the oDNA is a cluster of pseudogenes amid the other junk, but unlike most pseudogenes, these are fairly complete. Just dormant. And they remain dormant unless a certain mutation is present on one of the X chromosomes. In times of stress, this gene can awaken the oDNA and transform it from noncoding to coding."

"I don't understand what you mean by coding."

"Genes carry codes—templates, if you will—that the cell uses for making specific proteins. When the oDNA is stimulated from pseudogene status to an active gene, its codes start producing unique proteins that alter neurotransmitter levels in the brain, triggering violent impulses. We haven't worked out the exact mechanism yet, but we're pretty sure that's what happens."

"So you're saying these oDNA types can't help it if they're violent."

"I didn't say oDNA triggered violent *behavior*, I said violent *impulses*. There's a world of difference. One is the act itself, the other is a tendency toward the act. Other genetic and environmental factors that affect an individual's impulse control come into play here.

"The upshot is that all of us have some of oDNA in us, but the amount varies, so some are more 'other' than the rest. But the amount of oDNA has no effect on an individual unless he or she has the mutation that acts as a trigger.

"But take a large amount of oDNA, add the trigger mutation, mix with poor impulse control—or anything like alcohol or drugs which lower the impulse threshold—and you have a potentially lethal combination."

"Like Jeremy Bolton."

Levy nodded. "Jeremy Bolton is a perfect example."

"And that's why you need him for this clinical trial."

"Exactly. We don't know how to remove his oDNA—although someday we might be able to do just that—so we've targeted the mutated trigger gene. If we can suppress that, the oDNA will remain dormant, and Jeremy Bolton will be just like you and me."

"Speak for yourself, doc." Jack rubbed his eyes. "Your agency can't keep this oDNA a secret forever."

"It knows that. And when the news does hit, it will have devastating effects. Look at the problems caused by differences in pigmentation. Imagine what's going to happen when it's leaked that there are people among us with large amounts of alien DNA—and believe me, the *o* in oDNA will be quickly replaced by *alien* in the popular press. Not to mention what it will do to the criminal justice system. Chaos. Everyone behind bars or in court will be claiming their genes made them do it and will want to be declared not guilty by reason of defective DNA."

Jack hadn't thought of that. Jeez.

He said, "And since we no longer believe in personal responsibility in this country, the lawyers will have a field day."

Levy shook his head. "We're talking genetics here, not—"

"It always comes down to personal responsibility," Jack said. "Like you said, the oDNA triggers violent *impulses*. But there's one more step before the violence: You still have to decide whether or not to act on the impulse. And even if you're drunk or coked up at the time, you're responsible for deciding to drink or snort. So even though you have an impulse to drop a cinder block off an overpass, you don't cross the line until you release it."

Levy gave him a funny look. "Cinder block . . . ?"

"Forget it." Jack had a flash of a gray mass crashing through a windshield, smashing into . . . "Just an example that came to mind."

"All that aside, the government wants to be ready to offer a remedy. That's why the urgency to find a way to suppress the trigger. But there's a more practical use. We'll be able to formulate this into injections that will last three months. A condition of parole for oDNA positives will be the therapy. Imagine the reduction in recidivism."

Jack stared at Levy. Something in his voice didn't ring true . . .

"Is that the real reason?"

"Of course. What other reason could there be?"

Yeah. Definitely lying. But Jack figured it would be a waste of time to ask. Besides, he had a much more pressing question.

"Why are you telling me all this?"

Levy blinked. "Why . . . because we agreed to trade information: I'd tell you about oDNA and you'd tell me where you heard of it."

Jack didn't buy that. Levy had told him way too much. Could be he'd got carried away with his story, but that didn't wash. He hadn't prodded Jack once for his source on oDNA.

And then he knew.

"You want Bolton back in Creighton, don't you. And you want me to put him there."

Levy looked flustered. "I want nothing of the sort. I told you, this clinical trial is of momentous importance. Nothing must jeopardize it."

"Yeah, but you think it should be tried first on someone less volatile. You've got a wife and a daughter. Bolton knows you, knows where you live, and you know he's a Tate-LaBianca waiting to happen. Admit it: Bolton on the outside scares the crap out of you."

"I admit to nothing of the sort. As I told you—"

Jack waved him off. "Save it. You're looking for a patsy. You're hoping I'll do something to tip off the cops that Bolton's out—like maybe getting myself offed by him—and that'll solve your problem and leave your hands clean. Or at least looking clean."

Levy stared out through the windshield and said nothing.

"Okay," Jack said. "Let's do it."

Levy turned to him, looking puzzled. "Do what?"

"Out Jerry Bethlehem as Jeremy Bolton. But we do it so that neither of us is downwind when the shit hits the fan."

"How?"

Jack thought about that. Dawn was too gaga to be useful, and he couldn't use Christy to drop the dime because the agency overseeing all this would assume the source of the info was the guy she'd hired. Jack didn't want to be on their hit list.

He needed someone with no connection to him or Levy. The only other person Bolton would know on the outside was Hank Thompson.

Now there's a thought.

High-profile guy . . . low-profile guy . . . put them together . . .

And hadn't Thompson said the Dormentalists and Scientologists were after him because so many of their members were becoming Kickers? What if they had him under surveillance? And what if Thompson and Bolton were meeting on the outside? Maybe the rivals would want to know who he was meeting with. And when they investigated Bethlehem they'd find . . . Jeremy Bolton.

"Get me all you know about Hank Thompson."

Levy shook his head. "That's privileged—"

"You want this fixed or not?"

Levy hesitated, then shrugged. "I'll dig out whatever I've got."

"Do it tonight. I'll be doing a little digging myself."

"Where?"

"I'll let you know if I find anything."

Levy hesitated, then said, "There's something you should know about Jeremy Bolton."

"I'm sure there's plenty I should know about Jeremy Bolton. What've you got?"

"Don't underestimate him. He comes on as a laid-back, shit-kicking good ol' boy, but he tests high on all the intelligence scales, and he's done a lot of reading in the past twenty years. His major shortcoming is his impulsiveness. If you can keep him off balance, he'll act before he thinks. But give him time to think . . ."

"So I'm dealing with a smart but explosive sociopath."

Levy nodded. "With a lot of native cunning. Watch out."

Jack had every intention of doing just that. He'd handle Bolton from a distance.

"Thanks for the heads up. Now, how about driving me back to my car?"

Conditions permitting, Jack would be paying a visit to the Jerry Bethlehem crib tonight.

7

As he hit route 9, Jack fingered the bribe money in his pocket. He'd use it to discount the fee he was charging Christy. Checking his messages he found a frantic call from her telling him that her Dawnie had moved out and that Jack had to find something on Bethlehem now-now-now! Call her please-please-please!

So he called and ground his teeth as she told her tearful tale of doing everything he'd advised her not to, then compounding it by trying to buy off Bolton—and failing.

That took Jack by surprise. A guy like Bolton who'd been locked up all of his adult life had never seen anything like that kind of money.

Or had he? He did live awfully well . . .

The upshot of all this was that Dawn hadn't come home last night. But worse, when Christy had gone food shopping today she'd returned to find a lot of Dawn's things missing. She'd sneaked in and moved out.

Each sob was a blade of guilt. He could end Christy's pain with a single phone call, but that could mean the start of endless trouble for himself. He didn't see Bolton as a threat to Dawn—at least not yet.

He calmed Christy by telling her his plan to get close to Bethlehem and get to know him. Maybe he'd let something slip.

"I really screwed up, didn't I," she said.

Jack wanted to chew her out for not taking his advice but couldn't see how that would help matters. He wasn't about to disagree with her, however.

"Yeah, you did. You made accusations you couldn't back up."

Her voice rose in pitch. "My daughter's shacked up with a murderer!"

"You can't say that. He has an alibi." A shaky one, but an alibi nonetheless.

"I can't stand this! I don't know how much—!"

"Easy, easy," he said, using a soothing tone.

Too much of that kind of talk might trigger some oDNA-type behavior in Bolton.

A mutant trigger gene . . . oDNA . . . Jack shook his head. He couldn't believe he was thinking like this.

He said, "As I said, we don't *know* that he did it. Private eyes make enemies. I'm working on a number of angles, but they're going to take a little time."

"I don't have time."

"You may have more time than you think. He didn't take the money, and that wasn't chump change. To me that says Dawn means more to him than just a young girl he can . . ." He hunted for the right word.

Christy saved him the trouble. "Go ahead, you can say it: *screw.*"

Yeah. That and maybe . . . *the Key to the future* . . .

"The point is, if he means to harm her, he'd have grabbed the money, done his harm, and taken off. But he chose not to."

She sniffed. "I have to tell you, Jack, that baffles me. I know it sounds awful for a mother to say, but what does this guy see in Dawnie? Don't get me wrong, she has a sweet nature—although it's not too evident at the moment—and she's a smart, smart kid, but that's just it: She's a kid, and a naïve one at that. What does he see in her?"

Good question. Especially in light of the fact that Bolton had insisted on being relocated in Rego Park. Had he chosen the town out of the air, or did he have a specific reason? Like being next to Forest Hills?

Could Dawn have been that reason?

. . . *the Key to the future* . . .

But Bolton had been behind bars before Dawn was born. As far as Jack knew, she'd never been a media figure like the Long Island Lolita of yore, so how would he have even heard of her?

So if not Dawn, then what was it? What was so special about Rego Park?

He said, "I don't know what's going on in his head, so I can't answer that. But I think his refusing the money is a good sign that we're not in a dangerous situation here."

"Not yet."

"My point is, you've got to back off now. Sit tight, do your day trades, and let me do what I do."

"You've got something planned?"

"I do."

"What?"

"If I works out, you'll know. If not, it won't matter. Do you know Bethlehem's address?"

"I should. I've driven by it often enough."

She gave him directions to his townhouse and to the diner where Dawn worked.

Jack hung up just in time to turn into the Ardsley service area. He found a parking spot and watched the entry ramp. He hadn't seen anyone following him, and the only car that pulled in after him was a Dodge minivan. It parked near the food court and a horde of tweeny girls in soccer uniforms piled out.

Satisfied, Jack backed up to where Bolton had parked two nights ago. He grabbed an electric screwdriver and one of his real-fake license plates from under the front seat. He slipped around to the back and opened the trunk. While pretending to be searching for something, he substituted it for the fake-fake tag he'd put on this afternoon—one of half a dozen he'd bought from Sal Vituolo's junkyard on Staten Island. Then he reparked the car nose in, opened the hood, and switched the front plate.

No use in giving anything away to any curious types in Rathburg.

He got back behind the wheel and headed for Queens.

8

Jack had driven by Bolton's townhouse. Lots of lights on but was anyone home? He needed to be sure before he broke in. He'd checked the Tower Diner—brick walls, canopied windows, pillars at the entrance, and a clock tower, for Christ sake. What kind of a diner looked like that? More like a bank.

He'd looked through one of the windows and seen Dawn, but no sign of Bolton.

The next and last stop was Work. If he didn't find Bolton there, he'd have to assume he was home and put off the break-in for another night.

The place was crowded, with someone singing off-key over distorted guitars blasting from the sound system, but what did he expect on a Saturday night?

Jack wove through the crowd and made his way to the bar. He wasn't look-

ing for a drink, just a vantage point. He reached the corner and started looking around. He'd brought his camera just in case he found Bolton in a corner
with a lip lock on one of the waitresses. A photo of that might pry Dawn out of
his bed.

He did a slow scan of the front end—no sign of him here—and was starting toward the pool tables at the rear, when someone grabbed his arm.

Jack looked and found himself in the grip of a short but beefy biker type
whose breath reeked of Jack Daniels. He had a balding head and a huge red
handlebar mustache. Jack half expected him to shout, *Great horny toads!* or
call him a *varmint.*

"My girl says you was starin at her, you sonuvabitch!"

Jack could barely hear him over the music, but he knew the drill with
these guys. They got to feeling mean after a few shots and looked for any excuse to throw a few punches. If you admit looking at his girl, he punches you.
If you deny looking at his girl, he accuses you of calling him a liar and punches
you. A no-win situation.

The last thing Jack wanted was to draw attention to himself. He gave him
a close look.

"Sam?" he shouted over the music. "Is that you?"

The guy looked confused. "What?"

"You're not Yosemite Sam?"

"Ain't no kinda Sam, and you was starin at my girl."

"You might be right, but truth is, Sam, I don't know who your girl is."

"I ain't Sam, and that's her, right there."

He pointed to a busty babe in a skimpy black leather halter top watching
them with glittery eyes and a nasty smile.

"Oh, *her*. Her name wouldn't happen to be Cindy, would it?"

"Cindy? Hell, no. It's Roxanne."

"Weird, man. She's a dead ringer for a girl I knew in high school. I thought
it might be Cindy Patterson but I guess not."

As Sam digested these departures from the usual script, Jack looked
around for a way out. That was when he spotted Bolton leaning with his back
against the bar, staring off into space.

Thinking about the Key to the future, maybe?

And then a whole scenario leaped to full-blown life.

"But listen, Sam," he said, leaning close.

"I ain't Sam, goddammit."

"Oh, right. There's a guy down there been giving Roxanne the eye all
night. And I can't be sure, but I think she's been eyeing him back. You know,
like they know each other."

He cocked a fist. "You tryin to tell me—?"

"Hey-hey, I could be wrong. But if you and I get into a fight and get thrown out, that'll leave a certain someone a clear field with Roxanne."

He looked around. "Where is this guy?"

Jack nodded toward Bolton. "Down there—tall guy in the denims and cowboy boots. Watch out. He looks tough."

"He looks like a *pussy!*" he growled. "You wanna see what tough looks like, you watch!"

He started nosing through the crowd like a rottweiler called to dinner.

Go, Sam. Get that there varmint.

Jack watched him step up to Bolton and say something, saw Bolton shake his head and respond with a condescending smile. Sam's fist flashed out but Bolton dodged it and swung a fist of his own.

After that, things got confusing as women screamed and men shouted, some fleeing the fight, some moving toward it, a pair of bouncers homing in, and an infuriated, red-faced, out-of-control Bolton swinging a pool cue at a bloody and astonished-looking Sam. He checked the bartenders but none of them was calling the cops. Probably hoping their guys could control it.

Jack pulled out his officialdom phone and headed for the door.

Somebody had to be a good citizen and phone in this terrible, frightful melee before someone was seriously hurt.

9

Aaron Levy settled at his desk in his Creighton office and opened Hank Thompson's file. No easy task to find it. The clerical staff was long gone. The only people left were the skeleton medical crew and night security. And since Thompson's stay here had begun and ended before Creighton had gone digital, he wasn't in the computer. Aaron had had to retrieve the physical chart from the basement archives himself.

He shuffled quickly to the lab results.

Hmmm. Thompson had been a strong reactor to the fluorescent antibody test. Interesting. Newer tests could better quantify the content, but Hank Thompson might well be a contender for the upper echelons of the oDNA rankings.

It shouldn't be a problem to check. If everyone had done their job down through the years, blood and tissue samples from Hank Thompson should be sitting in the freezer.

Aaron smiled with pride at his foresight. He'd known biotechnology would progress by leaps and bounds, so he'd planned for the future. He might never have a chance to examine these subjects again in person, but he'd have their DNA at his beck and call.

He flipped through the documentation and was surprised to see his signature on the order to transfer him to Creighton. He shook his head. So many inmates over the years. Couldn't remember them all. But why Thompson? What had brought him to Creighton's attention?

A couple of more flips and he found it. The charge had been GTA. Not the typical Creighton-worthy offense. Then he saw it. Seemed young Hank had become violent when the cops pulled him out of his stolen car. Took five of them to hold him down so he could be cuffed, and even then he'd kicked and screamed and struggled. Had to put him in leg irons. Seemed they'd found a liberal application of the baton necessary to subdue him. His mug shot showed swollen cheeks and blackened eyes.

Yes, that sort of violence would trigger a look. Blood had been taken, he'd reacted with a strong positive, so off he'd gone to Creighton.

Only one admission, which meant no further convictions—because once a Creighton inmate, always a Creighton inmate. Any further convictions brought you straight back. Somehow Thompson had learned to control or sublimate his violent tendencies, or had managed to escape arrest and conviction. Or perhaps he didn't carry the trigger gene. They hadn't known the existence of the trigger at the time he was here. But Aaron would check for it now.

Vital statistics. Hmmm. Born January of the same year as Jeremy Bolton. Eleven months older. Interesting coincidence. Born in Selma, Alabama, to Diane Thompson. Father unlisted. No sibs. Another parallel: Both Thompson and Bolton grew up the only sons of poor single mothers.

Aaron made a note: *Check sib rate of high reactors. Does high oDNA level inhibit subsequent sibs?*

He'd just turned to the last page when his cell phone rang. He looked at the caller ID and saw no name. Robertson? He took the call.

"Yes?"

"*It's me. Our mutual friend was just led away from a bar in cuffs by the NYPD. Seems he got into a bad fight. He's being processed now at the hundred-and-twelfth precinct.*"

And then the caller was gone. But Aaron knew who it was.

He's done it!

Somehow, someway, Jack had succeeded in getting Bolton arrested. And making it look like Bolton's own fault, it would seem.

Amazing.

The routine fingerprint check at the precinct would set off alarms in Vi-CAP. The resultant firestorm would cause a PR nightmare for Creighton, but that wasn't his problem. The agency would have to handle it. One thing for certain: Jeremy Bolton was off the street for good.

Aaron leaned back. Thank God! Maybe now he'd be able to get a decent night's sleep.

As he sat there his gaze fell upon Hank Thompson's file and the discharge photo he'd opened to. Something familiar about his eyes . . .

And then it came to him.

Aaron felt his jaw drop as a cold wave of shock swept through him. He knew why young Hank Thompson looked so familiar. At least he was pretty sure. Had to confirm.

He lit up his computer terminal and tapped in the access code for Jeremy Bolton's highly restricted file. He paged down till he reached the intake photo, then leaned forward, staring.

Oh, yes. Oh, yes! This was wonderful. Not only would Bolton be back in custody, but Aaron had *this*!

Absolutely *wonderful!*

SUNDAY

1

Jack used a piece of toast to guide the last bits of his Everything Omelet—bacon, sausage, ham, mushrooms, onions, and hot peppers—onto his fork. Gia was at PT and Vicky had gone along with her. Abe slept in on Sundays, so he'd wandered over to the Highwater Diner in the West Fifties—so far west it was practically in the Hudson. He loved diners and the Highwater still sported its original chrome trim from the 1940s. But it and its kin were becoming an endangered species in Manhattan. He missed the old Munson on Eleventh Avenue—it closed in 2004. He liked the Cheyenne on Ninth down in the Thirties as well, but sensed its days were numbered too.

Figured he'd better enjoy the survivors while he could. Diner coffee, bacon, toast, two eggs over easy—was there a better meal in the world? And George Kuropolis, owner and chief cook, knew how to fry them with just enough easy on the over. But this morning Jack had celebrated with an EO.

He nursed his third cup of coffee at the counter while bald, chubby George fiddled with the radio, flipping from station to station, looking for who knew what. Not much happening radiowise on Sunday mornings.

Especially today. Why no story on Bolton? The one-twelve must have run his prints by now. The airwaves should be screaming the news about the life-imprisoned Atlanta abortionist assassin being arrested in a bar fight in Queens. But nothing. Maybe the cops were keeping it quiet till they double-checked the prints and called in the feds.

Sometime today it would hit. Had to. And then Bolton would be toast as far as the clinical trial was concerned.

Such a simple solution. He hadn't thought of it until Sam had started hassling him. With all that violence just bubbling under Bolton's skin, getting punched by some drunk was more than enough to set it free. After that—

"Whoa!" he said, waving to George as he heard a familiar voice. "Turn back. What was that?"

George gave him a look. "Since when do you care, Jack?" But he turned it back.

"There!" he said when he heard Hank Thompson's voice. "What station is that?"

He squinted at the dial. "Eight-twenty. Why?"

WNYC—the NPR station.

"Can we listen just a moment?"

"Usually we keep news on, but for you . . ."

Jack had done some work for George a while back.

"Just a few seconds."

He listened to Thompson's now-familiar rap, then heard the host say that he was "live in our studio"—as opposed to dead?—and would take some calls.

"Thanks," Jack said as he gulped his coffee, threw a ten on the counter—enough for the food plus a big tip—and headed for the door.

Where the hell was WNYC?

He called information and learned it was on Centre Street. Down by City Hall Park. He flagged a cab and headed downtown.

One Centre Street turned out to be a mini-skyscraper. He didn't know where WNYC was in the building and didn't care. All he needed was to spot Hank Thompson leaving.

He didn't feel properly caffeinated yet, so he ordered yet another cup of coffee from a street cart.

"To go," he added, just for fun.

The cart guy gave him a look. "It's way too early on a Sunday morning to fuck with me."

Whistling "I Love New York," Jack found a spot across the street where he could watch the entrance. He was just settling in when his phone rang—possibly the last phone in the city that still had a bell tone instead of music.

He checked the caller ID and saw a 914 area code.

Levy.

"We've got to meet," he said without preamble.

"We met yesterday. Any word yet on that matter I called you about last night?"

"Plenty. That's one of the reasons we have to talk."

Jack didn't like the sound of that. "Meaning?"

"He's out."

"Out?"

"As in free on bail."

"*What?* How the hell—?"

"I know how, and that's one of the reasons we need to meet again."

"That one's plenty. We don't need another."

"We do." Levy sounded excited. "I have startling—no, *amazing* news."

"You've already given me that."

"This might top it."

"Give."

"Not on the phone. Besides, you'll have to see to believe."

"Well, you'll have to come down to the city."

"It's Sunday. My wife—"

"If it's important enough you'll find a way."

A pause, then, "I suppose I could take a few hours . . . where will we meet?"

"I'm outside One Centre Street at the moment."

"But I don't know the city."

"Christ, you must have a GPS in that Infiniti. Use it."

"Oh. Yes. Right. Forgot about that."

"Set it for One Centre Street and go where it tells you. There's no traffic this hour on a Sunday. You'll be here in no time."

He thumbed the END button and returned his attention to the building entrance, but his thoughts were on what Levy had said.

Bolton free on bail . . . how the hell could that be? Somebody might have the pull to clamp down on the news, but nobody had enough to keep the Atlanta abortionist assassin from going back to finish his sentence.

Someone somewhere had screwed up big time.

And then this other thing . . . startling, amazing news that had to be seen to be believed . . . what was that all about?

Half an hour passed while he mulled these as-yet unanswered questions. He was debating a fifth cup of coffee when he spotted Thompson popping through the entrance and stepping to the curb. He flagged a taxi and Jack did the same, giving the driver a follow-that-cab line. The guy, whose name was Mustafa, looked like he was just back from the jihad. He didn't even blink.

2

Jeremy lay in bed and stared at the ceiling. He couldn't believe they'd let him go. When they'd slapped those cuffs on him at Work he had that same lost, helpless, panicked feeling he'd had way back in his teens when they'd cornered him for the Atlanta killings.

What had happened? Had they screwed up the prints? Did the computer burp while it was processing his and not recognize them?

Or had it been a higher power, guiding his fate?

Whatever the reason, he was glad he was out.

He stretched out his hand, expecting to touch Dawn. Instead he found an empty bed. Then he heard the toilet flush and Dawn stumbled into the room, looking pale.

"Somethin wrong, darlin?"

"Feel crummy." Rubbing her arms she crossed the room and closed the two windows. "It's freezing in here!"

He repressed a flash of anger. She hadn't even asked.

"You know I like fresh air."

An open window . . . no such thing at Creighton. Ever since he got out he'd kept one open in every room. Now, even though the window had been closed only a few seconds, he felt closed in. But he couldn't tell Dawn that.

She tumbled into bed and pulled the covers over her. Jeremy reached under and rubbed his palm over her ass.

"Too crummy for a little lovin?"

She pushed his hand away.

"Totally."

"Hey, you mad at me? That fight wasn't my fault. I was just—"

"If you were home here instead of hanging out at a bar while I'm working—"

Anger flashed through Jeremy but he controlled it.

"Hey, now, darlin. I told you to quit that job."

"And I did. I gave my notice but I can't leave them totally high and dry."

"Fuck 'em."

Truth was, he didn't want her or anybody else around all the time. Back at Creighton, day and night, twenty-four/seven, someone had *always* been around. Even though he craved his own time, needed to be able to drop into a place like Work and just hang, he had to act like the devoted, protective, take-charge boyfriend. He thought of playing that guy Joe Henry's video game yesterday—most likely wouldn't have been able to do that with Dawn along.

That guy was all right—a gamer and a Kicker to be.

"They've got two weeks, then I'm so gone. But what happens last night while I'm there? I get this call that you're in jail and need to be bailed out and I have to leave work and I'm a wreck and now I feel like shit so just let me sleep."

He gave her butt a gentle pat instead of the hard slap he wanted to.

"Will do. Sleep tight, darlin.'"

He returned to staring at the ceiling, wondering why he wasn't in shackles on his way back to Creighton, when her words came back to him.

. . . I feel like shit . . .

Could it be? Could she have morning sickness? If she did it meant for sure that a higher power was watching out for him. Freed from Creighton . . . released from jail last night . . . and now this.

He suppressed a giddy laugh.

Oh, please, yes. *Please!*

Oh, Daddy, wherever you are, this could be it!

3

They wound up on the Lower East Side, some side street off Allen, just uptown from Delancey and Chinatown. An old, old part of the city. That writer Winslow lived down here. Coincidence? Yeah, well, a lot of people lived down here—mostly Asian.

Thompson's cab stopped before an old stone building stuck amid brick-fronted tenements. A bedsheet had been strung between two second-floor windows. Someone had spray-painted the now too familiar figure of the Kicker Man on it.

This had to be one of the clubs Thompson had mentioned.

Jack had his driver cruise past and drop him around the corner.

Now what?

Was Thompson just visiting, or was this where he was crashing while in the city? He certainly could afford a hotel room, but maybe he wanted to maintain proletarian cred. Was this where he kept the *Compendium*?

Jack was staring at the building when a breeze caught the Kicker Man banner and flapped it up. He stiffened when he saw the carving beneath it: the Escherish seal of the Septimus Lodge.

The Lodge . . . that's what they'd called the one in his hometown . . . a secret society that supposedly predated the Masons and made them seem like an open book. Jack had sneaked into the local outpost as a kid and had a vague recollection of being unsettled by what he'd seen. Nothing like the fanciful tales whispered in the kids' underground, but definitely strange.

He hadn't known of a chapter here in New York, but why not? Should have expected one in this old part of the city. But what was their connection to Thompson? Was he a member? Or had some Lodge high-ups become Kickers? Jack doubted the latter. But for the Lodge to open its doors to outsiders . . . that spoke of an intimate connection.

Curiouser and curiouser.

He looked around for a vantage point with a view of the entrance. He figured a surveillance of Thompson was warranted by the Bolton connection. Probably best to set up on the same side of the street, where he wouldn't attract the attention of anyone looking out a window.

One building west he found a spot near the mouth of a narrow alley—a dead-end passage populated by half a dozen battered, empty garbage cans and most likely a colony or two of rats. But it offered a good view, and even a little sunlight. He'd worn his bomber jacket to ward off the chill of the early morning, but the day was beginning to warm.

As he waited his bladder started sending him the full-tank signal. All the coffee that had gone in wanted out, so he risked a quick trip to an Indo-Pak coffee shop down the street. Since the restroom was for customers only, he ordered some curried naan and a Pepsi.

Seated by the window, he had a narrow-angle view of the Lodge. He could have stayed but he needed to be out on the street if and when Thompson reappeared. So he made a quick trip to the head, then scooped up his food and headed back outside, hoping he hadn't missed Thompson's departure.

He was just polishing off the Pepsi when someone appeared on the steps of the club. He was disappointed to see it wasn't Thompson, but the guy did look familiar. It took him a few seconds before his face clicked. He had bed head and a few days' worth of facial stubble, but yeah: the missing janitor from the museum.

And he was coming this way.

Jack ducked back in the alley and rearranged a couple of the garbage cans, disturbing a trio of rats in the process. They squealed and fled toward the far end. Then he yanked a small wad of bills from his pocket. He dropped a couple of singles near the mouth of the alley, a fin a few feet in, and another even farther in.

Then he pulled out his Spyderco, flicked open the four-inch combination blade, and crouched behind the garbage cans to wait. If the mark was preoccupied or looking somewhere else, he'd miss the bait. Jack was betting a recently out-of-work janitor wouldn't.

He didn't. Jack heard footsteps stop at the mouth of the alley, then move closer. He hid the knife and let his head fall forward on his knees.

The footsteps stopped in front of him. He felt a poke and heard a voice say, "Hey, buddy. You all right?" Another poke. "Hey."

Jack remained immobile until he felt a hand worm its way into his jacket pocket. Then he moved, grabbing a handful of the guy's lanky hair and yanking him down. The janitor landed on his knees, face inches from Jack's, eyes bulging as the knife point pressed against his throat.

"Hey, I was just checking if you was all right!"

"Shut up!" Jack kept his voice menacingly low. "You have something of mine."

"No, I ain't! I never seen you before in my life!"

Jack pressed the point deeper. "Shut up! You speak when I tell you to, otherwise you'll never speak again. Got that?"

The guy nodded as best he could. He'd bought the threat and looked scared. Jack thought about this creep snatching the book—most likely from right under the unconscious professor—and taking off without letting anyone know the old guy was in trouble. He could almost see himself following through with the threat, slicing through his larynx and—

He shook it off.

"What's your name? Speak."

"M-Marty."

"All right, M-Marty, listen up. There's a book missing from the museum where you used to work. That book wasn't the museum's, it was mine, and I want it back. And since you stole it, I've come to you to get it." Jack had been watching his pupils. They suddenly constricted. Yep. He was the one. "Now, I don't want to hear any denials, like you telling me you don't know what I'm talking about, because I know you do. The cops are looking for you and you probably thought it would be a bad thing if they found you. But something far worse has happened. *I* found you first. The cops don't care about getting the book back. I do. Very much."

Had he laid it on thick enough? Yeah, probably.

"So, when I give you permission to speak, you'll tell me where it is and then we'll decide how you're going to get it back to me. Got that?"

Another nod.

"Good. Now speak."

"Look, I swear I didn't—ow!"

Jack gave him a little jab, just enough to break the skin.

"Remember what I said about denials."

"I know, I know. I was just saying that I didn't know it belonged to anyone. I thought it was just the museum's."

Jack refrained from getting into the basic distinction between mine and not-mine, but it might prove too esoteric for Marty.

"I saw it and I don't know what came over me. I only boosted small stuff before. I knew there was gonna be trouble, but . . ."

"But you saw the Kicker Man and just had to have it, right?"

The eyes widened along with the pupils this time. "How'd you know?"

"Where've you got it stashed?"

He flinched. "I . . . I gave it away."

"I know—to Hank Thompson."

The eyes widened further. "How do you *know* this shit?"

"Be surprised what I know."

Easy to figure, what with Marty and Thompson in the same building.

"Now—"

His phone started ringing. Who—?

Probably Levy again.

"You gonna get that?" Marty said.

Jack shook his head. "Later. Now, as I was saying, the question is, are you or are you not going to return my book to me? Think carefully before you answer."

"I'd love to, mister, I really would, but Hank ain't gonna part with it. He *loves* that book."

"You know where he keeps it?"

"Yeah. In his room, on the top floor."

Thank you for that tidbit.

"Well, steal it back. You stole from me, now steal from Thompson." He hardened his voice. "You're not going to tell me you won't do that, are you?"

"No-no-no! I'll do it! I'll do it!"

"Great."

Jack rose, pulling him to his feet. He put the knife away, straightened Marty's clothes, then pushed him toward the sidewalk.

"Get to it. I'll be waiting."

Marty looked as if he couldn't believe his luck. He rubbed the back of his hand against his throat, glanced at the smear of blood on his skin, then back at Jack.

"You're letting me go?"

"Yeah. How else are you going to get me my book?" He shooed him away. "Move-move-move. I'll be waiting."

Marty moved.

Jack peeked out the mouth of the alley and watched him dash back to the Lodge and up the steps. As soon as he disappeared inside, Jack stepped out onto the sidewalk and hurried the other way.

Yeah, he'd be waiting, but he hadn't said where.

4

Back at the Indo-Pak shop he grabbed a window seat and watched the street while listening to a pair of forever-virgin college kids at a nearby table argue whether Spider-Man could beat Wolverine in a fight. He checked his phone, recognized Levy's number, and called him back.

"Where are you?"

"On Centre Street. Where are you?"

"I moved." He glanced at the menu and gave Levy the address. "Meet me outside."

He watched the Lodge. In less than a minute Thompson appeared leading half a dozen men—Marty among them—wielding two-by-fours and other im-

provised clubs. They charged down the sidewalk and into the alley. A few seconds later they reemerged and stood in a group, talking and looking up and
down the street.

Finally they all trooped back into their building. Thompson was the last to
go in. He stood on the steps and scanned the street one more time.

Upset, Mr. Thompson? Rattled?

Hope so.

Levy's Infiniti showed up shortly after, pulling in by the fire hydrant in
front of the coffee shop. Jack hurried out and jumped into the passenger seat.

Levy looked at him. "Where do we go from here?"

"We stay put."

"But the hydrant—"

"If there's a fire, we'll move. A meter maid comes by, we'll move. Otherwise we stick. I'm watching for someone."

"Who?"

Jack wondered if he should tell him. Hell, why not.

"Hank Thompson."

Levy's eyebrows shot up above the frame of his glasses. "Isn't that interesting. Just the man I want to talk to you about."

Damn right it was interesting, but Jack wanted to talk about someone else.

"First tell me how Bolton slipped past the NYPD? Didn't they print him?"

Levy nodded. "Of course they did. But when they ran those prints they
came up empty."

"How is that possi—?"

"The agency had Bolton's record removed from ViCAP and the Atlanta PD
and anywhere else it might be."

Jack whistled through his teeth. "You said they were connected, but . . .
man."

"Yeah. That's why you don't want to get on their wrong side."

Amen to that, brudda.

He swallowed his disappointment—his perfect fix had flopped—and
moved on.

"What've you got on Hank Thompson?"

"I looked up his file last night. He'd been strongly positive for oDNA in
our earlier tests. So I had the lab dig out his old blood samples we've kept
frozen all these years and run them through our latest quantifying protocols."

"And?"

Levy smiled. "Through the roof."

"As high as Bolton?"

The smile broadened. He was starting to look like the Cheshire cat. Jack
wondered why.

"His equal. They're neck and neck. Plus Thompson has the trigger gene as well."

"So we've got two live grenades out there—and they've been talking to each other. How's that? Can they sniff each other out?"

"I couldn't say. But I want you to look at something."

He opened the laptop lying on the seat between them. Jack noticed it was plugged into the lighter socket. Levy hit a few keys and a picture popped up on the screen.

"This is Hank Thompson when we discharged him from Creighton. Take a good look."

Jack saw a guy in his twenties. His face was fuller, the hair shorter, but he still had that Jim Morrison look. Yeah, a young Hank Thompson.

"Okay. What about it?"

He tapped a few more keys and another photo popped up beside the second. "Guess who this is?"

The similarities, especially the eyes, were obvious.

"His brother?"

"That's Jeremy Bolton at age twenty."

"No way."

But as Jack stared at the photos, he realized that changing the hair, adding a beard and fifteen-odd years to the new guy would make him look very much like the Jeremy Bolton Jack had spoken to yesterday.

"They're *brothers?*"

Levy, still with that grin, shrugged. "Well, you're half right. They've got the same father."

A jolt of shock thumped Jack's chest. "That Jonah Stevens you told me about?"

Jack tore his gaze from the computer screen and checked out the Lodge. No activity.

"The same. Born in different states eleven months apart."

"Seems Jonah Stevens got around."

Definite family resemblance. But they reminded him of someone else. Who?

Levy said, "He stayed in contact with Bolton. Maybe he was in contact with Hank too, but I have no way of knowing."

"Sounds like he was a traveling salesman or something."

"Or something. We don't know what he did, but he had no arrest record. According to Bolton his father would visit and bring him a present every birthday when he was young."

"Did he tell him about his brother Hank?"

"Bolton never mentioned a brother. But he'd talk about his father's—his 'daddy's'—special gift. It seems Jonah was blind in one eye and told Jeremy that his bad eye could see things the good eye couldn't, things no one else could see. 'He could see what's coming.'"

"Didn't you tell me he was crushed by an elevator?"

"Something like that."

"That's one thing he didn't see coming."

Levy frowned. "No, I guess he didn't. But anyway, he told Jeremy he saw great things ahead for him, things that would come about because of the plan he had."

"What kind of plan?"

"Bolton was always cagey about that. I've interviewed him many, many times over the years, and I've approached this plan—always with a capital P when Bolton has mentioned it in writing—from every possible angle but I've never been able to make him slip. It's something he and his daddy cooked up. He didn't know his father was dead; he thought he'd just stopped visiting. When I told him, he was more upset about the Plan than his father's passing. 'Who's gonna finish the Plan?' he kept saying."

Jack remembered Bolton's remark about changing the world and the "Key to the future." Had he been talking about the Plan then?

"Maybe that's what he and his half brother have been discussing."

"I'm sure of it."

"Oh?"

"We had mics all around them whenever they'd meet, but they'd speak very low or whisper, and whatever we managed to pick up was cryptic. We did hear the Plan mentioned a number of times, however, and now in hindsight it seems a good guess that Jonah Stevens had discussed his Plan with his number-one son as well."

Number-one son . . . Jack shook off an audio flash of Warner Oland's bad Chinese accent and said, "Which makes it pretty obvious that they know they're related."

"No question."

"And I guess that clears up any questions about the source of Bolton's mystery money. The new question is: How do we use all this to put him back behind bars?"

Levy looked at him. "That's your department, I believe."

"Yeah, I guess it is. Thought I'd got that done last night but . . ."

Jack stared at the photos of the two men, wondering how he could turn their blood ties to his advantage. And as he stared, their features seemed to shift and blur and merge until, with a cold shock of recognition, he realized who they reminded him of.

Christy Pickering.

"Holeeee shit!"

He hadn't seen it in the adults, but those blue eyes plus the soft, hairless cheeks in the photos . . .

"What?" Levy said.

"The woman who hired me and Gerhard . . . she could be their sister."

"Really? Are you sure?"

"Of course I'm not sure. But there's a definite resemblance."

Levy paled. "But if Jonah Stevens fathered this woman as well, then Bolton is dating his . . ."

"Yeah. His niece. Was that why he wanted to go to Rego Park? To be near his niece? That's pretty damn—"

Levy held up a hand. "Aren't we getting a little ahead of ourselves here? We don't know that she's really a blood relation—it's an assumption based simply on a superficial resemblance from a couple of old photos. That's hardly definitive."

Jack had almost forgotten he was speaking with a scientist.

"Point taken, but—"

"We need proof."

Jack watched him. "Such as?"

"Some of her DNA. Do you know her well enough to get hold of a dozen or so strands of her hair?"

Jack had to smile. "You mean, well enough to snag some from her pillow or run my fingers through her lustrous locks? Hardly."

"We need something. There must be a way."

"Oh, there's a way." Jack already had a few ideas developing. "But why do you care? What's this do for your agenda?"

"Nothing. But it has everything to do with genetics. This super oDNA carrier Jonah Stevens could have been spreading his seed across the south for decades before he died. Who knows how many children he fathered, and how many of those are time bombs waiting to explode into killing sprees?"

"And you're worried about their potential victims, of course."

Right.

"I'm concerned, naturally, but I'm fascinated with the research possibilities. If I can identify his offspring, quantify their oDNA, and then assess their criminality or lack thereof—think about what that will do for my research, for our knowledge about the genetic basis of behavior."

"Is that the only reason?"

Levy looked at him. "There might be another. You probably wouldn't understand."

"Try me."

"Have you ever wanted to know something . . . know it simply for the sake of knowing . . . because it's hidden out there somewhere and you feel compelled to uncover it simply because it's hidden?"

"Too many times. Usually gets me in trouble."

"Throughout history it's caused many people big trouble."

"And that doesn't worry you?"

"Of course it worries me. But I need to know."

Jack was beginning to like Aaron Levy. Not a lot, but for a man who did a lot of lying, he had a core of truth.

"Okay, I'll get you your samples."

"Thank you. I—"

Jack raised a hand as he glanced again at the front of the Kicker club and saw the door open. "Wait."

"What?"

Hank Thompson stepped out and trotted down the steps. He had a backpack slung over his left shoulder.

What's in there, Hanky boy? A big old book, maybe? Taking it to someplace safer than the Lower East Side?

"Get ready to roll."

"Roll where?"

"Wherever I tell you."

Thompson turned away from them, quick walking up to Allen Street where he began waving for a cab.

"Recognize him?" Jack said.

Levy squinted. "Hank Thompson?"

"Yep. And we're going to follow him."

Levy shook his head. "I don't know . . ."

"This is one of those just-gotta-know things. And besides, he may be key to getting Bolton off the streets. Pull out and start rolling toward him. When he catches a cab, follow."

After a few seconds' hesitation, Levy complied, easing the car forward and heading for the corner. By time they reached it, Thompson still hadn't caught a cab. Levy slowed to a crawl. The light was green and a car behind them honked.

"What now?"

Jack hunched low in the seat. "Make the turn and pull over upstream. Soon as he's moving, we follow."

5

After a slow, frustrating trip uptown, mostly on First Avenue, Thompson's cab made a left on 39th Street and headed west.

Back to his publisher?

Could have a meeting, could be going out to lunch. That meant another lengthy wait. Jack wished he knew whether or not he had the book on him. If not, this was all a waste of time.

The cab pulled to the right and stopped, not before the Vector Publications building but a branch of the Bank of New York. Three words immediately tumbled through Jack's brain.

Safety deposit box.

Maybe Thompson had one, maybe he was about to rent one, but whatever the case, Jack couldn't let him stash the *Compendium* in a bank. He'd never see it again.

"Quick! Pull up behind him. Close as you can."

As Thompson paid the cabby, Levy eased to a stop and Jack crawled into the backseat. He lowered the rear passenger-side window and stuck his head out. Thompson was stepping out of the cab, swinging his backpack over his shoulder as Jack called.

"Mister Thompson! Hank!" Jack waved as Thompson turned. "Hey, buddy! Remember me?"

Thompson's curious expression morphed into a glare. "I remember you, you phony bastard!"

Must have done some checking up. Jack pretended not to hear.

"I'm so glad I ran into you. I have a couple of follow-up questions I'd like to—"

"You lying fuck!" Thompson was striding toward the car. Now that Jack knew they were brothers, he could see Bolton in his eyes. "What are you after?"

"Nothing. I—"

Closer.

"I mean, what's your game, man?"

"I just need to ask," Jack said, then let his volume fall. "Do you hang it to the left or right?"

Closer.

"What?"

"You deaf or something? Left or right? Does yours hang left or right?"

Jack eased back as Thompson pushed his face right up to the window opening, a definite Texas Tower look growing in his eyes.

"I want you out of my sight, scumbag! I ever see you again I'm gonna—"

Jack hit the window up button as he grabbed a fistful of his curly Morrison locks and yanked his head inside. Thompson tried to pull back but the rising edge of the window caught him under the chin, trapping him without quite choking him.

Thompson went wild. Red-faced with bulging eyes, he filled the car with incoherent screamed curses as he thrashed about like a trapped animal, twisting, kicking, straining, pounding his fists against the window and door and roof.

Jack slid toward the opposite side of the seat. He saw Levy's white face and wide eyes staring at him over the backrest.

"Dear God! What are you *doing*?"

"Only be a minute."

Jack slipped out the door on the driver side and stepped around the rear of the car. Few people were looking, and only long enough to nudge and point and grin. This was New York, after all.

Still, Jack hated this. He preferred subtle, preferred to operate shielded, from a distance, invisible. This was crude and it exposed him, but he couldn't stand by and watch the book sealed away in a bank vault. Sometimes you had to go with the most direct method.

Thompson made quite a sight with his head buried in the car and his limbs flailing and kicking in a pattern somewhere between the Charleston and an epileptic fit. His screams of rage were muffled out here but still audible. He'd dropped the backpack. Keeping an eye on the thrashing arms and feet, Jack picked it up and unzipped the rear compartment.

There she lay in all her metallic glory: the *Compendium of Srem*.

He pulled it free, dropped the backpack, and returned to the other side of the car. As Jack slipped back into the rear seat, Thompson saw the book and lost it.

"That's mine! That's-mine-that's-mine-that's-MINE!"

"Wrong," Jack said in a low voice. "Never yours."

Thompson squeezed his eyes shut and gave out a long, inarticulate roar.

Levy looked ready to jump out of his skin. He shouted over Thompson's screech. "What do we do now?"

Jack wasn't sure. He'd gone with his gut instead of his head. Never a good thing.

Well, at least he had the book. Now he had to come up with an exit strategy, a way to leave Hank Thompson in the dust. Sure as hell couldn't sit here much longer with a guy hanging out the window.

He checked out the street ahead. The cab was long gone, leaving the space ahead of them clear. The light was green but the pedestrian sign was flashing orange.

"Start moving . . . easy," he shouted back.

Levy gave him a panicked look over his shoulder. "But he's still—"

"Just do it. And be ready to floor it and make a left onto Fifth when I tell you."

As Levy put the car in gear and let it edge forward, Thompson stopped his screeching.

"Hey!" He had to start walking to keep up with the car. "What're you doing?"

"Going for a ride." He tapped Levy's backrest with his left hand while his right found the window button. "A little faster."

"No!" Thompson cried as fear started crowding the rage from his face. "No, don't! You can't!"

The Infiniti reached the corner just as the light turned orange. Jack lowered the window and gave Thompson's head a shove.

"Hit it! Go!"

Levy glanced back. When he saw that Thompson was free, he did indeed hit it. The Infiniti screeched onto Fifth Avenue.

"Dear God, that was awful! Who do you think you are? You can't go around doing that to people."

Jack didn't answer. He glanced back through the rear window and saw Thompson sprawled on the pavement.

"He's probably memorized my plates by now. He'll be calling the police and before you know it—"

Thompson didn't stay down long. In a heartbeat he was up and racing after them.

"He won't be calling the cops."

"Why not? You assaulted and robbed him."

"He's not about to report the loss of something he stole."

"Stole? From whom?"

"Me."

Ahead, the light at 38th Street turned green but cars were backed up, waiting to move. Levy slowed to a crawl.

Jack said, "If you check behind us you'll see an angry man coming our way."

"What?" Levy straightened in his seat and looked in the rearview mirror. "Oh, no."

"If you want to avoid another scene and perhaps some vehicular damage, I suggest you get moving."

The cars ahead began to move, but slowly.

Another backward glance showed Thompson gaining, and quickly. Murder in his eyes, veins standing out on his neck . . . his face was scarlet, his mouth working—looked like he was screaming a lot of words beginning with the letter F—and . . . was that foam flecking his lips?

"In your professional opinion, doc, would you say that we've yanked his trigger gene and his oDNA is in the driver seat?"

"Dear God!" Levy wailed.

Finally the traffic got rolling. A lane opened ahead and Levy darted into it, leaving Thompson in the dust, but still running, still screaming, still waving his arms as honking cars swerved around him.

"Guy could do with a little anger management."

Levy was panting as if he'd been running. "Now you know what happens when you push an oDNA-loaded man like Thompson over the edge."

Had to admit it had been an awe-inspiring exhibition of rage. Jack had had his share of rages over the years, but they tended toward the cold type—subzero cold.

Levy glanced over his shoulder. "You put us through all that for a book? Why?"

"Well, number one: He had it and it's mine. And number two: It's mine and he had it."

Jack resisted the urge to open the *Compendium* and leaf through it to the Kicker Man page. This was not the time or place.

"Where can I drop you off?" Levy said. "I've got to get back home."

"Not yet. I'm going to work on getting you those samples from my customer."

"Customer? You mean client?"

Something about having "clients" had always bothered Jack, but he was playing the private investigator now.

"Right. Client. If I can work a meet with her I can probably get you those samples. I want you around so I can give them to you. No sense in you driving all the way back in from Rathburg again when you're already here."

"Do you want me to meet her with you?"

"Hell, no. You don't see her, talk to her, come within a mile of her."

"Then what am I supposed to do while you're meeting her?"

Was he kidding?

"This is New York City, doc. You can't kill a few hours here, you're already dead and don't know it."

6

"I usually drink only Diet Pepsi," Christy said as Julio set a bar-draft tumbler, half filled with reddish liquid, before her. "But today I'm making an exception."

They sat at Jack's usual table, everything pretty much the same as the last time they'd met here. Except she didn't seem as prissy.

Jack nodded. "I can understand that."

She frowned at the tumbler. "Not the typical presentation for a cosmopolitan."

"Ain't got no martini glasses," Julio said and walked away.

"Not the friendliest person, is he."

"He's okay."

She sipped and made a face. "Ugh! Awful. And the glass is dirty."

"Just smudged. This place doesn't get much call for cosmos. He probably had to go online to find out how to make one." Jack took a swig of his Yuengling draft. "Pours a mean glass of beer, though."

Christy took another sip, shuddered, then pushed it aside. She gave Jack a hard look.

"So, am I to understand that you don't know *anything* more?"

Jack knew some and suspected a hell of a lot, but couldn't tell her anything until he was sure. He eyed her blond hair. If he could snag a few strands of that, he'd be on his way to certainty.

"As I told you, I have someone under surveillance."

He'd used that—and a supposed need for more expense money—as an excuse to have Christy come to him instead of him going to her, saying he didn't want to stray too far.

"But I thought the idea was to have *Bethlehem* under surveillance."

"So one would think. But if I can link this guy to Bethlehem, I might be able to get your boy in enough trouble to take him out of the picture for a while."

Christy leaned forward. "This man you're watching—what is he? A drug dealer?"

"I don't want to say yet."

"Look, I've been paying you. I have a right to—" She paused, frowned. "Oh, I see. Because I blabbed to Dawn you think I've got a big mouth. Is that it?"

"In a word, yes."

"I suppose I deserved that." She grabbed the cosmo and pulled it back toward her. "I don't care how bad this swill is."

She took a deep sip and only winced a little this time.

Jack said, "But it's been costly. Paying for information has run up my expenses."

She gave him another long, hard look. "You wouldn't be running a scam on me, would you, Mister Robertson?"

Jack returned her stare. "We need mutual trust here, Christy. I can't do my best work if I think I'm being second-guessed at every turn."

"Okay, okay." She reached into her shoulder bag. "I don't mind paying if I'm getting results."

She pulled out an envelope and slid it across the table.

"Cash, as requested."

Jack nudged it aside with a knuckle. "Great."

He noted with satisfaction that she'd sealed it—by licking it, he hoped. Levy had said he could isolate DNA from her saliva.

But what if she'd used water to wet the glue? For insurance, Jack had worked out a backup plan with Julio.

He finished his beer and waved the empty mug. Julio saw him and nodded. Jack pointed to Christy's half-empty tumbler.

"Want another?"

She shook her head. "Thanks, but I think I'll pass."

When Julio arrived with a fresh draft he bumped against the back of Christy's chair and spilled a couple drops of beer on her hair.

"*¡Ay, caramba!*"

Ay, caramba?

"I don't believe this!" Christy said.

Julio set down the beer and pulled a dishrag from his back pocket.

"I'm real sorry, lady. Today just ain't been a good day."

Jack watched as he began wiping the back of her head with the cloth.

"Ow!" She pushed his hand away. "I'm fine. I'd rather have beer in my hair than that cloth on it."

"Okay, okay." Julio glanced at the cloth, then grinned at Jack over her shoulder and winked. "Sorry."

Christy grabbed her bag and began to rise.

"We've got to stop meeting like this," she said to Jack, "and I think you know what I mean."

"Wait," he said, gently grabbing her wrist. "We need to talk a little more."

She gave him an uncertain look as she resettled herself.

"About what?"

"Your family, for one."

"What's my family got to do with this?"

"Maybe nothing." Jack thought of the resemblance between her and Thompson and Bolton: maybe everything. "But I'm working every angle and I've got to look into the possibility that there's something personal behind this."

She swallowed. "Personal? What could there possibly—?"

"I don't know. Have you ever seen Bethlehem anywhere before? Take away the beard, take off years . . . did you ever know him?"

She didn't hesitate. "No."

"You're sure?"

"Look, first off, it's not much of a beard, and second, ever see someone you know dressed up as Santa? Ever have a doubt as to who they were? If you know someone, a beard doesn't hide much close up. And I've been close up to Jerry Bethlehem. I've been in his face. I can tell you that if I ever knew him, it sure wasn't well."

That pretty well shot down one long-shot theory: That if they weren't related, maybe she'd known Bolton as a kid or teen and he was getting even with her for something.

"Okay, then. What about your husband?"

She stiffened. "I've never been married."

"All right—Dawn's father then?"

"He's never been a part of her life and he never will."

Something in her eyes, her tone . . . evasive?

"Why not?"

"Because he doesn't even know she exists."

"How can you be so sure?"

"Well, you can't be a hundred percent sure of anything, but I'm ninety-nine percent sure."

Jack pulled out the copy of *Kick* he'd retrieved from his apartment while waiting for her to make it in from Forest Hills. He showed her the jacket photo of Hank Thompson.

"Ever seen him before?"

She shook her head. "No. Why?"

Damn. Another long-shot theory down in flames. He'd hoped Thompson was connected to Christy and was pulling Bolton's strings to get even with her for something—like maybe running off with his daughter. Guess not.

"He might be connected to Bethlehem—another trail I'm pursuing." He leaned forward. "One last subject: your folks. Where are they now?"

"My mother died about five years ago, and I never knew my father."

Damn. He'd hoped she'd make this easy and come out and say his name was Jonah Stevens.

"What was your mother like?"

Another shrug. "I guess some would call her a free spirit, some just plain weird. Sort of a hippy. She belonged to the original Dormentalist commune before—"

"Whoa! Dormentalist? When?"

"Not sure. She quit when, as she put it, 'they went all corporate.'"

The Otherness again. The Dormentalist Church . . . Otherness connected . . . like oDNA?

"Did she keep in contact with any Dormentalists?"

Christy shook her head. "Not that I know of."

Now for the all-important question.

"You say you never knew your father, but did your mother ever mention his name?"

"Where's all this going? The only member of my family I want you interested in is Dawn."

"I'm looking for connections. Now, about your father?"

"Can't tell you much. Whenever I asked my mother what he was like she'd call him her 'pirate man.'"

"He had a criminal record?"

"No, because he wore an eye patch."

Jack felt a tingle of anticipation. Jonah Stevens had had a blind eye that he'd told young Jeremy Bolton he could see the future.

"Did she ever say anything else about him?"

She shrugged. "Whenever I'd ask why he wasn't around she'd tell me he'd been swallowed by a whale." She gave him a crooked smile. "Told you she was weird."

Jack leaned back. Not weird at all if she was referring to someone named Jonah.

That pretty much clinched it: Jonah Stevens had fathered Christy as well. What was he? Some sort of walking sperm bank?

She glanced at her watch and rose.

"I've got to go. The last thing in the world I feel like doing is rehearsing a musical, but a lot of people are depending on me. Call me tomorrow to let me know how this surveillance turned out. I need results, and soon."

"Talk to you then."

When she was gone, he looked up at Julio. "*Ay caramba?*"

The little man shrugged as he slid into Christy's seat. "What was I gonna say to the *blanquita*? 'Fuck'? I figure she watch *Simpsons*."

"You look more like Poncho than Bart."

"Poncho who?"

"Don't recall his last name. Cisco's pal. It was his expression."

"Cisco Kid? Like the song?"

"Yeah, but—never mind."

The TV show had been popular before either of them had taken a breath. Jack had caught some reruns on a cable channel. Leo Carillo used to say it all the time. Heard it from Ricky Ricardo a couple of times too.

Julio opened the towel and showed Jack the strands of hair trapped in the folds.

"This what you wanted, meng?"

Jack didn't want to tell Julio his efforts had been for nothing. That they'd only confirm what he already knew.

"Exactly. Nice job. Now, if you can get me a baggy and a pair of latex gloves, I'll be on my way."

Julio frowned. "Latex gloves . . . I don't know, meng."

"You've got to have them. Doesn't the health code say you need to wear them when you handle food?"

"We microwave. You know that. But I think we gotta box aroun' somewhere. We put it out for the health inspector."

He went into the back and returned a few minutes later with the baggy and a couple gloves. As Jack pulled them on, Julio sat and picked up the remains of the cosmo.

"She don' like my drink?"

Jack used his knife to slit the envelope.

"She loved it. She had appointments and had to go."

Julio took a sip. "Hey, not bad. Maybe I make these regular."

Jack removed the cash, then slipped the envelope into the baggy. The strands of Christy's hair followed.

"You can serve them by the pitcher."

"Yeah. But no martini glasses."

Jack tried to picture Julio's regulars with their pinkies raised as they sipped cosmos from long-stemmed glasses.

Oh, the humanity.

He sealed the baggy and stuck it in his jacket pocket.

"You being real careful, huh."

Jack nodded as he removed the gloves. "Any prints on that envelope are going to be run through the feds. I don't think I'm in any of their computers and I want to keep it that way."

He pulled out his phone to call Levy.

7

Levy picked Jack up on the corner of 72nd near the entrance to the Dakota.

"Isn't this where John Lennon was shot?" he said as Jack got in.

"Yeah. And where Rosemary had her baby, though they didn't identify it by name."

"Creepy-looking place."

Not creepy. Gothic. Jack would have loved to live in the Dakota. But even if he could afford it, the vetting process for all prospective tenants would keep him out. He'd never pass.

He pointed to his jacket pocket. "Everything you need is in here. Go on. Take it out."

Levy gingerly reached over and removed the baggy. He held it up to the light and smiled.

"Hair. Oh, perfect."

"It'll show that she's got the same father as Bolton and Thompson."

"She told you?"

"She doesn't know her father's name, but she told me enough to make book on it. But she's not telling me everything. She's holding something back. It may have nothing to do with anything else we're interested in, or it may. Maybe her fingerprints will tell."

Levy studied the baggy again.

"She handled the envelope?"

Jack nodded. "It'll carry her prints—and only hers. So don't waste your time looking for mine."

Levy gave him a sidelong glance as he stuffed the baggy inside his coat.

"You don't trust me, do you."

Jack smiled. "When did that occur to you? When I wiped down all the door handles and window buttons before I got out?"

"We should have at least a modicum of trust between us, don't you think?"

Sounded like what he'd said to Christy.

"At the moment, doc, we happen to have parallel agendas. That allows us to cooperate. But as soon as we come to cross purposes—and we might—you'll hang me out to dry. And you can count on me doing the same unto you before you can do unto me."

"Mutual mistrust . . . hardly an ideal working relationship."

"Works for me."

Jack pulled a paper towel from his pocket as he opened the car door. He wiped off the inner handle, then gave Levy a little wave.

"Call me with the results."

Before Levy rolled away, Jack wiped off the outer handle.

Mutual distrust . . . nothing wrong with that.

As he watched Levy turn uptown on Central Park West, he wondered how on Earth he was going to break the news to Christy that the man she knew as Jerry Bethlehem was her half brother.

The question was—did he know he was dating his niece? Had to. Couldn't be a coincidence. So the next question was *Why?*

Looked like he was going to have to pay a visit to Casa Bethlehem after all.

Whap!

Hank pictured again the face of that phony fuck John Tyleski on the leather of the heavy bag, and bashed it with a left and a right. The impacts rattled his arms all the way up to his shoulders. Then he pounded it again. And again. Good thing he was wearing gloves, otherwise his fists would be raw meat by now.

Earlier he'd attracted a lot of attention chasing after Tyleski or whoever he was—unwanted attention. Some plainclothes cop—a detective named Augustino or something like that—had pulled him off the street and ID'd him, asking him all sorts of pointed questions about his state of mind. Probably thought he was mentally disturbed.

Whap!

Yeah, well, he'd been pretty goddamned disturbed at the time. Still was. And worst of all, he hadn't been able to tell the cop the real reason why. Couldn't report the theft of a book he didn't own, so he'd had to make up some bullshit story about a package being stolen and then describe the wrong kind of car. Promised he'd come over to Midtown North and fill out a report. Fat fucking chance of that.

Whap!

Took everything he had to keep from tearing into the cop and the gawkers who'd gathered around. Couldn't risk letting go. Any bad publicity from him would attach to the book and the whole Kicker movement. So he'd walked away as cool as could be.

Whap!

But that had been on the outside. Inside he'd been boiling, building a pressure that had nowhere to go.

Whap!

He'd needed a drink but knew if he went to a bar he'd only pick a fight with someone. So he'd joined this health club and got on the heavy bag. Didn't know shit about boxing but it just felt good to hit something.

Whap!

Hit the bag, don't hit people. Right. Except for John Tyleski. If Hank ever saw him again he didn't care where or when it was, he was gonna open a big can of whup-ass on the bastard. Wouldn't know what hit him.

Whap!

The book—the damn book had been put in his hands for a reason. It had come to him because of the Kicker Man. So weird to see that same figure inside. He thought he'd dreamed it up on his own, but there it was. He hadn't understood what the book had said about it. But that wasn't why the book was important.

It had *answers*—answers to questions he hadn't even thought of yet. He'd had only a short, short time with it but he sensed—no, somehow he *knew*— it contained knowledge important to the future, to his and Jeremy's, but most of all to the Plan.

If only he'd taken the time to go through it. But he'd been so busy, and he'd thought he'd have all the time in the world for it after this damn book tour was done.

And he needed that knowledge now more than ever. Because Jeremy had

called this morning, so excited he could hardly speak because he thought
Dawn was pregnant. All part of the Plan as their daddy had described it.

Whap!

But he hadn't described it enough. Not nearly enough. He'd got only so far
and then he stopped coming around. Hank had looked for him and never found
him. Dead and gone. Had to be. But had he left anything behind that would tell
the rest of the story? Hank had found no trace.

Then the book had fallen into his hands and he'd known someone—
Daddy, maybe?—was watching over him.

Now the book was gone.

Whap!

But he was gonna get it back. Oh, yes. One way or another he was gonna
get it back.

9

Jack pulled to a double-parked stop outside the Tower Diner, wondering how
he was going to check out Bolton's presence or absence.

He'd already been to Work. Not that he'd expected him there after last
night's performance, but you never knew. He'd walked in, looked around,
walked out. No Bolton.

He couldn't help but smile when he looked at one of the front windows of
the diner and saw the man himself, sitting and sipping water.

Thank you, Jeremy Bolton.

Jack gunned the car and headed for Bolton's home. Christy's directions
led him on a winding course but eventually he arrived in a brand-new upscale
development of attached three-story townhouses in Rego Park. He cruised
around, getting the lay of the land, and not liking the well-lit streets.

Bolton's house was number 119. It sat third from the end and Jack noticed
that his row backed up to some woods.

That had potential.

He exited the development and explored some more. The woods weren't really woods. They proved to be little more than a hundred-foot-deep strip of wild oaks, elms, and underbrush that formed a buffer between the townhouses and a Woodhaven Boulevard strip mall on the far side.

Potential had become possibility.

He parked in front of a dojo and wandered over to the Italian restaurant/pizza joint that occupied the end unit. He pretended to read the posted menu while he scanned the vicinity. Assured that no one was about, he slipped around the side to the rear. No one there either, so he hopped the low retaining wall and made his way toward the townhouses.

10

Jeremy repressed a gag as he looked down at the plate before him. On a normal night he'd have his face all but buried in the pair of gravy-slathered country-fried steaks. They didn't serve anything like this in Creighton and he'd been sort of bingeing since he got out.

But tonight . . .

He swallowed hard against a wave of nausea. He'd been feeling a tad queasy all afternoon. It had started a little while after his lunch of extra spicy Buffalo wings at Work. The day shift there had heard about the fight and how one of the bouncers was pissed at him, but they didn't seem to care much. Could that be it? The wings? Or just some virus?

Who cared? All he knew was he was feeling crummy. It hadn't been too bad before, but the smell of the chicken-fried steaks seemed to crank up the nausea about ten notches.

He signaled to Dawn who came right over.

"Everything okay? You don't look so hot."

"I don't feel so hot, darlin. In fact, I'm feeling right poorly."

Dawn had started feeling better later this morning, but he'd been going downhill for a couple of hours now.

She frowned. "It's not the food, is it?"

"Naw. It kinda started before I came in." He pushed the plate away. "Why don't you give that to one of the Mexicans in the kitchen and bring me the check."

"You don't need to pay. I can say it was the food made you sick."

He smiled up at her. "Well, first off, I ain't touched it." You had to pay attention to details if you were going to lie. "And second, that ain't exactly honest now, is it."

"No, I guess not."

"Right. So you write me up the check and I'll call it an early night."

"Now I feel bad that I'm still working. If I'd just walked off I could take care of you."

"I don't need takin care of, darlin. When I get sick I'm like a dog—I just crawl under the porch or curl up in a dark corner till I get well. Now bring me that check. I need to be home."

Dawn made a face as she took the platter and headed back toward the kitchen.

Jeremy felt his gut cramp as it gurgled. Oh, no. Was he gonna have trouble on that end too?

He was gonna have to make pretty quick tracks back to his place.

11

Breaking in had been easy. Almost too easy. The place was wired with an alarm system, but Bolton hadn't activated it. Not only that, he'd left some windows open. Granted, they were on the top floor, but climbing atop a chair placed on the table on the deck outside the kitchen had put one of them within reach.

The only rough spot had come when Jack popped the screen and began to crawl in. The chair had toppled off the table as he'd levered himself up, creating a monster racket. He'd waited inside the window to see if any of the neighbors reacted. None had.

He couldn't go out the way he'd come in, but no biggie. He'd let himself out through a door. He replaced the screen and went to work.

With three floors to check, and a limited time to search, he had to make every minute count. The ground-floor garage was probably not the place to store anything personal; same for the kitchen and family room on the middle floor. Best to start with the three bedrooms up here.

The biggest bedroom was the only one with a bed—an unmade king—and so that was where he started. Holding a penlight in his mouth, he checked all the drawers, then pulled out the bottom drawers and checked in the space beneath. Next came the two closets—the one on the left held male clothing, the one on the right, male and female. He checked them high and low, going so far as to pat down the men's clothing.

So far, no good.

He moved to the other rooms. One was dedicated to video games. The furnishings consisted of a lounge chair, an LCD TV on a stand, a Wii, an Xbox, a PlayStation, and a GameCube, plus stacks of video games. The one closet was empty.

The bathroom was a melange of male and female toiletries.

The third bedroom at the front of the house looked like a storage locker. Bolton hadn't bothered to throw away any of his appliance boxes. Why not? Saving them for a move someplace else? Levy might find that interesting.

Using quick flicks of his penlight, Jack checked through the boxes. Most were empty, and the ones that weren't contained nothing but stray wires and Styrofoam packing. He moved to the closet and found it empty except for a backpack and a cheap tin lockbox stowed in the far right corner of the shelf. The backpack was empty so he moved to the box. The tip of the blade on his Spyderco made short work of the crude lock. He popped the top and looked inside. There he found an old composition notebook with the traditional black-and-white marbled cover and nothing else.

The first entry was about ten years old. He flipped to the last and found it dated just yesterday.

Just a single line: *The bird is in the hand.*

Something ominous about the vaguely smug satisfaction implicit in that simple sentence. Yesterday was when Dawn had moved in. Was she the "bird" in question?

Jack needed to read this. He'd have loved to take it home to pore over, but Bolton would know he'd been invaded when he found it missing. Or worse, he'd blame Dawn, and might get violent. Had to read it here.

He shut himself in the closet to hide his light from the street and began paging backward. Most of the more recent entries concerned his relationship with Dawn—pursuing her and winning her—but then they got strange. He came upon an entry where Bolton told of his plan to become a regular at the Tower Diner with the express purpose of meeting her.

How had he known?

Jack had an uneasy feeling as he paged back through his entries about the clinical trial and creating his new identity. Then Jack came to a page that stopped him cold. Nothing but the word "Dawn" written a hundred or more times, filling the page from edge to edge, top to bottom. It wasn't dated, but the neighboring entry was six months ago.

Jack stared at the page. Was that why he'd relocated in Rego Park? Just to hook up with Dawn Pickering?

It didn't make sense. How could he have known about her?

Jack found the answer on the preceding page:

> **Hank found her!**
> **Her name is Dawn!**
> **Dawn Pickering!**
> **She lives in Queens!**
> **Everything Daddy promised**
> **is coming true!**

Hank found her? Hank Thompson?

Had he hunted her up as a favor to his brother, or was he interested in her too?

Jack shook his head to clear it. This was like peeling the proverbial onion. Every time—

He froze at the sound of a door slam. He pushed open the closet door and heard pounding footsteps on the foyer stairs. They sounded too heavy for Dawn. Could only be Bolton.

Shit! Now what?

Jack slipped the notebook back into the lockbox and returned it to its place on the shelf, then stepped out to the window. The Miata in the driveway hadn't been there when he'd driven past before.

He sidled to the hallway door. From somewhere below came the sound of retching followed by the splatter of liquid hitting liquid.

Whoever had rushed in was making Jackson Pollock art in the main-floor toilet. Jack needed a way out. Couldn't use the route he'd entered, so he'd have to improvise. Maybe the vomiting would provide cover enough to slip past and let himself out onto the deck.

Moving in time to the retching and groaning, and pausing between, he reached the main floor. To his left the steps down to the front door beckoned. Immediately to his right lay a closet door, then a long console table, then the bathroom. Beyond that, the family room/kitchen area and the sliding doors to the deck.

Trouble was, the bathroom door was open. He didn't think it possible to vomit with your eyes open, so if he timed it just right, he might be able to flash past in mid-retch without being seen.

He was inching toward the door, waiting to make his move, when he heard the toilet flush. Bad news. He yanked open the closet door, ducked inside, and closed it after him—but left an inch-wide gap. Peering through it he saw Bolton lurch out of the bathroom and stagger away toward the family room. Now, if he'd only veer off to the kitchen for some water . . .

But no, he plopped himself in a chair in direct line of sight through the foyer. No way Jack could slip out unseen.

He weighed his options. He could wait and hope Bolton fell asleep. Or until Dawn came back and they went up to bed—and hope that no one opened the closet door along the way.

Another solution slithered to the fore.

He reached back and touched the grip of his Glock. He could step out of the closet, walk over to him, and tap a couple of nines into his brain.

Why not? Be doing the world a favor. The guy was a loaded gun ready to go off.

But Jack wasn't into doing the world favors.

Certainly would solve Christy's problem, though.

Of course, she'd be the prime suspect. If she didn't have an alibi—if she was home from rehearsal, sitting alone, waiting for her Dawnie to call—she'd be in big trouble.

Even though she'd eventually be cleared, he couldn't put her through that.

And after she was no longer a suspect, the agency behind Creighton might come looking for him. He hadn't been careful here. It had started out as a simple B and E with no one to be the wiser. A murder scene was a whole different animal. Who knew what kind of trace evidence he'd left?

He removed his hand from the Glock and rubbed his face. He used to have patience for this kind of waiting. Lately, though, his patience had gone south. He wanted out of here. And soon.

Had to be a way.

Jack tried a long-distance Vulcan mind meld to make Bolton move his ass toward the kitchen, but it didn't work.

He glanced down at the console table just outside the closet door, bare except for Bolton's keys. Must have tossed them on his way to the bathroom. No help there. Jack wanted *out,* not in.

Then he spotted the red button on the car remote. The panic button. Might be worth a try.

He dropped to one knee. Then, moving as slowly as possible, he widened the door gap a centimeter at a time until he could slip his hand through. Staying low, he stretched to the table, then to the keys. He pulled them a tad closer. When the remote was in reach, he pressed the panic button.

Outside, Bolton's car alarm started honking and wailing.

He ducked back as Bolton pushed himself out of his seat and stagger-stumbled into the foyer.

"Son of a bitch! Son of a bitch! I'll kill the motherfucker!"

Down the stairs, out the front door, and into the night.

Jack got moving as soon as Bolton was out of sight. Staying in a crouch he ran to the sliding glass door, let himself out onto the deck, and closed it behind him. He righted the fallen chair, slid the table back to where it belonged, then jumped to the ground.

A minute later he was on the far side of the fence and cutting through the woods toward his car.

But the question pursued him: What was so special about Dawn Pickering? Bolton's "Daddy," Jonah Stevens, the wellspring of his son's abnormal DNA, had promised his son something.

What?

12

There. Found it.

Jack sat alone in his apartment's front room, hunched over the *Compendium of Srem* at the round oak table with the paw feet. The glow from the hanging lamp lit the table and nothing else. The rest of the apartment lay dark around him.

He'd rather be doing this over at Gia's.

He pulled his copy of *Kick* over and compared its cover image to the one in the book.

Identical. He could have superimposed one on the other. But below the one in the book were printed five words: *The Sign of the Q'qr.*

It looked unpronounceable. *Que-quer?* Was that how you'd say it?

Everything else read as English. Why not that? Unless it was a word that had no translation. Like a name.

The verse below that was even more frustrating:

And then the Seven became One
But the One could not hold
And all with him were vanquished.
Yet though the Q'qr was cast down it endured
The Q'qr died yet lived on
The Q'qr is gone yet remains
Absent from sight
But present in deed
Present in spirit
Present in body.

What the hell did that mean? The lines might have rhymed or had some cadence in their original tongue, but now they were simply a clunky progression of contradictory statements about . . . what? A stick figure?

The author was obviously telling a story, but seemed to assume that the reader knew the details. Jack figured it was like showing a drawing of an egg sitting on a wall and reciting "Humpty Dumpty" below it. If you weren't familiar with the nursery rhyme and didn't know Humpty wasn't real, you'd be left scratching your head. Just as Jack was scratching his.

The bigger question that remained was where Thompson had come up with the figure. He'd said in a dream. If that was true, where had his dream come from?

Shaking his head, Jack copied down the lines and bookmarked the page. Then he began to leaf through the rest of the *Compendium,* looking for other appearances of the figure. The book was thick, the pages thin. He had a long way to go.

MONDAY

1

Jeremy awoke feeling rank. He'd puked three more times during the night and still had a funky taste in his mouth. But at least his stomach had settled. In fact, he felt hungry.

But not for Work's extra spicy Buffalo wings. He'd never try those again. From now on it'd be strictly sandwiches and burgers when he ate there.

He turned over and found the bed empty. Where was Dawn? She'd come home last night and gone straight into nurse mode. Got him some Pepto and rubbed his back and gave him sips of Gatorade. Nice try, but it all came back up again.

He heard the toilet flush and a few seconds later Dawn came in. She wore a short T-shirt and a thong and nothing else, and the sight might have put a little wood in Mr. Willy if she hadn't looked like hell. She wobbled on her feet and her face was the color of three-day-old grits mixed with some of that lime Gatorade she'd been spooning into him last night.

She groaned as she dropped onto the bed like a hundred-pound sack of corn feed and pulled the blanket up to her neck.

This was her second morning in a row like this.

"You okay?"

Another groan. "Like totally not. Like anything but. I think I caught what you have."

"Had. I'm feeling much better." He gave her arm a squeeze. "All thanks to you."

She pulled her arm away and pouted like a cranky child. "Sharing a bed's okay, but not a virus."

Virus . . . Jeremy had been under the impression he'd had food poisoning.

But Dawn hadn't eaten anything Jeremy had. Could you catch food poisoning? He didn't know all that much about medicine, but he didn't think so.

So maybe it was a virus. But if not . . .

He bolted upright.

"Puh-*lease!*" Dawn said. "Do *not* rock the bed!"

"Sorry. You . . ." Had to be careful here. Didn't want to spook her. "You felt this way yesterday too, didn't you?"

"What do you mean?" She looked at him. "Tell me you're trying to say I gave this to you."

"No-no. Not at all. But you know, these viruses, sometimes they hit you like a ton of bricks and sometimes they sneak up on you for days, and when they finally hit you look back and say, 'Oh, yeah, *that's* why I was feeling so crummy.' Was it anything like that?"

She closed her eyes. "I didn't feel so hot yesterday morning, but I didn't hurl or anything. Felt like I could have, though. Didn't even want my morning coffee."

Jeremy tried to hide his excitement.

Could it be?

Suddenly she was out of bed and running for the bathroom. He heard her puking. An ugly sound, but if the reason was what he hoped, it was like music.

He put on a concerned expression as she stumbled back to the bed and sat on the edge.

"You all right, darlin?"

She gave him a look. "Oh, I'm just fine. I just love totally puking up my guts. If I didn't know better, I'd be scared I was pregnant." She turned to face him. "You don't think I could be pregnant, do you?"

He wanted to scream *YES!* but kept his expression straight.

"I don't see how, darlin, what with me havin a vasectomy and all."

"I know, but I feel so totally rotten."

"It's the virus, I'm sure." He reached over and stroked her upper arm. "But you know what? Just so's you're not worrying about it—because if I know you, I know you're gonna dwell on it—we'll pick up one of those pregnancy test kits and give it a try."

"Oh man, that's scary. I do so not want to be pregnant. That's like the to-tally last thing in the world I need right now."

And the thing I need most, Jeremy thought.

2

"Well, you were right," Levy said. "Whoever those strands of hair came from, Jonah Stevens fathered her."

As usual, Levy had refused to discuss anything on the phone, so Jack had had to meet him for a face-to-face. He'd refused to go to Rathburg and Levy hadn't wanted to return to the city, so they'd compromised on Yonkers. Jack hadn't been to the Argonaut Diner in a while, and it seemed like a good choice, especially since he was heading for Forest Hills after this.

They'd grabbed a rear booth. The place had burned to the ground back in the late nineties, but was restored to its former tacky nautical-themed splendor. Jack had fond late-night memories of platters of Disco Fries—French fries slathered with melted cheese and gravy. Yum. He wondered if they were still on the menu. Yeah, he could check, but it was almost as thick as the *Compendium*.

Levy ordered a stack of buttermilk pancakes and Jack a western omelet with a pot of coffee. He'd been up late last night, poring through the *Compendium*. No luck on finding another Kicker Man. Hadn't seen another mention of Q'qr either. He'd leafed all the way through, but had barely scratched the surface of the text.

"Three kids in three states. How many towns did this guy alley cat through? How many more little Jonahs are running around?"

Levy shrugged. "Who knows? I'd love to find out. Turns out your client scores as high as her two half brothers—they make an unholy trio of oDNA carriers."

"So she could explode at any minute too?"

"Doubtful. She doesn't have the trigger gene."

Jack eyed him. "You said you couldn't discuss this over the phone. You could have simply said, 'Yep, Jonah's the daddy.' Must be something else is going on."

"There is. I—"

The waitress—a lot younger and tons better looking than Sally from

Moishe's—brought their orders. Jack watched fascinated as Levy drowned his pancakes in syrup and tore into them.

"Hungry? Haven't eaten since, oh, maybe the Depression?"

Levy swallowed a huge mouthful. "My wife's on this low-carb kick."

"I thought low carb's fifteen minutes were over."

"Not in my house. You can get scrambled egg whites and turkey sausage for breakfast—and it's not as bad as it sounds—but finding a piece of bread for toast is like searching for a pot of gold."

"So you make up for it when you're out."

"Better believe it."

Jack worked on his omelet awhile as Levy gobbled, then he ran out of patience.

"You said there's more. Give."

Levy leaned back. "Going on the assumption that the hair and the envelope came from the same woman, I had some folks at the agency run her prints."

"As expected."

"I discovered some interesting things about your client."

Uh-oh.

"Such as?"

"She was born Moonglow Garber."

"Moonglow?"

Christy had said her mother was weird, but Moonglow . . . sheesh.

"Raised by a single mother—just like her half brothers. Without the trigger gene she was pretty much like everybody else. Had an uneventful childhood up until somewhere around her eighteenth birthday when she disappeared for four weeks."

"Disappeared where?"

"Not known. According to police records she wouldn't say anything except that she'd been traveling around. Her mother had filed a missing person report and that was how Moonglow's prints got into the system."

"Find anything on the father of her baby?"

Levy shook his head. "No, but my guess is those four lost weeks were spent with him—she gave birth to a daughter nine months later."

"Dawn."

"Yes. Dawn Pickering."

"Wait. Is that the father's name?"

"It's a good possibility. Moonglow Garber had her name legally changed to Christy Pickering three months before the baby was born."

Jack could see her dumping the Moonglow, but why change the Garber unless she wanted her baby to have her father's name?

"So I suppose a search for Pickerings is on."

"In a desultory way. It's hardly high priority with the agency, but the good news is it's not a common name."

"Yeah? Somehow it rings a bell."

"You know a Pickering?"

"I don't know. I don't think so. It just sounds familiar."

"You don't think you could have known the father, do you?" He laughed. "Now that would be a coincidence."

"I don't believe in coincidences."

"Really? That's too bad, because you'll never guess where your client grew up."

"You're right. I won't."

"Atlanta, Georgia."

Jack felt a tightening across his shoulders.

"Was she there when . . . ?"

Levy was nodding. "When Jeremy Bolton was doing his dirty work. Do you think—?"

"She knew him? I asked her just yesterday if the guy she thinks is Jerry Bethlehem could be someone from her past. She says no, and I believe she's telling the truth."

"But she could be wrong. She and Bolton could have crossed paths somewhere when they were kids. It's just too much of a coincidence to think that this half brother of hers, who was in Atlanta when she was, should make a beeline for her daughter as soon as we lengthen his leash."

"No coincidence at all. He was looking for her. Or at least Thompson was."

Levy dropped his fork. "What?"

Jack explained what he'd found in the notebook.

Levy looked dazed. "He had his brother *looking* for her?"

"So it would appear. Last night I was asking myself why he was seeking out Dawn Pickering, but now it's even more complicated: Why was he seeking out his niece—or half-niece or whatever she is. To have an affair with her? It's sick. And for the record, Christy's never seen Hank Thompson before either."

Levy shook his head as if to clear it. "Three half siblings in a maze of interconnections that don't seem to go anywhere. I wonder what it all means, if anything."

"Maybe your people can look into it."

"Not without a more compelling reason than simple curiosity. If the answers don't impact on the clinical trial, they won't care to know."

"Swell."

That left Jack with the task of telling Christy Moonglow Garber Pickering that the guy dating her daughter was a close blood relative. Would she believe him? He doubted it.

"I'll need proof when I lay this on Christy."

Levy frowned. "I don't know what you mean."

"A lab printout saying in plain English that Bolton—or rather Bethlehem—and Christy have the same father."

"Dear God, I can't do that! The result is from Creighton's lab. No one can know Creighton is involved. It would mean my head—literally!"

"Can't you just white out the Creighton part?"

"That's not going to help you. No names are mentioned on the report. The specimens are referred to by number only."

"Well, can't you put names in? Not Bolton, of course—use Bethlehem instead."

"The computer won't accept names in the specimen ID fields. Of course you can say the numbers refer to Bethlehem and Mrs. Pickering."

"Nah, that's not going to convince Dawn that she's dating her uncle. The numbers could mean anybody."

Damn. Jack needed *something*. Even if Christy believed him—and that might not be an easy sell—she'd want to be able to prove it to Dawn.

He pointed his fork at Levy. "Look. Christy's trying to split up Bolton and her daughter. Simply dropping the brother bomb won't be enough. It's not going to mean a thing without documentation."

Christy had already derailed her own credibility with Dawn. Coming up with a wild story about Bethlehem being a blood relative but then being unable to prove it would not put it back on track.

Levy said, "If you want to help split them up, find a way to put Bolton back under lock and key."

"Easier said than done."

Especially when Jack had to work from the wings. Whatever happened to Bolton had to look like bad luck.

"Let's just say he's exposed. Where does that land you folks at Creighton?"

Levy shrugged. "All part of a government program. The fallout is the agency's problem. They'll handle it. They're good at that." He leaned forward. "Look, if you want documentation, let Mrs. Pickering drop the brother bomb, as you call it, and then challenge Bolton to prove she's lying. They can go to any commercial lab and run a paternity test. It will show they both have the same father. That way, you're out of it and so is Creighton."

Yeah, but would any of this be enough to break them up? Jack doubted it. He had a feeling it was going to take a lot more. Something really major.

But what?

3

"Come on now, darlin. You know you want to know."

"I *do* know. You had a vasectomy so it can't be."

They stood in the upstairs bathroom. Jeremy waved the home pregnancy test kit before her eyes like a hypnotist. He'd picked it up about an hour ago at the local Duane Reade. Now he had to convince Dawn to use it.

"Wouldn't be the first time something went wrong with a vasectomy."

Tears rimmed her baby blues as they fixed on the package like it was a cobra or something.

"You're starting to scare me, Jerry."

"Don't be scared now. Just get a little pee and see." He grinned. "Hear that? I'm a poet. Come on now—pee and see."

She snatched the package from his hand and pushed him toward the door.

"All right, all right! But you're not watching me pee. Nobody watches me pee."

He put on a hurt expression. "Not even me?"

"Especially you. Now get out of here while I do my business."

Jeremy stepped back and let her close the door. As soon as the latch clicked he raised his fists and punched the air.

Yes! It was gonna be positive. Had to be.

He waited, pacing like an expectant father. Hell, in a way he was an expectant father—father to be. He hoped.

His pits were soaked, his palms were so wet they were gonna start dripping soon. His whole life had been pointed toward this moment. Had some unexpected detours along the way—Creighton being one hell of a detour—but here he was, right where he was meant to be. But had he done what he was meant to do?

He waited near the door till he heard a flush inside, then backed away. Dawn came out holding a little wand, staring at it.

"It says we've got to wait. It turns either red or blue. If it turns blue . . ." Her voice choked off.

"What?"

"Blue is yes." She shook her head. "I don't believe I'm doing this. I . . . oh, shit!" She dropped the wand and buried her face in her hands. "Oh-shit-oh-shit-oh-*shit!*"

Jeremy swooped down and picked it up: Blue.

Yes!

He felt suddenly boneless. He leaned against the wall. He needed to sit down. But the feeling lasted only a few seconds. Then a wild mix of joy and pride exploded within, energizing him.

He'd done it! He'd damn fuck done it! He'd completed the touchiest, most difficult—and therefore the most important—part of Daddy's Plan. He wanted to run and tell Hank, wanted to jump around and whoop and scream in a crazy victory dance. But he resisted. Plenty of time for both later. Right now he had to deal with Dawn.

"There, there, darlin'," he said, slipping his arms around her and holding her tight against him. "No need to cry. We should be celebratin'."

She looked up at him with a blotchy, tear-streaked face. She wasn't a beauty to begin with, but she looked downright homely now. But looks didn't matter in this case. All that mattered right now was what she was carrying inside her.

"Celebrating? I'm *pregnant*! This wasn't supposed to happen!"

"Look at it this way: It's a miracle."

"No, it's a mistake, that's what it is. The test's got to be wrong."

"Yeah, you're probably right."

But Jeremy knew different. He knew all about pregnancy tests. He'd used them before, lots of them. But that had been pre-Creighton. These new ones were much better and accurate much earlier. Lots fewer false negatives.

Dawn backed away a step and wiped her face.

"I'm going down to the drug store and pick up a different kind—no, *two* different kinds. And then we'll see." Jeremy watched her shake her fists in the air just like he'd done minutes before, but with a different feeling. "I can't *believe* this!"

Jeremy kept his voice calm. "Worse things in the world, darlin'."

She stared at him with narrowed eyes. "Hey, wait a minute! Is this the same guy who told me he got a vasectomy because he didn't want to bring kids into this screwed-up world?"

"Yes, I did. I surely did. And I really and truly felt that way. But all that changed when I met you."

Her face softened. "Oh . . . that's so sweet. But I can't be pregnant! I just can't!"

You are, Dawnie-babes. You are.

"Maybe not," he told her. "But if you are, don't you think it's like a miracle?" She opened her mouth to reply but he rushed on. "I mean, don't you see the hand of god in this?"

"If you're talking about a virgin birth, I've got news for you—"

"No, I mean, you believe in god, don't you?"

He knew she did. Jeremy didn't. At least not in her god.

"Of course."

"Well, then, you can almost see his hand in this, can't you. I never wanted to have kids, then I meet you and start wishing I hadn't had a vasectomy because we're so perfect together and you'd make such a great mother, and now look what's happened."

"I'm not pregnant!" She started crying again. "I can't be! I'm not ready! And then there's the game—"

He hugged her tighter. "That's the great thing about software, darlin. You can do it from home."

She pulled away and headed for the stairs.

"I'm going down to the drugstore. When I get back we'll do it again, and then you'll see."

No, Dawn. *You'll* see.

And then would come the tough part. Once she was convinced she was pregnant he had to work on her to get behind having the baby and want it as much as he did.

Yeah, well, she'd never want it that much, and he could never *ever* tell her the whole story—man, would she freak!—but he'd have to convince her how special this baby was going to be.

That might not be so easy, but hell, she'd bought into everything else he'd told her. Why not that?

But more important, he had to keep an eye on Dawn, stay with her, watch her every minute. He had to protect the baby.

4

"Laurie! A round for the house! On me!"

Jack had been sitting in Work and sipping a draft pint while pretending to read a copy of *Kick*. He looked up and glanced around at the sound of Bolton's voice.

He'd been starting to think he'd been wasting his time, that Bolton would be persona non grata here after the fight, but apparently he wasn't the type to be easily deterred.

One good way to assuage hard feelings was to buy a round for the house.

Bolton had a distinctly unhappy-looking Dawn in tow. He spotted Jack on his way by, nodded, but didn't stop. Now he stood surveying the room as the two dozen or so habitués bellied up to the bar for a freebie.

Jack stayed where he was, watching Dawn. She stood at his side, holding a cola of some sort and looking embarrassed and red-eyed, as if she'd been crying. Trouble in paradise? If so, and if he could find out what it was, maybe—

"All right, everybody," Bolton said, holding a bottle of Bud aloft. "I want you all to meet my lady, Dawn."

Dawn's face reddened as the crowd murmured ragged hellos.

"I just want to let all of you know that today Dawn has made me the happiest man in the world."

Oh, shit. They're getting married? Christy would—

"Because today I found out that she's going to make me a daddy!"

Dawn turned crimson as everyone shouted their congratulations. Jack could only stare at the beaming Bolton as he lifted his glass higher.

"To Dawn!"

The crowd echoed the words and drank—all except Jack and Dawn. Her expression said loud and clear that she wasn't into this pregnancy. He had a feeling she'd be even less into it when she learned the father of her baby was her uncle.

And Christy . . . if he'd thought she'd go ballistic at the idea of a wedding, she'd be off the charts with the pregnancy, especially when she learned—

Then he noticed a grinning Bolton coming his way, dragging Dawn by the hand.

"Hey, Joe? Y'hear?"

"Sure did." Jack raised his glass and let Bolton clink his against it. "Congrats, man. And to you too, young lady." Dawn only nodded.

Bolton said, "This here's Joe Henry, darlin. Met him the other day. He's a gamer and a good one too."

"Pleased to meet you," Jack said. The next words resisted being spoken but Jack forced them out: "With you two as parents you gotta know it's gonna be a beautiful baby."

Pardon me while I find a shovel.

"More than beautiful—special. Special in so many, many ways." He pointed to the book lying on the table in front of Jack. "He'll never have to be dissimilated because he'll never be assimilated. A kick-ass Kicker from the git-go."

Jack tapped the stick figure on the cover. "Right on!"

"Ain't you finished that yet? You must be a slow reader."

"I'm studying every word. I can't tell you how much I'm enjoying it."

Jack glanced at Dawn's midsection. He now understood the "project," the "mission" Bolton had mentioned. Was this the "Key" he'd spoken of?

He shifted his gaze to Bolton himself and wondered what the hell was going on in his head. Then he finished his beer and rose to his feet.

"Wish I could hang around for the party, Jerry, but I've got places I've gotta be."

"Sure I can't buy you another beer?"

"Have to take a rain check."

Jack's plan had been to meet up with Bolton here and hang with him in an attempt to find out what he was up to and where he thought he was headed . . . glean a little more info before his meeting with Christy. The impending-fatherhood announcement had made that unnecessary.

It also had made Jack dread seeing Christy.

But he had an important call to make before he met her.

5

"Are you on a cell phone?" Levy said when he came on the line.

Jack leaned against the side of an open booth on Queens Boulevard. It had taken him a long time to find a public phone. They used to be everywhere. Now . . .

"I'm in one of the last telephone booths in Queens. Just listen. You know the fellow we're interested in—the one dating the young girl?"

Levy's tone was cautious. "Yes."

"Well, she's pregnant, and our friend is the father."

A pause, then a gasp. "Dear God, if she inherited her mother's . . ." He seemed to be searching for a code word, a neutral term, anything but oDNA. "Her mother's . . ."

"Special sauce?"

"We're not talking about a hamburger!"

"In a way, we are."

An exasperated sigh. "I don't believe this. Very well. If she inherited her mother's special sauce, and that combines with our friend's special sauce, then—"

"Then we wind up with one *hell* of a Big Mac."

"Yes . . . yes, we do."

"That's got to be what he's been looking to do all along: create a super sauce."

"You think this is intentional?"

"He went looking for this particular girl. What else can I think? This is kind of scary."

"Yes and no. Here's the thing: The girl might not have inherited her mother's special sauce. You don't inherit a carbon copy of your mother's genome; only half. The other half comes from your father. So there's always a chance the girl is sauce free."

"Unless, of course, the girl's father was heavy on the sauce."

"Yes. In that case the odds of inheriting a large portion of the sauce increase dramatically. *Dramatically.* You must learn who the father was and where we can find him."

"And if I do?"

"Then you obtain a sample of his, um, sauce and we find out what we're dealing with."

"And if I can't?"

"Then get a sample of the girl's so we can see how much she's carrying. If she missed out, then the experiment was a failure—thank God."

Something in Levy's tone bothered Jack.

"You sound upset."

"I am. There's genetic manipulation going on here—it's old-fashioned, barnyard-style breeding, but genetic manipulation nonetheless—and I want to know why. Someone has a purpose here, and I want to know what it is. Because that special sauce is potentially explosive. It's TNT, which is dangerous enough. But this makes me start to think that someone has spent generations trying to make an atom bomb."

To blow up what? Jack wondered. Who or what was the target?

6

"No!" Christy cried, feeling her heart leap into her throat. "That's not possible!"

They sat together on the front seat of her Mercedes, parked along the northern end of Meadow Lake, a peaceful haven hunkered between the roaring ribbons of the LIE, Grand Central Parkway, and the Van Wyck Expressway. Jack had thought it better if he stayed away from her house. He'd said Bolton, and now Dawn, knew what he looked like and either of them seeing him entering or leaving Christy's house would greatly complicate the investigation.

He'd said he had news, but she never dreamed . . . Jerry Bethlehem . . . her half brother? It was crazy!

"I'm afraid it's true."

She studied Jack's face. Was he up to something? Pulling some sort of sleazy scam?

But no. She sensed genuine reluctance in him. He hadn't wanted to be the one to tell her.

Her tongue tasted like tin.

"But . . . how?"

"The usual way, I assume."

Not funny.

"No, damn it! Where did you find out? *How* did you find out? And why did you even check?"

"I knew from my talk with Bethlehem at Work the other day that his father's name was Jonah and that he had one eye."

That rocked her. One eye . . . her father had worn an eye patch. At least that was what she'd been told. But millions of people had lost an eye.

"So?"

"When I spoke to you yesterday you said your mother told you your father was swallowed by a whale."

And there it was, smacking her in the face.

"Oh, God . . . Jonah."

He nodded. "Yeah. And since, as I told you, I was looking for some sort of connection between you and Bethlehem, that sent up a bright red flare."

"But you never said anything."

"Because I thought it was such a long shot, I didn't dare. Otherwise you'd have been looking at me like you were a moment ago—ready to call the booby squad."

"But how did you get a sample of—?"

"You left some hair behind at Julio's."

"And Bethlehem?"

"I snagged a spoon from Work."

She couldn't be certain but he seemed a little less sure of himself than before. Was that true? Could you get a DNA sample from a used spoon?

"I still can't believe this. Where's the lab report?"

He looked out the window. "I don't have it."

"What? Then how do you know?"

"Verbal confirmation. Hard copy will follow, but that won't help you. The samples are numbered on the report for confidentiality. Some sort of law."

"Then it could be a mistake."

It *had* to be a mistake.

He looked at her now. "The guy who did the test told me flat-out that the two specimens I gave him came from people with the same father but different mothers."

Christy closed her eyes and held her breath to keep from sobbing. This was getting worse and worse.

"How can something like this happen? I mean, what are the odds of my half brother coming to town and just happening to pick up on—?" She jolted upright and stared at him. "Unless he knows! Oh, Jesus, do you think he knows?"

"I'm almost sure he does. The odds of this happening by accident are astronomical."

"But why? I knew he was bent, but what possible reason could he have for dating his niece?"

"It has to be something in your past. And since you don't know Bethlehem, the only thing I can think of is some beef with Dawn's father."

No-no-no! she thought. Don't go there! Oh, please don't go there!

"Impossible."

"He could be getting even for something."

"By . . ." The word *fucking* sprang to mind but she couldn't bring herself to say it, not when it concerned Dawn. "By going with his own niece?"

"He's a twisted SOB. Who knows what's going on in his head. But the only way I can help you find out is by learning about her father."

"No!"

He looked annoyed and she could understand that. But she couldn't tell him.

"Come on, Christy. Who was he? Was he involved when you disappeared for those weeks?"

She looked at him. "How did you—?" Then she stopped and nodded. "Oh, right. You're a detective. But you're supposed to be investigating Jerry Bethlehem, not me."

"Just putting together all the pieces of this jigsaw you handed me. Now . . . what about those weeks? Was he involved?"

"Forget it. I don't even want to think about him. It was a terrible—it was the *worst* time in my life."

"It was bad for everyone in Atlanta around then. The abortionist assassinations, the—"

The abortionist assassinations? Why was he bringing them up?

The missing weeks, the killings, a brother she'd never known existed . . . too much. Panic blossomed, shutting off her air. Her heart rattled about in her chest, she couldn't breathe, the car was shrinking, closing in on her, pressing Jack closer until—

She yanked on the door handle, pushed it open, and scrambled out.

"Christy!"

"Leave me alone!"

She stumbled, found her feet, and began to run toward the lake.

7

Jack sat frozen, staring as Christy ran thirty or forty yards straight away across the grass to stop by a huge willow. She leaned against the trunk for a few heartbeats, then sank to her knees, sobbing.

He hopped out and hurried toward her. Out of the corner of his eye he saw a couple of old biddies out walking their dogs stop and stare.

Had to play it careful here. Didn't want any 911 calls about a domestic dispute going down in public.

When he reached Christy he squatted close but didn't touch her. He hesitated, unsure of what to say. What was up here? He decided the last thing he should do right now was push.

"If you don't want to talk about him, you don't have to." He glanced at the two biddies who were still watching. "But whatever you decide, let's get back to the car."

She wiped her eyes and looked at him, then nodded. Jack rose and held his hand out to her. She took it and he pulled her to her feet. As she and Jack walked side by side to the car, the biddies turned away and continued their stroll.

Back inside the Mercedes, Jack kept mum as he watched Christy and waited, mentally spurring her to spill. Finally . . .

"Why did you mention the Atlanta abortionist assassinations?"

Jack thought about that and didn't have a ready answer. All her problems revolved around Jeremy Bolton, the assassin, so he supposed it must have been running through his mind.

"I . . . when I was backgrounding you, it was the big story of the times in Atlanta."

"Well, I had nothing to do with killing anybody."

Why would she think he'd even consider that?

"I never thought you did."

"Yeah, well, for a while there the cops weren't so sure."

Jack stared at her. "You were a suspect?"

"I . . . I was connected to those doctors."

"Golden and Dalton?"

"You know their names?"

"Told you, I've been looking for someone from your past. What about the guy who killed them?"

She blinked. "Jeremy Bolton?"

"Now who's got the good memory."

She loosed a harsh laugh. "Oh, I'll never forget that name. When the cops finally caught him and found no connection between us, they lost all interest in me."

Jack hesitated. His next question might touch a nerve.

"You don't have to answer this but I've got to ask: Did you have abortions from the dead docs?"

She stared straight ahead. "No."

Something about the change in her tone . . . was she telling the truth?

"Being a murder suspect . . ." He shook his head. "That must be rough. That why you said it was the worst time in your life?"

"That . . . and other things."

"Dawn's father?"

"He's off-limits."

Remembering the last time he'd pushed her, Jack backed off.

"Well, if you change your mind, let me know so I can see where he fits in this puzzle."

"Believe me, he doesn't fit anywhere."

"What about the name change? Why did Moonglow Garber become Christy Pickering?"

"You're really on top of things, aren't you. Pretty damn thorough for so short a time."

"Just trying to give you your money's worth," Jack said without mentioning that someone else had done all the investigating.

"Well, the name change is my business."

"Another secret?"

She looked at him. "No. Just something I choose not to share."

Jack nodded. She was wound tight—maybe too tight. He decided to leave out the pregnancy part for now—it wasn't going to affect his course of action and it might drive Christy over the edge.

But since she wouldn't talk about Dawn's father, that put a sample of the mystery man's DNA out of reach. Levy's second choice was a sample of Dawn's. Jack had to figure a way to get it without triggering a barrage of questions. After a moment he came up with what he hoped was a plausible story.

He touched Christy's arm. "Did Dawn leave anything behind that might be carrying some of her DNA?"

She looked at him with an alarmed expression. "Why?"

"Let's see how close she and Bethlehem are—genetically, that is. Maybe the chance of birth defects—"

"Birth defects? Oh God, don't even think about her being pregnant!"

Jack took her reaction as proof his instincts had been right.

"You're the one who told me they were having sex."

"Yes, but *pregnant*?"

"One tends to follow the other."

"I can't even think about it."

"Well, then, think about this: You need to show her something. I have Bethlehem's DNA on file at the lab. If I can get some of Dawn's for a comparison, who knows . . . ? Maybe it'll change her mind, or at least give her second thoughts about getting too cozy with that close a relative."

Christy said nothing for a while, then nodded. "I'm sure I saw a hairbrush in one of her drawers after she left. Will that do?"

"Just fine."

"Then let's not waste any more time."

8

Jack sat in his car near the lake and waited. Christy had wanted to drive him over to her house to retrieve the brush but Jack had nixed that for the same reason he'd met her here today.

While waiting, he'd called Levy and told him Dawn's father was a no go but he'd have the girl's hair soon. Jack had expected an argument, with Levy wanting to put him off till tomorrow, but he'd jumped on Jack's suggestion to meet again at the Argonaut.

Levy seemed really into this possibility of a super-oDNA kid.

Jack closed his eyes and untethered his thoughts, letting them take random bounces.

Christy's panic attack . . . what had triggered it? His mention of the abortionist assassinations? Or something else?

She'd said she'd been "connected" to the two dead docs? What did that mean?

He let it all hang out and cooked up the wildest scenario he could imagine: Had they performed abortions on her and left her so wracked with guilt that she'd killed them?

No. He'd learned the hard way to judge character, and he just couldn't see Christy as a cold-blooded killer.

Then again, Levy said Thompson had told him Bolton was framed. What if it was true? What if Christy had been involved in the frame and now he was getting back at her?

But the cops and probably the feds as well had investigated her and cleared her. And, for whatever it was worth, she couldn't have known Bolton—he'd changed since going to the lockup, but not so much that she wouldn't recognize him as Jerry Bethlehem, beard or no.

He shook his head, baffled. This was making him crazy.

And making him even crazier was this idea of a super-oDNA kid. Clearly someone had designed this situation, but to what end?

And who? The mysterious Jonah Stevens? Who was Jonah Stevens? He pops up out of nowhere, does a Johnny Appleseed thing with his sperm, and dies—supposedly.

But did he die? With no body to exhume, who could be sure he was really dead, or even who he'd said he was?

He could have been Rasalom.

Jack shifted in his seat. Now *there* was a discomfiting thought: the Otherness's agent on Earth spreading some sort of toxic seed in the hope of creating a child to—what? Wake up everyone's oDNA and start Armageddon?

Was that the Plan? Was that what Bolton had meant by *the comin of the Key to the future . . . a new world*?

By "new" did he mean Otherness dominated?

Rasalom had been mounting attacks on multiple fronts to bring the Otherness to this sphere. Was the super-oDNA kid one of those fronts?

Up ahead he saw Christy's car approaching. She stopped next to him, driver to driver, and rolled down her window.

"Got it."

She handed him the brush. He checked it and saw plenty of hair wound in the bristles.

"I only need ten or so strands."

Christy shrugged. "Take the whole thing. It's old."

He looked at her. "Feeling better?"

She nodded. "Yeah, I think so. When do you think you'll have the results?"

"I'm going to get this rolling tonight. If all goes well I'll have some ammunition for you by tomorrow."

Her eyebrows rose. "Tomorrow? I've heard it takes weeks. Who do you know?"

He gave her what he hoped was a sly smile. "Low friends in high places."

9

When Christy got home and found Dawn's car parked in the driveway, her heart started thumping. Had she had a fight with that man? Had they split? She prayed the bastard hadn't hurt her. If he'd laid one finger on her—

She rushed into the house, calling, "Dawnie?"

Dawn came down the stairs and stood before her. She carried a full duffel bag. Moving more of her stuff out? She looked no worse for wear—no tears, no bruises, no quivering lower lip. She stared at Christy with a disappointed expression.

"I was totally hoping to get in and get out without a scene."

Christy's heart fell. "So, you're not back."

"I'm so not. Maybe someday I'll forgive you for trying to buy him off, but it's going to take a while."

Christy opened her arms and moved toward her. She wanted to take her little girl in her arms and beg her to come back, but Dawn sidestepped her.

"All right," Christy said. "I admit that was a bad move on my part. I regret it."

Dawn shook her head. "Why? Because it totally didn't work?"

Exactly!

But she couldn't say that. Could she say anything about the blood relationship? No. She wasn't convinced herself. She'd have to keep mum until she had proof. So she tried to lighten things up.

She held out her hand. "That's fifty cents you owe me."

Dawn simply stared.

Christy forced a smile. "Come on. Two totallies: fifty cents."

Dawn shook her head again. "That's so over, Mom. But speaking of money, where is it? Do you still have the cash?"

Oh, damn. She'd been so involved in this mess that she hadn't returned it to the bank. Tomorrow . . . tomorrow for sure.

"Yes. Why?"

"I want to see what it looks like."

Christy didn't know where this was going but decided to play along. Anything to keep her here a little longer. She hurried upstairs to her room, pulled the bag from the bottom drawer of her dresser, and returned to the first floor. Without a word she handed it to Dawn.

Dawn took it, reached inside, and removed a few stacks of bills. She stared at them, then looked at Christy with tears in her eyes.

"This is what you thought I was worth?"

"Oh, God, no! You're priceless to me. I thought that would be more than you were worth to *him*."

"But you were totally wrong, weren't you."

Christy remembered something Jack had said.

"Maybe he has another agenda more important than money."

"Like what?"

"I don't know, but I intend to find out."

Dawn's face hardened as she crammed the bills back into the bag and shoved it at Christy.

"What? Another detective?"

"Yes. And he's learned a few things."

Dawn pushed past her on her way to the door.

"He'll have to go some to beat the first's whoppers."

Christy didn't want to say it but it slipped out.

"He's your uncle, Dawn!"

Dawn stopped and did a slow turn. She looked stunned.

"*What?*"

"He's my half brother. I never knew he existed."

Her face twisted. "You expect me to believe that?"

"Sadly, no, I don't. But it's true. Not only is he a dangerous, violent man and old enough to be your father, but he's your uncle!"

"You're just jealous because you have no man in your life and I do! And did you ever think that maybe I'm with a guy old enough to be my father because I never had one and my mother *won't tell me a fucking thing about him?*" She screamed the last words.

Christy felt her heart breaking but she kept her voice calm. They'd been through this a million times over the course of Dawn's life. Time to remove the sugar coating without telling her the whole truth.

"Your father has never wanted anything to do with you or me. What more do you need to know?"

Truth. He wouldn't even know of Dawn's existence.

"I'd like to hear that from him."

"Well, then, you'll have to find him. His last contact with me was before you were born. I have no idea where he is."

True.

She shook her head. "Why do you hate him so?"

"I don't. He gave me you."

True again.

Dawn's expression softened for a moment. "He married you and dumped you. That's totally cold, I know, but . . ."

More than cold—pure fiction. She'd never married and the supposed husband and father—Dennis Pickering—never existed. She'd never even met a Dennis Pickering, let alone married him.

But she'd keep that to herself . . . forever.

She took a step closer to Dawn.

"Stay for dinner?"

She backed up a step. "Can't. I'm still too pissed about the money. And this uncle thing just makes it worse. Prove it."

"I can't right now."

She rolled her eyes. "Mom! You must think I'm totally stupid!"

"I know you're very bright." Something Jack had said clicked in her mind. "I don't expect you to believe me. I hardly believe it myself. So prove me wrong. Take some of your hair and some of his hair and give them to the lab of your choice—I'll even pay for the test—and have them run a check on how similar they are. If I'm wrong, the laugh will be on me."

Dawn's face reddened as she yanked open the front door.

"You think I'm going to totally insult him by asking him to prove he's not my uncle? Forget it!" She turned on the front step and pointed at Christy. "Better get used to him, Mom. He's the father of your grandchild!"

With that she turned and ran to her car.

Christy wanted to chase after her, but her body wouldn't respond.

Oh no! Oh, please, God, NO!

10

Jerry rubbed a hand over his mouth. "She really told you I'm your uncle?"

Dawn couldn't tell if he was amused or totally pissed. She'd watched him carefully while she told him and his face had been like stone throughout the whole thing.

"Yeah, but she's lying, right? I mean, it's totally not possible, right?"

He slashed the air with a hand. "It's completely impossible! Where does she get these ideas? Has she always been a loon?"

Normally Dawn would so get on the case of anyone who called her mom a name. But this was different. This time Mom *was* acting loony.

"No, but you and me . . . it's like unhinged her."

He looked totally upset as he began stalking back and forth across the room.

"Unhinged, hell! She's lost it! First she says I killed one guy and kidnapped somebody else. Now—" He stopped short and stared at her. "Did she have any kind of proof—bogus proof?"

Dawn shook her head. "No. She said she couldn't prove it."

"Well, well, well. If nothing else, your momma is consistent. No proof I killed someone, and no proof I'm her brother."

"Half brother."

His face hardened as he waved a hand. "Makes no difference. This has gotta stop."

He stepped to the closet and pulled out his jacket. Dawn grabbed his arm.

"Where are you going?"

"To see your momma."

"Bad idea, Jerry—*totally* bad. If you've got to talk to her, call her on the phone."

"I do better in person, darlin. You know that. I want some face time with her to warn her about spreadin any more of her shit."

"Don't do anything . . ."

He looked at her. "What? Stupid? Like making a scene and throwin things?" He shook his head. "I'm just gonna let her know that if she keeps this up, she'll be hearin from my lawyer."

He kissed her, hugged her, then he was on his way. She watched him stride out the front door, slamming it behind him.

What a mess. What a mad, godawful mess.

She felt a sob building as she thought about how totally she'd screwed up. Pregnant! She did so not want to be pregnant. She didn't want to be a mother—not yet, at least. The idea terrified her. Maybe later on she'd be ready to be totally responsible for another person, but now? No way. She could barely take care of herself. She had some living to do before motherhood.

But Jerry . . . Jerry was *so* into this baby.

She thought about how he'd danced around this morning when the other tests she'd bought all came out positive. Kept saying how it was a miracle and how the stars had aligned to make this happen and how it was meant to be and talking crazy about destiny and the baby ruling the world. And always "he" when he referred to it. Why not "she"?

He quieted down later, but he'd been just as happy, dragging her out to Work to celebrate, wandering around the place grinning like a drunk.

Like a drunk . . . Jerry all of a sudden wanted her to be a teetotaler. Not even a beer. Well, fuck that bullshit.

She went to the kitchen and pulled a can of Bud from the refrigerator. But as she reached for the tab she stopped.

Could alcohol really hurt a baby? She'd heard that, but was it true? Maybe she'd better investigate first. She didn't know what she was going to do about the baby yet, but if she decided to keep him—she was sounding like Jerry now—she didn't want to cause any birth defects.

She returned the beer to the fridge.

Shit. This pregnancy thing totally sucked.

11

"Hearin from my lawyer," Jeremy said as he drove along. "Yeah, that'll be the day."

He shook his head in disgust. Why couldn't things go smoothly just once? Just *once*. The day had started out so great, and now it was turning to shit. Goddammit, why couldn't Moonglow mind her own goddamn business?

Okay, okay, her kid *was* her business, but couldn't she just lay off? And where was she getting all this info? Who'd have thought anyone would be looking at his DNA.

The world had turned into a science fiction movie during his time on the inside.

He needed to talk to someone. He picked up his cell and thumbed Hank's number.

"Yeah?"

"It's me. Remember that good news I had for you this morning? Well, here's a little bad to go with it: Someone told Moonglow that I'm her half brother."

"Shit! Who?"

"Don't know. The detective she hired, I guess. But who's feeding *him*? I got a feeling it's someone from our old living quarters, if you know what I mean."

"I know what you mean, but it doesn't have to be. DNA testing is done everywhere these days. Hair, a little saliva—hey, you watch CSI. *You should know that."*

Jeremy knew, but a picture of Doc Levy kept popping into his head.

"One thing I do know is we don't want anyone doing any more, do we?"

"Sure as hell don't."

"Well, if it ain't the folks upstate, then it's the detective she hired. I'm on my way to Moonglow's place now and—"

"Are you crazy? She's got it in for you. You go in there and she could beat herself up and say you attacked her. Then where'll you be?"

Jeremy had thought of that. Moonglow—*Christy*, damn it! Calling her

Moonglow would botch everything. Christy didn't seem the type to pull something like that, but anything was possible.

Still, he needed a face-to-face to get a line on this detective of hers. And thought he had a way to pull it off.

"I'll be careful—real careful. But I hope I can count on you for some backup if I need it, bro."

A long pause on the other end, then, *"I'll do what I can, man, but I've got other obligations."*

Jeremy's hands tightened on the wheel. Hank and his fucking Kickers. Jeremy loved the Kicker idea of dissimilation, but there had to be a limit. You had to have priorities. The two of them had already had a couple of arguments about this—damn near came to blows one time—but Hank didn't want to risk getting his hands dirty with anything, even if it meant backing off from Daddy's Plan. Way back when, he'd promised to do his part, but then when the time came he'd welshed. Said his Kickers were an adjunct to the Plan. Adjunct . . . Mr. Writer-man.

"Fuck your fucking obligations, this is crucial."

"I told you—I'll do what I can."

"Yeah, right."

He cut the connection and bounced the phone off the passenger window.

Hank . . . useless piece of crap. Oh, yeah, he'd been all full of praise and compliments this morning when Jeremy had told him about the baby, saying stuff like, *"You da man, Jeremy! Told you you didn't need me. You da MAN!"*

Yeah, I'm the man all right. The only one of us who is.

12

Jeremy pressed Christy's front doorbell, then retreated to the bottom of the steps where he waited while the front lights came on. He saw her face peer through one of the sidelights, then the door opened. Slowly.

Christy stuck her head out, glanced at him with a worried expression, then looked around as if someone else might be hiding in the bushes.

Not likely. And not likely that he was coming within ten feet of her. Still plenty of light, easy for any nosy neighbor to see him standing out here in plain sight, not even in spitting distance.

"What are you doing here?" she said.

He looked up at her. "We need to talk."

"I have nothing to say to you."

"Yeah, you do. This bullsh—" He cut himself off. Some of the neighbors might be listening. He didn't want any calls going out to NYPD. Didn't want another run-in with them. "This craziness has got to stop. You just can't go around spreadin lies about me."

"Who says they're lies?"

"I do. And you know they are. You and me related—that's a laugh."

That was a whopper. Daddy had told him all about little Moonglow Garber when he was a kid.

Her mouth twisted in disgust. "It's anything but a laugh—it's a horror."

"There are laws against this kind of thing. I'd be suin you now for libel—"

"You mean 'slander.' Libel is in print."

"Whatever. You'd be hearin from my lawyer instead of me right now if you wasn't Dawn's mother. But this is the last time. This is your last free pass. Next time, we go to court."

She smiled. "Fine with me. The only way I can get hurt in court is if what I'm saying is untrue. And it's not, is it."

Bitch. How could Daddy have sired such a dumb cow?

Well, maybe not so dumb. She'd found out he was her half brother. No, wait. *She* didn't find out—her detective did. Jeremy had to get the name of this guy. Couldn't handle him like Gerhard—that, he admitted, had been stupid—but maybe he could get Vecca to pay him off.

"Who's feedin you all this crap?"

"A friend."

"The same guy who fed you that other line of bull?"

"Maybe."

"Tell me who he is. I need to have a heart-to-heart talk with him, straighten him out on a few matters."

Her mouth twisted. "Like you talked to Mike Gerhard?"

"I never heard of this Gerhard guy. Let me talk to your PI. Talk—nothin more. Just give me his name."

She laughed—*laughed*—then said, "You've *got* to be kidding."

Rage exploded in Jeremy—a white-hot burst of flame spreading from his chest into his limbs. He wanted nothing more than to run up these steps and wipe that smile—

She must have seen something in his face because her smile did disappear as she took a quick, small step back inside the door.

"You want to hit me, don't you."

The words struck like a bucket of ice water. Almost as if she'd read his mind. He looked down and saw his foot on the first step.

She stepped out again and gave him a contemptuous stare.

"Go ahead, *brother*. Do your worst."

Another explosion. Jeremy teetered on the edge of doing just that. This bitch had no idea what his worst could be. He started to raise his other foot to take the next step but stopped himself.

A voice in his head shouted, *No!*

That's exactly what she wants. She wants you to lose it and pound the shit out of her. Because then she'll have won. You can double-talk your way out of unsubstantiated accusations and lab reports, but take a few pokes at Dawn's momma here in public and you'll not only lose your freedom, but you'll lose Dawn as well. For good.

He backed off the step—damn near the hardest thing he'd ever done—and kept a calm expression as he looked up at her.

Maybe Daddy hadn't done such a bad job siring her. She'd done what she was supposed to: Birthed a baby girl and raised her and protected her. She was even ready to take a beating for her.

I take back the "cow" remark, Moonglow. You've grown into one hell of a woman.

And with that he felt something stir in his loins. He realized he wanted her—wanted to rip off those clothes and take her.

That too was off-limits. But it gave him an idea. A wonderful idea.

"This is getting us nowhere. Be warned. And be warned about somethin else. Dawn says she told you about the pregnancy. Well, if you ever hope to lay eyes on your grandson, even for a second, you'd better make the best of things as they are and leave us alone."

He took huge satisfaction in Moonglow's stricken expression as he turned away and sauntered toward his car.

13

"Well, did you tell her?" Dawn said when Jeremy stepped through the door. "Did she get the message?"

He put on an uncertain look. As before, he had to play this carefully. Even more carefully than the last time.

"I . . . I don't think so. I don't think she'll ever leave us be."

Dawn stepped closer, a concerned look on her face.

"What do you mean?"

Jeremy looked away. Now the touchy part. Had to hold back and let her think she was prying it out of him.

"Nothin."

"*Nothing*? Come on! You threatened her with a lawyer and what did she say?"

"It's not what she said. It's what she did."

"What, damn it!"

He loosed a long sigh. "I'm not sure how to tell you this . . . not sure I even want to."

"What do you mean?" Dawn took a step back. "She didn't try to hurt you, did she? Did she have her gun?"

Oh, this was perfect, perfect.

"I almost wish she had."

"What are you *saying*?"

Another sigh, then he turned and gave her a forlorn look as he hit her with the money shot.

"She came on to me."

The color drained from her face. *"What?"*

"I was afraid you wouldn't believe me. You thought I was lyin about her tryin to buy me off and—"

"No!" She waved her hands. "No, it's just—are you *sure*?"

"Well, she was wearin some sort of red robe that she took off and there she was, standin right in front of me bold as day in her birthday suit."

Jeremy knew about the robe from his explorations of the house the few times he and Dawn had had the place to themselves.

"No! She'd never! What did she say!"

"Nothin. But she knelt down in front of me and started pullin at my fly, and . . . and I guess that kind of said it all. I—"

Dawn waved her hands again. "Stop it! Stop it! I'm going to be sick!"

"I knew I shouldn't have told you."

"Ohmigod! But this is so not her. Mom's just not into that. I mean, she's gone out like maybe twice in the last two years."

Careful . . . careful . . . need just the right tone here . . .

"Maybe that explains it."

Dawn looked at him like a kid who's just been told there is no Santa Claus. "She stripped down right in front of you? That's so totally not my mom."

He decided to risk going out on a limb to add the finishing touch.

"I was floored myself. Did you know she's got this cute little butterfly tattoo"—he touched his lower abdomen, just below his belt line—"right here."

Dawn pressed her hands against her eyes. "Stop! I've seen it! I've seen it! Damn her!"

He slipped his arms around her.

"Go easy on her, darlin. She seems like a real confused woman. Don't be too mad at her."

"Too mad? Oh, I'm not too mad at her, because mad doesn't even come close. I'm like totally pissed out of my mind!" She bit her upper lip as she blinked away tears. "My own mother. I can't believe this."

"I'm so sorry, Dawn."

And for an instant he meant it. She was hurt, crushed. So although he wanted to take a run up to Vecca's and find out where this detective was getting his info, he couldn't leave Dawn right now.

She'd just had the rug pulled out from under her life. But Jeremy was going to give her a new rug—a Persian carpet.

14

The phone rang. Christy checked the caller ID and saw Dawn's number.

Now what? As much as she loved her daughter and wanted to speak to her, she had a feeling this would not be pleasant. Not after the way they'd parted this afternoon. Not after the smirk on that man's face as he'd left earlier.

After hesitating for a few heartbeats, she picked up.

Dawn . . . screaming incoherently . . .

Christy's heart climbed into her throat. Had something happened? Had he done something to her?

"Dawnie-Dawnie-Dawnie! What is it? Are you hurt?"

"Hurt?" she screeched. *"How can you ask that? I'm not hurt—I'm CRUSHED! My own mother! How could you DO that?"*

"Do what? What are you talking about?"

"You know damn fucking well what I'm talking about!" The screech broke off in a wrenching sob. *"How could you, Mom? How could you come on to Jerry like that? You of all people!"*

What? Come on to that man? Never in a million years!

"I don't under—"

"He told me all about it!"

The bastard! The sneaky, lying bastard!

"Then he's lying. I didn't even let him in the house!"

"No!" The screech again. *"YOU'RE lying! You took off your clothes right in front of him!"*

"I did no such thing!"

"STOP LYING! He told me about the butterfly! How else could he know about the butterfly if you weren't stripped down in front of him!"

Butterfly? What was she—?

Her tattoo—she'd got it on a crazy whim at seventeen . . . high . . . at the beach . . . wearing a bikini . . . going to a tattoo parlor with her friends . . . they all got inked . . .

But how did that man know about it?

She'd worry about that later. Right now she had to break through Dawn's hysteria. Christy struggled to keep her voice calm, her tone rational.

"It's all lies, Dawn. He's trying to make you hate and mistrust me. I didn't do anything like that. I never would! You *know* me better than that."

"I thought I did."

"You've known me for eighteen years and him for what—a few months? Who are you going to believe?"

"He knows about the butterfly, Mom! How else could he know about it?"

"I have no idea. Maybe he's been peeping on me or—"

"Stop it! You're crazy! STOP IT!"

And then the line went dead.

Christy tried to call back but Dawn wouldn't answer. She thought about going over there but decided against it. What would that accomplish? More screaming, more he-said, she-said, and Christy unable to explain how that man knew about her tattoo.

A chill ran over her skin. *Had* he been peeping on her?

But how? She never walked around undressed. The only time she was un-clothed was for a shower, and her bathroom was on the second floor and she kept the blinds drawn, so even if he climbed a tree—

A camera . . . he knew computers and video games . . . had he installed some sort of minicam in her bathroom? She'd read where they could be hidden in something as simple as a box of tissues.

It sounded so paranoid, but look at what that man had done in so short a time: He'd stolen Dawnie and turned her against her. Tonight's lie proved that nothing was beneath him.

She'd have to search her bedroom and bathroom inch by inch. But first . . .

She grabbed her phone and dialed Jack's number. She no longer wanted him as an investigator. She prayed he'd hire out to do something else—something more direct, more . . . final.

15

"Carb loading again?" Jack said as he sat down.

He'd arrived at the diner and found Levy's car in the lot, but no Levy. He checked inside and found him chowing down at a table for two along an inner wall.

Levy looked up from his platter of latkes and applesauce. "These are fabulous."

"Have I got a friend for you."

Jack hid his annoyance. He'd wanted to meet outside, give him the hairbrush, and be off. Now there'd be chit-chat and exhortations to join in on the eating. Jack wasn't hungry and in less of a chit-chatty mood than usual, which meant approaching zero.

A waitress showed up, older and not as pretty or perky as the last one, and asked what Jack was having.

"The latkes," Levy said. "I'm not kidding. They're loaded with little bits of onion and fried to perfection. You've got to try them."

Jack looked at the oily lumps of potato and decided to pass. He ordered coffee.

He slipped the brush out of his pocket and, touching only the bristles, slid it toward Levy along the rear edge of the table.

"This belongs to Dawn."

Levy's mouth was too full for speech so he simply nodded and shoved it into a side pocket of his suit jacket.

"When can I expect results? I promised tomorrow."

He swallowed. "Promised? Who did you promise? I hope you didn't—"

"Don't worry. Didn't mention Creighton. But I needed Christy's help to get the sample. I implied I had an in with a commercial lab."

"Tomorrow might be pushing it. We have a queue for DNA analysis."

"So, pull rank."

"Already did that with the last sample. Too often might attract attention. I'd like to keep this to myself for the time being."

Jack watched him. "Planning a palace coup?"

"Not at all. But I don't want a certain camel sticking her nose into this particular tent. You know how that story goes."

Jack hadn't the vaguest.

"Enlighten me."

"It's an old Arabian tale about a desert traveler who beds down in his tent on a cold night. His camel asks if it can stick its nose in the tent to keep it warm. The guy says yes. Later the camel asks if it can put its head inside. The guy says yes. Then come the front legs, then the hind legs. Soon the Arab is out on the sand and the camel has the tent all to itself."

Jack had to smile. "Are you telling me Doctor Vecca's got a hump on her back?"

"No, but she's a camel nonetheless."

"What do you think you'll find, gene-wise?"

He shrugged. "We know Christy's chock full of oDNA. If Dawn's father had a fair amount, that could mean Dawn is loaded. If she is, and she mates with Bolton—also packed with oDNA—that baby could be off the map."

"If . . . could . . . you don't sound very sure."

Levy looked annoyed. "If I knew, I wouldn't have to run tests, would I? Look, if Dawn's father is a regular Joe like you or me, he probably didn't pass on much oDNA. That said, if he fertilized an ovum from Christy that carried very little of *her* oDNA—don't forget: Only half of a parent's genes wind up in any given ovum or spermatozoon—Dawn would be relatively oDNA free. And thus her child, even with Bolton as a father, could have no more oDNA than Bolton contributed."

"So these generations of barnyard breeding, as you called it, could be for nothing."

"Absolutely. It has a hit-or-miss aspect to it. Let's just hope we're dealing with a series of misses."

"Why?"

Jack knew why he didn't want Jonah Stevens's plan to succeed. Any scheme that involved the Otherness had to mean bad news for the world as he and Gia and Vicky knew it. But what did Levy care? He knew nothing of the Otherness, and Jack would have thought he'd be fascinated by the outcome.

Levy looked uncomfortable. "It's hard to say. Jonah Stevens . . . what could he have known of his genome? No one knew about oDNA thirty-odd years ago. So how could he know he carried something different?"

Jack shrugged, trying to look nonchalant. "Maybe he didn't. Maybe he just sensed he was 'special' and wanted to preserve his bloodline."

"*Concentrate* his bloodline is more like it. There's a certain primitiveness about this, a certain sense of cunning purpose that makes my skin crawl." A

fleeting smile. "Not very scientific sounding, is it. But this isn't a rational de-
duction. It's a gut reaction."

Jack regarded Levy. Here sat a guy who dealt in chemicals and proteins,
dissecting how they were structured and interacted, and oDNA should have
been just another of those proteins. Yet his primitive hindbrain, the ghost of
reptiles past, sensed something wrong, something threatening, something
other.

"Never hurts to listen to your gut now and then, I al—"

Jack's phone rang. Gia? He checked the readout. No . . . Christy.

"Yeah?"

"Jack, I've got to talk to you."

"What's up?"

"Not on the phone. Can you meet me at the same place as this afternoon?"

"I guess so. Tomorrow morning?"

"No! It's got to be tonight!"

Back to Forest Hills? Tonight? No way.

"What's the emergency?"

"Everything has gone to hell. That man is the devil himself." She sobbed.
*"Please, Jack. I may have lost Dawn for good. This can't wait till tomorrow.
Please?"*

He sighed. He'd been looking forward to kicking back at Gia's, putting his
feet up, cracking a brew . . .

"All right, but I'm north of the city. Let's make it someplace midway. Do
you know where Van Cortlandt Park is?"

"Sure."

"Good . . ."

16

They'd parked in a well-lit section of the main lot and, as before, Jack moved into Christy's car where she recounted the events since they'd parted.

It never ceased to amaze him how quickly things could go from bad to complete crap.

Had to hand it to Bolton, though. Dirty as it was, telling Dawn that her mother had come on to him was a sick masterstroke. But one that could have backfired had he not known about the butterfly tattoo.

"So you see," she said finally, "this changes everything."

Jack wasn't following. "I don't see how."

She looked at him with teary eyes, gleaming in the glow from the street-lights. "I've lost her. She'll never trust me again, and she'll certainly never come back home again unless . . ."

"Unless what?"

"Unless she's got nowhere else to go."

Jack hoped this wasn't going where he sensed it was. He decided to let her fill in the blanks.

"How does that happen? Get Bethlehem to kick her out?"

She shook her head. "That won't happen either." Her voice hardened. "That man has to die."

He raised a hand. "Whoa, now. I hope you don't think I'm going to—"

She lifted the Talbot's bag that had been lying between them on the front seat and thrust it at him.

"There's a quarter of a million in here. It's yours if you make it happen."

Jack didn't touch it. "Sorry. I don't—"

"Then find someone who will!" she said, her voice rising in pitch and volume. "You must have contacts, you must know somebody—"

"Forget it. Keep pushing and I walk."

She stared at him a moment, then slumped back against the seat and barked out a harsh laugh.

"What is it with this money? Is it cursed or something so that nobody will take it?"

"It's the same money you offered Bethlehem?"

She nodded. "He wouldn't take it, you won't take it . . . God, it's a quarter of a million bucks and no one wants it!"

"Let's put aside murder for the moment and look at this from another angle . . ."

Murder . . . if someone knocked off Bolton, the mysterious "agency" connected to Creighton would have Jack down as the most likely suspect.

"What other angle is there?"

Bolton knowing about the tattoo bothered him. Christy had told him her theory about a hidden minicam. Jack had trouble buying into that. Where would a guy who'd been locked away his entire adult life learn to install something like that?

But if no minicam, where had he learned about the tattoo? How many men had Christy had sex with over the years? Could one of them be involved with Bolton?

Or was it someone else? Someone from way further back in her past?

"We can't play games with this any longer, Christy. I need to know about Dawn's father."

He heard a sharp intake of breath. "Oh, God! I can't!"

Jack saw her stiffen. She squeezed her eyes shut as her breathing tempo picked up. Starting to hyperventilate. Looked like she was going to have another panic attack.

That must have been one traumatic relationship.

He put her hand on her shoulder.

"Easy, easy. Just say his name, give me a few vital statistics, and that's it. I'll take it from there."

Actually, Levy would take it.

Slowly she calmed herself. She swallowed, took a deep breath, and spoke in a tiny voice.

"I have no idea who her father is. I was raped."

17

Silence ruled the car for an endless moment. When Jack recovered from the shock he turned to her.

"Jeez, Christy, I had no idea. Let's just drop it. Forget I asked. If I'd had any clue—"

"No. It's time. I thought I'd put it behind me. I've locked it away for so long I'd almost forgotten it happened. But it did."

Jack made no comment, giving her time and space to say her piece. She stared straight ahead through the windshield. After a minute or so, she cleared her throat and spoke in a soft monotone.

"I was kidnapped right off the street one night in downtown Atlanta. I was a senior. My school was putting on *Jesus Christ Superstar*. I was going to play Mary Magdalene. I was on my way home from rehearsal. One moment I was walking along, passing a van, the next I had a burlap bag over my head and was yanked into it. I was tied up and driven somewhere. It could have been near or far, I don't know. Then I was bundled into a windowless room—it was damp so I figured it was a basement—and chained to a bed. Then I was stripped naked and raped. I was raped every day, sometimes twice a day, for weeks."

"Christ." That explained the weeks she disappeared as a teen. "The same guy?"

She nodded. "Yes. He wore a ski mask, but I could tell. The same guy."

"Did he beat you?"

"Yes and no. If I fought him he got rough. And I learned real quick that whether I fought or not, he was going to have his way, so after a while I stopped fighting."

She seemed ashamed. Jack reached out to touch her arm but pulled back. Probably not a good idea.

"You had no choice."

"I know. But it goes beyond that. I began . . ." She cleared her throat again. "He fed me three meals a day. Always fast food—Wendy's, Mickey-D's,

BK—with plenty to drink. That was how I knew what time of day it was—the arrival of an Egg McMuffin meant it was morning. The chain was about ten feet long and attached to my wrist by a padded cuff."

That startled Jack.

"Padded?"

"Padded. And get this: I had a bedpan which he removed and replaced with every meal."

"Christ, that's weird."

She nodded. "I was like some sort of pet—except for the rape part. I was so scared and lonely down there in that room, thinking he was never going to let me go, that I began to look forward to his visits, even if he was going to rape me. I can't say I enjoyed it but then again, sometimes I did. God help me, a couple of times near the end I . . ." Her voice drifted off.

"Don't beat yourself up. It's called the Stockholm syndrome."

She nodded, still staring out the window. "I know. I learned about that later. But at the time I was so ashamed of myself."

"How did you escape?"

"I didn't. The sex—the rapes—stopped one day. The man still fed me regularly, but for three days he didn't touch me. Then on the fourth day I fell asleep after dinner—I figured out later I'd been drugged—and woke up on a bench in Piedmont Park dressed in the clothes I'd been wearing when he kidnapped me."

Jack leaned back and joined her thousand-mile stare through the windshield.

It didn't make sense. Why go to all the trouble to make a sex slave of Christy and then let her go? Someone sociopathic enough to do that wouldn't want to run the risk of the victim leading the cops back to him. The safest and smartest thing would have been to kill her.

But the creep had let her go. Why? Why take the risk of kidnapping her and then compound that risk by freeing her? A mouth breather who wanted a sex slave wanted her forever, or at least until he tired of her or she died from the mistreatment. But this guy had fed her well and even gone so far as to give her a bedpan. Emptying his slave's bedpan . . . something so incongruous about that. Almost as if he'd planned all along to let her go.

Wait. He *had* planned to let her go. Wearing a mask clinched that.

None of this made sense. What had made him decide it was time to let her go?

Jack turned to her. "Why didn't you report it?"

Still staring out the window: "I told you—I was ashamed. I'd become a compliant pet. I was afraid they'd find out. Emotionally I was a basket case, but physically I was unmarred. I didn't even have a mark where I'd been cuffed. I thought people would think I was lying. Tawana Brawley was still fresh in everybody's minds back then. I was just a teenager—I know you're considered an adult at eighteen, but I was just a scared kid—and I was so afraid they'd think I'd been off on some sex-and-drug binge and was trying to pull a Tawana."

Jack could almost understand her thinking, but he hated the idea of the son of a bitch getting off scot-free.

"I could've said I was raped, but how could I prove it? There'd been no sex for days. The only proof I had was being pregnant, but I didn't know that till a month or so later."

Jack bolted upright as if he'd touched a live wire. Lights were going on, enough to make him feel like the Christmas tree at Rocky Center.

"Oh, jeez!"

Christy looked at him. "What?"

"Um . . ." He couldn't tell her. Not yet. "Just thinking about Dawn—does she know?"

Christy glared at him. "No, and she damn well better not learn. You're the only one I've ever told, so if she does find out, I'll know the source."

"You're forgetting—the rapist knows."

"Whoever it was only knows he raped me. He doesn't know he made me pregnant."

Don't be so sure, Jack thought as she returned to staring out the window.

He maintained an outer calm, but his insides were fired up.

There it was, laid out before him—the whole plan: Young Moonglow Garber hadn't been kidnapped to be a sex slave; she'd been kidnapped to be impregnated.

That explained the gentle treatment, the regular meals, and most of all, the bedpan: The rapist was testing her urine. When the pregnancy test turned positive, his work was done. Probably waited a few days to recheck just to be sure, then let her go.

Jack knew—or was at least ninety-nine percent certain—that the rapist, Dawn's father, was Hank Thompson. Jack was equally sure that Jeremy had been on hand to help.

It all fit now. The mysterious Jonah Stevens had been behind this. A super-oDNA being had been his plan all along. And he'd fathered three children—at least three that Jack knew of—to make it happen. The sons must have been indoctrinated early on, the daughter kept in the dark. Maybe the boys didn't even know Moonglow Garber was their half sister. If they had, would it have made any difference? Somehow, Jack doubted it.

He could see how it might have gone down: Jonah Stevens tells his boys that there's this girl with special blood, and they need to mix their blood with hers. So, one boy would impregnate this special girl named Moonglow Garber. Then, assuming the resulting child was female, the other would wait until she was old enough and then impregnate *her*.

Jack thought about what kind of man would use his kids that way. But then, Jonah probably saw them as tools rather than children. Jack didn't use the term *sick fuck* very often, but surely it applied here.

The result of this plan—if the right sets of genes were passed on—would be a baby packed with a dose of Jonah Stevens's oDNA.

But what if Moonglow's child had been a boy? No way outside of a test tube to guarantee the sex of a child, so Dawn very easily could have ended up Danny. Then what? All that trouble, all that planning, all those years of waiting, for nothing.

Unless . . . unless Jonah had procreated more threesomes as a sort of insurance. Like discrete terrorist cells—homegrown, indoctrinated since birth, probably unaware of each other—dedicated to breeding a genetic bomb.

To what purpose? Had to be a purpose.

Did Bolton and Thompson even know what it was? Bolton had talked about a Plan and mentioned a Key, but was that simply an image, a metaphor, or was this baby supposed to unlock some doorway and cause apocalyptic change?

Two years ago Jack would have written off Jonah Stevens as a madman. No longer. He'd seen too much over the course of those years to dismiss anything as mad. Something was in the wind. He'd heard from a number of sources that an Armageddon was gathering over the horizon. Was Dawn's child a harbinger of all that?

Would stopping the child slow the advance of Armageddon?

The thought triggered a question. He turned to Christy.

"You never thought of having an abortion?"

Christy rubbed her temples and groaned. "Oh, God, please let's not go there. You've just made me relive the rapes. I don't want to revisit that nightmare too."

"I'm sorry, Christy, but this is important. I'm trying to make connections here."

Her head snapped toward him. "My daughter is shacked up with her uncle or half-uncle or whatever the hell he is. Isn't that enough of a connection?"

He didn't understand her reaction. What was he missing?

"Please. I need to know. What was this nightmare? Did you consider an abortion?"

"Hell, yes! No way was I giving birth to a rapist's child, so I went to an abortion clinic run by a Doctor Golden. I was examined, had blood tests, and was given an appointment to have it done. But before it happened someone put a bullet through his head. His death closed his clinic, obviously, so I went to another, this one run by a Doctor Dalton. And would you believe the same thing happened? The day before I was scheduled to have it done he was killed too."

Jack nodded. Everything was falling into place. Christy's trip to an abortion clinic must have thrown the two boys into a panic. They had to stop her from terminating the pregnancy so they did what had to be done. Jeremy might not have committed both murders, but once caught he took the fall for them.

Christy shook her head. "I mean, it was almost like God was saying, 'You have to have this child.'"

"God?"

"Hey, I don't mean that like it sounds—I mean, like my rape-baby and I really mattered in the grand scheme of things—but the timing was so creepy, it pretty near unnerved me. And don't think the cops didn't notice that timing. They questioned me again and again to see if I was connected to the killer—as if I'd somehow set the doctors up. With nothing else to go on, they weren't buying that it was all just a coincidence."

Coincidence? Oh, no . . . nothing of the sort.

It's sitting right in front of her, Jack thought, but she can't see it.

That didn't make her a dummy. Not by a long shot. The truth was too outrageous. Hell, if he didn't know what he knew, he might not be seeing it either.

"Didn't they want to know who your baby's father was?"

"Yeah, but how could I tell them? And I hadn't reported the rape, so I made up a name. Told them we'd hooked up and driven around in his van for weeks, then parted ways."

"They bought it?"

"Had a statewide manhunt for a guy who didn't exist. But then they caught the guy who did the shootings and found out we had no connection, so they dropped me, thank God."

"So all this made you decide to keep the baby?"

"Not really. But getting an abortion in Atlanta was almost impossible for a while, and what with all that time with the police questioning me and telling me not to leave town, by the time everything settled down it was too late for an abortion."

"So you kept the baby by default."

She shook her head. "I'd resigned myself to going through the pregnancy but no way was I keeping her. I had her all set up for adoption by a rich couple. The money I'd get for her would stake my trip to New York where I was going to take Broadway by storm."

"I can guess what happened."

Christy nodded as tears filled her eyes. "I took one look at her and couldn't let her go."

"So she's the reason you changed your name."

She nodded. "Yeah, well, the name change came about because I was afraid she'd happen upon some old account of the murders and see my name mentioned as someone being questioned in the case. I mean, how could I get away with explaining that? Say it was someone else named Moonglow Garber?"

Jack nodded. "Good thinking."

"So the name had to go." A fleeting smile. "I was hanging out at a friend's house and the *My Fair Lady* sound track was on—"

Jack snapped his fingers. "That's it! That's the connection!" He now knew why Pickering sounded so familiar. "Let me guess: 'A Hymn to Him' was playing and you heard, 'Pickering, why can't a woman be more like a man?' Right?"

"Yes! You *sure* you're not gay?"

Jack smiled. "Why? Because I know a song from a musical?"

"Well, my friend was, and he was heavy into theater and sound tracks. And you knew all about *Promises! Promises!* too."

"Credit my mother. She loved musicals and *My Fair Lady* was one of her favorites. Played it all the time while I was growing up."

Jack could hear the overture right now. Part of the sound track of his youth. A shiver of melancholy tingled through him. Mom . . . he could almost hear her voice from down a long hallway . . . humming along.

Christy said, "Anyway, it seemed as good a name as any, so I became Christy Pickering and my daughter became Dawn Pickering." She sighed. "And I'm so glad I kept her. She's been a constant source of joy . . . until now."

Jack didn't have the heart to tell her that what he suspected was much worse than she thought: That Christy and her daughter were part of some incestuous breeding experiment wherein Dawn had been impregnated by a man who was a full uncle, not just a half.

Nor could he tell her that he had the answer to the question of how Bolton knew about her tattoo: He'd seen every inch of her when he and his brother imprisoned her.

"So that's my tale of woe," Christy said.

And some tale it was. She'd been through a nightmare ordeal— kidnapped, imprisoned, and raped multiple times. And yet she'd bounced back. Changed her name, changed her life, become a loving mother and successful day trader.

"You should be proud of the way you handled it. You could have let it define your life, started identifying yourself as a victim. But you didn't. You beat it."

She shrugged. "You think so? I was just doing what felt I had to do to survive. My mother was furious with me for screwing up my life by keeping the baby. I suppose I could have told her about the rape, but I didn't think she'd believe me at that point, and if she did she'd really want me to give Dawn away. She was driving me crazy so I decided to leave. Me and my baby—we were going to make it. But I spent years in terror that it would happen again. I never walked when I could drive, even when it was a block away. And when I was on the street I walked way inside with my shoulder practically brushing the buildings, eyeing every van whether parked or driving along the street."

"Do you still?"

"I've relaxed a little, but not completely. I keep a gun hidden in my bedroom and I know how to use it."

"Good for you."

Jack wished he could get Gia interested in learning how to shoot. He couldn't be around her twenty-four/seven, and a pistol, even a small one, was a mighty equalizer. But she had something akin to a phobia about them.

"I still dream about them, though—those weeks. I still look at Dawn now and then and wonder about the unknown half of her gene pool and what diseases are hiding there. Cancer? Heart? Diabetes? Insanity?" She looked at him. "Do you think any of that will show up in the genetic testing you're doing?"

Jack fumbled for a quick reply. "I—I doubt it. I only asked for relationship testing. I don't even know if those other tests exist."

"Well, if they don't, someday they will. And maybe we can track down her father."

Jack didn't dare look at her. "And if you found him . . . what then? Start another search for a hit man?"

"I don't know. Would my life have been different if he hadn't done what he did? Absolutely. Would it be better? I don't know . . . I just don't know." She shook herself. "But enough about the past, what about the present? What are we going to do about that man?"

"Before we go there, I just want to make sure we've taken killing him off the table. Have we?"

She loosed a long sigh. "Yeah, sure. I went a little crazy, I guess. I feel so trapped. I'm boxed in by this big lie he's told about me and I can't see any way out. It's almost like being chained up in that cellar again. Killing him seemed like the easiest way out."

Jack needed to drive the no-killing concept home.

"Not easy at all. After what's been going on between you and him, you'd be a prime suspect. Even with an alibi. And if they catch the hit man he'll give you up in a heartbeat. And then where will Dawn be? Single and pregnant with no one to turn to. Sound familiar?"

She nodded. "Yeah. Too. So if we're going to let him live, what do we do about him?"

Jack didn't have a plan. This new wrinkle had muddied the water. He needed time.

"Let's wait and see what the DNA analysis shows. Maybe Dawn will change her tune when she sees how closely related they are. Maybe pushing information about the increased chance of birth defects from mating with a relative will put her off."

"I don't know . . . she's completely taken with this guy."

"In the meantime I'll sift through my notes and see if I can come up with a backup plan."

She was staring at him.

He stared back. "What?"

"You really seem to care." She smiled. "You have no stake in the outcome here, but it really seems to matter to you."

Lady, if you only knew.

18

Jack sat at the table in his front room and arranged his notes before him, trying to construct a timeline.

Jonah Stevens first fathered Hank. Then less than a year later, Jeremy. And a year after that, Christy—or Moonglow.

Eighteen years later Moonglow is kidnapped by the boys and Hank repeatedly rapes her until she becomes pregnant.

Moonglow tries to get an abortion but the boys kill off the two abortionists she visits. Jeremy is caught, locked away for life, and winds up at Creighton.

Hank, meanwhile, gets tagged for interstate GTA and also winds up at Creighton.

Coincidence? Not according to Levy. They both tested positive for oDNA, so they became instant candidates for Creighton. But the timing . . .

Did Hank arrange to have himself arrested on a federal beef so he could visit his brother?

No, that didn't square. He didn't know about the oDNA project at Creighton so he couldn't know he'd be sent there.

Jack checked his notes for the date of Bolton's arrival in Creighton, then opened his copy of *Kick* to the section covering Hank Thompson's wild, criminal youth.

When he saw the date of his capture, he checked back to the timeline for Jeremy's arrest and saw that Hank had been locked up in Creighton when Jeremy was nabbed . . . locked up for six months.

Jack's mouth went dry.

He rechecked the dates of the weeks Moonglow Garber had gone missing. When he found those, his stomach took a dive.

"Oh, shit."

TUESDAY

1

Dawn sat alone at the kitchen table and sipped a Diet Pepsi. Nothing else would stay down during her first couple of hours after rising.

Were you supposed to get morning sick this early in a pregnancy? Did it mean something might be wrong with the baby?

She didn't know. But then, she didn't know a thing about being pregnant. All she knew was that she hated feeling this way. How long would it last? Not the whole nine months—please!

And school. She'd missed yesterday and could so not bring herself to go today. Not that graduating would make much difference once they finished their video game idea and got it sold, but she'd worked hard for four years and totally wanted that diploma to show for it.

She bit back a sob. She felt so *alone*! God, she wished she had someone to talk to about this. Couldn't mention it to any of her friends—it'd be totally all over school in like two seconds. Under normal circumstances Mom would have been the obvious choice, but these circumstances were nothing like normal.

She shook her head. Still couldn't believe it. Coming on to Jerry. Her mother had gone crazy. That was the only possible explanation.

Well, crazy or not, she was so never speaking to that woman again.

Which left her with no one to talk to about being pregnant—at least no one who'd been there. Oh, she could talk to Jerry about it all day, but he didn't seem to care about what she was going through. All he wanted to talk about was the baby and how *he* was going to rule the world.

Sometimes she thought Jerry was as crazy as Mom.

And where was he, anyway? He'd said he had an important meeting in the city with some people from Electronic Arts—or "EA" as he called it—but left her home because the time wasn't right yet to bring her into the picture, whatever that meant. Was that really where he was? Normally she'd take him to-tally at his word, but she'd noticed that somehow every Tuesday he'd disap-pear for about four hours or so. He always had a plausible reason, but it occurred to her that his meetings always seemed to be timed for late morning to early afternoon.

Coincidence or . . . ?

Or what?

Did he go to AA meetings? No, he wasn't an alcoholic. He drank only beer and never got sloshed. NA? Nah, he didn't even do weed.

A real uncomfortable thought snuck up on her: What if he was visiting a parole officer or something like that? Yeah, that was what Mom would say. To-tally. But no way . . .

Come to think of it, what made her so sure he *wasn't* an ex-con? What did she really know about him? She'd asked him about his family but he'd totally killed the subject by saying no brothers, no sisters, folks dead, 'nuff said. Like he'd come out of nowhere.

She realized the same could be said of her. She'd never seen even a photo of her father, and now, in a way, she no longer had a mother.

All she had was herself.

And a baby.

Oh, God, a baby. I don't want to have a baby.

She couldn't go through with it. She had to do something about it . . . something to stop it.

But she couldn't let Jerry know. God, he'd have a fit. She'd have to do it on the sly and tell Jerry she'd miscarried.

Without giving herself time to think, she rose to her feet. A wave of nausea rolled through her stomach as she headed for Jerry's computer. Yeah, she had to do something about this. She'd look up the nearest abortion place. Had to be a zillion of them around.

2

"Doctor Vecca?"

Julia looked up to see her assistant standing in the doorway.

"What is it, Toni?"

"Mister Bethlehem is here. He wants to see you. Says it's important."

Jeremy? Why on Earth—?

Oh, yes. It was Tuesday—time for his weekly injection of D-287. The clerical staff—and most of the medical staff, for that matter—knew him by his new identity. The personnel in the max security section who knew Jeremy Bolton thought he'd been transferred and they'd have no contact with an outpatient like Jerry Bethlehem.

But even so, Julia preferred that he spend as little time as possible at Creighton.

"Send him in."

A moment later Jeremy strode through the door and slammed it closed behind him. He looked frazzled. That made Julia a bit uncomfortable. A frazzled Jeremy Bolton could be a dangerous Jeremy Bolton, even with his trigger gene suppressed.

"Get Levy in here," he said. "We need a powwow."

"Something wrong?"

"Yeah. Lots."

Julia didn't like the sound of that.

"Care to share?"

"Damn fuck right I care to share. Soon as Levy's here I'll be sharin like crazy."

Normally the idea of allowing an inmate, even one as special as Jeremy, to give orders was unthinkable, but she decided to make an exception in this case. She wanted to find out what was upsetting him and then send him on his way as soon as possible.

Julia buzzed Toni. "Call Doctor Levy and tell him I need him for a conference with Mister Bethlehem."

Jeremy stepped to her window and stood staring out at the grounds.

"Coffee?" she said.

He shook his head. "Just Levy."

Rather than twiddle her thumbs while they waited, she turned to her computer and called up the Jerry Bethlehem file. Yes, he'd been receiving his injections as scheduled, and he'd been testing negative for drugs—any THC or opiates in his urine and the clinical trial would be cancelled. Couldn't allow drugs to muddy the water.

Jeremy was being a good boy.

Aaron came in a few moments later. He looked almost as spooked as that night last week when Jeremy had tried to kidnap him.

Get over it, she thought. Jeremy's dangerous but not *that* dangerous.

"Good morning, Aaron," she said, indicating one of the chairs on the far side of her desk. "Jeremy has something to say to us."

Aaron seated himself gingerly, as if he feared the cushion might be wired with electricity.

"What's up?"

Jeremy had ignored his arrival. He turned now and fixed each of them in turn with his ice-blue stare.

"That detective is still fuckin with me. I thought you told me you were gonna get him off my ass."

Damn that man. Just a few minutes with that Robertson character had been enough to convince her he was trouble. When she'd run his license plate and found it defunct, she'd been sure. First Gerhard, now another one. Couldn't these idiots simply take the money and mind their business?

"Fucking with you how?"

"First he tells my girl's mother that I killed Gerhard, and now he's doin DNA testing on me."

Shock shot her to her feet. She slammed her hand on her desk.

"*What?*"

She glanced at Aaron who looked as alarmed as she.

"You heard me," Jeremy said.

She dropped back into her chair as an icy tremor shuddered along the walls of her heart. It couldn't be for oDNA—no one knew about it and Creighton had the only means to screen for it. Still . . .

"What—" She swallowed around a dry tongue. "What sort of DNA testing?"

Jeremy suddenly looked uncomfortable. "Just looking into my family tree, that sort of thing."

"What did he find?" Aaron said.

"Nothin. Nothin *to* find. Thing I want to know is, where's he gettin this information?" That cold look again, shifting from Julia to Aaron. "You got a leak here?"

Julia forced a laugh. "Here? You must be joking!"

"This ain't no jokin matter, lady. Because I got to thinkin about how you two've been awful damn interested in my DNA and my family tree ever since I got here, and now along comes this detective, right out of the blue, and all of a sudden he's got the same kinda interest. Kinda makes you wonder, don't it?"

Aaron cleared his throat. "We paid him *not* to do any further investigation on you." He turned his watery gaze on Julia. "Didn't we, doctor."

Didn't we, doctor . . . always so formal.

"We damn well did. Paid him handsomely. Looks like he's been taking us for a ride. I think—"

"I don't give a damn about your money. He's lookin into my DNA and I want to know why."

Aaron cleared his throat again. He seemed to do that only when Jeremy was around.

"Well, one reason might be because he tried to find something incriminating through your fingerprints and couldn't. Doctor Vecca had the foresight to have them erased from ViCAP, so he came up blank."

Jeremy looked at her. "Pretty smart, doc."

Julia allowed a small smile. "I thought so."

"With fingerprints a dead end," Aaron continued, "maybe he's going the DNA route."

Jeremy turned his gaze on him. "What's my DNA going to tell him?"

"Well, if he has a contact in one of the police departments, he could have it checked against the DNA database of sex offenders."

"Well, he ain't gonna find me there."

Only because you've been locked up the whole time it was being compiled, Julia thought. If you'd been out there . . .

"Of course not," Aaron said. "We know that, and you know that, and now he knows that. But it was a good thought on his part. Imagine the leverage he would have had on you if he found a match to someone with a sex offense conviction. Or better yet, a match to an unsolved crime."

Jeremy glared at him. " 'Better yet'?"

Aaron shrank half an inch deeper into his chair. "I meant for him."

Julia wondered about that. Aaron had seemed to be warming to the subject of Jeremy taking a fall for a sex offense.

Julia said, "What does he say he found in your DNA?"

Again that cagey look. "Just a bunch of personal junk that don't mean nothin."

Julia kept her tone as level and soothing as possible. "Then why are you so upset?"

"Because I want to know where he's getting this information. And where's he getting my DN-fuckin-A?"

Aaron said, "Many commercial labs do DNA analysis. And as for obtaining a sample, all this detective would need was some of your hair or blood or saliva."

Jeremy shook his head. "I ain't had a haircut or cut myself recently and I never developed the spittin habit." His mouth twisted. "When you're inside and you spit, you're spittin where you live."

Julia had noted a thickening of his redneck accent during the course of the conversation. Over the years she'd noted that it usually occurred when he was upset. She'd come to see it as an unconscious affectation to put people off guard, make them underestimate him.

She said, "He could get saliva from an envelope or a fork or a spoon."

Jeremy looked at the floor and shook his head. "Shit. That means someone's been followin me and I ain't had a clue." When he looked up again his expression was fierce. "Where can I find this sonuvabitch?"

Julia glanced at Aaron and found him looking at her.

"We don't know," she said.

Fury blazed in Jeremy's eyes as he took a step toward her.

"Bullshit!"

It was all Julia could do not to flinch. But she held his burning gaze as she blurted a reply.

"It's true. He calls himself John Robertson, says he's a licensed private eye, but the man who holds the license is dead."

"You ain't gonna tell me he's a ghost, are you?"

"No, just someone who's very good at hiding his tracks." She thought about that. "I guess in a way he *is* a ghost."

Jeremy's expression became frustrated. "Well, what about this agency you're always threatening me with? Can't you sic them on this guy?"

"There's nothing I'd like better, but we've got nothing to go on. He wears gloves, so we have no fingerprints. The plates on his car are not registered to anyone. The only thing I might be able to give them is his physical description, but that's no help. He looks like a million other men his age."

"And what age is that?"

"Yours, I'd say. Average height, brown hair, brown eyes. No distinguishing features. Very average looking, wouldn't you agree, Aaron?" She looked to him for support and found him staring at her with a shocked expression. "What?"

He shook his head. "Nothing."

What was eating him?

"What about his face?" Jeremy said. "Big nose, little nose? Fat lips, thin lips? Scar? *Anything?*"

Julia shook her head. "Nothing. An eminently forgettable face."

"Fuck! And you have no idea where I can find him?"

Julia looked at him. Jeremy had unsettled her. Time for a little payback.

"Somewhere in your general vicinity, I imagine. Not now, not here, but sometime during the course of the rest of the day I would suspect he'll be watching you."

The flash of uncertainty in Jeremy's eyes was gratifying, but didn't last nearly long enough.

"Well, now that I know he's watchin, I'll catch him at it. And when I do . . ."

Julia pointed at him. "Don't do anything foolish. If you think you've spotted him, keep your distance. Call me instead. Anytime day or night—call me and I'll have him taken care of."

"I can handle this myself."

"I'm sure you can, but you mustn't. You were able to get off easy with that barroom fight. But if you assault this man, you'll be locked up again and we'll have to cancel the clinical trial. And then where will you be? Be sensible, Jeremy. If you spot him, you make the call, and that's all. Understand?"

He nodded. "Oh, yeah. I understand."

Julia wondered if he did. Only time would tell.

Without another word he walked out, leaving the door open behind him.

Julia turned to Aaron and found him staring at her again with that shocked look. One of her mother's favorite expressions came back to her.

"Close your mouth, Aaron. You're catching flies."

"I don't believe you did that."

"Did what?"

"Gave him Robertson's description. You might as well have served him up as a sacrificial lamb."

Julia shook her head. What an old woman.

"Think of it as a provocative stimulus. How can we know whether or not the suppresser therapy is working if we don't challenge it?"

"You did the same with Gerhard, and now you're condemning Robertson to the same fate."

"Not necessarily. If the higher dose of suppresser therapy is working, Jeremy will call in and we'll handle Robertson."

"And if it's not working, Robertson could wind up dead."

Julia had had just about enough of this.

"And if he does, so what?" She remembered his crack about her underwear. The bastard. "He's been playing us for fools, Aaron. He's not supposed to be anywhere near Jeremy, so if he's caught snooping around, it's on his head, not ours. Besides, I see it as a win-win situation."

"Not for Robertson."

"No, for us. If Jeremy removes Robertson, not only will we have him off our backs, but we'll also have an indication that we need to up the dose of two-eighty-seven."

"But what if he's clumsy about it and gets caught?"

"We'll clean things up before he gets caught—just like last time."

"Last time we were lucky."

"We *must* provoke him, Aaron. And think about it: If he calls in instead of attacking, not only will we know the suppresser is working, we'll have an idea of the proper milligram-per-kilogram dose. I don't see a downside."

"Unless you're Robertson."

"Why do you care about that lying swindler?"

"He's a fellow human being. Isn't what we're doing here supposed to make the world a safer place for our fellow human beings?"

Julia sighed. "Yes, I suppose it is."

But not that particular human being.

3

Jeremy's brain blazed as he spun the Miata's tires on the way out of the Creighton front gate and headed back to the city. He checked his rearview mirror to see if anyone pulled into the lane behind him, and scanned the road ahead for cars parked on the shoulders.

Someone had been following him around, picking up little souvenirs here and there and using them to test his DNA.

Shit!

Worst part was he hadn't had a clue.

He checked around again. He had the road to himself. But what did that mean? This Robertson guy could be waiting down near the Thruway, knowing he'd have to come that way to get back to Queens. The guy could pull in a few cars behind him as he got on and Jeremy would never know.

That hunted feeling . . .

Reminded him of his last free days in Atlanta. He'd thought he was in the clear, thought he'd covered his tracks. Everyone was looking for a religious nut, a wild-eyed right-to-lifer, and Jeremy was anything but. But . . .

Yeah. Always the *but*.

But someone had seen someone near the second shooting and gave a description that shared certain features with someone else seen in a photo taken on the street shortly before the first shooting, and a sketch was circulated in a door-to-door canvas and finally a newsstand guy thought it looked like someone who came by regularly to buy cigarettes.

Like a jerk, he'd held on to the gun. Yeah, it was stupid, but with the feds all over the place he'd have no way to get his hands on another piece on the outside chance Moonglow decided to try yet another abortionist. One thing led to another and, when he felt the circle tightening, he decided he had to get rid of it. He was nabbed before he could.

And now someone else was trying to tighten a noose around him.

Maybe he shouldn't go back to Queens—at least not yet. He needed to talk to fuckhead Hank about this gene-testing shit, and the sooner the better. Why not head for the city?

He pulled onto the shoulder and grabbed the map from the glove compartment. He'd learned his way around the Forest Hills area, but up here was still pretty much a mystery. He located Rathburg and noticed that if he headed east from here he could get on the Saw Mill Parkway. Going south on that would take him to 9A which led right down the west side of Manhattan.

Perfect.

He got rolling again and pulled out his cell phone. Time to call big brother. He'd try to find some excuse not to meet, but he wasn't weaseling out today. This was too important.

4

Aaron pulled into the lot of the Argonaut, found a space, and parked. Instead of heading inside he sat with the motor idling. To tempt himself out of the car and into the diner, he conjured images of Belgian waffles dripping with syrup and topped with powdered sugar and strawberries and maybe even some whipped cream, but he felt too queasy to eat. So he sat and wrestled with the question that had been plaguing him all through the hours since the meeting in Julia's office.

Should he tell Jack that Julia had given that pervert Bolton his description?

On one hand, he felt he owed it to him; after all, they'd been working together on putting Bolton back behind bars, but beyond that, he liked the man. He seemed a decent sort, as well as clever and resourceful.

On the other hand, they weren't getting anywhere against Bolton. If Bolton pegged Jack as the detective who'd been causing him so much trouble, he might try to do him serious harm. Enough harm to get himself locked up, thereby aborting this whole outpatient fiasco.

Might *try* to do Jack harm . . . that was where the struggle came: the *try*. Bolton had a couple of inches and maybe twenty pounds on Jack, but Aaron had a feeling the man could take care of himself.

For all he knew, Jack might put Bolton in a hospital. Might pound the living shit out of that deviant, amoral bastard. God, wouldn't that be wonderful? For not only would Bolton be suffering some well-deserved pain, but physical incapacitation might also prove enough to end the outpatient trial.

On the other hand, if Aaron warned Jack, he might back off on his surveillance, reducing or perhaps even eliminating the chance of a confrontation. Aaron dearly wanted to see Bolton hurt.

He jumped and squealed like a girl at the sound of a rap on the passenger window. He shrank against his door as he looked.

Jack.

Relief flooded him. If it had been Bolton, God knew what he would have done.

He hit the unlock switch and Jack slid into the passenger seat.

"Jumpy?"

Aaron nodded. "You could say that."

"Thought I'd find you inside. Actually it's better here. I don't feel like eating."

"Neither do I. Especially after seeing the DNA comparison between Dawn and Bolton."

"You mean the father-daughter thing."

Aaron gasped and stared at him. He'd said it so matter-of-factly.

"You know?"

A nod. "Since last night."

"But how could you? And how can this be? How does something like this happen? How could her mother not know?"

He realized he was babbling, but the questions had been pounding against the inside of his skull since he'd seen the printout.

Ninety-nine point nine nine percent probability of paternity.

Aaron listened in horrified fascination as Jack told about how Moonglow Garber had been abducted and repeatedly raped for weeks until she was pregnant, then released. And then he saw it all.

"The abortionist assassinations! They finally make sense!"

Jack nodded. "Finally."

"But that doesn't explain how you know Bolton is Dawn's father. Hank Thompson could have been the rapist."

"That's what I thought. Then I sketched out a timeline last night and realized that Hank was locked up in Creighton during the weeks Moonglow was missing."

Aaron leaned back. "Dear God."

He thought of Moonglow. That poor girl. Kidnapped, raped daily, probably in terror for her life. And then Bolton, father of her child . . . he thought of his own daughter and wanted to be sick. This only confirmed what he'd known all along: Bolton was a monster.

Jack's fingers were knotted into fists. "The sick, sick, subhuman son of a bitch. How does anyone *do* that?"

For no good reason, Aaron said, "Do you have a daughter?"

Jack looked up at him and Aaron recoiled at what he saw in his eyes. He didn't know what it was—pain, certainly, but nestled in a terrible seething darkness that urged him to flee and never look back.

"I almost did," he said in a low, barely audible tone. "I sort of do." He closed those terrifying eyes, took a breath, then opened them again. The darkness was gone. "You have a printout of the comparison with you?"

The abrupt change caught Aaron off guard. "Uh, um, yes. Why?"

"I want to see it."

He pulled it out of his pocket and watched as Jack unfolded it, studied it, then looked up.

"Ninety-nine point ninety-nine percent probability. Not much wiggle room there."

Aaron shook his head. "Not a bit. But I don't get it. If Moonglow's child was to be later impregnated by one of her uncles, why not have Thompson do it? With a half uncle as the father, the chance of autosomal recessive traits coming to the fore are increased, but nowhere near what could happen to a baby whose father is not only its grandfather, but an uncle as well. It's not only sick, it's . . . counterproductive."

"Refresh me on 'autosomal recessive traits.' "

"An autosomal recessive gene is a genetic defect you inherit from one of your parents. For want of a better term, it's half of a genetically mediated disease. Let's say for example that you inherited a cystic fibrosis mutation from your mother. You don't show signs of cystic fibrosis because your mutation is paired with a normal gene from your father that overrules the mutation. This makes you a *carrier*. Should you impregnate a woman without a similar mutation, there's a fifty-fifty chance of the child being a carrier too, but *zero* chance it will wind up with cystic fibrosis. You following?"

Jack nodded. "Because there's no chance of my mutation getting paired with another like it."

"Correct. But should you impregnate a woman *with* a similar mutation, there's still a fifty-fifty chance of producing a carrier, but also a one-in-four chance of producing a child with cystic fibrosis. This is why first-degree relatives—parents, children, siblings—shouldn't mate."

"More chance of sharing recessives."

"Right. Hemophilia is a recessive that ran rampant through the royal families of Europe due to intermarriage."

They sat in silence for the moment, then he noticed Jack refolding the printout and slipping it into a pocket.

"Hey, you can't have that."

"I'll need it to show Christy. She'll never believe me without it."

Aaron felt a stab of panic. It had "Creighton" printed in large, boldface type across the top of the sheet.

"No! If she shows it to Bolton he'll know it was me!"

"Relax. I'll show her a Xerox with the logo folded out of sight. You'll have no connection."

Not good enough.

"But it won't help you! It has no names!"

"I've got to show her *something*, doc, and this is better than nothing. Be cool. I don't want to see you hurt. You're my man on the inside. I'll keep Creighton out of it. Trust me."

Trust him? He didn't know if he could trust anyone at this point. Except maybe this man.

Not that he had a choice. He couldn't very well take it from him.

More silence as Aaron wondered what Jack was thinking. Then he realized he hadn't got an answer to his previous question.

"Why *didn't* Thompson impregnate Dawn? Did Bolton *want* to bed his own daughter?"

Jack shrugged. "Maybe he's sterile. Maybe they don't know about recessive traits. But then again . . ." His voice trailed off.

Watching him, Aaron saw a look of growing wonder on Jack's face.

"What? What is it?"

"Maybe they want to match up certain recessive genes. Maybe that's been the whole purpose of this scheme all along." And then he shrugged. "And maybe not." He smiled. "Too bad I can't simply ask Bolton next time I run into him."

Aaron opened his mouth, then closed it again. Here was the perfect time to say something to Jack about Julia giving Bolton his description. He should say something. Really he should . . .

But he wanted that showdown, wanted Bolton hurt.

Of course it might be Jack who wound up getting hurt, maybe even killed.

Bolton could walk up behind him and gun him down just like he did the abortionists.

But he held his tongue. He'd have to trust that Jack had more street smarts than Bolton. A good bet, since Bolton had been off the streets for the last eighteen years.

Still . . . all the street smarts in the world wouldn't stop a bullet in the back.

Sometimes Aaron hated himself.

5

Jeremy watched Hank as he stood at a window and peeked through the blinds.

"You *sure* you weren't followed?"

"Absolutely."

No way was Jeremy absolutely sure, but he was reasonably sure. He wasn't exactly an expert at this sort of thing. But he'd made a lot of turns coming down here to this Lower East Side Kicker crib, and he'd watched carefully the whole way. He hadn't seen anyone following him.

Hank let the blind slat drop and turned to him.

"All right, what's so important that we couldn't discuss this over the phone?"

"Like I told you, someone's been testing my DNA and knows I'm related to Moonglow."

"So she knows—?"

"Yeah, she knows. Question is, how long before he tests my DNA against the girl's?"

Hank pressed his palms against the sides of his head and began to walk in a circle about the room.

"Oh hell! Oh damn! Oh shit! Who is this guy? We've got to get to him, make him stop!"

"Vecca and Levy already tried that. Paid him off but he still keeps snooping. Almost like he's got some sort of hard-on for me. I mean, like it's personal."

Even though Jerry Bethlehem hadn't been around long enough for anyone to have something personal against him, the thought didn't sit well.

"Yeah. Funny, I've run into someone like that too."

Here we go. Can't let this get too far from rich, famous, too-important-to-get-my-hands-dirty Hank. His attitude sucked. Jeremy resisted the urge to pop him one.

"Well, unless he's threatening to take a shit in the Bloodline, like my guy, maybe we should forget about him for the moment."

"Okay, okay. What do we do?"

"Well, since I've never seen him, we'll have to try to beat him at his own game. That's where you come in."

Hank's tone turned cautious. "Yeah?"

"Well, he's been following me. So what we do is have you follow me too, only you'll know where I'm going so you can hang back and watch for anyone on my tail."

Hank was nodding. "Sounds like a plan." Then he frowned. "But what do we do when we find him?"

"Then *we* follow *him*. And we convince him that he doesn't want to stick his nose in my life anymore."

"And if he doesn't listen?"

Jeremy shrugged. "Then he disappears."

Hank was shaking his head. "Oh, no. Not while I'm within a hundred miles. Include me out."

Jeremy felt his temper heating.

"You gonna let me down *again*, bro? You gonna let *Daddy* down again too?"

He remembered his talks with his daddy whenever he'd come to visit. A scary man, Daddy, what with that patch over his bad eye and the way he'd fix him with the bright blue of his good one. But once he got talking, his smooth voice would wrap around Jeremy and caress him like a warm breeze, making the scaredness go away. Jeremy knew he'd inherited some of Daddy's gift for persuasion, but only some.

Daddy knew things no one else knew, saw things with his dead eye that no one else saw. He'd talk of gods—not the gods that everyone had heard of. Those were just stories, he'd said. He spoke of other gods, the Others, locked out from the world, waiting for ages to return.

He told of the special blood that ran through his veins, and ran through his children's. They all were part of a special Bloodline that made them shine in the eyes of the Others, but their Bloodline had been diluted and polluted over the ages. It had to be concentrated and purified.

Daddy would tell him over and over about his Plan to do just that, and about the parts Jeremy and his half brother Hank were to play, and how together with a girl named Moonglow they would create the Key, a pure-blooded child who would unlock the gates that prevented the Others from returning to the Earth and reclaiming it.

And when they did return they would reward those of the Bloodline who had made it possible. Daddy would ascend to the throne of Earth and Jeremy and Hank would be his princes.

Daddy's soothing voice had stayed with Jeremy, repeating the story and the things they must do to bring the Plan to fruition, and left him with never a moment's doubt of its truth. But then Daddy stopped coming around. He'd warned that there might come a day when that happened, and he'd made Jeremy swear by the blood of the prince within him that he'd see the Plan through to its finish.

Jeremy had sworn. So had Hank. But obviously Hank's promises didn't mean much.

"We're not going to get into this again, are we?" Hank said. "I told you—"

"You told me you had your own thing going and that Daddy could shove his Bloodline up his ass!"

"I never said anything of the sort. What I'm doing is just as necessary to the Plan as what you're doing."

"Bullshit! The Plan was this: I knocked up Moonglow, so you were supposed to knock up her kid."

Hank rolled his eyes. "I know, but I'm identified with the Kicker movement—right now the movement is *me*—and I can't risk getting involved with knocking up an eighteen-year-old."

"So I'm left with the job of fucking my own kid."

Hank smiled. "And doing a damn fine job of it too."

Jeremy felt heat rush into his face as his hands curled into fists. "You son of a—"

"Easy now. You got the job done, didn't you? And as for boffing your own kid—first off, if she's eighteen she's not a kid; and second, it's not like you raised her or anything, or saw her even once when she was growing up. She was a complete stranger when you met her."

Jeremy felt himself relax a little. Hank had a point. Dawn could just as easily have been someone else's kid.

"That may be, but it didn't stop me from feeling weird and maybe even a little perverted the first few times."

"That's because in the everyday world it's a big taboo, and everyone's all uptight about it because if you do that sort of thing too much you can wind up with a bunch of FLKs."

"Eff-ell—?"

"Funny-looking kids. But because you two share the Bloodline, that changes all the rules. That means it's not only okay, it's *necessary* for you two to get together and have a kid."

"It also means that I had to do everything myself. *I* had to kidnap her, *I* had to get her pregnant, *I* had to keep her from getting an abortion, and *I* wound up getting sent up for life for it!"

Realizing he was shouting, he clammed up.

He remembered his confusion at the time. Hell, he was only nineteen when he'd tracked Moonglow to Atlanta. He tried to get in touch with Hank to tell him the good news, but Hank was nowhere to be found. They'd been meeting maybe every six months, talking about how to carry through Daddy's Plan, and now he seemed to have vanished—just like Daddy had.

But somehow he'd known Hank was still alive, somehow he'd sensed him out there.

Hank said, "I would have helped you if I could have, bro. You know that."

"But I didn't know it then. I knew you wasn't dead, so I thought you'd run out on me."

He later found out that Hank was in jail, but he'd been pretty shaken at the time.

Hank shook his head. "Never. But isn't it strange, this connection we have? I know you're around, and you know I'm around. Weird, huh?"

"Yeah. Weird. But that made it all the worse when I had to do everything myself."

"I wish I could've been there with you, bro. Things would have been different then, and they'd be different now."

Damn right, they'd be.

The Plan had been for Hank to charm his way into Moonglow's pants and get her pregnant. They'd marry and have the baby. If it wasn't a girl, they'd try again. When they finally had one and she grew old enough to have a baby of her own, Jeremy would move in. One way or another—by charm or by force—Hank's daughter would have Jeremy's child.

And that child would change the world.

But Jeremy had panicked when he couldn't find Hank. He had no confidence in his ability with girls. That was Hank's strong suit, not his. Or so he'd thought at the time. He now knew that he could turn on the charm just as well as his older brother.

Not knowing what else to do, afraid that Moonglow might get knocked up by some other guy, he'd chosen the only route he could think of—the most direct. And when she'd started looking for an abortionist, he'd done the same.

He'd never believed he'd get caught. When he did he'd thought the Others had deserted him.

But then, last year had come word of a special therapy that the high-ups at Creighton wanted to test. And the testing would require that Jeremy be freed into the world.

He'd known then that the Others hadn't deserted him. They'd only been waiting for the proper moment. They'd arranged for him to be released in time to help Hank do the final purification of the Bloodline by fathering the miracle child.

But Hank had balked. His Kickers were more important.

"I still can't believe how when it came to choosing between the Bloodline and these losers, you chose them."

"What I'm doing, I'm doing for the Bloodline. In my dream—"

"I don't want to hear about any stupid dreams."

"You keep saying that, but it's time you listened. I keep having this dream about a baby. It's in danger. It's screaming in fright. And then along comes the Kicker Man, and he takes it in his arms, and it stops crying. How do you interpret that, Jer?"

Jeremy felt a chill as he pictured the powerful image. If it really was a dream, he could see only one way to interpret it, but he couldn't bring himself to say it.

"I interpret that as your way of easing a guilty conscience, or, better yet, making excuses for yourself."

Hank took a step closer. "The dream is real, Jer. It's been coming to me off and on for the past year, and every night for the past two weeks. *Every night.*"

"So?"

"So, how long has Dawn been pregnant?"

Jeremy got another chill, stronger this time, as he remembered the instructions on the testing kit's box saying it took a minimum of two weeks after the start of pregnancy to turn positive.

He hated giving him the answer. "Two weeks or so, I'd guess."

Hank grinned. "Doesn't that tell you something?"

"It tells me you're kidding yourself."

"It's a message from the Others and you know it. I couldn't be sure before, but it's clear as day now: They sent me the sign of the Kicker Man and inspired me to write my book, and now they're telling me why: Because the Kickers are going to pave the way for the return of the Others. But they have an even more important mission than that: They're gonna protect that baby from the enemies of the Bloodline."

Could Hank be right? Was all this Kicker shit part of the Plan to bring back the Others? Were they some sort of palace guards, or maybe the shock troops of the Others?

Was that Hank's job—captain of the guard? Then who was he—father of the Key?

Yeah. *Father of the Key.* That sounded pretty good. Maybe all this was going to work out right after all.

As long as no one got in their way.

"You think there really are Enemies out there like Daddy told us about?"

Hank's expression was grim. "I've given this a lot of thought. Daddy told us plenty of stuff that would sound crazy to other people, stuff that other people would laugh at. But we believe it. Why?"

"Because Daddy told us, and because it's the truth."

"Yeah, we believe it's the truth, but why do we believe these things that no one else believes? That no one else has even heard of?"

Jeremy was losing patience. "I'm sure you're gonna tell me."

"It's because the Bloodline is so strong in us. We heard these things and we believe them because our blood *knows* they're true. That's why, even though I've never seen an Enemy, I *know* they're out there. And so do you."

Jeremy found himself nodding. Yes, he did know. Daddy had talked about Enemies of the Others who had almost killed off the Bloodline in the past and would try again.

"You think that's what happened to Daddy? You think it wasn't an accident—that the Enemies got to him?"

"I don't know what else to think."

He'd known Hank was still alive when he couldn't find him back in Atlanta. He just didn't know where. He remembered having a feeling as a little kid that Daddy wouldn't be coming back because he wasn't . . . *there* anymore.

Hank said, "Those bastards have probably been looking for us ever since."

And then Jeremy had an unsettling thought. "This guy that's been dogging my trail, testing my DNA . . . do you think he could be one of the Enemies?"

Hank started pacing again. "Could be . . . could be . . ." He stopped and stared at him. "Shit!"

"What?"

"The guy who stole my book—I'll bet he was one. As a matter of fact I'm sure he was."

"What book?"

"It's a long story. Suffice it to say it was old and contained a drawing of the Kicker Man. Might even had contained information on where it came from— something I'd really like to know—but it's gone now, stolen away by a guy who pretended to be a reporter."

"Hey. Maybe the guy after me is just pretending to be a detective. Maybe he's just pretending to work for Moonglow when what he's really doing is hunting down the Bloodline."

Hank spun and kicked the wall. "Shit! What does yours look like?"

"Never seen him. But I got a description from Vecca."

Hank barked a harsh laugh. "Vecca! That vampire bitch. You gonna believe anything you hear from her?"

"She seemed pretty pissed that someone was testing my DNA. Like they were horning in on her territory."

"Her territory—that's us, all right. She's always seemed like a big eye gazing down on the rest of us through a microscope. I mean, don't you get the feeling when she looks at you that she's not seeing a person, but just a conglomeration of cells?"

Jeremy stared at his brother. He'd nailed Vecca—to the nth degree. But damned if he was going to hear that from Jeremy.

"That's downright poetic, Hank. Maybe you should try your hand at being a writer someday." He got a kick out of Hank's reddening face. "But there's a chance we've got a couple of Enemies bird-dogging us, so why don't we stick to that?"

"All right. Let's do that. What did Vecca say yours looked like?"

"She wasn't much help. My age, brown hair, brown eyes, and about average height."

Hank frowned. "That could describe my guy too."

"Maybe they're the same guy—or twins."

Hank snapped his fingers. "Twins! Did Daddy ever mention twins to you?"

"Not that I recall."

"He did to me. Said the chief Enemies were twins. Do you think these could be the guys he was talking about?"

"One way to find out: You trail me back to Queens and see if anyone's following me."

Hank glanced at his watch and shook his head. "Sorry, bro. I'm supposed to speak to a Kicker gathering in about an hour."

Jeremy stiffened. Hank wasn't going to leave him high and dry again.

"So? Cancel it."

"No can do. This is a big crowd. Been set up for weeks. I can't back out now."

Jeremy felt that familiar heat again. "I've got an Enemy chewing my ass who could mess up everything. If he finds out I'm Dawn's father and goes and tells her, the shit will really hit the fan. She'll go running back to her momma and start looking to get an abortion. I can't go knocking off abortionists again, Hank. That worked once, but it won't work again. I do one and the Creighton folks'll be all over me. That'll leave the dirty work to you. Got a gun, Hank?"

Hank seemed unmoved.

"I'll come out your way tomorrow and follow you around all day if you want. But today is out of the question."

He realized if he stayed here another second he'd be strangling Hank. He turned and headed for the door.

"Fuck you!"

6

Jeremy kept a death grip on the Miata's steering wheel as he crossed the Williamsburg Bridge. He shifted his gaze between the road ahead and his rearview mirror, keeping an eye on a silver PT Cruiser that had been staying two cars behind him since he'd left the Lodge.

Was that an Enemy? The so-called detective? Or just another guy on his way to Brooklyn?

Fuck Hank for weaseling out and making him do this all on his own. They were supposed to be a team, damn it.

He tried to see through the PT's windshield but the glare reduced the driver to a featureless silhouette.

Damn! If he could just get—

He glanced at the road, saw red lights, and slammed on his brakes. As his car screeched to a halt just inches shy of the bumper ahead of him, he heard other tires screeching behind him and braced for a rear-end collision.

It never came. The cars stopped in time. He checked for the PT, saw it pull out into an open lane and roll by to his right. The college-age girl behind the wheel didn't even glance his way as she passed.

He pounded his steering wheel. He could have been killed. And then what? Would Dawn keep the baby—the Key—if he was gone?

Like hell. She didn't seem all that crazy about being pregnant. In fact, she seemed downright unhappy about it.

The Key . . . aborted . . . its remains tossed out like garbage.

Unthinkable.

He heard a toot and looked around to see that his lane was moving again. Keeping his eyes trained on the road, he resumed his trip. But his thoughts remained on the enemy.

Average height . . . brown hair . . . brown eyes—

"Shit!" he cried.

Joe Henry . . . the guy hanging around Work . . . the video gamer. He fit

Vecca's description to a T. But lots of guys did. He bet he could wander through Work and—

Shit!—the guy had been reading Hank's book. That clinched it. He knew they were brothers. All a fucking setup.

He pounded the steering wheel in near-blind rage until a honk warned him that he was veering out of his lane. He straightened the wheel and drove on, seething.

The guy had played him like a fucking five-string banjo.

What had Vecca said his name was? John something . . . like two first names . . .

John Robertson. Yeah.

He bared his teeth. You and me, John Robertson . . . I think we got us a score to settle.

7

Jack reached Forest Hills and went looking for a copy shop or office supply store. He found a Staples on Queens Boulevard and, as promised, made a copy of the DNA comparison with the Creighton letterhead folded out of sight.

Then he called Christy. Her voice mail picked up on her home number; he left a message and tried her cell. The cell's voice mail picked up on the second ring—a reliable indication that it was turned off. He left another message for her to call him ASAP.

A worm of unease wriggled in his gut and he didn't know why. Bolton had Christy right where he wanted her: on the far side of a chasm from her daughter. No reason to make a physical move against her.

Should he go over to her place and check it out? No. Didn't want to take the risk of being seen peeking in her windows.

Most likely she'd forgotten to charge her phone or turn it on. Or maybe she was rehearsing for that play she mentioned. Could be a rule that all cell phones are turned off during rehearsal. Made sense.

Kind of a relief in a way. The news he had to give her deserved—no, *de-manded* to be delivered in person. He was dreading the prospect of sitting across from her and looking her in the eye while he told her that the father of her child, the man who abducted her and raped her when she was eighteen, was the same man who'd just made her daughter—*their* daughter—pregnant.

He'd almost rather wear a red shirt through a Crips neighborhood.

But he'd keep trying her phones. Meanwhile, he had time to kill. He didn't want to return to the city and then come back out again. So he drove around for a while, then decided maybe it was time to become Joe Henry again and pay a visit to Work. He had mixed feelings about the possibility of running into Bolton. On one hand he wanted another chance to get into the guy's head, see what made him tick and hope he'd let something slip about this baby of his; on the other, just thinking about the guy made his skin crawl.

He called both of Christy's numbers again. No answer.

Time to go to Work.

8

Jerry was on edge. Totally. Dawn had seen him flare up before, but he'd always cooled off pretty quick. This was different. He couldn't sit still. He was like in a chair one minute and out of it the next, turning on the TV, surfing a few channels, then turning it off. He looked like he was ready to totally explode or something.

"You okay?"

He stopped between the TV and the easy chair and stared at her.

"Yeah, darlin. Why?"

She shrugged. "I don't know. You seem, like, tense."

"Got a lot on my mind."

"Something go wrong at the meeting?"

"Meet—?" He looked confused.

"You know. With EA?"

"Oh, that." He shook his head. "No, everything's fine with EA. I'm just bothered by all this friction with your mother. I wish there was a way we could straighten her out and get her on board."

"That's so not going to happen. Way too late."

But how sweet of him to care. So totally typical of him to be worried about a crazy woman who'd accused him of awful things, then tried to seduce him.

Which made Dawn feel totally worse for what she planned to do about the baby.

She'd found a place called Women's Choice right here in Rego Park. They said she could come in for an interview and paperwork this afternoon. Then they'd schedule her for tests, and then . . .

She'd totally hate herself doing it, but she knew she wasn't ready to be a mother and couldn't see any other way.

"Why don't you play a game or something. Maybe that new FPS." Dawn couldn't remember the title—a new Doom or Half Life or Call of Duty? No matter. First-person shooters always relaxed him.

He shook his head. "Not in much of a gamin mood. Feel more like doin the real thing."

She blinked. "Shooting people?"

He grinned. "Just kiddin."

The look in his eyes . . . Dawn wasn't so sure.

He said, "Maybe I'll just check my e-mail and surf a little."

A spasm of uncertainty gripped her. Had she closed the Women's Choice Web site? She wasn't sure. God, if she'd left that window open . . .

"Good idea," she said, turning and dashing upstairs. "I've got some errands to run."

She ducked into the extra room and checked the computer screen. The screen saver was running. She hopped over and wiggled the mouse. The desktop appeared with no open windows.

Knew I'd signed off.

Light with relief, she passed Jerry on his way in. He was giving her a strange look, but she spoke before he could say anything.

"I'm running out. Need anything from Pathmark?"

After a couple of seconds he said, "Yeah. Pick me up some beef jerky—the peppery kind. I feel like chompin on something."

She gave him a quick kiss. "You got it."

She grabbed a sweater from the bedroom and hurried downstairs. She'd go to Women's Choice first, then swing by Pathmark on her way—

"Dawn!"

Something in his voice froze her. She didn't turn as she heard him race down the stairs behind her. He grabbed her shoulders and spun her to face him.

"Women's Choice?" His eyes were wild. "Women's fuckin Choice?"

She couldn't speak, only yammer.

He said, "I thought it was kind of funny, you checkin the computer before

I got to it, so I opened the browser history." His grip on her shoulders tightened as he shook her. "*Women's Choice!* I can't believe it! You want to kill my baby!"

"It's not like that! And it's my baby too! You don't have to carry it! I do! And I'm so not ready for that!"

He wrapped her in his arms and cooed in her ear. "Oh, darlin-darlin-darlin! If you only knew what this baby means to me."

The sob that had been building burst free. "I know, I know."

"And not just to me. To us. To the world. Our baby is the Key. He's gonna change the world!"

"You keep saying things like that and they're . . . they're totally scary. The key to what?"

"To the future. You'll be known the world over as the Mother of the Key. Millions of people will worship you and pray to you to speak to your son on their behalf."

He was getting scarier by the minute.

"What do you think I'm gonna be—the Virgin Mary? News flash: I'm so not a virgin and this was a totally *maculate* conception."

He pushed her back to arm's length. His face was filled with joy as his wild blue gaze bored into her.

"Darlin, you're gonna be better than any Virgin Mary. You know why? Because you're *real*. But the only way you're gonna get to be the queen mother is if you have our baby."

"Jerry—"

His grip tightened as the joy faded from his face.

"And you *will* have this baby—"

His grip tightened further and now she saw no joy in his face, only growing rage as he bared his teeth.

"Jerry, you're hurting—"

"—because if you don't . . . if you *ever* do *anythin* to hurt my baby, you will wish you'd been born dead, darlin. You'll wish it 'cause I will hunt you down like a bitch cur and I will see you dead. But before you die I will see you suffer the tortures of the damned for killin the prince of the Bloodline. You'll suffer so long and so bad that you'll *pray* to die, you'll *beg* to die."

His face had gone crimson, spittle speckled his lips, and his eyes . . . in their pale-blue depths she saw exactly what he'd do to her. A scream was surging into her throat when he suddenly let her go and stepped back. He licked his lips and smiled as his complexion faded to normal.

"But of course, that's all idle chatter 'cause nothin's gonna happen to my baby, right? Right?"

Dawn could only nod. He was back to talking normally now. She so wanted to scream and run but didn't dare move a muscle—couldn't. Her limbs were frozen in position.

He leaned closer and sounded like the SpongeBob pirate. "I can't heeeeeear you. *Right?*"

She found her voice and croaked out a feeble, "Right."

What had just happened? He'd gone from totally normal to totally insane, then back to totally normal again in less than a minute. She'd never seen that side of him, hadn't even guessed it existed.

Women's Choice . . . the idea of aborting his child—why was it always *his* child?—had like totally set off a bomb in his brain. Made him mad crazy.

Well, maybe he had a right to be pissed that she was going to end the pregnancy without telling him. The baby was half his, after all. But only half. What about *her* half? And he wasn't the one who was going to get all fat and bloated.

But he'd been totally more than just pissed. He'd been insane. And he hadn't been kidding about killing her. A shudder passed through her like an earthquake. She knew from his eyes and the way he'd said it that he meant every word.

"Well, darlin," he said with his usual warm, friendly smile. "Long as you've got your sweater and were on your way out, what say we take a trip down to Work. I feel like gettin myself a couple of cold ones."

"Not me. It's totally boring. And you won't even let me have a beer."

"That's right, darlin. No more booze for you. Like those signs in the bar say, *When you're pregnant, you never drink alone.* You're not going to get my baby boy drunk. You can have some of that Diet Pepsi you and your mother like so much."

"But—"

"Hush now. I've got another reason I want to visit Work tonight. Want to see if a certain someone is hanging around, waiting for me."

As he propelled her toward the door, Dawn wondered what she'd got herself into. And if there was a way out.

9

Jack stood at the bar nursing a watery Coors Light as he went over his options. At least it was better than an even more watery Bud Light from the ruinators of Rolling Rock.

The neon Corona clock on the wall behind the bar said 6:30. Still about an hour until sunset. But from what Christy had told him, if Bolton was coming in, he would have shown by now.

Reminded of Christy, Jack pulled out his phone and called her numbers again. Still no answer. Rehearsal was dragging on. At least he hoped it was rehearsal.

Someone eased over and leaned against the bar beside him: Dirty Danny.

"Need any party supplies?"

"Nope. Sorry. No one's invited me to any parties lately."

Danny gave him a yellow grin. "Well, then have one of your own. That's what I'd do."

"Why am I not surprised?"

"Well, you need anything, you know where to find me."

Danny moved on and Jack decided he was tired of Queens, tired of wasting his time waiting for people to answer their phones or show up in bars. Time to head home and see if Gia had any plans for dinner. If nothing was on the stove yet, they could head down to Little Italy where Vicky could chow down on Amalia's mussels in garlic sauce.

He left the rest of the beer wannabe on the bar and headed for the door.

10

A parade of what-ifs were tying Jeremy's stomach in knots as he maneuvered into a parking spot down the street from Work.

What if he hadn't checked Dawn's browser history?

What if she'd gone ahead and had the abortion?

What if she tries again?

It was like the past was repeating itself. But at least this time he wouldn't have to go around killing doctors. He hadn't been able to reveal himself to Moonglow. With Dawn it was different. She knew he was the father, so he could stay close and watch over her.

Watch over her . . . what a job that would be . . . nine months of hell until—

No, wait. Maybe only a few months of hell. He knew abortions weren't done after a certain point in a pregnancy. He didn't know that point, but he'd sure as hell find out.

The thing was, he'd have to stay right on top of her, not let her out of his sight until that point was reached. Could he do that? How could he get up to Creighton every week for his injection if he couldn't trust her alone? What was he going to do—chain her in the basement?

He didn't want her along now—not if he was going to have to deal with that Enemy posing as Joe Henry—but he didn't dare leave her home.

"Shit!"

"What's the matter?"

He looked at Dawn and wanted to kill her for wanting to kill the Key. She'd come so close to ruining everything. He saw the fear in her eyes and realized that might be the key . . . the key to protecting the Key.

Fear.

Make her so afraid of him that the thought of an abortion will never cross her mind again.

But before the fear . . . marriage. That way he could have some legal say about the baby. But marrying her wouldn't be an easy proposition after the way he'd blown up earlier. He knew he'd scared her bad.

"Nothing, darlin. Just mad at myself for losin it the way I did. You've got to understand that though I never wanted a kid, I do now. And like I said, it's a miracle. I—"

He squinted through the windshield at the man who'd just stepped out of Work: Joe Henry. No . . . his name wasn't Joe Henry . . . Moonglow's detective, John Robertson. Or maybe not just a detective. Maybe an Enemy of the Bloodline. And here he was, practically walking into Jeremy's arms.

The Others must be watching over me.

"What's wrong?"

"I'm looking at a guy who's been causing me trouble."

Dawn leaned forward and pointed. "Him? You introduced me to him yesterday. I thought he was a friend."

"So did I. But I've learned different."

He heard Vecca's voice in his head telling him to make the call, then follow the guy until folks from her mysterious, all-powerful agency grabbed him. He heard another voice telling him, Yeah, that would be the smart thing to do because he couldn't be a hundred percent sure that Joe Henry wasn't really Joe Henry. He might not be a detective or an Enemy, might just be some everyday shlub who liked beer and video games and was reading *Kick*.

Shit! Hank's book! That was the key. He was carrying it around as a prop—a goddamn *prop*—because he thought it would make Jeremy lower his guard and let him get in close where he could screw up everything.

Well, it almost worked. It almost fucking *worked*.

Jeremy felt his blood begin to heat.

Come to think of it, the guy probably didn't know shit about video games either, because he'd let Jeremy do all the playing.

The only thing Robertson had played was Jeremy—like Hendrix played guitar.

He knew his face was reddening.

And Robertson wasn't just some smart-ass detective, he was an Enemy. Carrying *Kick* around proved it, because only an enemy could know Jeremy and Hank were connected. Must know about the Bloodline too, and the Key. That was why he was here—to mess up the Plan.

His vision took on a red tinge.

"The *fuck!*"

Dawn jumped in her seat. "Jerry! What—?"

Jeremy ignored her as he hit the trunk release and jumped out. He ran around to the rear and yanked on a ring in the floor. Beneath, in the spare well, he found the tire iron and hefted it. Good solid feel, the lug-wrench end nice and heavy.

As he started after Robertson, Dawn lowered her window.

"Jerry, what are you doing?"

"Just stay here. This'll only take a minute."

"But—"

"Be right back. I owe somebody something. Gonna settle up with him."

His blood sang in his ears as he hurried through the dying light toward Robertson, long, quick strides eating up the distance between them. The guy was oblivious, just ambling along the sidewalk like he hadn't a care in the world. Yeah, well, he was about to have a care—a big care. He was about to get messed up.

Jeremy stepped over the curb and onto the sidewalk a dozen feet behind him. He glanced around. Nobody nearby, nobody looking his way except Dawn.

Nine feet to go . . . six . . . he tightened his grip on the tire iron and chose a spot on the back of the guy's head. He could almost hear the crack, feel the crunch, see the spray of red when steel hit bone. He took a two-handed grip and raised it high as he closed in.

This was gonna be good. This was gonna be easy. This was gonna be quick and clean. One skull-crushing shot, plus one more for good measure as he went down, then Jeremy would keep moving, barely breaking stride, walking away as if nothing had happened. Someone would find the guy leaking his brains out onto the sidewalk and call EMS. If he survived, he'd most likely never wake up, and even if he did he wouldn't remember shit, and be good for even less.

Jeremy raised the iron higher then and, putting his arms, shoulders, and a good deal of his body behind it, swung—

And missed.

At the last second the guy spun and ducked to his right. Jeremy had been set to connect with something hard and solid. Instead the iron whipped through empty air, leaving him stagger-stepping ahead.

There—to his left.

He half turned and saw something flashing toward his face—the palm of a hand. Jeremy tried to react but he was off-balance, tilting forward as the heel of that palm caught him square on the nose. He heard a sickening *crunch* as pain detonated in his face—a July Fourth finale of brightly flashing lights that left him blinded and disoriented. He quit his two-handed grip as he raised his left to fend off another blow while the right tried a feeble backhand swing with the iron. But almost immediately a fist that seemed aimed at his spine or maybe at a place somewhere behind him rammed into his gut, doubling him over. He grunted with the pain, blinked, turned away defensively as he tried to clear his vision for a swing at this guy, wherever he was. That was when something hard slammed against the outside of his left knee, bending it a way it wasn't supposed to go. The leg gave out and he went down, dropping the iron to put his hands out to break his fall. As he landed on hands and knees some-

thing heavy rammed his back, knocking him flat. Then a shoe against the back
of his neck, pressing his face into the pavement.

He's gonna kill me, he's gonna curb me then he's gonna break my neck
and then the Plan'll die because sure as shit Dawn'll have an abortion before
I'm cold in the earth.

"What the hell's up with you?"

Jeremy's vision cleared and he found himself face-to-face with the tire of
one of the parked cars. And the guy was talking to him instead of kicking the
shit out of him. Good sign.

He knew he should lie still and look like he was beaten down and wait for
a chance, but then he thought again of how this guy had played him and the
rage rushed back full force.

"You motherf—"

He tried to roll and rise but pain shot through his knee like someone had a
knife in it and the foot pressed harder, grinding his cheek against the concrete.

"Easy, there. What I ever do to you?"

"I know who you are, you lousy—"

"And just who is that?"

"I don't know your real name but I know it ain't Joe Henry and it ain't
John Robertson—"

The pressure against his neck increased.

"Whoa! Let's back it up there. Where'd you hear the name John Robertson?"

"What difference it make? I know it's fake. I know you and your friends
been doggin my ass for months now, tryin to kill the Bloodline, but it ain't
gonna work."

More pressure. Jeremy thought his jaw was going to break.

"Months? You need some heavy medication, dude. I don't know anything
about a Bloodline and I never heard of you until last week."

"Bullshit!" He had to speak through forcibly clenched teeth.

But the guy's voice carried a ring of truth. Something in his tone said he
hadn't heard of Jeremy before. So what was the deal? Was he just a detective
like he said?

"Then why you been doggin my ass? Why you been messin with my life?"

"It's what I do."

He realized then that the guy wasn't going to kill him, because if that was
what all this was about, he'd have picked up the tire iron and be doing to Jeremy's skull what Jeremy had been planning for his. If he just lay still and shut
up, he'd live to fight another day.

But then he thought of how this jerk had suckered him into looking bad in
front of Dawn and his mouth started running.

"Better kill me now, asshole, because there ain't no place you can hide from me. It's me or you, so you might as well end this right here and right now, otherwise—"

Jeremy hadn't thought the pressure on his neck could get any worse, but it did, and for an awful second he thought he'd gone too far, pushed too hard, and the guy was really going to do it.

But then the pressure eased . . . very slowly . . . as if it took every smidgen of the guy's will not to do as Jeremy had suggested. He heard a laugh—as forced sounding as any laugh Jeremy had ever heard.

"You mean kill you? You're not worth the hassle."

And then the pressure was gone and he heard fading footsteps. He looked up and saw the guy walking away with his back to him, just leaving him here, and not even looking over his shoulder—not once.

What's he think I am? Cow shit he can just scrape off his shoe and walk away from? No way.

He saw the tire iron less than half a dozen feet away. Yeah. No funny stuff this time, no surprise moves. This time he'll wish—for the last two seconds of his life—that he'd finished him when he had the chance.

Jeremy pushed himself up from the pavement and—

His knee—a bolt of lightning shot through it again. He'd forgotten about his goddamn knee.

He wasn't going nowhere.

As he rubbed the swollen joint he stared at the tire iron he'd never reach and at the retreating figure of the mystery man who still hadn't looked back. He wanted to scream.

And then he heard running footsteps and Dawn's voice coming up behind him.

"Ohmygod! Ohmygod! Did he hurt you?"

He felt like such a jerk. How the hell was he going to spin this?

11

Jack noticed his hand still shaking as he went to fit the car key in the ignition.

He'd forced himself to walk away from a living, breathing Jeremy Bolton—an act that ranked near the top of his Hardest-Things-I've-Ever-Done list—and leave the scene.

Alibi or no alibi, Jack was sure now that he'd killed Gerhard.

Every fiber of his self-preservation instinct had screamed to kill the son of a bitch and end it there, but a higher center had warned that he was too exposed, that some concerned citizen might have seen all or part of the attack from a window or across the street and called 911. Witness accounts of who was the aggressor would depend on when they'd tuned in. If they missed Bolton swinging for the fence with his tire iron, then Jack would be listed as the assaulter instead of the assaultee. But even if not, Jack wanted no part in a police report.

The cautious end of his brain had also reminded him of the agency behind Creighton that would come looking for him.

So he'd walked away, fighting head-to-toe adrenaline shakes as he forced himself to maintain a cool saunter. No worry about Bolton sneaking up behind him on that knee—his sneaking days were over for a while. When Jack had reached the corner, he'd trotted for his car. He'd parked it well out of sight of Work.

He turned the key and pulled out, moving away from the area.

When he'd left Work he'd spotted Jeremy out of the corner of his eye, crossing the street as he came his way. The fact that he hadn't called out, and the way he was holding his right arm tight against his side, told Jack that something was up, something not good.

So he'd listened to Bolton coming up behind him—those cowboy boots weren't built for stealth—and made his move when he heard a sudden increase in footsteps.

Jack had been surprised at first at how fast Bolton folded, but thinking about it now he realized he should have expected it. Bolton had been locked up since his late teens. Whatever street smarts he might have had were long atrophied. And life at Creighton had weakened them further. While the place's maximum security lockup wasn't exactly a country club, it was a long, long way from hard time. Even if Bolton had worked out—and it looked like he had—strength wasn't enough in a fight. His oDNA might make him mean but it didn't make him fast or tough or smart. He'd folded like a cheap lawn chair.

But that wasn't the most striking thing about the encounter.

I don't know your real name but I know it ain't Joe Henry and it ain't John Robertson . . .

The words echoed silently through the car. How had Bolton heard the name John Robertson? Certainly not from Jack, so that left only two other possibilities: Levy and Vecca.

But right now he was worried more about Christy.

After putting about a mile between himself and Bolton he tried Christy's numbers again, and again got no answer. He didn't feel right leaving town without at least going over to check on her place. No reason anymore to stay away—his role as Bolton's new video gamer friend was dead.

He had Christy's address but these streets were confusing as hell. She lived on 68th Drive, but that ran parallel and next to 68th Road which ran next to 68th Avenue. Finally he found it—a decent-size, older, well-kept, stucco-walled house with high-peaked gables and an attached two-car garage. Worth a gorgeous penny.

No lights on inside. Not encouraging. He pulled into the driveway, got out, and went to the front door. He rang the bell three times and used the brass knocker between rings.

No answer.

A vision of Christy lying dead or close to it inside began to form.

One more place to check. He'd noticed that the two-car garage had small windows placed high in the metal doors, too high to look through. He walked around the back and found a double-hung window into the garage. His penlight revealed that it was empty.

Relieved, he returned to his car. If her Mercedes had been there he would have felt obligated to break in for a look-see. Its absence made it most likely that she was at rehearsal with her phone off.

He headed for Manhattan. She'd have to wait till tomorrow to learn the truth about the father of her grandchild.

Looking on the bright side, Jack had just been given a reprieve of sorts.

12

"I still think I should have called the cops," Dawn was saying as she applied an ice-filled baggy to his swollen knee. "Why didn't you let me?"

"Okay, for the fourth time," Jeremy said—damn, his voice sounded like he was holding his nose—"I don't want them thinkin I'm some kinda trouble-maker. You know, like every week I'm gonna be in some kinda fight."

That, for once, was the truth. The second was that someone might have seen him with the tire iron. Why make a bad situation worse?

"Yeah, but, well, that guy's totally dangerous. I don't think I've ever seen anybody move so fast. One minute you were coming up behind him, a second later you were on the ground. For a moment there I wasn't sure what happened. I thought you'd disappeared."

Go ahead, he thought. Rub it in.

But he knew that wasn't what she was up to.

She'd changed from the frightened girl in the car to instant caregiver. Like seeing him hurt had flipped some sort of switch inside, and suddenly she couldn't do enough for him. She'd helped him to his feet and brought the car to him, saving him a painful walk. Then she'd driven him home, stretched him out on the couch, and had been playing nurse ever since.

"And why won't you tell me what's up between you and that guy? I thought you were friends."

Couldn't before—his head had been too fuzzy to come up with something. But he had a story now.

"Not friends, acquaintances. I didn't know it but he scammed a friend of mine in the city—duped him out of a small fortune—and now he's come out here to set me up." He did an embarrassed shrug. "I don't know what hap-pened. I saw him and thought of how he just about ruined my buddy, and I guess I lost it."

"Well, he just about ruined you. Look at your nose," she said for the tenth time, clucking over him like a mother hen. "It's like twice its normal size. That's so got to hurt."

"Like crazy."

Not true. Kind of numb, really, but why tell Dawn that? Maybe this was the key to keeping her under control: Get hurt, be needy, bring out her mothering instincts, let her think she'd taken charge. He was pretty sure he could find ways to keep it up until the baby was too old to be aborted, then he'd take over again.

"Poor thing. Do you think it's broken?"

"Absolutely."

"We've totally got to get you to a doctor."

Like hell. Last thing he needed now was a doctor.

"I'll be all right. But maybe just a little more ice for the nose . . . to help the swellin."

"You got it," she said and hurried off to the kitchen.

Good. He needed to be alone for a couple of minutes. Needed to think and that wasn't easy with her yakking and hovering over him like a hummingbird on speed.

The guy . . . Jeremy figured he'd call him Robertson for now, because he'd seemed concerned that Jeremy knew that name . . . maybe he wasn't an Enemy. He'd sounded baffled when Jeremy had mentioned the Bloodline . . . and had sounded sincere when he'd said he'd never heard of him until last week. If he was an Enemy, wouldn't he have killed Jeremy while he had the chance?

Maybe he was just what Vecca and Levy had said he was: a detective.

It's what I do.

Yeah . . . a detective. And one who knew his business. He'd somehow connected Jeremy and Hank—his carrying that copy of *Kick* around sort of proved that—but how?

Creighton. Had to be. All those meetings Hank and him had had, with Hank pretending to be researching a book. Had Vecca or Levy ratted? He didn't see why they would, but he didn't trust those two, especially not Levy.

Well, however he'd found out, he was tough—Jeremy's swollen nose proved that—and smart. And it was plain he was going to keep on digging and poking and meddling until he screwed everything to hell.

Only way he'd stop was if he met with a fatal accident. Or got fired—and Jeremy couldn't see Moonglow doing that. As long as she was paying him, he'd keep—

Hey, what if he stopped getting paid for another reason besides being fired? What if the lady doing the paying suddenly stopped signing his checks . . . because she was dead?

Jeremy thought about that for a few seconds, then rejected it. Wouldn't work. Too risky. Some neighbor might have seen them arguing. She got killed, someone might mention that. Dawn might be on the outs with dear old

Mom at the moment, but her bad feelings would go poof when she heard she was dead. And if she got even the tiniest idea in her head that Jeremy might have had anything to do with it—after seeing him with the tire iron, she might not think that was so far-fetched—she'd be on the first train to Abortion City.

But what if it looked like an accident?

No. Better yet—what if it looked like suicide?

Jeremy raised himself to sitting. He liked that. Moonglow had been acting crazy lately, and no one knew that better than Dawn. If Mom offed herself, Dawn would think it was partly her fault. She'd go on a major guilt trip, and with no family, there'd be only one person she could turn to.

Oh, yeah, he liked this a *lot*.

"What are you smiling at?"

He jumped at the sound of Dawn's voice. He looked up and saw her approaching with a fresh ice baggy. Had he been smiling? Yeah, probably. Why not?

"Just thinkin about what good care you're takin of me."

Inspiration struck then—he grabbed his neck and groaned.

"What's the matter?" She was at his side in a second. "You all right?"

"My neck—that guy must have crunched it harder than I thought."

"I'll get you some Advil."

"This ain't Advil pain, darlin. I'm gonna need something stronger—a lot stronger."

"But we don't—"

"Yeah, I know. But I know where we can get it."

"Where?"

He winked at her. "Dirty Danny."

"Oh, no. Not him. He looks like a total scuzz."

"He is. But he has the real thing." Grimacing, he struggled to his feet. "I'll score a few Vicodins to get me through the night."

"Are you crazy? You can't go down there now. You sit here and I'll go."

"No way, darlin. I'd rather suffer all night than let you anywhere near the likes of Dirty Danny. Gotta be me."

Dawn shrugged with annoyance. "All right, so it's gotta be you. But no way you're driving. I'll take you down there—right up to the door."

Jeremy hid a smile. Exactly what he'd figured she'd do. Exactly what he'd intended her to do.

13

"Jerry boy!" Dirty Danny said, catching Jeremy's limp as he approached, then fixating on his nose. "What the fuck happened to you, man?"

True to her word, Dawn had dropped him off at the front door and was double-parked outside now, waiting for him. He'd had a bad moment when he'd stepped inside and hadn't seen Dirty Danny at the bar, but then he'd spotted him moving away from one of the booths, stuffing something in his pocket along the way—a completed sale.

"Guess," Jeremy said, looking him in the eye.

Danny grinned and shrugged. "I dunno. Get hit by a truck or something?"

Apparently no word had got back to Work about what had happened. Good. He didn't want to be embarrassed to show his face here.

"Close enough. I'm hurtin a bit. Got any Vikes?"

Danny grinned as his hand slid toward his pocket. "Does the pope shit in the woods? You want brand name or generic?"

"What's the diff?"

"Brand goes for three times more. Same stuff in the pill, but some people just gotta see that VICODIN stamped on it."

"Not me. Dozen generics'll do." He kept his voice level, casual. "Could use a few roofies too."

Danny's eyebrows rose. "You want to forget about the accident?"

"Maybe. How much I need for a good night's sleep?"

He'd pulled out half a dozen little snack-size baggies and was sorting through them.

"A one-milligram tab oughta do it."

"And what if I want some heavy forgetting?"

Danny grinned again and nudged him with an elbow. "Looking to get into someone's panties?"

Jeremy gave him an offended look that was only part put-on. He didn't need a date-rape drug.

"You think I can't get there on my own?"

"No-no. I think that young thing you've got hanging on you—"

"Name's Dawn."

"Right. Dawn. I think she proves you've got mucho mojo."

"The forgettin dose?" Getting info out of this asshole was like pulling teeth.

"The fer-sure dose is five migs with booze, a few more without. Goes to work in fifteen-twenty minutes."

"Gimme a dozen."

"You got it."

14

Back in the car, after giving Dawn an edited version of the buy—no mention of the roofies—Jeremy pulled out his phone.

She glanced at him. "What are you doing?"

"I've decided you're right. I'm gonna call the cops on this guy."

She smiled. "Finally you're listening to reason."

He made a show of dialing, then shook it and tried again.

"Shoot. Must've done something to it when I hit the ground. Mind if I borrow yours?"

"Go ahead."

When he dug it out of her handbag, he punched in Moonglow's number. He figured if she saw Dawn's name come up on caller ID she'd pick up sure. But she didn't. She could be in the shower or something, but this was a sign that she might not be home.

He cut the connection.

"What's the matter?" Dawn said with a laugh. "Cops not home?"

"Bad connection." He turned to her, all sincere and vulnerable. "I don't know if this is such a good idea."

"Try again. Just hit redial."

"Okay."

And he did. Still no answer at Moonglow's. He cut the connection again.

"Nope. Can't do it. Just realized that my friend doesn't want to press charges 'cause he feels like such a jerk. So what's the point?"

Dawn sighed. "Yeah. Maybe you're right."

She sounded disappointed. So what? Jeremy had something more important on his mind: Moonglow wasn't home.

Interesting. Tonight could be the night. The sooner the better.

15

"Say, darlin," Jerry said from where he was stretched out on the couch.
"What've we got to drink?"

Oh, no, Dawn thought, giving him a disapproving look. No way.

"You are so not going to mix beer and Vicodin—not while I'm around."

He smiled. "Yes, dear."

She couldn't believe what a totally different person he'd become since he
got the crap kicked out of him. Almost like he'd had the mean beat out of him
too. She'd been a little scared of him before—a *lot* scared after he'd threatened
her—but when she'd seen him go down some fierce protective instinct had
surged to life. If that guy had stayed around he'd have found Dawn clinging to
his back, clawing at his eyes.

Yeah, Jerry had threatened to kill her, but that was just talk. Hyperbole.
He'd never hurt her. He'd said he'd die for her and she believed him. He'd just
been shocked she'd been thinking of aborting his baby. That was all—the
shock talking, not Jerry.

"Darlin, how about a glass of that diet junk you drink?"

Her Pepsi? Was he kidding?

"But you hate that."

"Hey, I'm desperate and I'm not in the mood for water. Let me try some of
that. If I can't finish it, you can."

"Okay."

She went to the kitchen and poured him a glass from the big three-liter
bottle in the fridge. Poured herself a short one and gulped it down.

God, she totally loved this stuff. She checked the level: Getting low.

Okay, face it, girl: You're addicted. You've got a major Pepsi jones. Another thing she could blame on Mom. Better remember to pick up more tomorrow. Running out would be like tragic.

When she brought the glass back to Jerry she found him closing up her cell phone.

"Calling the cops again?"

He smiled. "Forgot to check my voice mail earlier."

She handed him the glass and watched as he took a sip. He grimaced.

"Maybe it'd be better if it had some ice in it. Could you get me a couple of cubes?"

She sighed and reached for the glass. "Sure."

He held it back. "Just the cubes. I'll keep this here, okay?"

"Yeah. Okay."

Kinda weird, but . . .

She got him the cubes. When she returned she found him swirling the glass. Didn't he know that would make it go flat? She dropped the cubes in and he swirled them around before taking a baby sip.

He shook his head. "Nope. Can't do it. Tastes like medicine." He held out the glass to her. "You finish it."

Some people . . .

She took it back and chugged half of it.

"Best stuff in the world."

He smiled. "I knew you wouldn't let it go to waste."

"Better believe it."

She felt his eyes on her as she finished it off.

Then he yawned. "I'm beat." He laughed. "In more ways than one. I think I'll turn in. Want to come snuggle with me?"

"Are you sure you're up to—?"

Another laugh. "Not tonight, darlin. When I said 'snuggle,' I meant *snuggle*."

She wasn't tired, but there wouldn't be much else to do with Jerry conked out. Why not?

"Okay. Let's snuggle."

16

Jack was halfway across the Queensboro Bridge when his phone rang. He checked the ID and hit TALK when he recognized the number: Christy. What a relief.

"Where've you been, lady? I've been calling all day."

"I know. I just got your message. Sorry. I've been out on the beach at Montauk."

What had she been doing way out on the eastern tip of Long Island?

"Not exactly swimming weather."

"No, but this time of year it's a good place to be alone and do some thinking. And as you well know, I've got a lot to think about."

Jack chewed a lip and thought, Not nearly as much as you'll have after you hear the latest.

"So you turned off your phone?"

"Of course not. What if Dawn needed to reach me? No, the battery ran out. I forgot to charge it. I'm so scattered lately. I guess I didn't hear the warning beeps over the surf. I sat on the beach and stared at the ocean, walked up and down the waterline, found a fish place and had fried clams for lunch. When I checked it and found it dead it took me a while to get back to the car. Got it plugged into the charger now."

"Come to any decisions?"

"Well, the big question was, What do I do next? What *should* I do next? Should I do anything? Dawn's eighteen, which means she's an adult in the eyes of the law. She can make her own decisions and I have no legal right to interfere. So should I just back off and wait till this whole tawdry affair falls to pieces—as it must—and she comes back home?"

Fall to pieces? Jack knew Bolton wasn't about to let that happen—at least not until his baby was born.

"I can't see you going for that."

"Damn right. I couldn't. Dawn may be eighteen, but she's *only* eighteen. She may be legal, but she's still just a kid inside." Her voice rose. "I can't

stand it! And I can't stand by and watch her ruin her life! I've got to keep trying, I've got to find some way to make this right!"

Jack clenched his teeth. He was just a quarter mile from Gia's place—
warm smiles and hugs from his two ladies. If he was smart he'd wait till tomorrow to break the news. But he heard the pain in her voice, the naked need to
save her daughter.

What he had to tell her might very well break up Dawn and Bolton for
good, but it would be a live grenade dropped into the heart of her life.

*Christy, the man who raped you every day for weeks and weeks is the same
man who has made your daughter—yours and his—pregnant.*

How was he going to look her in the eyes and force those words past his lips?

But she had to know. She had a right to know. Because she'd asked him to
learn whatever he could about the man bedding her daughter, and this was
what he'd discovered.

Jack decided then that he wanted—*needed*—to get this over with, to remove this burden of truth and send it home. Tonight.

"Maybe I've found that way."

Eagerness crowded her words. "You have? What? What?"

"It's not for the phone."

"Come on, Jack. Please?"

"Trust me." He thought of the copies of Levy's printouts in his pocket.
"This needs show as well as tell."

"Okay, then. I'm about an hour from home. Where can we meet?"

"Your place is as good as any."

"But I thought you didn't want to be seen with me."

"He's on to me, so it doesn't matter anymore."

"I can be there in an hour—maybe less if I hurry."

Jack had reached the end of the bridge and began looking for a way to get
back on the Queens-bound lanes.

"All right. I'm on my way."

"Hurry. I can't wait."

Yes, you can, he thought. You'll wish you'd waited forever.

17

It didn't take long for Dawn to fall asleep. Jeremy listened to her slow, even breathing for about ten minutes, then got up and limped out to the living room to find her phone.

Time to call Moonglow again.

If she was home, he'd just wasted a roofie on Dawn. Even if not, this still might turn out to be a waste.

He hit REDIAL for maybe the sixth time tonight—every time Dawn had left the room. And this time turned out the same as the others: no answer.

Excellent.

He went back into the bedroom and gave her a nudge. She didn't stir. Not even a little.

Double excellent.

Earlier he'd gone into the bathroom and dissolved one of the olive-green roofies in some hot water in a medicine cup. When he'd sent Dawn back for the ice cubes, he'd poured it into the Diet Pepsi. Odorless, tasteless, she hadn't a clue . . .

She'd be out till morning.

His only worry was whether or not the roofie would hurt the baby. He couldn't see how one milligram could matter.

Now . . . to Moonglow's place.

He slipped out, taking a pair of winter gloves plus Dawn's phone and keys. He took her SUV—no way he'd be able to bend his swollen knee far enough to get into the Miata. Damn good thing it was his left knee too—he'd never be able to drive if it was the right. He dashed to the Home Depot where he bought a cheap utility knife, all razorbladed up and ready to use.

When he reached Moonglow's he called again. Still no answer.

He parked down the street and limped back in the dark. He made a circuit of the outside of the house and found no sign of anyone home. So he pulled on his gloves and let himself in with Dawn's house key. Easing the door closed behind him, he stood listening.

All quiet.

He went straight to the kitchen and opened the fridge where he found the ever-present bottle of Diet Pepsi. Like mother, like daughter. This one was two-thirds full. Moving quickly—she might pull into the driveway any minute—he emptied it until only eight ounces or so remained. A single glass.

Even though the kitchen faced the backyard, he didn't want to risk putting on the lights. So, using the open fridge to show the way, he took a disposable plastic cup and crushed eight roofies in it with a spoon. He dissolved the powder in an ounce of warm water, then poured the solution into the Pepsi.

As he was swirling the bottle he heard a hum. He stopped and listened, then realized it was the garage door opener.

Shit!

Moving as fast as he dared or could, he stowed the Pepsi back in the refrigerator, then rinsed the spoon and dropped it into its drawer. After crumpling the plastic cup, he shoved it into his pocket as he hopped-limped for the back door. He eased it closed behind him and found a dark corner of the backyard that allowed a good view of the kitchen.

Lights went on as Moonglow crossed the dining room and disappeared.

Where'd she go? Not straight to bed, he hoped. Too early. Maybe the bathroom?

After a couple of minutes she reappeared and he pumped a fist as she went straight to the fridge and pulled out the Diet Pepsi. He tensed as she paused and held up the bottle. Had he left any sediment? No. The roofies had been completely dissolved when he'd poured in the solution. She must be thinking she'd left more in the bottle.

She shrugged and emptied the bottle into a glass, took a long gulp, then carried the rest to somewhere else in the house.

Yes!

He'd give it time to work before he got down to business.

And then it would be bye-bye Moonglow.

18

"Come *on!*"

Jack sat behind the wheel and fumed. Traffic had come to a standstill, leaving him trapped on the eastbound LIE between Mount Zion Cemetery and Maspeth. He'd passed this way just an hour ago traveling west and everything had been fine. Had to be an accident.

And then he heard sirens and saw flashing lights in his rearview mirror. A cop cruiser and an ambulance passed him on the shoulder.

Swell. An accident with injuries.

He turned off his car and reached for his phone. Better call Christy and tell her he'd be late. Just what he wanted to do: Draw this out.

No answer. Probably taking a shower, something he wished he were doing.

He plugged his iPod into the radio, selected shuffle, and let her rip. Nilsson's voice filled the car. Vicky's favorite viewing these days was a DVD of the old TV special, *The Point,* and Jack had become a fan of the sound track.

"This is the town and these are the people . . ."

19

Jeremy heard Moonglow's phone start to ring. He knew from his multiple calls tonight that her voice mail picked up after the fourth. He counted four rings.

Time to check her out.

He limped up to the dining room window and peeked in. Empty. But it offered a line of sight into the living room at the front of the house, and there he spotted her, sprawled on the couch.

Excellent.

He let himself in and made his way to where she lay with her eyes closed and mouth open. He nudged her.

Nothing.

Nudged her again—hard.

Nothing. Completely conked out.

Excellent.

He slipped his arms under her and lifted. Groaning with the pain in his knee, he carried her upstairs, stopping ever few steps and leaning against the wall to relieve the weight on his leg. Finally he made it to the master bathroom where he laid her gently in the tub—didn't want any bruises.

As he stepped back to stare at her, she began to snore.

Decision time: clothes on or off? Tough one. Different people did it different ways. Much as he'd love to see her naked again after all these years—what a fine piece of ass she'd been as a teenager—he decided to keep it simple.

Leaving her clothes on, he started the water, nice and warm.

While the tub was filling he returned to the kitchen where he loaded two baggies with ice cubes—Dawn's first aid for his bruises had given him this idea—then limped back upstairs. He arranged Moonglow's arms and hands on the edges of the tub, palms up, then placed an ice bag over each wrist.

During his seemingly endless years at Creighton, Jeremy had devoted a lot of time to planning his own suicide. He'd been sentenced to two consecutive life sentences with no possibility of parole, so he was sure he'd never get out, and just as sure that he'd failed his daddy and the Bloodline. So what was the point of living—especially if it meant spending another thirty or forty years like that?

Of course if he'd known he was going to be let out for this drug trial, his attitude would have been different.

He'd been allowed to draw books from the Creighton library with all its medical texts, and he'd read a lot about suicide, especially accounts of failed attempts and the reasons they'd failed. Often it was ignorance—taking non-lethal doses of drugs or cutting a vein in the wrist instead of the artery, not knowing that a vein will often clot up long before the person bled to death. More often it was failure of nerve—the rope is tied to the beam and knotted around the neck, but the clown just can't make himself step off the chair; or the pistol is loaded and cocked with the muzzle pressed against the side of the head, everything in place except the guts to pull the trigger.

Jeremy had known he'd never have a chance at a gun, but getting hold of something sharp enough to slice through his skin was not all that far-fetched.

The most surefire way was to slice through one of the big arteries in the neck, but Jeremy wasn't sure he could cut his own throat. And if he botched it—if his hand faltered and he didn't cut deep enough to get it done—he'd be on suicide watch the rest of his life.

He could slit his wrists, though. At least he thought so. So he'd studied up on wrist-slitting techniques, learning why the failures failed and the successes succeeded. The key was something called the radial artery. It lay closest to the surface at the wrist, on the near side of the base of the thumb—where doctors and nurses like to take the pulse. Put a deep long cut into one—or better yet, both—and life would pump out of you pretty damn quick.

The ice packs were his own innovation. He didn't know how far down the eight roofies had put Moonglow, so he figured the numbing effect of the cold would keep her still. The last thing he wanted was her waking up and starting to struggle when the blade bit into her arteries. The whole idea was to make this look well thought out and deliberate on her part: Her only child was pregnant and had moved out after a terrible fight. Her behavior had become increasingly weird. Finally, in a fit of depression, she took her own life.

Boo-hoo-hoo.

Poor Moonglow. Or Christy. Or whoever.

The water level had risen almost to her chin. He shut it off but left the ice packs in place a little longer—the more numb her wrists, the better. To kill time he wandered through the house, keeping an eye peeled for a certain Talbot's bag. Had she put that quarter mil back in the bank? If not, it sure as hell would come in handy. No good to her after tonight, that was for damn sure.

He found it lying on its side in the bottom drawer of her dresser. Take it or leave it? Who knew she had it? He, Dawn, her bank, and maybe—this was a long shot—her detective. Who had she told she was planning to use it to buy off her daughter's boyfriend? The bank? Hardly. The detective? Maybe, but he'd have no reason to believe she hadn't redeposited the money, and no way to find out.

He grabbed the bag and returned to the bathroom. He'd find a safe spot to stash it at his place for the big rainy day that was sure as hell on its way.

Okay. Let's get this over with.

He removed the ice bags, then pulled the utility knife from his pocket. He wrapped the fingers of her right hand around the handle, then guided the point of the blade toward her left wrist—she was right-handed so it made sense that she'd cut her left first. As he pushed it beneath the surface, he felt water fill his glove. Taking a breath, he made a deep, long cut along her radial artery. She gasped as crimson spurts swirled into the water. Her eyes opened and gave him a glassy stare that lasted maybe two seconds, then closed again.

Quickly he switched the knife to her left hand and sliced open her right wrist. Another gasp, and this time she twisted in the water, but that was over in a few heartbeats and she returned to snoring.

He let the knife slip from her fingers and fall to the bottom of the tub. He dumped the mostly melted contents of the ice packs into the bathtub and shoved the empties into his pockets. He removed his sodden gloves and wrung them out over the water, then settled back to watch.

He stroked her forehead. Sorry, sis. Why'd you have to interfere? Everything would be fine now and you'd be going about the rest of your life if you'd only minded your own damn business.

He realized her death would cut off a branch of the Bloodline, but it couldn't be helped. And Moonglow wasn't a branch that was going to bear more fruit anyway, so no big loss.

He watched her face grow paler as the water grew redder. She stopped snoring. Then she stopped breathing, or at least it seemed that way. Her body shuddered, then relaxed. As her mouth and nose slipped beneath the surface, he knew she was gone. He watched a couple of minutes longer for insurance, then gathered up his gloves and the money bag and started for the back door. As he stepped out onto her rear patio he heard her phone begin to ring.

He heard her outgoing message in his head: *I'm sorry, I can't come to the phone right now . . .*

Damn right you can't.

He'd thought he'd feel happy. After all, he'd just removed a big obstacle to the Plan. Instead he sensed a deep sadness and a vague queasiness, as if he'd done something terribly wrong. But how could anything done to preserve the Bloodline be wrong?

No . . . as the feeling persisted he realized that it wasn't quite that he'd done something wrong, it was that he'd made a terrible blunder. As if with this act he would set in motion a force that would destroy him.

Ridiculous. He'd been careful, he'd been thorough. He'd left nothing to connect him to what he'd already begun referring to as "that poor, troubled woman's suicide."

20

Jack pulled up in front of Christy's house and parked. The traffic had put him on edge—this trip had taken twice as long as it should have, and hours spent sitting in traffic were hours he'd never get back. Christy's refusal to answer her phone hadn't helped. What was it with this woman?

He sat a moment. He'd had plenty of time to prep himself, but still he hesitated. This was going to be rough.

Finally he forced himself out the door and up the walk to her front step. He knocked, he rang . . . nothing. He tried the door—locked.

Well, the lights were on. Wasn't anybody home? She had to be. She was expecting him. Why would she leave?

The nape of his neck tingled as he hurried around the garage to its rear window. He shone the little flashlight through the glass. Christy's Mercedes sat to the right.

He moved to the back door and knocked. Still no answer, so he tried it: open. He stepped inside.

"Christy? Christy?"

No response.

She had to be here.

With his gut steadily tightening, he did a quick check of the first floor and found a glass containing a remnant of what looked like cola, but nothing else. He hurried upstairs.

"Christy?"

He froze in the doorway to the master bathroom. He saw red-red water, saw the upper half of a woman's head. Jack had an inane flashback to the scene from *The Tingler* when a hand rose slowly from a blood-filled bathtub.

A lump formed in his throat as he stepped forward. He knew who it was, recognized the ash-blond shade of hair, but had to be sure. He saw her half-open blue eyes staring across the top of the water; her mouth and nose hidden beneath.

Beneath the shock and dismay lurked a growing sense of déjà vu—Gerhard dead in his tub.

He knelt beside her. No way Christy could be alive, but just to be 110 percent sure he touched her eye. No blink.

Her hands had floated to the surface. He lifted one by an index finger and saw the two-inch-long, lengthwise incision over the artery. She'd known what she was doing.

Or at least someone had.

Had *she* done it? He couldn't believe that—not now, not when she was waiting to hear what he'd learned. Later, after she knew the awful truth, it might have been in the realm of possibility. But not now.

He released her finger and stepped back to survey the scene, looking for signs of foul play, a struggle. But no . . . everything looked neat and in place. She'd filled the tub and made the cuts beneath the surface, preventing the arterial spray from splattering the walls. Perfectly in keeping with Christy's orderly personality.

But he still didn't buy it. It reeked of Bolton.

Okay . . . if Jack was going to create a scene like this, how would he go about it?

His mind ranged over the possibilities, and came up with only two: Force Christy to kill herself under the threat of death or worse to someone she loved more than life; or drug her into oblivion and fake it.

Jack couldn't see how there had been time enough for the first, so that left the second . . .

And, remembering the glass downstairs, what was the one thing Christy could be counted on to drink?

He stared at her a moment longer, feeling again the lump in his throat as he fought a sense of failure. He hadn't failed her in a true sense. She hadn't hired him for protection, only to gather information, and he'd gathered that—in spades. Yet still he felt he'd failed her. How could he not? She'd been alive when she'd come to him and now she was dead, by either her own hand or someone else's. In neither case could he be held responsible, so why this sense of guilt?

Because.

Sometimes that was reason enough.

He had to know what happened here. To find out, he needed to learn if Christy had been drugged.

He went downstairs. Using a paper towel to avoid leaving prints, he bagged Christy's Diet Pepsi bottle and almost-empty glass. He wiped off the doorknobs as he left.

Back in his car, he got moving and called the local police to tell them that
if they went to a certain address they'd find the owner dead. He closed with,
"Be sure to run drug and tox screens."

He didn't know if they could. He didn't know if she had any blood left in
her for testing, or if the blood in the bathwater would be of any use. What he
did know was that his call would raise the official index of suspicion and have
them treat Christy's house as a crime scene.

Maybe they'd turn up something, maybe they wouldn't. Either way, Jack
intended to pursue his own course. For that he'd need Levy's help.

And Levy would help—whether he wanted to or not.

21

"Is something wrong, Jack?"

He looked up and found Gia standing at his side, staring down at him. He
realized he'd been lost in thoughts about Christy.

"Sorry. I've been lousy company, haven't I."

"If you mean being here in body alone, yes."

He'd returned late after driving to Rathburg and placing Christy's glass
and bottle in Levy's hands. Gia had reheated some of the veggie stir-fry she'd
made for dinner and filled a couple of tortillas with it. He guessed he hadn't
said much then. Vicky had gone off to bed and now they sat in the library with
something playing on the tube and Jack staring at the screen without seeing it.

"You know that woman I told you about, who wanted information on her
daughter's boyfriend? I found her dead tonight."

"Good God!" Gia stepped closer and laid a hand on his shoulder. "Please
don't tell me she was murdered."

"It looked like suicide, but I don't know."

"And if you find out it wasn't?"

He looked up at her. "I don't know."

That was true—at the moment. He'd put off making plans until he heard
from Levy.

She settled herself on his lap and clasped her arms around his neck.

"Whatever you do, be careful."

"What makes you think I'd be anything but?"

"You have a look in your eyes . . . not the look you had when you learned Vicky had been taken to that ship full of monsters—God, I don't ever want to see that look again—but there's something a little scary in your eyes right now."

Vicky . . . Kusum . . . the rakoshi . . . it would be two years this coming summer. Where had the time gone?

Where had his family gone? Bolton was supposedly obsessed with his bloodline. Jack had never given much thought to his own, but now, when he considered it, his had been virtually wiped out. The only one left that he knew of was his uncle Gurney, and he wasn't all that closely related—his mother's uncle.

"I—" He froze as he saw the label on Gia's water bottle: Ramlösa. "Where did you get that?"

"The Gristedes down on fifty-seventh. Why?"

The name . . . Ramlösa . . . an anagram of Rasalom. And Rasalom was always playing games with his name. He'd called himself Sal Roma when Jack first met him.

He grabbed the bottle as calmly and gently as he could. "What do you know about it?"

"Well, it's good, and it's sparkling. What else do you need?"

The label said it was established in 1707. But labels could lie. And Rasalom had been around forever.

"I don't know if you should drink this."

She laughed. "I've been drinking it for a month now."

"You have?" He'd never noticed.

"Yes, and I'm fine. Look, I've been thinking . . . about you coming up from underground."

Jack had known the subject would rear its head again sooner or later.

"Abe and I have discussed—"

"I don't think you should."

Jack paused, wondering if he'd heard correctly.

"Did you just say what I thought you said?"

She nodded. "Yes. Abe's plan—it's too dangerous. You'd be in a country where you didn't speak the language, dealing with hardened international criminals who might find it simpler to kill you and take your money should things start to go wrong."

She had a point. Even though Abe vouched for his contacts, the process of sneaking into the Balkans and reemerging with a dead man's identity was fraught with risks.

"Besides," she added, "it doesn't matter."

Jack stiffened. "What do you mean, it doesn't matter?"

She shrugged. "It just . . . doesn't."

They'd gone around and around about this before her pregnancy, but the baby had brought matters to a head: Jack could not claim fatherhood without an official existence. And in today's world a man simply could not appear from nowhere, with no Social Security number, no history of 1040s filed, no work history or licenses or documentation to prove his identity, and not wind up in serious trouble with Homeland Security, the IRS, the FBI, INS, and other denizens of officialdom's Acronym City. Thus the elaborate Balkan scheme.

"We might have another baby, Gia."

She hugged him tighter. "We might. But it still won't matter."

"I don't get it."

"I don't either. Before the accident I thought it was so important. Now . . . it's not. Maybe it was the coma that did it. Maybe it's the dreams I had when I was so near death."

"Dreams? You never mentioned dreams."

"That's because I don't remember them. I remember having dreamed, but not about what. I don't know whether it was the brain trauma or the dreams or the combination of the two, but the world seems different. The future seems . . . shorter. Does that make any sense?"

The words chilled Jack. He'd heard something like it before. Someone who supposedly could see the future revealed that he could not see next summer, or anything past it—next spring ended in a wall of darkness.

Gia had been pushed to the threshold of death. While she'd teetered on the edge, had she looked across and seen what was coming? And had that vision mercifully been blotted out, leaving her with only a vague sense of impending doom?

What was going to happen next spring? It sounded like the end of the world.

And if indeed it turned out to be the end of the world, then Jack's becoming a citizen . . .

. . . wouldn't matter.

He squeezed her close.

"You, me, and Vicky—we matter, Gi. We matter."

WEDNESDAY

1

Dawn came out of the bathroom after her morning retch. Nothing had come up and the nausea didn't seem so bad this time. Maybe it was easing off. But she was like totally exhausted. She could so fall right back into bed this minute, but her mouth was parched.

As she passed through the bedroom, she glanced at Jerry, still asleep. She stopped short and stared.

Ohmygod, his nose! What happened to—?

Then she remembered. How could she forget that beating he got? His nose looked awful. Worse than last night. At least she thought so. Last night was a little fuzzy, almost as if she'd been drinking. But no chance of that with Jerry around.

She went downstairs and flipped on the TV on her way to the kitchen. She gulped Diet Pepsi straight from the bottle, then carried it back to the living room. She sipped more as she watched some news story about a "suspicious" suicide in Forest Hills. The woman's identity was being withheld until next of kin were notified. The suicide was deemed "suspicious" because of the phone call that had tipped off the police.

A strange feeling swept over Dawn as she listened. For some reason she thought of her mother.

Mom? No way. She so wasn't the suicide type.

Yeah, she'd been acting totally strange lately, but she'd never . . .

A wave of nausea rippled through her stomach—a different sort of nausea. She went cold.

Mom?

She hunted for her phone, found it on the kitchen counter—didn't remem-

ber leaving it there, but whatever. She speed dialed her home. She wasn't going to speak to her, just hear her voice and hang up.

One ring . . . two . . .

Come on, pick up—

A man's voice came on after the third ring.

"Pickering residence. Who's calling, please?"

Dawn's voice locked and her heart froze. Her mouth moved but made no
sound.

"Hello?"

"Is . . . is Mrs. Pickering there?"

"Who's calling, please?"

"I-I'm her daughter."

"You're Dawn Pickering?"

"Yes." She felt her knees softening. "I-I-I want to speak to my mother."

*"We've been trying to get hold of you since last night. I'm afraid I have some
bad news."*

Dawn dropped the phone and began to scream.

2

"Your suspicion was spot on," Levy said as he made a sandwich out of his side
orders of toast and hash browns. "That cola was loaded with flunitrazepam."

"Never heard of it."

"Its brand name—it's not legal in the U.S.—is Rohypnol."

"Ah." Jack nodded. It made sense now. "Roofies."

"Is that the street name? It's also a date-rape drug. With the amount she had
in her, that woman could have been gang raped and never remembered a thing."

At least she'd still be alive, Jack thought.

"How do you know how much she had in her?"

Levy took a huge bite and spoke around it. "I don't. But the assay calculated
a concentration of zero-point-zero-three milligrams per cc. That comes out to
about one milligram per ounce. If she'd had a typical serving of eight to twelve
ounces . . ." He shook his head. "You could do just about anything to her."

"Including slit her wrists?"

"Obviously."

Right. Obviously.

Jack clasped his hands in his lap to keep from smashing his coffee cup into Levy's face.

"You son of a bitch."

The second half of Levy's potato sandwich stopped halfway to his mouth. "What?"

"You lied to me about the alibi. You never had any idea where Bolton was when Gerhard was killed."

"Okay, th-that's true. But I was under orders. I had no choice."

Should have followed his gut when it told him Bolton had done Gerhard. But no, Levy's lie had let him feel it was just safe enough to leave Bolton on the street a little longer.

Shit.

Jack leaned forward. "A good woman, a concerned and loving mother is dead, murdered by someone you were supposed to lock away until the sun went out. She's dead because you helped slap a fresh coat of paint on that human Dumpster and put him back on the street. Now here you sit, stuffing your face with as much concern as if one of your lab rats died."

Levy leaned away from him. "I—I had to alibi him. I have a family, a life, an identity. I'm more vulnerable than you."

Maybe, maybe not.

Jack stuffed his blooming rage back into its cage, took three deep breaths, then . . .

"Will they pick up Rohypnol on a routine drug screen?"

Levy blinked and looked confused by the change of subject. "I . . . don't . . . know. I'd expect it to send up flags in the benzodiazepine category, which is a part of just about every screen, but I couldn't guarantee it. It would depend on what sort of blood sample they were able to obtain. Urine would be the best, since the drug's excreted by the kidney. Of course, if they don't have any blood or urine to work with, they could always try her CSF."

"Which is?"

"Cerebrospinal fluid. It's the liquid that bathes the brain and spinal cord. I don't know if that would work, but it's worth a try."

Jack would make a call and suggest that to the ME as soon as he left Levy. That decided, he had another concern.

"What haven't you told me about what this agency and the DoD are really up to with this oDNA?"

"I've told you—"

"Yeah, yeah, you've told me a lot, not all of it true. You say if you can control the trigger gene you can turn them all into Alan Alda. But there's got to be another agenda. I mean, it's not the Department of Public Health and Safety we're working with here. What are they really going to do? Create oDNA-loaded soldiers and control their trigger genes so they're all milquetoasts during peacetime, then stop treatment and let the dogs out during combat?"

Levy dropped his sandwich. "Wh-where did you hear that?"

Jack stared at him. He looked bloodless.

"I just pulled it out of the air. You're not telling me—?"

"Of course not, of course not. I . . . I just thought . . . I mean, I was just wondering where you might have heard something so far-fetched and ridiculous." He pushed his plate away. He seemed to have lost his appetite. "The, um, crime scene. You were there. Any sign that he left evidence?"

Levy apparently wanted a change of subject. Jack let it go. If it were true, he could do nothing about it. And with the way this so-called therapy was working, the plan would never get off the ground.

"Not that I could tell. What about the Pepsi bottle? Any prints?"

"I'll hear today."

"And if his are on it, will that be cause enough for your people to haul him in?"

"If it were up to me, absolutely. But it will be Julia's call, and I can almost guarantee she won't. She'll say it's just an indication to up the dosage."

Jack clasped his hands tighter.

"From where I sit, Vecca's as bad as Bolton. She pointed him in Gerhard's direction, didn't she? Why? To test the suppresser therapy?" Levy's expression told him he'd hit a nerve. "That was it, wasn't it. Rattle his cage and see what he'd do. Did the same to me. Maybe *she* should be on this therapy. Anyone ever test her for oDNA?"

Levy shook his head. "I wouldn't know. I wouldn't be surprised if she had none."

Jack lowered his voice. "She's a killer, damn it! She might as well have slit Christy's wrists and held Gerhard's head under water herself."

"Oh, she could never do that. She's not violent—and that's the hallmark of oDNA-influenced behavior. But I do believe she's a sociopath—a scientific sociopath. She sees life as a series of well-coordinated chemical reactions. And death is merely the cessation of those reactions."

"That doesn't make her less responsible. She fingered me, and so Bolton thought he had to stop me. When he couldn't do that by his usual direct means—killing me—he did it indirectly by killing the person who'd hired me. I'm laying that right on Vecca's doorstep."

"What are you working up to here? I hope you're not thinking of doing anything so foolish as taking reprisals on Julia. You could get us both in a lot of hot water."

"Hot water? Two people are dead. Gerhard might not have been the most savory character, but he didn't deserve what happened to him. And Christy . . . I liked Christy."

"Please don't do anything rash."

"Me?" Jack said. "Rash? Never."

"So you'll stay away from Julia?"

"Won't harm a hair on her head."

But he couldn't speak for Jeremy Bolton.

That guy, that detective, that Robertson . . . had to be him.

Jeremy fumed in silence as he comforted a sobbing Dawn in the police station. The two of them were seated at the desk of a detective named Cullen—*homicide* of all things—who'd just explained the circumstances of her mother's death. Balding, overweight, sweating, Cullen was obviously uncomfortable as he described how they'd found her, and the wounds that had killed her.

"B-but the news said something about 'suspicious,'" Dawn said. "What does that mean?"

"It means the circumstances are unusual enough to warrant an investigation. We received a call informing us of your mother's death. That's certainly unusual in a suicide. And the caller told us to run drug and tox screens on her."

The fuck! How could he know?

Jeremy felt a scream of rage building . . . wanted to start smashing things . . . but forced himself to remain calm and cool.

"But what does that *mean*?" Dawn said.

"It means we have two possibilities." He ticked them off on his fingers. "Someone found your mother after she committed suicide, wrongly suspected foul play, but didn't want to get involved; or someone found her dead, rightly suspected foul play, but didn't want to get involved. The second possibility means that someone killed your mother and made it look like suicide."

"But who . . . ?"

"That's what we'd like to know. The caller used a pay-as-you-go cell phone, so the call is untraceable."

Jeremy could tell him who owned that phone. Robertson . . . that fuck Robertson must have paid a visit to Moonglow soon after Jeremy left, found her dead, and made the call. A simple suicide had now become a possible murder. And if they checked her blood as suggested . . .

Jeremy said, "If she was killed—I can't imagine a soul in the world who would want Mrs. Pickering dead, but let's just say she was—how do you know it wasn't the killer himself who called?"

"That would be even more unusual, but nothing's impossible." He squinted at Jeremy and then pointed at his own nose. "Have an accident, Mister"—he checked his notes—"Bethlehem?"

"Tripped on the stairs yesterday. Racked up my knee too."

Cullen's expression said nothing. He turned to Dawn.

"Did your mother seem depressed recently?"

Jeremy jumped in before Dawn could reply. "She was very unhappy that Dawn had moved in with me." He looked at her and squeezed her hand. "I don't think I'm talkin out of school when I say she's been actin real strange ever since we became involved. Without gettin into particulars, she seemed to become downright unglued when she learned Dawn was pregnant."

Cullen made some notes and said, "Unglued how?"

Jeremy cut Dawn off again. "She never threatened suicide, if that's what you mean. At least not to me. How about you, darlin?"

Looking dazed, Dawn shook her head. "No, never. She did hire a detective, though."

Shit-shit-shit! Never should have let her speak.

"Right," Jeremy quickly added. "We don't know who she hired and we don't know why—I asked but she wouldn't tell us."

Cullen was nodding. "We'll look into that."

Jeremy wanted to shift the subject away from the detective before Dawn said anything about her mother's accusations against him.

"You say the caller mentioned drug and tox screens. Has anything come up?"

"No results back yet." Cullen looked at him. "Why do you ask?"

"Well, it's just that—"

Cullen's phone rang. He answered it, muttered and grunted a few times, then said, "I'll be damned. Keep me posted."

He hung up and looked at Dawn.

"Looks like our mystery caller is back again. He called downstairs and said we should check your mother for Rohypnol."

Jeremy almost jumped out of his seat. How the hell—?

When Moonglow came up positive for roofies and the word got out, Dirty Danny was sure to hear about it. He'd put two and two together in no time.

Looked like Danny was going to need an accident.

Shit!

This was getting more complicated by the minute.

"What's that?" Dawn said.

"An illegal downer. Was your mother into downers?"

Dawn glared at him. "My mother wasn't into anything. She was like totally antidrug."

"Yes," Jeremy said. "I'd be very surprised if you found anything. The only thing Mrs. Pickering seemed hooked on was caffeine."

Cullen shook his head and sighed. "Okay. In the meantime, for the record: Where were you two last night?"

Jeremy had known this was coming—family members, especially those like Dawn in line to inherit, were always prime suspects—but he put on a shocked look.

"You can't think Dawn would have anything to do with this terrible thing!"

Cullen didn't react. "As I said, for the record."

"We were home," Dawn said. "Jerry was hurting from his, um, fall, so we went to bed early. When I got up this morning . . ."

She broke down again. Jeremy put a comforting arm around her quaking shoulders.

"She heard a news story about a suspicious suicide in town. And since her mother had been actin weird, she gave her a call, just to check on her, and, well, you know the rest." He gave Cullen a pleading look. "Can I take her home now?"

"Sure. I have your contact numbers. Miss Pickering, I'll keep you updated on developments."

Still sobbing, Dawn nodded.

Jeremy struggled out of the chair—the knee hurt worse today than yesterday. The good news was that he didn't look like a guy who'd be sneaking around faking someone's suicide.

But knee or no knee, he had to do something about Dirty Danny. And then he'd have to track down Robertson. He wanted Robertson for a lot of reasons. Payback topped the list, but he also wanted to know where he got his information. Especially how he knew about the roofies.

4

"You don't need a man of my not inconsiderable talents for something like this," Russell Tuit said as he positioned the paper on the glass. "You could teach yourself in less than an hour."

He'd adopted a put-upon look, but Jack knew he got off on anything with a whiff of scam or illegality. He'd done some soft time for bank hacking and one of the conditions of his parole was a ten-year ban from the Internet. Russ had found ways around it—like helping the guy next door set up a wi-fi network in his apartment last month and making sure the signal was strong enough to penetrate the wall they shared—but he swore his hacking days were over. He did *not* want to go back inside.

"But I don't have one of those thingamajigs, Russ."

"This thingamajig is called a scanner."

Jack knew that, but he liked to pull Russ's chain.

"Right. Don't have a scannamajig. Don't even have a printer."

He shook his head. "How anyone can have a computer and not a printer is beyond me. I mean, what if you need to print out something like Mapquest directions?"

Russ was not the stereotypical mouse potato—no taped glasses or pocket protector—but he tended to get so wrapped up in his keyboarding that he'd forget to bathe. The fact that he lived over a Second Avenue Tex-Mex restaurant was sometimes a good thing.

"Not much of a traveler, Russ. And if I need directions to anywhere I can write them down."

"I suppose I'd be crazy to ask if you've got Photoshop."

"Certifiable. I mean, I've heard of it—a lady friend of mine who's into art has been using it—but I can't see myself ever buying it."

Gia had started toying with computer art before the accident. She probably could have done this for him but he didn't want her involved. The less she knew the better.

Russ smiled, showing yellow teeth. "Buying software . . . what a concept. I guess you do need me, Jack."

He closed the cover and moved to one of the three computers in the room. A few key taps and a glow began to move along the scanner's edge. A barrage of taps and then Russ motioned Jack toward the monitor.

"Okay. There it is. What do you want to do with it?"

Leaning over him he realized that Russ had been procrastinating in regard to his next shower. No biggie. Couldn't hold a candle to a rakosh.

On the screen he saw an image of the lab report he'd taken from Levy, showing Bolton's positive paternity test with Dawn. He pointed to the screen.

"See that logo? Can you copy that onto a blank sheet to make it look like stationery?"

Mouse-click-mouse-click-tap-tap.

"There you go."

Jack blinked. "That's all it takes? I can type a letter on that?"

"I'll save it as a file and you can write dozens of letters from the . . ." He squinted at the screen. "Creighton Institute."

Jack wasn't crazy about Russ connecting him to Creighton, but the guy wasn't a conniver. And the truth was, Russ having Creighton's logo on his computer was a greater liability to him than to Jack.

"Do it."

Mouse-click-tap.

"Done."

"All right. Back to the lab report." He touched the screen. "See those code numbers? Can you substitute names for them?"

Russ looked up at him. "You're kidding, right?"

"I didn't think I was."

"You weren't kidding." He shook his head as he turned back to the screen. "You really do need me, Jack. At least until you join the twenty-first century."

"I'm not some sort of Luddite. I own a computer, I use it, I enjoy it, but it's not a way of life." He was sure he hadn't tapped one percent of its potential, but getting into it took time—hours before the monitor or reading manuals that he didn't care to surrender. "I've got other things to do. I mean, why should I spend my time learning this Photoshop thing when I can pay you to do it for me? You're better at it than I'll ever be, so it's worth the money."

"Never looked at it that way," Russ said as he moused and clicked. "You're right, man. Save that computer of yours just for e-mail. I can always use the money." He started tapping on the keys. "Okay. We got rid of the numbers, now we've got to match the font and the text size and we're in business. What names we using here?"

Jack grabbed a pen and pad from the desk and jotted down *Dawn Pickering* and *Jerry Bethlehem*.

"Make sure Dawn goes in the second spot—she can't very well be anyone's father."

Russ spoke as he typed. "You never know, Jack. You never know. So, you running a number on this Bethlehem guy?"

"Better you don't know. And even better you forget you ever heard these names."

"Gotcha. Okay. There you are: Some girl's found her daddy—or vicey-versey. I'll print this out along with the stationery. How many copies you want?"

Jack thought about that. He needed only one letter, but a number of copies.

"How about I type it right here, and then you print it out."

"Sure thing." Russ rose and gestured toward the keyboard. "Be my guest."

As Jack seated himself he pulled a slip of paper from a pocket and handed it to Russ.

"While I'm doing this, why don't you make yourself useful and look up the next of kin of these folks."

"Don't want me to see what you're writing, right?"

"Right."

"No problem." He looked at the names on the slip and whistled. "This might take a while."

Jack looked up at him. "Then you might want to get right to it. Besides, you're blocking my light."

As Russ wandered away, Jack began to type. He had a two-finger style—slow, but it got the job done . . .

5

"You sure your phone's turned on?" Jerry said.

"Yes, I'm sure." Dawn hid her irritation. "That's like the tenth time you've asked me."

What was up with him? He knew her phone was never off. Never. The way he kept getting up and limping around his living room, and then sitting down again was getting on her nerves, and she didn't have many left.

Mom . . . dead . . . even after identifying the body—which had to be the totally worst moment in her life, ever—she still couldn't wrap her mind around the idea that she wouldn't be down the hall at home or at the other end of the phone anytime Dawn needed her.

God, she wished things between them hadn't got so out of hand.

If I'd been home . . .

Guilt enveloped her like a cold, damp cloud. She couldn't shake it. A sob burst free.

"It's my fault . . . all my fault. If I'd been there . . . if I hadn't moved out . . ."

Jerry stopped his pacing and stood over her.

"Now, darlin, we been through that. Your momma was on the edge, havin strange thoughts, doing strange things. We didn't recognize the signs. If it's anybody's fault, it's mine. I shouldn't have fallen in love with you. I shouldn't have taken you away from her."

Dawn grabbed his hand and pressed it against her cheek. She needed Jerry now, more than ever. She felt so sad, sad beyond words, beyond belief, and maybe even a little—she didn't like to admit it—angry at Mom for abandoning her. She'd left her totally alone, with no father, no sisters and brothers, no grandparents, nobody. She couldn't even go back to her house because it was a crime scene and the police were still working on it—they called it "processing." Or so they said. Maybe she was the prime suspect and they didn't want her back, covering her tracks.

God, that was totally sick!

"I so should have known something was going haywire with her."

"Look, darlin, I been around crazy people and I know the signs, and your momma wasn't givin a clue that she had this in mind."

Dawn stared up at him. He never spoke about his past. This was the first clue he'd ever given. Despite her fog of depression, she jumped on it.

"You've been around crazy people? When?"

He looked confused for a second, maybe even flustered.

"My momma had a major breakdown when I was in my, um, twenties. Broke my heart when we had to stick her in a loony bin, but we just couldn't handle her. I'd go visit her every day and, believe me, I saw loads of craziness."

"What was wrong with her?"

"I'd rather not talk about it. You're *sure* your phone's on?"

She wanted to scream. "Yes! Why do you keep asking?"

"I'm just wondering what they found on the tox screen. This mysterious caller—is he right? 'Cause if he is, how does he know? Unless your mother *didn't* kill herself." He put his hands to his head. "I can't handle this. It reminds me too much of my own mother. It's freakin me. I gotta go out."

"Where?"

"Just out. I need some air."

"I'll go with—"

"No. I just need a little time. I'll be better when I get back. I need to be alone."

"And I need *not* to be alone."

"Hang on there, darlin. I'll be just a little while."

As he limped toward the door she thought of a way to stop him.

"But you can't drive with that leg!"

"I'll manage. I'll take your car."

And then he was gone.

Dawn picked up the nearest thing she could find—the universal remote—and hurled it at the door. The battery cover popped off when it hit and the batteries went flying.

How could he do this? What was so important that he had to leave her now of all times? It was like totally heartless.

An awful thought crept up on her. What if he didn't love her as much as he said? What if he was sneaking off to see someone else? He'd been looking at his watch as if waiting for a certain time.

No way. Don't be stupid, Dawn. You—

The doorbell rang.

She smiled. So he couldn't drive after all. Told him.

But why was he knocking?

She hurried down the foyer steps and opened the front door. Instead of Jerry, a stranger stood there. She eeked in surprise and went to slam it closed but stopped herself. He held a clipboard and a manila envelope and didn't look the least bit threatening. Longish blond hair and one of those gay little mustaches, wearing some sort of coverall.

"Special delivery. Is a"—he checked the clipboard—"a Dawn Pickering here?"

"Yes. That's . . ."

Should she identify herself to a stranger? The guy looked harmless enough. Even looked a little familiar. Maybe she'd seen him making deliveries before.

Oh, WTF.

"That's me."

He handed her the envelope. "Then this is for you. Just sign here, please."

"What is it?"

He smirked. "They never tell me and I didn't open it."

"Who's it from?"

"From whoever's on the return address, I'd guess."

She signed. The guy gave her a little salute and was off.

"Wait. Am I supposed to like tip you?"

"Don't worry about it. All taken care of."

She closed the door and looked at the return address: A sticker carried the logo of something called the Creighton Institute. The name J. VECCA, MD was typed under it.

Never heard of either.

She tore open the envelope and pulled out two sheets of paper. The first was a letter, dated today.

Dear Ms. Pickering—

I hate to be the bearer of bad news, but I fear if I don't tell you, no one else will. And you must know.

Dawn's gut crawled. Was this about Mom?

It concerns the man you know as Jerry Bethlehem. That is not his real name. I am restricted from giving you his real name, but I can tell you that he was recently an inmate at this facility. When you look us up, as I'm sure you will, you'll find that Creighton Institute is part of the federal penal system.

Oh, God. This couldn't be true. It had to be some awful prank.

The man you know as Jerry Bethlehem was released as part of a special experimental program. He has been under observation. We know that your mother was having him investigated. We tried to discourage that because it jeopardized our release program. But when she discovered that the man you know as Bethlehem was her half brother, we became curious.

You see, we'd wondered why he had gone straight to your town upon his release, and why he had sought you out. The reason was not his blood relationship with your mother, it was his blood relationship to you.

What . . . because he was my uncle?

Now we come to the difficult part. The man you know as Jerry Bethlehem is a rapist. We weren't certain before, but our tests have confirmed that he raped your mother 19 years ago. She never saw him so she never could identify him. You were conceived during that rape. This is why she could never tell you who your father was. She didn't know.

The paper shook in Dawn's hands. No way . . . no fucking way.

I know what you're thinking. No way. We felt the same. But genes don't lie. Unknown to you, I obtained a sample of your hair and did some testing of my own. The man you call Jerry Bethlehem is your father.

Oh, this was sick. This was *so* sick.

But even stranger and more baffling than that is the fact that he wants you to have his baby. Please look at the accompanying DNA paternity analysis. It leaves no doubt.

Dawn did just that. She saw her name . . . Jerry's . . .

Probability of paternity 99%.

A fake! It had to be!
She went back to the letter.

I know you're thinking that a report like this can be faked. I assure you it isn't. I also assure you that I am genuinely concerned for your well-being. Especially after what I suspect he did to your mother last night.

Mom? What?

I cannot prove it yet, but I am reasonably sure that he murdered your mother. She had ordered a DNA comparison between you and him (possibly to try to show you the genetic dangers of involvement with a man she assumed to be your uncle). The test results would have shown her the awful truth—that he was not your uncle but rather your father. And at last she would know the identity of her rapist. We believe he drugged her with Rohypnol (the street name is "roofie," I believe— perhaps you've heard of it) and staged her suicide.

Lies! A pack of lies! Had to be!
But then she remembered that this wasn't the first time Jerry had been accused of murder. Mom had said he'd killed her first detective. Dawn had

laughed at the idea back then—Jesus, was it only a week ago?—but she wasn't laughing now.

> *What I'm telling you is easily verifiable. Simply bring samples of his hair (a dozen strands or so from a brush or a shower drain will do) and yours to any commercial lab and ask for a paternity DNA analysis. The results will confirm what I've told you.*
>
> *I assure you this is not a hoax. I am a real person and you may call me at the above number at any time to discuss this, or I will be glad to meet with you in person. I must warn you, however, do not mention this to your father. He has a history of violence. Perhaps you have seen evidence of that, perhaps not. Nevertheless, I assure you it exists, and he can explode when things do not go his way.*
>
> *I have initiated procedures to rescind his release and return him to this facility, but that will take time. Once he learns of this, his personality may become unstable, his behavior unpredictable. I suggest you vacate the premises. We can offer you shelter until he is safely incarcerated again.*
>
> *Remember, you can call me at any time if you have questions.*
> *Julia Vecca, MD*
> *Director of Medical Services, Creighton Institute*

"Oh, really, Julia Vecca, MD?" Dawn said aloud. "Maybe I'll do just that."

She ran back up to the main floor and grabbed her phone. This had to be some sort of scam cooked up by Mom and her detective before she died. More proof of how far her mind had slipped.

But that would mean she'd known she was going to commit suicide . . . and planned to use it against Jerry.

Dawn's mind balked at the improbability.

Make the call.

She looked at the number on the letterhead. *As if.* She wasn't born yesterday. The letterhead was probably a total fake and she'd bet the number would be answered by someone coached to repeat all this bullshit.

She called information and asked for the number of the Creighton Institute in Rathburg, New York. Never even heard of Rathburg.

To her shock, the operator gave her a number—the same one on the letterhead.

Her finger shook as she punched it in. She reached a voice mail tree that informed her that the medical offices were closed but if this was an emergency she should hit "0." She did and found herself speaking to a woman with some sort of accent. Yes, a Dr. Vecca was on staff—head of the medical department—and no, she was not available until tomorrow. Another doctor was on call. Could he help?

Dawn hung up and stood there feeling gooseflesh run up her arms as she told herself it couldn't be, it totally couldn't be. Jerry couldn't be a criminal . . . but what did she know of his past? He always avoided talking about it. It had made him deliciously mysterious before. But now . . .

As for being her father . . . they so didn't look anything alike.

And killing Mom? Dosing her up with roofies and killing her? Come *on*! She knew about roofies—heard a million warnings to be on the lookout for someone slipping a date-rape drug into your drink at a party. Where would Jerry even—?

OMG! Dirty Danny! She herself had taken him down to score some Vicodin. He could have picked up some roofies too.

Wait-wait-wait. He was with her all night.

Or was he? He could have slipped her one and knocked her out for the night. Was that why she'd felt so totally groggy this morning? And she'd thought he couldn't drive, but he was out driving right now. Last night, while she was zonked, he could have slipped out and—

No. Stop. This is insane.

But putting the letter together with what had been going on . . . they fit too well. And he seemed so interested in the results of the drug screen. Was that because . . . ?

Coincidence. Had to be.

But if Jerry *had* bought roofies, where would he hide them?

God, she hated herself for doing this, but she was going to have to search the place. Not finding any wouldn't mean anything, of course—he could have used them all or taken them with him—but she hoped it might ease her mind.

6

Jack had removed the wig, the mustache, the nostril dilators, and the cotton pledgets from inside his cheeks. He hadn't been sure how well Dawn would remember him from their one meeting in Work, but decided not to take any chances.

What a stroke of luck that Bolton had left Dawn home alone on the first day of surveillance. He'd expected—and been mentally prepared for—a wait of up to a week.

He wondered what had drawn Bolton out tonight. Didn't matter—it had given Jack a chance to put the letter and test results in Dawn's hands. Whatever happened next would be a matter of luck and circumstance. Dawn's youth and naïveté would work in Jack's favor.

Ideally, she would swallow the whole story—why not? It was all true—and come running out of the house.

More than likely she'd be in complete denial at first; but after a while she'd start to recognize a few parallels between her experience and the letter.

Even if she was so enthralled with Bolton that she stayed in denial and showed the letter to lover boy, it would cause a major disruption in Bolton's life, maybe even enrage him enough or panic him enough to do something stupid enough to throw a big-enough monkey wrench into the Creighton clinical trial to shut it down.

One thing Jack knew he wouldn't do was hurt Dawn—because what hurt Dawn would hurt the baby.

But no matter what she did with it, that letter was going to rock Jeremy Bolton's world.

7

Jeremy sat at a corner table in Work sipping a Bud and waiting for Dirty Danny to show. The guy was usually here by now, bothering everybody to buy his shit. Where the fuck was he? An hour here and no sign of him. Jerry couldn't ask about him because that would connect him and Danny—the last thing he needed. But it hadn't stopped people from asking what had happened to him.

"How's the other guy look?" . . . "What happen? Step in front of a truck?" . . . "Dawn catch you with another babe?" . . . and on and on.

He felt like he was going to explode.

He didn't have a firm plan yet. He figured it best to play it by ear. Get Danny to meet him outside . . . tell him he had a customer for him, real paranoid but with a major jones. Anybody else and Danny might be suspicious. But he knew Jeremy, knew he wasn't hurting for dough or drugs. He'd come along. Drive him to a secluded spot, use the trusty tire iron—no surprises this time—then strip him of his wallet and of most of his stock. They'll call it a drug deal gone bad. Another pusher gone. No loss.

But the damn guy had to show first. And Jeremy had to wait. Couldn't risk putting it off till tomorrow. If word got out tonight that the cops found roofies in Moonglow, tomorrow would be too late.

Getting rid of Danny would do it. Then he'd be home free. Dawn was his alibi against any suspicions the cops might have about him and Moonglow, and even any she herself might have. He'd dropped the gloves in a strip mall trash bin; they were probably in the county dump by now. The roofies had gone down a storm drain. Nobody and nothing to connect him to the dead Mrs. Pickering.

Yep. Home free after tonight.

8

"Oh, God!" Dawn wailed. "Oh, *NO!*"

She knelt outside the closet in the extra bedroom—"the shit closet," he'd called it. Seconds ago she'd been on her feet, but her knees had given way.

She'd started going through Jerry's backpack, looking for roofies. She'd come up empty everywhere else, and then she'd unzipped the main compartment.

She hadn't found drugs. She'd found something a lot worse.

A Talbot's bag containing a quarter million in cash.

She'd seen it before. At Mom's place. Only one way Jerry could have got his hands on this.

She screamed.

Oh, God, he killed Mom. But she was already out of their lives. He had no reason to hurt her. Unless—

Oh, *shit!* If the letter was right about him killing Mom, it could be right about *why* he'd done it.

To keep her from finding out that he was her rapist, that he was Dawn's father.

My father?

This was a nightmare, a total nightmare. Had to be. She was going to wake up any second and find herself next to Jerry and write this off as the worst dream of her life.

But even if that happened, who *was* Jerry, really? She didn't know.

One thing she did know was that she could so not count on this being just a bad dream.

A line from the letter came back to her: *I suggest you vacate the premises.* Totally.

Clutching the wall for support, she struggled to her feet and lurched toward the hall. Thoughts cascaded through her brain in a jumbled avalanche, tumbling, bouncing off each other without connecting, without coherence. She had to get out, find a place away from here to think, sift out truth from lies, if she could.

If she could . . .

But how could she know—ever really *know* the truth about this?

What I'm telling you is easily verifiable. Simply bring samples of his hair . . . and yours to any commercial lab and ask for a paternity DNA analysis.

Just what she'd do. Because she totally had to know.

She stumbled to the bathroom and found his hairbrush. He used it a lot, saying he was afraid it was thinning on him and he'd read where regular brushing would stimulate it. She used to think it was cute, but now nothing seemed cute.

She grabbed a comb and cleaned the brush, removing a lot more than a dozen strands. She stared at the tangle in her hand.

What if this proved that Jerry was really her father?

For God's sake, Dawn, he's old enough to be your father!

How many times had Mom said that?

Other memories followed . . . straddling him in ecstasy, sucking his—

She leaned over the toilet and vomited.

Had to get out of here. But Jerry had her car. So what? She'd take his. Do anything to get away and stay away until she'd figured this out.

But stay where? Her house was out. A motel? But she didn't have much money.

The bag.

She rushed back to the shit closet and grabbed the bag from where she'd dropped it, then hurried down to the main floor. She grabbed a set of Jerry's keys from the bowl and was heading for the door when she saw lights sweep across the windows. She peeked out and saw her Jeep pulling into the driveway.

No! No, she couldn't confront him, couldn't even face him or stand being in the same room with him until she knew the truth. Had to get out.

Since she couldn't take his car, her first thought was to run—go out the back door and keep on going. But that wasn't going to work. And even if she could somehow get to her car, he'd only chase after her in his.

She looked down at the bowl where they tossed their keys when they came in, and had an idea.

9

Jeremy sat behind the wheel of the Jeep and composed himself. Had to be cool and calm and pretend like nothing was wrong.

That asshole Dirty Danny hadn't shown. Jeremy had finally broke down and asked for him. Nobody had seen nothing of him today.

Damn it!

Okay. Be cool.

He'd work things out. Who knew? Maybe Danny was already dead, killed in a real drug deal gone bad.

Wouldn't that be a kick?

He got out and took deep breaths all the way to the front door. By the time he let himself in he was the Jerry Bethlehem everyone knew and loved. Well, not everyone.

"I'm home, darlin."

No answer.

His foot kicked a piece of paper. He looked down and saw a torn-open envelope. He picked it up. Dawn's name on the front and . . .

His mouth went dry and his heart stuttered when he saw the return address: Creighton Institute. And Vecca's name.

What the—?

Dawn! Where was she? He limped up to the main floor calling her name, but still no answer.

Was she gone? What had been in that fuckin envelope?

He made it up to the second floor, going from room to room. All empty. He checked the bathroom last and found two sheets of paper on the floor. As he bent to snag them, he heard a car engine roar to life outside.

"No!"

He hurried downstairs as fast as his damn knee would allow and reached the front door just as Dawn and her Jeep reached the curb.

"Dawn! Wait!"

He went to run after her but his knee crumbled beneath him and he tumbled to the grass in a blaze of pain.

Dawn never looked back . . . just raced away.

"Shit!"

He pushed himself off the lawn, regained his feet, and hobbled back inside. He went straight for the key bowl. The Miata would be murder on his knee but he'd have to grit his teeth and put up with it. Couldn't let Dawn get too much of a head start. Had to chase her down and—

The keys! Where were his keys? Both sets were gone.

The bitch! She'd taken both sets to the Miata, leaving him just the cycle, but that was out of the question. He was stranded.

Fuck!

What was going on?

He had a pretty good idea how to answer that.

He found the sheets he'd dropped on his way outside. He sat on the stairs with his bad leg stuck straight out, and began to read.

With each sentence his fury grew . . . fury mingled with disbelief . . . and fear.

I have initiated procedures to rescind his release and return him to this facility.

What was Vecca thinking? Had she lost her fucking mind? What about her precious clinical trial? She was throwing it away. Why? Because she suspected he'd offed Moonglow? Gerhard hadn't bothered her. Why Moonglow?

But far worse was telling Dawn he was her father. Vecca had no business doing that. And how the hell did she know? How had she found out?

That was the same question he'd asked about the detective—where had he got his info? Now he knew: Vecca. Vecca had been working with him, feeding him all along. It didn't make any sense, but who could figure Vecca? She always seemed to have a hidden agenda.

Thing was, he didn't care *why*. He knew *what* Vecca had done—it was all here in black and white—and that was enough.

He'd have to pay her a little visit. But not until he'd made things right with Dawn. He didn't know how he was going to do that—yeah, swear everything in the letter's a lie, but how to prove that? He had a gut sense in this case he'd be guilty until proven innocent.

You'd think she could have given him the benefit of the doubt, given him a chance to explain. But no, she'd upped and run without even—

His mind flashed back to the spare bedroom when he'd peeked in while searching for her. The closet door had been open with his backpack sitting on the floor.

"Shit!"

A painful rush back upstairs to check again. There it was, everything unzipped.

She'd found the money. Never mind how, it had iced the case against him.

Again, he could explain, he could talk his way out of it—out of just about anything with that girl—if only he could find her. That had to be priority number one. But he had no fucking car!

Wait. The spare key he'd stuck in the wheel well after that time he'd locked himself out. He'd forgotten about that.

Down the steps again and outside. He reached up into the well and yanked out the little magnetized box. Opened it, pulled out the key, and he was on his way.

He had a pretty good idea where Dawn would go to ground.

10

The chain of events puzzled Jack.

First Bolton had come home and gone inside. Then Dawn appeared on the far side of the garage, coming around from the backyard. She got in her Jeep, started it up, and raced off, leaving Bolton facedown in the turf. When Bolton limped-hopped back inside, Jack expected him to return right away and take off after her.

But he didn't.

Which left Jack in a quandary: Go after Dawn or wait for Bolton's next move.

The issue was solved when Bolton came back outside holding a couple of sheets of paper. That explained the delay. He'd found the letter. Jack had printed up a couple of extra copies just in case Dawn never showed it to him. Because a big part of Jack's plan hinged on Bolton seeing the letter.

This was working out better than he'd hoped.

He watched him remove something from his wheel well, then ease into the car and drive off.

Jack followed. He was pretty sure Bolton wouldn't hurt Dawn, not when she was carrying the baby he'd worked so hard to create. As long as the baby's life was linked to hers, she was safe from harm. At least physical harm. He wasn't so sure about abduction and imprisonment, though.

Bolton made a beeline for Christy's house and parked in the driveway. Jack slowed as he passed. The house was dark—not a single light on inside or out. No sign of Dawn's car either, but it could be in the garage. Bolton didn't even check. He walked to the front door, unlocked it, and stepped inside.

Back to the scene of the crime.

Seemed awfully risky. Yeah, Dawn was undoubtedly worth it to him, but no sign she was there.

Jack went to the end of the block, hung a U, and cruised back. He needed a place to park but didn't want Bolton to see his car. Needed to know if Dawn was inside, though.

Hell with it.

He parked at the other end of the block and quick-walked back. Slipped around back and blinked his key-chain flash through the window.

No Jeep.

Okay. Good. That meant Dawn had gone somewhere else. As for what Bolton was up to inside, as long as he wasn't in the same house as Dawn, Jack didn't much care.

He headed back to his car. Figured he'd do some cruising, pass the house every so often, and follow Bolton when he left. No telling which way he'd tip but, sure as night followed day, Bolton was going to tip.

11

"Dawn, darlin. Where are you?"

Dawn held her breath to keep from screaming. She'd almost died when she'd seen him pull into the driveway. How had he started his car? Didn't matter. Somehow he had. But how did he know she was here?

"Come out, darlin. No sense in hidin. I know you're here. I mean, where else you gonna run to?"

Wait a minute. *Where else you gonna run to?* That sounded like he didn't know she was here—more like he was just guessing. Because how could he know? She'd parked her Jeep in the Jacobsens' driveway around the corner. It was curved and she'd parked at the apex behind the big clump of rhododendrons in their front yard. Her car was hidden from the street, and no one was home to see it from the inside—the Jacobsens were retired and spent January into May in Florida. Dawn knew because they always asked Mom to keep an eye on their place while they were away. No big deal—the back of their house was visible from the kitchen window.

So all Dawn had had to do was park behind the bushes, then run through their backyard and hop the fence into her own.

Jerry couldn't know about that. So maybe she had a chance.

She'd crawled under the sofa—her favorite secret spot as a kid when playing hide and seek. Her super safe spot, because Mom could never find her here. Later on she came to realize that Mom had known exactly where she was all the time and only pretended to be unable to find her.

A lot tighter squeeze now. She could barely breathe. But she could see a good expanse of the floor beneath the lower edge of the dust ruffle. She saw Jerry's boots as they strolled across the room.

"I found that letter, darlin. Felt like I was readin sci-fi or somethin. I never heard of this Doctor Vecca. I bet she don't even exist. Or if she does, she's in cahoots with that detective your momma hired. Even though she's dead, Lord rest her soul, she's still tryin to come between us."

Dawn felt a pang. What if that was true? What if—?

What about the money?

She'd left the bag stuffed beneath the seat of her car.

Explain the money, Jerry.

He kept talking but his voice faded a little as he moved from the living room into the dining room. It seemed he'd read her thoughts.

"There's somethin I oughta tell you, Dawn. When your momma came on to me the other night, well, she offered me that cash as well as herself. I gotta confess, I took the cash. I know it was wrong, but I figured it might come in handy if the game project fell through. You know . . . tide us over until things picked up again. I never told you because I was kinda embarrassed."

Could that be ture? It wasn't totally impossible, but somehow it didn't ring true. Something in his voice . . . like not only did he not believe it, but doubted she'd believe it.

Liar!

She wanted to scream it in his face, but didn't dare. Because if he was lying, it meant he'd killed Mom. And that meant she'd been living with and was now hiding from a murderer.

Her bladder spasmed, begging to empty. But it calmed as she heard him trot upstairs. She wondered if she should make a run for it.

No. Stay put. If she ran, he might catch her. If she stayed hidden, he'd cross this off as someplace to look for her.

"Dawn, darlin," he said as he came down the stairs. "Where are you, damn it."

His voice had changed. The sweet-talking tone had developed an angry edge. He was getting pissed.

He limped through the living room and headed for the kitchen. She heard the door to the garage open. She guessed he'd been so sure she was here that he hadn't bothered to check for her car. About time.

The door slammed closed.

"Shit!"

More footsteps, louder this time.

"That bitch! That fucking cow! Where the fuck is she!"

Tears sprang into Dawn's eyes. So now it came out. Now she knew what he really thought of her. Still cursing, he slammed out the front door.

Dawn stifled sobs as she waited for the sound of his car leaving. When that died down she crawled out from her hiding place. But instead of getting to her feet she lay on the carpet and cried.

What a fool she'd been, what a total jerk. How could she have let herself be sucked in like this? Jerry didn't care for her. He had some whole other freaky agenda going on.

After crying awhile longer she struggled to her hands and knees and crawled through the house. She'd been feeling her way in the dark before Jerry came. But he'd left the lights on. Still, she didn't dare stand. Someone might see her from the street.

She crept upstairs to her old bedroom—no, her new bedroom, her *only* bedroom now. She stopped at the door to Mom's room and stared at the yellow crime-scene tape across the master bathroom doorway. It pulled her closer.

Here was where Mom had died—not killed herself—*been* killed. Murdered. She was sure of that now. Just as she was sure it was all her fault.

She crumpled to her knees and stared at the tub.

I'm sorry, Mom. I'm sorry for believing that asshole instead of you, I'm sorry for believing that you'd *ever* come on to Jerry. God, that must have totally hurt you. I so should have listened. You were right all along and I acted like a total jerk. You'd be alive now if I'd paid attention.

Mom dead, because her Dawnie had been sleeping with her own father. Her life had turned to shit.

God! Somebody shoot me!

Shoot . . .

Mom kept a gun hidden somewhere. Dawn had found it once as a kid. A little silvery automatic or whatever they called those things. But empty at the time—Mom had kept the little thing with the bullets somewhere else. A good idea because Dawn might have hurt herself had it been loaded.

She rose and hunted until she found it in a wooden box. This time it was loaded—the slot at the bottom of the handle had been empty before, now it had something in it. What did they call it—a clip? Guess she'd felt safe leaving it loaded now.

See you soon, Mom.

Without giving herself time to think, she raised the gun, pressed the muzzle against her temple, and pulled the trigger.

But it wouldn't pull. She tugged on it again. Wouldn't budge.

She lowered it and looked at it. She didn't know anything about guns. Was it locked or something?

With a cry she hurled it across the room.

What a total loser. She couldn't even shoot a gun when she needed to.

She'd have to find another way. And she would. Because she couldn't stand being who she was, or even being with herself. One way or another, she was going to end this nightmare for good.

She totally deserved to die.

12

Jack had seen the garage light go on during his last pass. It finally must have dawned on Bolton to check for Dawn's car. Now he'd either settle down and wait—assuming he was sure she'd show up—or go looking for her.

Betting on the latter, Jack had pulled around the corner and waited where he had a view of the house. Turned out to be a short wait.

Sure enough, a minute later Bolton came storming out and drove off, chirping his tires as he accelerated. He looked like he had a destination in mind.

Jack followed. If Bolton knew where Dawn was hiding, Jack wanted to be there when they met up.

He trailed him out of town onto the Grand Central where he headed north. When he switched over to the Deegan, still going north, Jack had a pretty good idea where he was headed. When he segued onto the Thruway, Jack was sure.

Destination: Rathburg.

And the only reason he'd be heading there tonight would be to see the author—the supposed author—of that letter.

You wanted to see what a provoked Bolton would do, Dr. Vecca? Well, lady, you're about to find out.

13

"Hey, doc. How's it going?"

Julia sat up in bed with a start. That voice. She knew it. She fumbled for the lamp on her nightstand and turned it on.

Her heart nearly stopped when she saw Jeremy Bolton sitting on the foot of her bed, some folded sheets of paper in his hand. She slept in an oversized T-shirt and comfy pants, revealing nothing, yet for some reason she found herself clutching her sheet and blanket up to her neck.

Two black eyes and a bruised, swollen nose made him look even more threatening.

"Jeremy. What . . . what happened to you?"

He sneered. "As if you didn't know."

She didn't know . . . why would he think she did? But a more important question arose.

"Why are you here?"

"Ohhhhh, I think you know."

She forced some indignation into her voice and hoped it sounded convincing.

"No, I don't, Jeremy, and I want you out of my house right now."

"That ain't gonna happen." The finality in his tone jarred her. "We got things to discuss."

"Well, whatever they are can wait till morning. Call my office first thing and I'll—"

"Tonight, doc. *Tonight.*"

Something in his eyes frightened her. She'd always felt in charge with him—as much as anyone could be in charge of someone with that much oDNA—but tonight was different. Someone or something had unchained the beast in him. A very scary thought.

She considered screaming but dismissed that. No one would hear her, and it would immediately relegate her to a subordinate position. She had to maintain her rank as his overseer.

"Very well, then. Let me put on some clothes and I'll meet—"

"No. Here. Now."

And now she detected a new undertone in his voice, his expression. Fear? Had he got himself in trouble?

Robertson!

Had he gone wild and done something that could be connected to him?

"You didn't do anything foolish to that detective, did you?"

"*To* him? No." He pointed to his nose. "But he did a tap dance on me—as you knew he would."

"Don't be ridiculous. You didn't . . . do to him what you did to Gerhard, did you?"

"No. Not yet. But I ain't here about Robertson. I'm here about you." Fury lit in his eyes as he raised the papers. "And these . . . your recent correspondence."

She shrank back. "What?"

He tossed them at her. "Tell me what the fuck you were thinkin when you wrote that."

She grabbed them, retrieved her glasses from the nightstand, and began to read. Astonishment warred with cold, sick dread as the words flashed through her brain.

Dear Ms. Pickering . . . the man you know as Jerry Bethlehem . . . recently an inmate at this facility . . . special experimental program . . . raped your mother . . . is your father . . . have his baby . . . murdered your mother . . . have initiated procedures to rescind his release and return him to this facility . . .

Signed with her name—only that wasn't her signature. Not even close.

She looked up at him. "I never wrote this! It's pure fiction! It's . . . it's deranged!"

"Don't gimme that!" he gritted through his clenched teeth. "Only you could have figured it out."

" 'Figured it out'?" And then the meaning came through with a cold shock. "You mean it's true? That girl is your daughter?"

He shot to his feet and leaned over her. That was when she noticed some sort of iron bar in his hand.

"Cut the shit! You know damn well she is—you did the test!"

Julia shrank back against the headboard. "I did no such—"

"Shut up! You think I'm stupid? You think I go around givin out samples of my DNA?" He pointed the metal bar at her. She could see now that it was a tire iron. "No, it was you. It could only be you. You been suckin my blood and lookin at my genes since I got here. You gotta full file on me. You're the only one who coulda put this together."

. . . he murdered your mother . . .

She didn't doubt he had. Was this homicidal madman the Jeremy Bolton that girl's mother had seen before she died? And Gerhard—had he felt the fear slithering through her right now?

His diction had gone south—far south. And that, she knew, meant trouble. She glanced at her phone—no help there. Was he going to kill her? No. He couldn't. He wouldn't.

Why was this happening? Who had set her up like this?

And then she knew.

"Please, Jeremy! Don't you see? Doctor Levy's framed me. He wrote that letter, trying to goad you into attacking me." She almost said "killing" but didn't want to put the idea in his head if it wasn't already there. "If you do, the agency will track you down and put you away."

And if he did kill her, Aaron would step into the void. It all fit.

He stepped closer, his eyes wild.

She held up a trembling hand. "Stop, Jeremy! It's a trap! For both of us!"

He didn't seem to be listening.

"It was my daddy's Plan—to purify his Bloodline and to bring the Others back here where they belong."

" 'Others'? What are you—?"

"My brother and me, we been part of it. And now when it's all come true, when the baby—the Key to the future—is finally on the way, you come along and ruin it!"

"Baby? You mean she's pregnant?"

"You *know* damn fuck well she is! You said so right in your letter."

Julia didn't know about that, but a part of her brain, a part that wasn't scared nearly as senseless as the rest of her, wanted to examine that child, test it, observe it, watch it grow.

Key to the future? Who knew? But it might be the key to her survival.

"I can help you with your child."

Another step closer. Foam flecked his lips as his voice rose to a shout.

"There ain't gonna be no child! Because now, thanks to you, Dawn knows I'm her daddy, and sure as shit she's gonna get rid of my baby! You've ruined everything! *Everything!*"

With that he raised the tire iron.

Now Julia screamed. "Jeremy! Please! NO!"

"Yes!" he said as he swung.

She raised her arm and screamed in pain as her ulna cracked. He swung again. She tried to fend him off with her other arm but couldn't raise it fast enough.

The last thing she heard was the *crunch* of her skull as it caved in.

14

Finally Jeremy stopped swinging. He didn't know how many times he'd hit her but his arms had tired.

He looked down at what was left of Doc Vecca: Below the neck she was undamaged; above . . . another story. Mostly bloody goo with chunks of bone. Gonna need fingerprints to identify this one.

Now, with the rage-fire cooling, he started to realize what he'd done, how he'd royally screwed himself.

This agency Vecca kept talking about . . . if they were half as tough and connected as she'd said, they'd be after him as soon as her body was found— probably no later than mid-morning tomorrow when she didn't show up for work.

Had to get out of here and disappear. Fast.

Shit. If he only had Moonglow's two hundred fifty K. Easy to disappear with that. For a while, at least. He'd have to make do with what was in his bank account. Clean that out first thing tomorrow and hit the road.

But first . . . one more score to even.

Levy.

Maybe Vecca had been telling the truth. Maybe she hadn't signed the letter. Maybe it had been Levy instead. One way or another that weasel had to be involved. He'd always had it in for Jeremy, always against using him for the clinical trial.

Might as well make as big a splash as possible before dropping out of sight. In for a dime, in for a dollar, as Daddy used to say.

Levy had a date with Vecca in that great laboratory in the sky—tonight.

15

When it became clear where Bolton was headed, Jack had been tempted to turn around and head home. No question about Bolton's first stop. But would he make a second?

The possibility bothered Jack, so he found a place near the woods where he had a view of Levy's street, fished a brand-new goody from the spare tire well, and made himself comfortable.

After a while his eyes wanted to close and he'd had to shake himself awake a couple of times. But the drowsiness fled when he saw a silver Miata pull up in front of the house.

Bolton, damn him.

Jack's plan had been to put a couple of degrees of separation between him and Bolton: Light his fuse, point him at Vecca, and let him deliver the payback for Gerhard and Christy. That done, Jack could sit back and watch from afar as the agency reeled him in and threw away the key.

But that wasn't going to be possible now.

Wait. Why not? Levy was almost as responsible as Vecca. Why not let him take a hit?

Because he wasn't alone in there. Bolton might very well kill everyone in the house.

Shit.

Jack was going to have to get his hands dirty. Just what he'd wanted to avoid.

He eased out the door and hurried toward Levy's house. When Jack caught up to Bolton—carrying that same old tire iron—he was halfway across the lawn, silhouetted in the light from the lamps flanking the front door. He stopped a dozen feet behind him.

"There you are! I've been looking all over for you!"

Bolton froze, then turned. Jack couldn't see his features, but knew Bolton could see his.

"You!" He started toward Jack at a limping run. "You ain't gonna sucker me this time, motherfu—!"

"Hey, now, wait!" Jack said, backpedaling. "That was all a big misunderstanding!"

He slowed enough to let Bolton get close, then speeded up as he took a swing.

"I'll show you a misunderstanding!" Bolton said as the iron cut through empty air.

Jack was off the curb now and backpedaling toward his car with Bolton in hot pursuit. He was glancing over his shoulder, making sure he was on course, when Bolton lunged forward for another swing. Jack felt the breeze from the tire iron, but no more. The move cost Bolton, though, twisting his knee and worsening his limp.

Just a little farther . . .

As Jack backed around the rear of his car, he pulled a Taser M-18. When Bolton reached the trunk area, he fired it. The darts flashed out and pierced the T-shirt and the skin beneath, sending fifty thousand volts into his central nervous system. The tire iron went flying as Bolton hit the pavement doing an epileptic variation on the worm. Jack released the trigger and he lay still.

He looked at Bolton, then at the Taser.

"Whoa."

First time he'd tried one. He tended to favor a blackjack or sap for this kind of work, but Abe was always going on about how unreliable they were— hit too hard and the joe never wakes up, or not hard enough and you've got to give him a second tap, which might put him in vegetable land as well. After all, the reason for a sap was to put someone down, not dead. So Abe had lent him this baby on a trial basis. Jack was sold. The Taser was a keeper.

He glanced up and down the empty street. No one about. He popped the trunk, then lifted Bolton and dumped him inside. One thing about this trunk: Plenty of room. Enough for three or four Boltons, easy. Maybe more. Could be why Vinnie Donuts liked Crown Vics.

After slipping into a pair of gloves, he grabbed his roll of duct tape and quickly fastened Bolton's wrists behind him. Then bound his ankles, then his knees—lots of tape. As he worked he envisioned this piece of crap drugging Christy, slitting her wrists, and watching her bleed to death, all after seducing her child—*their* child, for Christ sake.

No more community theater for Christy, no more listening to *My Fair Lady* . . .

He looked at this smear of human scum with a legacy of four corpses and a pregnant teenage daughter and sensed the darkness he kept bottled up breaking free. He felt his lips retracting, baring his teeth. He glanced over at the bloody tire iron lying in the gutter, temptingly near.

Don't lose it . . . don't lose it . . .

. . . yet.

He wrapped the tape extra tight, and as he worked, Bolton's eyes fluttered open. He gave Jack a dazed look, then tried to move. When he realized he couldn't, his eyes widened in shock, then blazed with anger.

"Pussy motherfucker! Can't even fight me straight up and fair!"

Jack tore a short strip of tape off the roll.

"Fair? You mean as in meeting on a field of honor? This from a guy who shot two unarmed doctors in the back, water-tortured a detective, and murdered his own sister while she was unconscious. Fair? You gotta be kidding."

"In a fair fight my bloodline'd kick your bloodline's ass!"

Jack fought the driving urge to shove the tape down Bolton's windpipe. Instead he slapped it across his mouth.

"A fair fight presupposes I've got something to prove to you. Dream on."

Bolton's eyes blazed with wild hatred as he began kicking and thrashing. The Taser darts were still stuck in his chest. Jack reached down, grabbed the pistol, and gave him another dose.

Bolton began a different sort of thrashing.

16

Lying awake in bed, Aaron heard something that sounded like a car door slamming outside, then the roar of a big engine racing away. He got up and peeked out the front window.

Nothing moving out there. Could have been anybody.

He'd been jumpy lately. Well, why not? Bolton had killed again and might not be through. Who knew what he'd—

Aaron started as he noticed an arc of reflected light just beyond the corner of his front yard, behind the big junipers. It looked like the fender of a car. No one was supposed to be parked out there.

With his heart thumping he padded downstairs to his study where he grabbed his pair of mini-binoculars and focused them on the car. He gasped as he recognized a Miata.

Bolton had a Miata.

Aaron stood paralyzed for a moment, then snatched up his phone and punched in 911.

17

Jack cruised the Thruway truck stop lot till he found what he was looking for: an idling eighteen-wheel rig parked facing the food court and between two others of its kind. He backed up to the space between it and its neighbor to the right, then opened his trunk and hauled Bolton out. He grabbed the coil of half-inch nylon cord he'd just picked up at a Home Depot along the way, then crawled under the refrigerated trailer, dragging the struggling Bolton behind him.

He'd gone on autopilot along the way, feeling nothing, almost as if he were watching himself from afar as he looped the cord around Bolton's taped legs, tying multiple knots on knots, then secured the other end to the cab's rear frame rail. All through the process Bolton twisted and thrashed, breath snorting through his nostrils as he made frightened squeals and moans behind the tape.

When Jack finished, he looked at him. Couldn't make out his features in the dark; all he saw was a wriggling, oblong shape making faint, muffled, panicky noises.

"Having a bad day, Jeremy?" he said, raising his voice above the sound of the engine as he patted him on a shoulder. "It's about to get worse."

More whining and thrashing.

"I want you to take this personally. I'm sending you off to your greater reward this way because I don't want you identified for a while, maybe not ever. I also don't want you to die too quickly. It won't take you near as long as it took Gerhard, but long enough."

He crawled out from under the trailer and stood listening: The noise from the idling cab drowned out Bolton.

Jack returned to his car and parked it halfway between the truck and the on-ramp to the Thruway. Then he took out a sheet with the phone numbers Russ had found for him.

Two names, two numbers, two women. The widows of Doctors Horace Golden and Elmer Dalton. Nancy Golden had remarried, Grace Dalton had not. Never ceased to amaze him how many secrets could be ferreted out through the Internet.

He dialed Nancy Golden—now Nancy Emerson—then Grace Dalton. He gave them both the same message: Jeremy Bolton has disappeared from Creighton. No one's talking because no one knows where he is. Then he hung up.

Exactly thirteen minutes after the second call, a lean man in a cowboy hat and boots strode up to the cab, flicked a cigarette away, and climbed in.

Jack got out and stood by his door as the driver did some revving, then ratcheted into gear and started moving. Bolton must have worked the tape off his mouth somehow, because Jack heard him. His scream dopplered up, then down as the truck accelerated past.

He got back in and followed. The rig had barely made it to the entrance ramp when Jack's headlights picked up a gleaming line of red winding from beneath the trailer.

A line of blood . . . a bloodline.

. . . my bloodline'd kick your bloodline's ass!

Jack stared at the red streak.

There goes your bloodline.

But this was not the end of Bolton's bloodline—or Jonah Stevens's. It lived on in Thompson and in Dawn, especially in her baby. Where was Jonah's bloodline headed? The man had concentrated it for a purpose, aimed it toward some end. What?

He couldn't help thinking of Emma and his own bloodline. Where would she have taken it?

Nausea tickled his stomach. He pulled over and onto the shoulder, stopped for a few deep breaths.

Bloodline . . .

Had to call Levy tomorrow . . . set up a meet . . . needed some info only he could supply.

18

Hank broke off in midsentence and looked around. He'd not only forgotten what he'd been about to say, but where he was.

He looked down from his makeshift stage and saw seventy or eighty faces staring up at him. Now he remembered . . . he was speaking to a Kicker group in the basement of a clubhouse in Howard Beach.

But what was he supposed to say next? How could he have forgotten? He'd given this speech so many times he could repeat it in his sleep.

Something was wrong. But what?

And then he knew: Something . . . some*one* was missing.

Jeremy . . . Jeremy was gone.

He didn't know how or why or where, but Jeremy's light had flickered out. Hank felt it, knew it. Just as he'd known, so many years ago, that Daddy was gone and never would be coming back.

Had an Enemy gotten to him? That was the most logical explanation.

Hank searched for grief but found only fear. He'd never been that close to Jeremy, hadn't even liked him, to tell the truth. He was more concerned about being next on the Enemy's list.

He looked again at his audience. Could one of them be lurking in the crowd, waiting for a chance to kill him too?

He fought the urge to turn and run. That would be stupid. He was safe here among the Kickers. This would be the last place the Enemy would try for him.

He calmed himself and resumed speaking. But not his usual spiel. He started telling them about a young woman—alone, afraid, no family, pregnant, thinking she hadn't a friend in the world. But she did have friends and family—the Kickers. He told them how she and her baby were important to the future of the Kicker movement, to the future of the whole world, and how the Kicker family would find her and shelter her and protect her from those who feared and hated the dissimilated.

THURSDAY

1

Hank stood by the copy machine and watched as it started to spit out the brightly colored sheets. He grabbed one to double-check.

Dawn's photo looked grainy but that couldn't be helped. He'd enlarged it from one of the shots he'd taken when he'd tracked her down while Jeremy was in Creighton. The text said she was missing and offered a thousand bucks for any information leading to her discovery. He'd set up a special voice mail account for the calls. He knew a lot would be cranks, but he had plenty of manpower at his disposal to check them out.

He handed it to the nearer of the two Kickers who had accompanied him.

"This is what she looks like. This is who we're looking for."

The guy studied it for a few seconds, then handed it to his companion.

Later today he'd start handing out stacks of the flyers to the Kickers at the Lodge. They in turn would distribute bunches to all the Kickers they knew, who would spread them to all the Kickers *they* knew, and so on and so on.

He turned back to the newspaper he'd brought along. Still no report of the death of Jerry Bethlehem, or Jeremy Bolton. But he did find mention of an unidentifiable body dragged along the Thruway beneath a truck last night. Could that be Jeremy?

He shuddered. From now on, he wasn't traveling anywhere alone. He'd find a reason to have at least two Kickers with him at all times.

Just to be on the up and up, he'd filed missing persons reports with the NYPD on both Jerry Bethlehem and Dawn Pickering. Hank had been surprised at how seriously the cops had taken his reports. He later learned that their disappearance made them prime suspects in Dawn's mother's faked suicide. Hank had tried to glean more details but failed.

What a damn mess. The only upside was that he'd have both cops and

Kickers on the lookout for Dawn. His big worry was that she and the baby had died along with Jeremy. But he didn't think so. Through the night the tenuous link he'd had to Jeremy had been replaced by a link to the baby. He sensed it was alive and well. That meant Dawn was alive and well too. And thus findable.

Hank was going to find her first. And then, just as in his dreams, the Kicker Man would snuggle that baby in its arms and protect it from all Enemies.

2

Dawn eased herself into the warm water of the tub.

Like mother, like daughter, right?

But Mom hadn't had a choice. This was Dawn's idea, her own doing.

She felt like total hell. She'd been up all night drinking rum and Diet Pepsi. Sure, the rum wasn't good for the baby—at least that was what she'd heard—but nowhere near as bad as what was about to happen to both of them.

She'd agonized over what to wear until she'd realized she was just delaying the inevitable.

She listened for any sounds from the house—like anybody trying to get in. About an hour ago, as she was working up the nerve to get off her butt and do it, she'd heard sounds outside. Thinking it was Jerry, she'd slid back into her hiding place.

But it hadn't been Jerry. Two men, strangers. She didn't know how they'd got in, but they had, and they were searching the place. They hadn't said a word, but she'd seen their feet. They went through the whole house, silent as shadows. And then they left. She'd waited a long time before coming out again.

Who were they? Had they been looking for her, or for Jerry? Whatever, it had totally spooked her into action. Get it done before someone else came nosing around—like the local cops "processing" the crime scene—and totally ruined her chance.

So now, dressed in the same clothes she'd worn all yesterday and last night, she unwrapped the razor blade she'd found in the garage and held it up to the light. It looked so *sharp*. Little bits of rust flecked the edges. Couldn't rust give you tetanus? Not that it mattered.

Okay . . . had to get up the nerve to do it.

She'd known girls in school who cut their arms with blades like this. How did they do that? Why? Yeah, short, shallow little slices that probably didn't hurt too much, but it had so never made sense to her.

Had to do this now before she totally lost her nerve.

She placed the razor's corner point against her left wrist, just below the base of her thumb, and lowered her arm into the water. Closed her eyes, took a breath, and slashed the blade across.

She cried out with the pain. God, that hurt! Hurt like crazy!

She opened her eyes and looked. All those glasses of rum and Pepsi threatened to come up when she saw the scarlet billows flowing from her wrist.

Scarlet billows . . . that was in some song Mom used to like . . .

A blast of panic flashed through her as she watched her blood, her life flowing out of her. What had she done? This was crazy. She—

No. She so deserved this, had it coming for being a total jerk. No way she could live with herself after all the pain and death and misery she'd caused.

She looked at her right wrist. She'd intended to slit that as well but the first cut had hurt too much. And with the way the left was bleeding, she doubted she'd need it.

An odd sort of peace slipped over her like a warm blanket. She'd done it. In a few moments her cares and troubles would be totally over. No more worries, no more guilt, no more heartbreak.

Just . . . peace.

3

Doc Levy looked like hell in the late afternoon light coming through the Argonaut's window. Off his feed as well. Hadn't ordered anything but a glass of seltzer.

Jack had left voice mail about how they needed to meet—pronto. He'd known something was bothering Levy when he'd called back. Sounded frazzled. Jack had a pretty good idea why.

Levy hadn't been able to get free until now, and so here it was, four-thirty, and he looked like he hadn't slept in days.

Jack hadn't had much sleep either. He'd hunted for Dawn most of the day and come up empty.

"Something bothering you?" Jack said.

For all he knew, he looked as jumpy as Levy. With good reason, considering what was to come in the next few minutes.

"Bothering me?" Levy chugged some seltzer and gave him a funny look. "Don't you listen to the news?"

Jack shook his head. He let Abe filter much of his news. "Depresses me."

"Obviously you haven't heard then. Remember Doctor Vecca? You met her when—"

"I remember."

"Well, she's dead. Murdered. Head splattered all over her bedroom."

"How awful."

He hoped he sounded sincere.

"But you know what's worse? Maybe I shouldn't say 'worse,' because she's dead and I'm not—no, it *is* worse: They found the murder weapon—a tire iron coated with her blood—on the street outside my house."

"Bolton?"

He paused, then, "How'd you know?"

"Seems to like tire irons. Came after me with one, or have you forgotten?"

He ran a shaking hand through his dark hair. "To tell you the truth, I had. His prints were all over it. The blood was Julia's and traces were found inside his car—also outside my house."

"No wonder you're upset."

"As if that isn't enough, someone called the Golden and Dalton families and told them that Bolton had escaped and no one had reported it. They're screaming bloody murder. That news should be hitting the airwaves any minute. Not that you'd hear."

"Sounds like you'd better catch up to Bolton. Anybody have any idea where he is?"

"No. And that's what frightens me. The local cops and state police are looking for Jerry Bethlehem, who's listed as the owner of the car. But the agency knows to look for Bolton and has been scouring the area without finding a trace of him. Even sent a couple of agents to comb his girlfriend's house. Nothing."

Jack wanted to know more about their search. Had they found Dawn? He took an oblique approach.

"Well, he either ran off or was given a ride. The only ones I can think of who'd give him a ride are Dawn Pickering and Hank Thompson."

"Thompson checks out. The girl's gone missing. House is empty. They think she might be dead too."

Jack shook his head. "Can't see him doing that. It'd mean the end of the baby as well."

"I agree. Which means he hasn't gone far." Levy looked around. "I drove here looking over my shoulder the whole way. I've got a guy from the agency watching my house—my wife, my little girl . . ."

A twinge of pity prompted a little reassurance from Jack.

"Relax. You've got nothing to worry about."

Levy's eyebrows shot up. "Oh no? He left his car and the murder weapon in front of my house!"

"'Left' is the operant word. He's on the run. He won't be back."

"I wish I could be so sure."

Jack figured it was time to get down to the real reason for this little meeting. His palms began to sweat.

"You bring your little test kit?"

"Hmm?" Levy pulled himself back from somewhere else. "Oh, yes. Here."

He reached into his pocket and pulled out a small box, maybe the size of a bracelet jewelry box. He set it on the table and lifted the lid to reveal a little eyedrop bottle and a square card with what looked like a coffee stain at the center of its glossy surface.

Jack stared at it. "That's it? That's all there is to it?"

"What did you expect—test tubes and a gas chromatography unit? Yes, that's it. And as I told you on the phone, it can't leave my sight. Only Creighton staff and certain screeners for the agency are allowed access to these kits."

"What do I do?"

"All we need is a drop of your blood." He patted his pockets. "I could have sworn I brought a packet of lancets—"

"Never mind." Jack pulled out his Spyderco and flipped it open. "This oughta do."

Levy stared at the blade. "I said a *drop* of blood, not a whole unit. A finger stick, not surgery."

Jack didn't smile. This wasn't funny.

Levy said, "You sure you want to do this? What are you going to do with the result?"

"They say knowledge is power."

"Not in this case. Whatever the result, there's nothing you can do about it."

Jack knew that. But he had to know.

He wiped the blade with a paper napkin, then made a quick short slice in his fingertip. Barely felt it. As blood welled in the slit he looked up at Levy.

"Now what?"

"Without touching the card, let a drop fall on that beige area."

Jack complied and watched the drop expand on the glossy paper. Levy took some sort of oversized toothpick and began mixing the blood into the beige residue.

"It's a variation on the old latex agglutination method. Basically a yes-or-no test. If we get clumping, it's positive. No clumping—negative."

"No telling the amount?"

He shrugged. "Sure. The more clumping, the more positive, but that's too crude and too subjective to rely on. The gold standard is a full quantitative analysis."

After stirring the blood and the beige, he took the little plastic bottle, removed the cap, and squeezed three drops of clear fluid onto the mix. He picked up the card and started tilting it this way and that. His cell phone rang. He handed the card to Jack.

"Just rock it back and forth to mix it."

Jack took it and looked. His breath caught as he saw little flecks begin to form in the fluid. He heard Levy's voice faintly, as if he were sitting four tables away.

"You what? You found him? Wh—? . . . Oh, dear God . . . But how—? . . . Yes, I see . . . No, not at all. Thanks for calling. It takes a load off my mind, but dear God. Who could have—? Okay, okay. As soon as I get back."

His gut acrawl, Jack watched the flecks enlarging, sticking to each other, forming clumps.

"Jack? Jack?"

Levy tapped him on the arm and Jack looked up.

"What?"

"Bolton's dead."

Jack almost said, *Yeah, I know*, but caught himself in time. He returned to watching the clumps expand while Levy prattled on.

"The agency heard about a body found dragging beneath a truck on the Thruway. Most of his skin was gone so they had no fingerprints or even facial features to go on. But since the truck's last stop had been a few miles from Rathburg, they ran a quick DNA and damn if it wasn't a match for Bolton."

"Uh-huh."

Jack felt a vague disappointment. He'd wanted Bolton to go unidentified for a while, preferably forever. That way Vecca's agency would concentrate on finding the escapee and forget about Christy Pickering's investigator.

Levy ran a hand across his face. "This is incredible. He'd been tied there, but God knows by whom."

"Uh-huh."

Levy craned his neck. "What's going on?" He reached for the card. "Let me see that."

Jack pulled it back. He didn't want Levy to see it—didn't want anyone to see it.

"Come on. Give it over."

What the hell. Jack laid it on the table and slid it toward him. Then watched Levy's eyes widen.

"Dear God!" He looked up at Jack, then back to the card, then at Jack again. "You're playing tricks on me, right? What did you do—sprinkle something on this while I wasn't looking? That's it, right?"

"I wish."

Levy did the up-and-down look again.

"Dear God, this can't be true! I've never seen agglutination like this! It puts you right up there with—" His phone rang again. He checked it, then pointed at Jack. "I've got to take this, but do not leave, understand?"

Jack felt boneless—he wasn't going anywhere.

"Yes?" Levy said, jamming the phone to his ear. "What? What sort of letter? Read it to me."

As Levy listened, Jack stared at the clumps—the *agglutination*, as Levy put it.

Last night, after following the line of Bolton's blood until it petered out, he hadn't felt a shred of guilt or regret or remorse. Why not? Easy: Because Bolton had suffered a fate he'd have had no hesitation inflicting on someone else.

Then an ugly thought had bobbed to the surface: Didn't that make him just like Bolton?

No. Of course not. He hadn't wanted to do it, had planned a hands-off solution that would force the agency to take out Bolton for killing Vecca . . .

. . . which Jack had put him up to.

But Bolton's arrival at Levy's, bloody tire iron in hand, had left Jack no choice.

Could have simply shot him and buried him.

Bad option. Too many chances to leave trace evidence.

But to tie him under a truck? That was something one of Levy's heavy oDNA carriers would do.

Right.

The possibility had sickened him, but he needed to know. So he'd asked Levy to bring one of his screening kits.

"Dear God!"

If he says that once more . . .

"Not her signature? Then who—?" He looked at Jack and paled. "I'll follow up on this later." Without taking his eyes off Jack he folded the phone and placed it on the table. "They found a letter in Julia's bedroom, the room where she was murdered. It's signed but the signature isn't even remotely like hers. It tells all about Bolton's paternity to Dawn and . . ." He shook his head. "Only two people knew about that: You and I. And I didn't write that letter, so that leaves . . ."

"Why are you looking at me?"

"Because you—"

"Forget this letter jive. What about my test?"

Levy glanced at it again.

"What's to tell? You're in the Jeremy Bolton league of the oDNA tournament. I'll bet you even top him."

Jack leaned back. Just what he'd been afraid of, what he hadn't wanted to hear but sensed he would.

Levy was pointing—no, jabbing a finger in his direction, his face even paler, his voice a hoarse whisper.

"You! It was you! You tied Bolton beneath that . . . you wrote that letter to set him off . . . you knew he'd come looking for Julia and—"

"How can you know whether the therapy's working if you don't provoke him? Wasn't that the gist of her approach?"

"Yes, but—oh, dear God—"

"Would you please come up with another expletive or exhortation or whatever? Please?"

He wasn't listening. "Bolton came to my house after killing Julia! It wasn't the Pickering girl or Thompson who gave him a ride, it was you. Oh dear God!"

"Didn't I ask—?"

"You tied him to that—oh dear God." He shrank back against the booth's rear cushion. "What kind of a man does something like that?"

Jack didn't offer an answer. They both knew: One carrying a load of oDNA.

Levy gathered himself. "But then again, you probably saved my life."

"*Probably?*"

Levy glanced away. "Okay. Definitely."

"Let's say all of what you say is true. That leaves me with a problem, doesn't it."

"What?"

"You."

Levy flinched. "M-me?"

"You know an awful lot about me. Maybe too much. What am I going to do about that?"

Levy's face was alabaster white now. Even his lips.

"Look, I'm in this as deeply as you. The agency will want to know who wrote that letter and I'll be the first one they come to."

"And you'll tell them . . . ?"

"Nothing. What can I say about you without incriminating myself?"

Just what Jack wanted to hear.

"Good. Because if they come looking for me, I'll flip you in a New York second—as the source of the letterhead, all the DNA information, etcetera. I suggest you get back to your lab and start deleting certain results. I go down, you go down. Remember that." He waved at the test card between them. "And remember this."

Levy swallowed. "Will do."

"Good." Figuring he'd made his point, he pointed to the agglutinations. "Does this mean I'm one of them?"

"Them?"

"Someone in the Jonah Stevens's line?"

"In his direct bloodline? I doubt it. But somewhere in the distant past you might have shared an ancestor."

Jack sighed. "Swell."

"This test is qualitative and only crudely quantitative. Come by my office someday after this all settles out and I'll run a full analysis."

"That's okay."

"I'm serious.

"I'm sure you are."

"But—but don't you want to know if you carry the trigger gene?"

Jack gave him what he figured was a bleak look. "You really think that's necessary?"

Levy looked uncomfortable and averted his eyes.

"No, I guess not."

"Neither do I."

4

Dawn awoke choking and gagging.

"Wha—?"

She was wet—totally soaked—up to her chin in water—pinkish water—

She bolted upright and raised her arm. The cut on her wrist hadn't like healed or anything, but it had stopped bleeding. Maybe a little oozy trickle, but nothing of any consequence.

A while ago she'd felt herself weakening, so when she'd closed her eyes she'd thought she was slipping away. But she guessed all she'd done was doze off.

She looked around. She was alone, but somehow she didn't *feel* alone. Like someone was here—or had just been here.

Come to think of it, she'd had a vague sense of someone standing beside the tub looking down at her just before she'd come fully awake. She straightened in the tub. And the feeling of a hand on her head, pushing her down . . .

But that was crazy. No one was here, and no one besides herself was trying to hurt her. In fact, when her lips sank beneath the surface it had awakened her and—

Then she realized the truth and screamed and slammed her hands against the bloody water.

Failed again. What a total loser! Might as well paint a big red L on her forehead. God, she hated herself more than ever now.

She looked around for the razor blade. Where was it? She'd show them.

When she couldn't find it, she tried to pull herself to standing but fell back in the tub, sloshing water all over the place. So weak. She must have gotten like halfway to dead. Just a little ways to go. If she could find the blade she could finish the job.

Then she saw it, lying on the bottom of the tub. She reached for it, but stopped.

Who was she kidding? No way she was going to cut herself again. It hurt too much.

She began to cry—huge racking sobs that rippled the water around her.

She had to end this. She had to find a way.

And then she knew.

5

Jack had left Levy at the diner and spent what was left of the afternoon and the early evening searching for Dawn—but circumspectly. He couldn't ask too many questions, couldn't put word out on the street. Not with the agency looking too. If they heard someone else was asking about the same girl, they'd want to know who that someone might be.

Whatever. The search had been fruitless. Dark had fallen with not a sign of her Jeep. For all he knew she'd left the state. But that seemed unlikely. She had no family. Where could she go except home or to a friend? No sign of her at home, and Christy had said she didn't have many friends, but that didn't mean she wasn't crashing somewhere.

Jack had a feeling she wasn't far from home. So he kept searching. Sooner or later he'd spot that Jeep.

But not in the dark.

The Queensboro Bridge loomed ahead. And beyond that, the blaze of Manhattan. Gia would be waiting, but he couldn't face her now. She'd know immediately that something was wrong and quiz him till he told her. He had to get used to this oDNA thing.

Used to it . . . odd way to think. He'd carried it all his life but now he had to get used to it. No, he had to get used to *knowing* about it.

He called her and told her he'd be spending the night at his own place.

"How come?" she said.

"This thing I'm working on. I might get called during the night and I don't want to disturb the whole house."

He didn't mind lying to other people, but he hated lying to Gia. Sometimes the nature of his business made it necessary. Tonight the reasons were personal.

"Don't worry about that."

"It's better this way."

A pause, then, "What's wrong?"

"Nothing."

"Something's wrong, I can tell. You're in danger, aren't you, and you're afraid to bring it here."

"No, it's nothing like that, I swear."

They went round and round on that for a while until Jack semiconvinced her that he wasn't in danger and that everything was cool. He ended with a promise to see her tomorrow—if not for breakfast, definitely for lunch.

He hung up and approached the on-ramp to the bridge feeling like he'd swallowed fishhooks.

Go jump off the Brooklyn Bridge . . . what a total cliché.

But why not?

Except she'd just driven over the Brooklyn Bridge and didn't see any way to jump into the river off its raised walkway. So she'd headed uptown.

But now, as she drove along, she had this weird growing sensation that she was being followed. Very much like the feeling she'd had in the bathroom when she'd felt she wasn't alone. Had Jerry somehow spotted her?

Feeling totally freaked, she locked her doors and pulled over to let traffic pass and see if anyone else stopped. But everyone behind her went by and kept on going.

Must have been her imagination.

She parked her car in a garage near the Queensboro Bridge. Who cared what it cost? She wouldn't be around to pay for it. Then she started walking toward the center of the span among the bicyclists and other pedestrians, moving slowly, stopping every so often to rest. So tired. She hadn't lost enough blood to kill her, just enough to make her weak. The center was so far. Half a mile at least.

Nice going, Dawn. Talk about doing a half-assed job.

Just her luck she'd pass out before she reached the middle. The EMTs would arrive, see the cut on her wrist, and take her to the loony bin in Bellevue where she'd be locked in under a suicide watch.

Yeah, that would be perfect. Totally in keeping with the mess she'd made of the rest of her life—mess up her death too.

No, not this time. But when she reached the middle—what?

She hadn't counted on the chain-link fence. It had to be like seven or eight feet high. She'd have trouble climbing that on a good day. Today—forget about it.

But she had faith in the destructiveness of some of her fellow New Yorkers and in the quality of the city's maintenance: Somewhere along the way she'd find a gap large enough to squeeze through.

As she neared the middle she found one. She could do this. All she needed to do was climb to the top of the chest-high railing, squeeze through the opening, and take that one giant step. That was all. Just one step and gravity would do the rest. She'd read where people who jumped from this high hardly felt a thing—like hitting a brick wall at a hundred miles an hour. Or something like that.

She waited for a break in the pedestrian traffic. Not too many strollers at this hour. She'd never walked the bridge before so she had no way of knowing if this was a light night or a heavy night. No matter. As long as they gave her enough time to climb the railing and—

Climb the railing. Oh, God, could she even do that? She felt so weak.

She shook her head. She'd find a way.

She looked around. Nobody nearby on either side, nobody closer than half a football field. This was it, this was her chance. Do it now or never.

As she stepped onto the first of the three railings she heard a voice behind her.

"Dawn! Dawn, thank God I've found you!"

She turned and saw a big black car. It had stopped and a man was looking at her through the open passenger window. She couldn't quite make out his face.

"How—how do you know my name?"

"I worked for your mother. She hired me to investigate your boyfriend."

Dawn screamed, "Then it's *your* fault!"

He shook his head. "We both know whose fault it is."

His words cut so much deeper than the razor ever had.

"Me? You think it's my fault?"

He opened the passenger door. Cars started backing up behind him. Long, angry honks filled the air but he didn't seem to notice. Or if he did, he didn't care.

"Not at all, Dawn. You were a pawn. Jeremy's to blame."

A line from the letter flashed in her brain: *The man you know as Jerry Bethlehem . . .*

"Jeremy? Is that his real name?"

The man nodded. "A creep with a long ugly history."

"And I totally fell for him. Like a jerk."

"He has a natural talent for seduction. Get in and I'll tell you all about him."

The light wasn't good, but she could see now that he had dark hair and soft eyes. The other drivers were swerving around him, honking, screaming, giving him the finger in various combinations.

He smiled as he glanced at them, then sniffed. "Road rage . . . it adds a certain sweet tang to the air, don't you think?"

When Dawn saw him rising out of the car she pressed back against the fence.

"No. Don't come near me! I'm so ready to do this and no one's gonna stop me!"

He stood by the open door and raised his hands.

"Not one step closer, I promise. Just listen."

Something in his voice, his eyes . . . he was kind of good looking but not too. She had an odd feeling she could trust this man. But—

"Nothing you can say is gonna change my mind."

A guy on a bicycle slowed as he approached. He was looking straight at her.

"Hey, you gonna jump?"

"No, she is not," the man said. "Keep moving."

The cyclist speeded up as he passed, muttering something about never having any luck.

The man said, "Your mother asked me to look after you."

"What? You're lying!"

"I didn't understand it myself at the time, but now I believe she had a premonition that she was going to die. She said if anything happened to her I was to find you before you did anything foolish—"

"No way! Now I know you're lying. She—"

"Those were her exact words—I swear. She seemed to sense that you'd blame yourself for whatever happened to her and she wanted you to know that she never stopped loving you."

Dawn began to cry. "I totally hurt her! I deserve to die—I *need* to die!"

"She seemed to know you'd feel that way." His voice was like a soothing caress, stifling her sobs, drying her tears. "And she wanted me to tell you that if you love her, you will not do this."

"But I have to!"

"She's watching you, Dawn." He pointed toward the night sky. "From up there. She was a good woman. Don't you think she's suffered enough? Do you want to compound her misery by making her watch you die?"

"But then I can be with her!"

He shook his head. "I wouldn't be too sure of that. From what I've heard and read, suicides aren't treated too kindly in the afterlife."

She'd heard that too. Totally.

He said, "Don't you think it's time to stop thinking about yourself and start thinking about your mother—what *she* might want?"

"Yeah . . . I guess. But how do I know what she wants?"

"Easy. She told me she wants you safe and asked me to keep you that way."

Dawn bristled. That totally sounded like Mom—no faith in her.

"I can take care of myself."

"Not with Jeremy on the loose and looking for you."

Panic jolted through her chest. Jerry . . . Jeremy . . . she remembered that look in his eyes when he learned she was thinking of an abortion.

. . . if you ever *do* anythin *to hurt my baby, you will wish you'd been born dead, darlin . . .*

She felt the tears welling up again.

"What am I going to do?"

The man turned and opened the rear door of his car.

"Allow me to take you to a safe place until that monster is found and brought to justice."

Dawn stared at the open door. It looked warm and safe in there. But could she trust this man?

She looked into his eyes—fell into them was more like it. Two warm, welcoming pools of comfort and safety. No hint of danger there. He wanted only to protect her, wanted only what was best for her. And he knew so much about her. He had to be Mom's investigator.

Yeah, she could trust him. Totally.

As she took a step forward he made a flourish toward the rear seat.

"Your carriage awaits, madam."

He offered his hand as she tried to climb up from the walkway. He was strong, practically lifting her through the air. A few steps and she reached the car. As she ducked her head to enter, chill spiders of foreboding ran over her skin. She hesitated.

"I don't—"

She felt his hand against her back—not pushing . . . guiding.

"Go ahead, Dawn"—his voice was a warm pool, his touch balm, banishing her fear—"everything will be all right now."

Right . . . nothing to be afraid of. She slipped inside and settled onto the soft leather of the seat.

The car darkened as the door clicked shut behind her—darker than she would have expected. Tinted windows maybe? The blaring horns silenced as if someone had twisted a volume dial.

She realized with a start that she wasn't alone in the car.

7

"Now what?" Jack said as traffic on the bridge slowed.

Another accident? Couldn't people pay attention when they got behind the wheel? City traffic was bad enough without dumbasses banging into each other.

He reigned in his irritation and forced himself to relax. He wasn't on the clock, nowhere he had to be.

Chill.

Then he felt a chill—literally. A vaguely familiar one, last experienced in January when Rasalom had paid him a visit to sup on his rage, grief, and despair. Emma was gone and Gia and Vicky were on the fast track to join her. Jack had provided a movable feast of negative emotions.

And this was very much like the chill he'd experienced as Rasalom had fed.

Was he nearby?

8

Alarm raced through Dawn as she noticed another man sitting in the driver seat.

"What—?"

"Not to worry," the first man said as he climbed into the front passenger seat and slammed the door. "This is my driver, Henry."

Henry nodded without looking around. Dawn heard the doors auto lock. She tried her handle—useless.

"Am I locked in?"

"What?" The man laughed, sounding embarrassed. "Oh, sorry. Child locks."

"You have kids?"

"Not yet, but I've had some young passengers recently. Don't think of it as keeping you *in*side—consider it protection against anyone getting in from *out*side."

"This is so totally weird. I don't even know your name."

He reached his hand back. It held a card. She took it and angled it into the scant light coming through the side window.

MR OSALA

That was it—no phone number, no address, just his name.

"It doesn't say you're a detective."

Henry put the car in gear and they began to move.

"That's because I'm many things. Sometimes I'm an investigator, and sometimes I'm a guardian—like now."

"You mean like a bodyguard?"

"Exactly."

"Are you taking me home?"

"Not at the moment. That would be unwise. Jeremy knows where you live."

"Yes, but—"

"Your mother wanted me to keep you safe, and the best place to do that right now is my place."

A warning bell rang.

"*Your* place?"

Another laugh. "Not to worry, I have no designs on you. You'll be staying in a beautiful duplex penthouse on Fifth Avenue where my staff will take excellent care of you."

Duplex penthouse? Fifth Avenue? Staff?

"You sound like totally rich."

"I am."

"Then why—?"

"—am I helping you? Because that is my mission in life—I exist only to help those in need. I was helping your mother, now I'm helping you."

She hesitated to ask, but he knew everything already, so why not?

"Do you think you could help me get an abortion?"

A pause, then, "I don't think that would be a good idea at the moment."

"Are you totally kidding? I thought you knew the story here."

"I do. I know—how shall I put this?—I know that the child you carry is also a sibling."

Dawn thought about that. Yeah, he was right. How totally gross and sick.

"Right. So then you can understand why I want it gone."

"Yes, but the child is your protection. Jeremy wants that child and will do you no serious harm while you carry it. Think of it as an insurance policy. If you abort it—"

"But I want it gone, out of me. He told me he'd been fixed but that was obviously just another of his lies."

And I swallowed every single one, she thought.

She wanted to retch. Lies weren't the only things she'd swallowed.

"There will be plenty of time to terminate the pregnancy once he's caught. As soon as we hear of his capture, I shall personally take you to a private clinic that will fulfill your wish."

"When do you think that'll be? I want this so over with."

"Not too long. And who knows? In the meantime you might change your mind and spare the child."

"Spare? Are you kidding?"

"Well, it's not the baby's fault. Why take it out on him or her?"

Him or her . . . she'd thought of it only as an *it*.

"You never know," Mr. Osala was saying. "Your baby might turn out to be someone famous. An Einstein or a Madame Curie—someone who'll change the world."

Change the world? Where had she heard—?

Our baby is the Key. He's gonna change the world!

"Jerry said something like that. Why doesn't anybody want me to get rid of this baby?"

Mr. Osala half turned and his hand darted toward her. For an instant she thought he was going to hit her, but his fingertips only brushed her forehead.

"Hush, now. You're exhausted. Get some sleep."

An overwhelming lethargy enveloped her. She fought to keep her eyes open but the lids suddenly weighed like tons.

Mr. Osala, the car and its driver, her cares . . . they all drifted away.

9

The odd chill faded, so quickly that Jack wondered if he'd imagined it. Whatever had been slowing traffic on the bridge must have been cleared because the cars began moving again.

Jack shook off thoughts of Rasalom and cruised into Manhattan. He parked the car in the garage down the street and walked to his apartment. Along the way he glanced at a flyer tacked to a tree. He passed it, stopped, then stepped back.

A picture of Dawn and a reward for any useful information.

He yanked it free and took it with him.

Entering his apartment, he didn't turn on the lights. Simply sat in the dark by the front window, watching the street as he let his thoughts wander into darker places.

He tried to keep them from Emma but they strayed there anyway. How much oDNA would she have wound up with? Would it have affected her, commandeered the helm of life as it seemed to have done with her father's? Would she—?

A familiar figure stepped into view on the street below—not the only pedestrian, but now the only one who mattered. He wore a homburg and an overcoat, and used a walking stick. As usual the brim of his hat shadowed his face, but Jack thought he caught a glimpse of a gray beard this time.

Let him stand there and stare all he wanted. Jack wasn't going after him. Not tonight.

He turned away and thought about where next to search for Dawn. The flyer meant he wasn't the only one looking for her. Hank Thompson had to be as well. And he had loads more manpower than Jack.

But somehow Jack had to find her first.

And then what? What would he do if he succeeded? If she'd gone ahead and already aborted the baby, he'd need do nothing. But if she hadn't, if for some reason she intended to have the baby, what then? If she was indeed carrying this so-called Key to the future—a future hell on Earth for humanity—he'd have to convince her to end the pregnancy. And if he couldn't . . . ?

He didn't want to think about that now. He'd worry about it after he found Dawn—if he ever did. One thing he knew: He'd keep looking.

After all, in some odd, distant way, she and her baby were family.

<www.repairmanjack.com>